SUCH A BAD INFLUENCE

SUCH A BAD INFLUENCE

a novel

Grace Demyan

This is a work of fiction. Names, characters, organizations, places, events, and incidents are either products of the author's imagination or are used fictitiously. Otherwise, any resemblance to actual persons, living or dead, is purely coincidental.

Published by Lake Union Publishing, Seattle
www.apub.com

EU product safety contact:
Amazon Media EU S. à r.l.
38, avenue John F. Kennedy, L-1855 Luxembourg
amazonpublishing-gpsr@amazon.com

ISBN-13: 9781662529061 (paperback)
ISBN-13: 9781662529078 (digital)

Cover design and illustration by Sarah Horgan
Cover image: © Kovalov Anatolii, © Andychi, © YamabikaY / Shutterstock
Interior image: © MUHAMAD_KHOTIBUL_UMAM / Shutterstock

Printed in the United States of America

To my mom, Kelly:
Life wouldn't be nearly as much fun without you. I love you.

FIRST
Alex

The time had come, to get arrested.

The security guard clocked me as I entered the department store—*that profiling bastard.* Between my baggy clothes, unwashed hair, and aura of teenage rebellion, he'd taken one look and decided I was trouble. His mall-cop uniform and shiny bald head did little to mask his surveillance when he followed me across the first floor and onto the escalator.

He couldn't bag a criminal if they walked up and asked to be handcuffed.

I'm going to be his first catch. Picturing a smile on Mr. Shiny Head's face, I almost called the whole plan off.

Almost.

Unless I wanted to beg in the streets after spending my last three dollars on a soft pretzel at the food court, my grand scheme needed to work.

On the second floor, shoppers buzzed through the store like bees in a hive. Two men tried on shoes, boxes piling up beside them. An employee emerged from the fitting-room area with an armful of unwanted clothing. A plastic hanger clattered to the floor. To my left, a woman and a teenage girl browsed through formal dresses, looking happy and carefree, like two actors at the end of a commercial for antidepressants.

I, on the other hand, roamed in and out of the clothing racks, fingers drifting across the fabrics.

Like a vagabond.

With security hot on my trail, I wandered into the kitchen section, pausing to examine a crystal vase that had potential. The sticker read $29.99. I returned it to the shelf with a thud. As with everything in this world, the crystal exterior was fake and cheap. An empty promise of grandeur.

Nothing in this store suited my needs—an item expensive enough to warrant an arrest, but not so lavish that my life would be ruined if *she* didn't show up.

My eyes flicked toward the mother-daughter pair scanning dresses. Queasiness bubbled in my stomach. She'd show. She'd have to. Felicity had called my cell phone every damn day for over a year, leaving sobbing, trivial voicemails that I never responded to. Day after day I had to listen to her perceived tragedies, wondering why this stranger's purpose in life seemed to be annoying me. Felicity owned a blueberry farm in the Middle of Nowhere, Ohio, like a Hallmark character—she didn't have any real problems.

Unlike me.

"Can I help you?" an employee asked. She stood behind the jewelry counter. Silver and gold glinted beneath the glass exterior. *These trinkets will do quite nicely.*

My fingers smudged the glass surface when I pointed to a set of earrings. "Let me see those."

The woman placed the necklace she'd been fiddling with on a velvet cushion, then bent and removed the tray of earrings.

"You have good taste," she said. "These pearls will go well with your complexion." She smiled by way of encouragement, nodding once toward the earrings, practically nudging them into my hands.

The white dots lay in my palm. "How much?"

She adjusted the white tag on the tray. "Three hundred and fifty dollars."

It should've been easy to take the earrings and run, but doubt rooted my feet to the floor. Would she get fired for unknowingly aiding in my theft? The pearls had been secured behind glass—not meant for just anyone. Certainly not for me. Only a pretentious fool would spend hundreds of dollars on ear decorations.

I rolled a pearl between my fingers.

Now. Go. Flee.

"I don't have my ears pierced." I returned the earrings to the tray. Six months of planning down the drain. What would I do now? How would I get Felicity's attention?

"If you're over eighteen, we can remedy that." She retreated toward the register. "Let me grab the form. Can't use those earrings at first, though, but I'll place them on hold for you."

My phone rang.

The volume of the ringtone made me flinch. Looking over my shoulder, I saw the security guard take a step in my direction like I'd triggered an alarm.

My fingers moved before I could stop them, taking the necklace off the velvet cushion. The metal felt cold against my clammy hand. And solid.

Using a second I didn't have, my gaze dropped to the jewelry in my grasp. Diamonds set in a gold band sparkled up at me. *Fuck.* Stealing this necklace would be a felony.

"Wait," the woman said, holding a hand out in desperation. "Don't—"

Too late.

I lurched across the linoleum floor, running from the shouts. I shoved a cardboard stand over in the hope of slowing their pursuit.

An old lady gasped as I hurtled into her, sending shopping bags flying in every direction.

With no time to apologize, I sprinted toward the far end of the store. Footsteps thudded behind me at different rhythms. More than one person had given chase.

Where's the exit? Where's the exit? I'd intended to get caught, so I hadn't bothered to work out an escape route. The footsteps and shouting grew louder.

"Stop her!"

"She took the necklace!"

"Everybody out of the way!"

Fingers grasped my bicep, but before they could squeeze, I threw myself sideways into the menswear section, toppling straight into a set of mannequins. Momentum sent me crashing to the floor in a heap of plastic limbs. Landing hard on a synthetic leg, I felt the necklace slip from my fingers.

"Don't move," Mr. Shiny Head wheezed. He doubled over, hands on his knees. Three additional store workers surrounded us, blocking my escape.

I'd no intention of listening. Instructions, even those given by someone with authority, had no effect on me. All my former school teachers could attest to this. "Obstinate," Mrs. Rutledge had called me during a third-grade parent-teacher conference, which had been kinder than Ms. Krane calling me "pigheaded" two years later. The incident with Ms. Krane and the hamster had gotten me grounded for a whole month.

Mr. Shiny Head grabbed my arm and hauled me upright.

Sweaty, gasping for air, looking on the verge of a heart attack—the bastard still managed to smile.

I kicked his shin, and he called me a word far worse than *pigheaded.*

ONE
Felicity

Thirty-six hours later . . .

I'd written the words *Don't run* on my palm.

Shifting uneasily in the beach chair, I resisted the urge to switch on the flashlight as my eyes adjusted to the pitch-black blueberry field. At twenty-seven, I hadn't outgrown my fear of the dark, especially when the wind hissed through the bushes. I half expected something dark and sinister to spring from the shadows and drag me away.

But after two months of theft on the northern edge of the property, I could no longer handle this problem in my usual style: hiding in my two-story farmhouse, the doors locked and curtains drawn. If Rodney, that fool of a sheriff, couldn't catch the culprits, it was time I took matters into my own hands. It had taken weeks to build up the courage, but tonight I wouldn't cower inside.

Tonight, the thieves, so unheard of in Elswood, would be afraid of me.

Crack! Crack! Crack!

Twigs snapped in the distance. Leaves rustled, and whispers swept across the field.

This is happening. They're actually here.

I waited for half a heartbeat, not understanding the foreign sensation of adrenaline in my bloodstream. The last time I'd waited in the dark to catch criminals was never.

What would I do if I caught them? What if these criminals were more than simple blueberry thieves? What if they were armed? All I had was a flashlight.

Mud gripped my boots, preventing me from bolting to safety.

I looked up and down the rows of blueberry bushes. All my life, this spot of land had been my home. And a good, solid home at that. Now it was being ransacked by thieves.

If I fled and let this night pass, if I let them get away with stealing from me, then everything would slowly disappear—the house, the yard, the blueberries. Everything that had once belonged to my mother would be lost, replaced by an emptiness that would leave me truly and inescapably alone.

Don't run. Don't run. Don't run.

Lifting my boot from the mud, I took a single step toward the noise. Then another. And another. Ducking below the bushes, I hid my approach.

Whispers grew louder the closer I stalked. The blueberries smelled like sweet, tangy jam in the summer heat as I separated a batch of stems. I peered through the gap, counting four figures roaming in the darkness. Blueberries thudded against the bottom of a bucket.

I exhaled, chest expanding with relief. My worries of being bludgeoned to death were forgotten quicker than a police report on the sheriff's desk. These thieves were shorter than I'd expected, no older than children. And children could be scared off by an angry adult. At their age, I'd have peed my pants if I'd been caught trespassing on someone else's property. Where did kids get the nerve to cause trouble?

I lifted my phone to take a picture. Digital proof would go a long way, especially since the sheriff didn't believe me. *I'll show him.* My fingers twitched with anticipation. Any second and they'd be close enough. I needed to get around one bush, and I'd have them.

A branch snapped under my foot. Against the silent backdrop, the splintered wood sounded like an explosion.

"What was that?"

My muscles tensed as blood pulsed in my ears. *Oh no. Oh no. Oh no.*

"I think it was the wind."

"No, I heard something over there."

"You're hearing things, Tim."

Tim? In such a small town, the odds were already high that I knew the kids; from his name alone, I identified one of the thieves: the Callaway boy. If I remembered correctly, little Timmy Callaway had recently celebrated his ninth birthday.

Sensing danger, the kids retreated a few steps. I couldn't wait any longer or I'd miss my opportunity. A bead of sweat dripped down my forehead. It was now or never.

I leaped out of the bushes, flashlight switching on as my feet sank into the mud. Who knew I was so coordinated? "Freeze!"

When the nearest kid screamed, I was so overcome with fright that I screamed, too.

Scrambling, the kids took off in different directions.

My longer legs did little to help me as I chased after Timmy. When did kids get so fast?

"Stop! Please stop!" *Don't be so polite, Felicity!*

Timmy dropped his bucket and fled toward the woods, the tree line marking the edge of the blueberry farm. *Not the dark woods.* The treetops, black against the night sky, scared me more than anything.

Fear made my legs move faster. I reached for Timmy's shirt, fingertips brushing the fabric. He twisted, throwing me off-balance. My hand shot past his shoulder as my foot caught an exposed root. I crashed face-first into the mud.

Timmy climbed over the fence, shaking the prominently displayed No Trespassing sign. He and his accomplices regrouped on the other side of the fence. Despite fleeing in different directions, they'd ended up in the same spot.

The distinct slap of a high five rang out in the night.

Mud clung to my clothes, and my ankle was likely sprained, but in that moment, my deflated pride hurt the most. I peeled a leaf off my forehead, watching the children disappear into the trees. Outsmarted by nine-year-olds—with my luck, it seemed about right.

I rolled onto my back and breathed deep in the warm summer air as I stared at the night sky. My fingers, still clutching the phone, dialed my mother's number, a force of habit even after three years of unanswered calls. I had no one else to call when life grew unbearable. I didn't even have a cat, which, given my proclivity for sitting inside and judging my neighbor, would come as a shock to any observer.

Cats didn't live forever—and my emotional state couldn't survive another loss.

A generic voicemail answered. Why did the new owner never pick up? Had they blocked my number after years of unwanted messages? Perhaps they could no longer stand my rambling, sobbing conversations with my dead mother.

Beep.

"You won't believe the night I'm having."

If my mother had been on the other end of the line, she'd have responded with, "What's wrong, sweetie?"

But no one answered, so I shared my miseries unprompted.

"Welp, I didn't catch the thieves. A huge shocker, I know." My voice sounded as miserable as I felt. I couldn't even defend her beloved blueberry farm from degenerate children. "I know you'd tell me that it's fine, not to worry about a few stolen berries, but those berries, this place—it's all I have left of you. It's our home."

A mixture of grief and loneliness caught in my lungs, halting my speech. Tears pricked my eyes. These one-sided phone conversations always turned me into a sobbing mess. Four hundred and seven times, I'd dialed her number and received no response, causing me to ramble on about how pathetic my life had become.

But not tonight.

Tonight, I'd made a promise to myself that I'd start fighting back.

So, if my mom was listening—and it helped to believe she was, even if the rational part of my brain knew otherwise—I didn't want her to know about my misery and pain. She'd said that when her child hurt, she hurt, and the only good thing about her passing away was that the pain had ended.

"I swear to you, I will find a way to protect the farm. I'm going to fix this. For you and for me."

I closed my eyes and let her love wash through me, finding just enough strength to end the call and carry on for one more day without her.

"Until tomorrow, Mom."

TWO

The modest three-bedroom farmhouse had no air-conditioning unit, which made it warm even in the early morning. The blue siding needed to be replaced, and the bottom porch step had splintered after I dropped a two-gallon paint can on it last year. The sound of crunching wood still haunted me every time I had to hop onto the second step like a gymnast to enter the house.

But the deteriorating outside hadn't crept inside—I'd made sure of that. My mother had put a lot of care and energy into making the house feel warm and welcoming. It was my home, my one safe and sacred space in the chaos happening around me. Nothing bad would happen so long as I kept the interior exactly as it had looked before she died. The furniture, the pictures hanging on the walls, the books we'd piled on the staircase—all of it remained untouched. I hadn't even removed her work schedule from the front of the fridge.

My mother had inherited the house and farm from her grandparents, who had received the deed under suspicious circumstances. *Very* suspicious circumstances. My great-grandparents had immigrated to the United States from France after the First World War. Legend had it, they brought two handfuls of blueberry seeds with them, and once they arrived in Ohio, they found the best soil in the area and planted a few rows of bushes. Twenty years later, after my family built a house on the property and cut down trees to facilitate the farm's expansion, the landowners discovered the squatters.

The Callaways had not been pleased, especially when the judge ruled that adverse possession, the common law property doctrine of granting landownership to trespassers, applied. Since my ancestors had illegally occupied and worked the land for over two decades, the legal rights to the property transferred to them. My family, the Lavignes, had paid nothing for twelve acres of prime Ohio soil—from the back edge of the woods to the front of the farmhouse. Legally, the land was ours.

But the law didn't stop the Callaways from sullying my family's name, calling us criminals and thieves at every opportunity. Four generations later, the Callaway clan still considered the blueberry farm and all its profits rightfully theirs. It had taken all of two days after my mother's passing for Jonathan Callaway, the town's esteemed mayor, to show up on my doorstep with a tuna casserole and an offer to buy the place.

The bastard had lowballed me. Why pay full price for stolen land?

Jonathan had no idea that I'd never sell the place. Not for a hundred million dollars. He'd have to claw every single blueberry from my cold dead hands before I sold him so much as a blade of grass.

The irony of Timmy Callaway, the youngest member of our century-old feud, stealing blueberries from my property didn't make it any easier to limp down the stairs the following morning, ankle swollen and bruised.

The first and only item on the agenda involved a trip into town to deliver berries. Local business owners, more out of pity than need, purchased a few cartons from me every other day. This money kept me going, even as I opened the fields for self-picking, which had yet to hit its stride.

My swollen ankle protested when I pulled the wagon to the side of the house. Across the street, Wade Londergan, my only neighbor, had the hood of his truck propped open. The two of us occupied a side street on the northern edge of Elswood. The unpaved road, marked by a faded street sign, was typical of roads off the main square. I couldn't find it using GPS, but everyone in town knew the streets by heart. The mailman, at least, had no issues finding the house when he delivered my bills.

I limped toward the road, hoping he wouldn't notice me or my injured ankle. Wade had found my issues with the thieves amusing, insisting for weeks that the culprits were no more than children. He'd double over with laughter if he knew how badly I'd failed last night.

"Well, well, well. If it isn't the Elswood vigilante." He poked his head around the truck's hood. "I thought for sure this morning's headline would read 'Blueberry Bandits Caught at Last.'" He laughed at his joke. "Or 'Kids Caught Blue-Handed.'"

I skipped over his attempt at humor, focusing on the unbelievable instead. "You read the newspaper?"

"I canceled my subscription after Herman stopped including a cartoon section."

That made more sense. I turned to leave, knowing it was better to avoid Wade than stand around arguing with him. If only it had always been so easy. Adult me could put aside his good looks and find his immaturity repulsive, but fifteen-year-old Felicity had fallen hard for the high school quarterback. And I wasn't the only girl in town who had succumbed to his "charms."

"Was that you I heard screaming bloody murder last night?" Wade walked around his truck to prolong the conversation. Standing at over six feet tall, with broad shoulders and dirty-blond hair, his admittedly attractive body stunned my comeback for half a heartbeat.

"That was the thieves."

"Right." He smiled in a way that said he didn't believe me. He used the inside of his elbow to wipe the sweat from his forehead. "You know, if you're scared, you can stop by my place tonight. I'll protect you."

"Ugh." Thank goodness I'd skipped breakfast. "Never. I'd rather die in the fields." I started walking away, before turning back to add, "And I'm not scared. I can handle a couple of kids."

"You sure? That hitch in your step says otherwise."

"I'm made of steel, Wade. Made of steel."

The two-mile walk into town led me past three cornfields, the edge of Regina's horse stable, and across a river. Cars zipped past as I trudged along the gravel. I'd sold my car two years ago, unwilling to pay for the added expenses when nearly everything I needed was a short walk away. Gone were my weekend trips to Lake Erie, Crocker Park, and the farmers' market two towns over—the one with half-priced Honeycrisp apples and cilantro so fresh I had to store it on the porch or the whole house would smell like guacamole for days.

Elswood, Ohio—with exactly one grocery store, one hair salon, one bakery, and *two* tourist shops dedicated to selling snow globes—had become my entire world that I didn't venture beyond.

My calf muscle cramped by the time I reached the town square—a rectangular pitch of grass that ran across the center of town, with sidewalks along the edges that connected in the middle at the white gazebo. Shops and restaurants ran parallel to the grass, enclosing the open square. Elswood had a subtle but outdated charm. Tourists would find no corporate-owned stores or chain restaurants within the town limits, and the local business owners remained adamant about maintaining Elswood's wholesome appeal.

Nothing said *small-town charm* like a family-owned bakery—my first stop of the day. Late June in Northern Ohio could be muggy, and my T-shirt clung to my damp lower back. The bakery's air-conditioning gave me goose bumps after so much time in the summer heat.

Philomena, who was on the verge of retiring after running the bakery for over forty years, headed to the register before the door had closed behind me. I placed her usual five containers on the counter.

She moved quickly—no small talk, no inquiries about my health or the weather. By now, everyone in town conversed with me as little as possible. Besides my spats with Wade, people ignored me, letting me sink further into the depths of my depression. I had nothing to discuss anyway, unless the topics of weeping in the shower or disposing of rotten blueberries interested them.

A stack of Founders' Day flyers sat on the counter. I'd forgotten about the Founders' Day Festival—my mother's favorite town event. A weeklong celebration of all things Elswood, complete with games, junk food, and carnival rides. The festival's crown jewel, the Elswood Man of the Year competition, served as both entertainment and an election. A member from each of the town's founding families—Callaway, Londergan, Wilkinson, Menke, and Haskall—competed for the chance to become mayor.

While normal places held free and fair elections, we chose our leader through a series of athletic games, an art auction, and a fairly dangerous tractor derby. Not exactly legal, but no one dared challenge this sacred Elswood tradition in a court of law.

Despite our family name's duplicitous reputation, each year my mother had secured a spot in the festival for her blueberry-pie table, landing between the salad stand and the medical tent. She hadn't complained, because for her, the blueberry business was about making people happy, not getting rich.

Inside the bakery, people enjoyed their Saturday morning over a cup of coffee and a fresh pastry. My insides twisted. They looked happy. Relaxed. Carefree. I, on the other hand, had bloodshot eyes from crying all night in my painfully empty home.

I leaned my elbow on the counter, biting my lip to keep my emotions from running out of control. Experience had taught me that random bursts of crying made people uncomfortable.

Then I saw him.

At a table near the window sat Timmy Callaway. The little thief himself.

Something surged through me. A sensation I'd never felt before. Later, I would describe it as rage, but it was more than that. I *hated* the nine-year-old boy who came up to my elbow. *Hated.* Before that moment, I wasn't sure I'd truly hated anyone. Yet the pressure in my head threatened to explode as he ate his breakfast—a croissant, of all things. At least be a normal kid and eat a doughnut.

My feet, with a mind of their own, marched straight for him.

I never initiated confrontation, especially not with the Callaways, who already thought they were better than everybody else in town. But

Timmy and his friends had gone too far. It was one thing to mess with me, but another to steal from my dead mother's blueberry farm. Loyalty to her memory demanded action.

"Did you pay for that croissant or steal it, too?" I bent down, one hand on the table, looking Timmy in the eyes. "Answer me, you little punk!"

Cheryl Callaway, his mother, hastily swallowed her coffee from where she sat across from him. "What on earth?"

I'd known Cheryl all my life, and she'd always been annoying. Since third grade, she'd played Mary in the annual Christmas show, pretending to be a savior for all of Elswood. Her delusions of grandeur became more pronounced once she married Jonathan Callaway and secured her seat on the town council—a group of women who oversaw the town's ridiculous and often embarrassing events. She'd spent taxpayer money on "beautifying" the town in preparation for May Flower Day, which meant hiring landscapers to sculpt the bushes into geometric shapes and archways. An unnecessary expense that scandalized residents after the bushes outside the bank took on what could only be described as a phallic shape. But, as her husband was the mayor—the only person with the ability to veto council decisions—Cheryl's power had gone unchecked for years.

Apparently, little Timmy was just as annoying and entitled as his mother.

"I caught him stealing blueberries from my farm last night." My voice trembled. "He's been stealing from me for weeks."

The bakery had gone silent. No one dared to question the Callaways, especially not "the Elswood Doormat," Felicity Lavigne. My nickname had cropped up about a year ago, the moniker's creator still unknown.

My encounter with Timmy and Cheryl jeopardized its accuracy, but no one in the bakery had any illusions about me winning this argument. Until Cheryl squashed me, I was purely entertainment on a Saturday morning before college-football season began.

Cheryl took a deep breath, as if merely listening to my hysterical accusation were beneath her. "You're mistaken, Felicity, like usual. Tim knows better than to steal. Don't you, Timmy?"

Timmy nodded, but his cheeks turned red.

He's not even a good liar. "He and his friends were in my field last night. I saw them."

"You're a crazy lady who sees things," Timmy interjected in a squeaky voice.

The insult didn't bother me; most people in town thought I'd lost it. Overcome with grief, I'd trapped myself in a house full of memories that I wouldn't leave for anything other than farm business. Rumors of my mental decline weren't entirely wrong.

What irked me, though, was Timmy's tone. His spoiled, unapologetic tone. He'd inherited the trademark Callaway arrogance, and I wouldn't stand for it.

When Cheryl stood, chair scraping against the floor, I directed my anger at her. "You owe me money for the missing berries—at least five hundred dollars, maybe more."

"If Tim took the berries, which I'm not saying he did"—she added the second part louder so the onlookers couldn't mistake her words as an admission of guilt—"it wouldn't be a fraction of what your family owes ours." She moved around the table and took Timmy's hand. "Do yourself a favor, Felicity, and let this go before you have another mental breakdown." She paused, looking me in the eyes. "And if you ever threaten my son again, I will go straight to the sheriff."

"Go ahead! Call the sheriff! And while you're at it, why don't you tell Rodney what your kid has been up to!"

Cheryl shook her head in exasperation as the door closed behind them.

My chest heaved; I was well aware that the atmosphere in the bakery had changed. The relaxed morning vibe had evaporated like steam from one of Philomena's coffeepots. My hands trembled, and tears filled my dark-brown eyes. Living in Elswood felt like being in perpetual high school: Gossip swirled uncontrollably, appearances mattered more than substance, and most important, some people were considered better than others for inexplicable, sometimes nonexistent, reasons.

Unfortunately for me, I'd utterly failed to navigate teenage social circles, and adult life hadn't proved much better. In the decade since graduation, I hadn't outgrown my insecurity, still preferring to hide behind my chestnut-colored hair and unfashionable attire, which never seemed to hug my curves in a flattering way.

I turned back to the counter, hoping to appear unflustered. I couldn't cry—not with everyone watching. A baffled Philomena opened her mouth, paused for half a heartbeat, then closed it.

I held out my hand for the cash. "That'll be twenty dollars."

THREE

I'd planned to catch up on the sleep I'd lost thanks to my failed stakeout, but the earplugs didn't work. Rock music drifted through the walls, the bass shaking the windows. Agitated, I removed the pillow from atop my head so I could see the clock. 10:37 p.m. Wade's house party, which had been going strong for three hours, showed no signs of slowing down.

Wade accentuated his less-than-charming presence with a party every three to four weeks. Like a teenager whose parents had left him alone for the weekend, he cranked up the music, poured cheap booze, and didn't care about disturbing the neighbors. My complaints had been thoroughly ignored as Wade attempted to relive his high school glory days, replaced instead with an invitation to join the party. That would never happen. I didn't socialize with people I liked, let alone Wade Londergan and his high school football buddies.

Unable to sleep, I trudged downstairs to add fresh ice to my water bottle. I jumped, and not from the loud crash of ice cubes into my canister. A howling came through the front door, the barking soon replaced by a scratching noise.

"Juno!" How had I forgotten about her?

I found Juno, Wade's border collie, on the porch. Her tail wagged when she saw me. She hated the loud music, too, and whenever he threw a party, she found her way to my house. With everything that had happened today, I'd forgotten to check for her.

She bolted inside, heading for the kitchen, where I kept her water bowl. She knew the routine: water, two treats from the cupboard, then straight to bed. She licked my hand in thanks as she padded over to the stairs. If I had the energy and resources to permanently take care of her, then Wade wouldn't get Juno back. He didn't deserve such a well-behaved, sweet dog. The man couldn't remember to feed himself, let alone take care of another living creature. The rescue shelter must've been desperate when they approved his adoption application.

I followed Juno up the stairs when my robe pocket buzzed, startling me. I fumbled for the phone as the ringing made my headache worse. Who was calling at this hour? There weren't many nighttime emergencies in the blueberry business.

The phone number flashed across the screen: 440-221-6746.

My mother's phone number.

Blood rushed to my head. My legs gave out as I stared at the screen, not believing my eyes. I sat on the top step, unable to move. Juno whined, ready for bed.

The phone buzzed again.

Should I answer it? Should I let it go to voicemail? What if they were calling to tell me never to call again? Did I want to know who was on the other end of my pathetic, sobbing rants?

The answer to the last question was definitely no, but I couldn't bring myself to decline the call. There was something about seeing her number on the screen—a number that hadn't called me in years—that I couldn't ignore.

My fingers shook as I accepted the call. "Hello?"

No one answered.

"Hello?" I tried for a second time, hearing nothing on the other end. It was a wrong number. All that panic for nothing.

I was about to end the call when a female voice said, "Felicity?"

I nearly dropped the phone. She sounded anxious—frightened, even. Of me? This was a hallucination, surely. I'd truly done it and lost my mind. A smart person would've hung up, called the police, and waited to be admitted for psychological evaluation.

Instead, I responded with a tentative, "Yes?"

"Um . . . my name's Alex. I didn't have anyone else to call . . ."

I swapped my pajamas for sweatpants and my slippers for tennis shoes. The walk to Wade's house was short but irritating. Cars were lined up in his driveway, half of them spilling onto my yard, the tires leaving divots in the grass. His front door—ajar, of course—leaked music outside.

His house was as filthy as I remembered—red cups on every surface, stained carpet, and mismatched furniture scattered across the interior. It was the kind of decorating a man would do to convince other men the place had never had a woman's touch. Which of course it hadn't. Wade had moved here a year after divorcing Monica. I'd never thought highly of the woman, who worked part-time at the drugstore, but at least she'd been smart enough to avoid this place. College frat boys would've appreciated his tastes.

People were crammed inside, standing in groups, holding cups, and talking loudly over the music. My head pounded, sensory overload making me nauseous. A crowd had formed around someone playing *Guitar Hero* in the living room. Potato chips pelted him from all angles to break his concentration. A few people glanced curiously in my direction, taking in my casual attire as I searched high and low for Wade.

I found him at the back of the living room, on the couch with a red-haired woman. The details of her face were lost to me—because he was glued to it. His back was turned to me as his hands glided up her side. I tapped him politely on the shoulder.

No response. I poked him again, harder.

I didn't know if I imagined the sucking noise as he came up for air or if it really happened, but either way, he looked annoyed as he searched for whoever had intruded on this obviously private moment they were having in the crowded living room.

"What do you . . ." He did a double take. "Felicity?"

"Hey, Wade," I said as if I'd encountered him in the grocery store aisle. "Can I have a word?"

"What are you doing here?" He removed his arm from around the woman, disentangling himself.

"I need to talk to you."

He pushed himself off the couch, wiping his mouth with the back of his hand. The redheaded woman, Cynthia Porter, looked aggrieved. "What the hell, Felicity?"

"Don't worry, I'm not keeping him. He'll be back in a minute."

I walked toward the hallway, hand gripping the front of Wade's T-shirt as I dragged him behind me.

"Am I drunk, or are you really at a party?" he asked.

"Yes, you're drunk, *and* I'm at the party. But I'm not here for that." I paused, unsure the words would pass through my vocal cords without choking me. "I need a favor."

He leaned his shoulder against the wall. "I'm not turning down the music. I have till one a.m. That was our agreement."

That was absolutely not the agreement. And even if it was, he'd never stuck to that time limit, normally playing music till the next morning, when he woke up hungover. All of this I wanted to point out, but his constant annoyances would have to wait. For the first time in a long while, I had something important to do.

Before I could get the words out, he asked, "Do you want a drink?"

When he stepped closer, I backed up, holding my hands in front of me. I didn't want his beer breath in my face. "You couldn't pay me to drink anything you gave me."

His eyebrows creased with confusion. Perhaps he'd expected a simple yes-or-no answer. I could tell when my statement connected in his mind, about three seconds later than it should have.

"What do you want, then?"

I worked to keep my tone even. I needed a favor, after all. "Can I borrow your truck?"

"For what?"

"Can I borrow it or not?" I should have told him what I needed it for; he'd forget by morning anyway. Only, I didn't know how to get the words out. I was having trouble wrapping my head around the phone call, and I didn't need Wade's take on any of it.

"Are you in trouble?" He looked me over. Then he shifted so he could see out the side window of his living room. He had an unobstructed view of my yard and front porch. I'd been meaning to plant a row of trees to block his view but hadn't gotten around to it. "Is it those kids again?"

"No, I just need your truck."

"If you're going to commit manslaughter, you'll have to get a rental."

"It's not the kids!" My temper flared, as it always did when we interacted. Why wouldn't he cooperate? He obviously wasn't driving anywhere tonight. I took a deep breath and reminded myself that I was speaking to an overgrown man-child. "Give me the keys. I'll be back in a few hours. You'll never even miss it."

"Have a drink first."

I ran a hand through my hair, thoroughly exasperated. I wasn't going to drink and drive; that was illegal. Didn't he know I was responsible? "I don't have time for a drink. I need to get moving. Unlike you, I don't have all the time in the world."

"One drink; then you can have the keys."

Why was he toying with me?

"Forget it, Wade." I shook my head and headed toward the front door, leaving him to negotiate with himself. He called after me, but I'd already pushed through the sea of people in the living room.

Luckily, I'd borrowed his truck a few times and already knew where he stashed the keys. His bottle-opener key chain sat on the hallway table, under a substantial stack of mail, magazines, and bills. I ducked outside, not looking back, and hoped no one would be on the road at this hour.

FOUR

Cleveland was forty minutes from Elswood, if abiding by the speed limit—which, of course, I did. I didn't have the nerve to commit theft *and* break traffic regulations on the same night. If I took this reckless behavior any further, I'd be jaywalking by the end of the week. Where would it end?

I drove without music so I wouldn't be distracted. My hands shook on the steering wheel for the first few miles, but when I didn't immediately crash, I relaxed, settling instead for staring at the road with catlike focus.

The front tire bumped into the street curb as I checked the building number against my hastily scratched Post-it note. I checked again. And again. The numbers matched.

1300 Ontario Street.

The Cleveland Police Department.

Here goes nothing, I thought, putting the truck in park and heading inside. A counter surrounded by plexiglass dominated the entryway. Two police officers stood beside it, deep in conversation. I ignored them, focused on the man sitting behind the glass staring at his cell phone.

His eyes flicked upward, then back to his screen. "State your business."

My throat had gone dry. "Hello, I'm here to pick up Alex Norse."

"Pickup times are between eight a.m. and six p.m. You'll have to come back in the morning."

I bit my lip, thinking of a clever or charming remark to get special treatment. I didn't want to drive back out here in a few hours. Traffic would be unbearable at eight a.m., assuming Wade hadn't reclaimed his keys by then. Sleeping in the truck was an option, but the dark, deserted street frightened me, even if it was mere feet from a police station.

"Can you make an exception?" I knew the answer before I asked. My voice didn't ring with the kind of authority that garnered an exception to rules. I basically had *won't make a fuss* written in bright letters across my forehead.

"Pickup times are between eight a.m. and six p.m. You'll have to come back in the morning."

I stood there as the moments passed, unsure whether I had it in me to ask for a supervisor. But I'd have to. It would be worth a shot. Maybe if I explained the situation, someone would take pity on me.

"You're here for Alexandra?" One of the officers had stopped his conversation to address me. I nodded, heart lifting at his tone.

"I'll take this one, Cory." He leaned forward so Cory could see him through the glass. Cory returned to his cell phone before the other officer could lean back.

He led me to his desk and introduced himself as Officer Frank Heathman.

"You family?"

"Um . . . a friend." It sounded like a question.

He unlocked his computer and started typing. "Real piece of work," he muttered. At first, I thought he meant the computer, which looked like it was from the early 1990s, but then he looked me in the eye and said, "Your friend caused quite a bit of trouble when we arrested her three days ago."

My curiosity increased, but so did my anxiety. What was I getting myself into?

"Got her in front of the judge yesterday, but she refused to call anyone until she had her cell phone. Not exactly protocol, but she wore me down. The sooner she's out of here, the better."

"What did she do?" I crossed my fingers. *Please don't let it be anything too heinous.*

"Attempted shoplifting."

I uncrossed my fingers. That wasn't so bad. It wasn't like she'd committed armed robbery or killed someone.

"Then assault on a department store clerk, resisting arrest, and threatening a police officer. Multiple officers, actually."

I swallowed. I'd been too hasty in my relief. But for some reason, I didn't bolt for the exit after hearing her list of crimes. Alexandra had made some mistakes, but she also had my mother's old phone number, and that outweighed any potential danger she posed to me. The moment she called, I'd decided to meet her, no matter what crimes she'd committed, because perhaps this was my mother's way of finally returning my calls.

"What happens next? Do I need to post bail or anything?"

He consulted the computer screen. "Judge set bail at three thousand."

"Dollars?" The lights of the station blurred. I'd have to sell a kidney to get that much cash.

"She's eighteen and a flight risk. If she returns for her court hearing, the money will be returned to you."

If she returns? Three thousand dollars was more than I had to spare, and I didn't know if Alexandra—whoever this girl was—would show up for her hearing. Giving Officer Heathman even a dollar was a gamble. And I'd never been much of a risk-taker. Until tonight, it seemed.

I unzipped the top of my purse. "Do you take credit cards?"

He nodded, and I tried not to think about forfeiting the last of my savings and the overdue property taxes on the farm.

Before I could change my mind, he took my card and typed on his keyboard. "Is she staying with you?"

"Hmm?"

"Is Alexandra staying with you? She didn't provide an address when we arrested her."

"Uh . . . I don't know." *Would* she stay with me? There was no plan here; there wasn't even the beginning of a plan. I was winging this entire thing and way out of my element.

He retrieved a document from the printer, and my eyes roamed the precinct. The desks surrounding Officer Heathman's were either empty or quiet. A couple of officers drank coffee, clacking on their keyboards, and another spoke on the phone with someone, his voice low. I did my best not to listen to the conversation, uncertain if one could be arrested for eavesdropping on a police officer.

Heathman returned, startling me from my thoughts. "Sign here, here, here, and here." He indicated with a pen on the forms. "And here, then initial here."

My sloppy signature covered the pages as I rushed to sign before I could rethink my decision. I slid the papers across the table, and he looked them over.

"I'll get her to sign this, and then we'll release her. You can wait here."

I thanked him and remained perched on the edge of my seat. I fiddled with my purse strap. It was old, fraying at the sides, but I used it every day. Ever since I was a kid, I'd been a perpetual creature of habit—eating the same foods, wearing the same clothes, having the same conversations with the same people. I'd trapped myself in a tiny world where I controlled everything.

Sitting in a police station, waiting for Alexandra—a teenage delinquent—went beyond my tiny, controllable world. Yet I stayed in the chair, holding my hand out, palm upward. The blue ink had faded, but the letters were still visible, as if the message had permanently sunk into my flesh.

Don't run.

Three years of grief and loneliness had led me to this moment, and if I ran away without meeting Alexandra, I'd regret it forever.

A loud buzz disturbed the quiet. "She's coming out now, ma'am."

I stood, feeling shaky and breathless as I got my first glimpse of Alexandra Norse. She didn't look like a criminal—not that I knew what a criminal should look like. Tattooed? Multiple facial piercings? Wearing a leather jacket with a gang symbol etched onto the back? She possessed none of those clichéd indicators.

Her dark-brown hair was greasy, probably from her time in lockup, and her small frame was hidden under a baggy T-shirt and black yoga pants. Her clothing appeared old and worn, like my purse. But what really struck me was how young she looked. She hadn't been lying to the officers about her age. Had I looked that young at eighteen?

As I was the only person not dressed in a police uniform, she stepped toward me, clutching a plastic bag with papers inside.

I cleared my throat, all sense of tiredness gone. For some inexplicable reason, I had to fight the impulse to hug her. "Alexandra?"

"Alex." Her tone made me flinch. She looked me over with curiosity, then said, "Did you drive here?"

"Yes."

"Then can we leave before they arrest me again?"

She strode past me, not looking back in my direction, and headed for the door. No thank-you, no explanation, no hint as to what she wanted or why she'd called me in the middle of the night. Unable to stop myself, I chased after her. My purse bounced on my shoulder, sliding down my arm as we approached the truck.

"This is yours?" She looked at the truck with skepticism.

"Borrowed it." I clambered into the cab and unlocked her door. Would she respect me more if I told her the truth about stealing it?

She climbed inside, and I waited expectantly. "Where am I taking you?"

Alex looked out the passenger-side window. "The nearest bus station."

"You don't live around here?"

"Nope."

"Where do you live?"

"At the moment," Alex said, clutching the plastic bag in her lap, "the nearest bus station. I think there's one about five miles away. So head straight, then take a right at the corner."

She indicated the route with her hands.

I didn't start the engine. Why had she called me and not someone else, like a family member or a friend? She was too young to be on her own. Was she a college kid going to school in the city? Had she run out of money to get back home?

"Where's your family?"

She paused, clearly thrown by my blunt question, and I swore her sarcastic demeanor cracked ever so slightly. "My mother lives in Florida."

"And your friends?"

"What friends?" she asked, looking between insulted and incredulous.

"Whoever you're staying with."

"I'm not staying with anyone. Now, can we leave before the police decide to charge me with another crime I didn't commit?"

Her voice demanded action, but I couldn't let her get on a bus and leave the state. She had a court hearing in Cleveland in a few weeks. I needed that $3,000 back.

"Officer Heathman said you had to appear in court. Shouldn't you stay in the area?"

"I think I'll pass."

"Well, I had to pay a lot of money to bail you out. I maxed out my credit card, and I only get the money back if you go to your hearing."

Alex took a deep breath like I was being purposely difficult. "I'll show up for the hearing, okay? Now, can we get moving?" She gestured toward the windshield.

An unsettling feeling flooded my stomach. Not about the money, which I doubted would ever be returned to my bank account. I'd have to beg Laurel Montgomery, the town treasurer, to grant me another extension on my property taxes.

The feeling ran deeper than any financial implications. It seemed vital, like I wouldn't be able to continue on if Alex left for Florida. "What if you stay with me until the hearing?"

"I'm not a charity case."

"It's not charity. In exchange, you could help with my farm."

"You mean, your blueberry farm?" She looked me over from head to toe with incredulity. "And get trapped there like you did? I think I'll pass."

I leaned back in my seat. Why was she acting like this? Officer Heathman had been right: Alex *was* a real piece of work. But that wouldn't scare me off. Not tonight, when I was breaking all the rules. "Beats getting on a bus and avoiding your problems till they eventually catch up to you, which of course this will. You can't steal something and then expect everyone to look the other way. You have to deal with your problems like an adult."

"Whatever," she muttered, looking anywhere but at me.

Despite my irritation, a plan was forming in my mind, growing clearer by the second. Alex wasn't the only person in the truck with problems. Every week, thieves ransacked my farm, bleeding me dry. Last night, I'd made the decision to stop hiding in my house and do something—anything—to stop the culprits. Only I'd failed.

But what if I had a little help? From someone who clearly didn't mind bending the rules?

"Would you consider yourself a good thief?" I asked. "This incident aside."

"I'm not a thief. Those cops are lying." Her face darkened as she stared out the windshield.

"Okay, sure," I responded, trying to calm her. But I believed Officer Heathman. Perhaps my personality didn't let me question anyone in a position of authority, but he hadn't come across as a liar. "I'm having a problem at the farm, and I could use your help."

"My help with what?"

The moment I spoke, I knew it would be trouble. Alex had only minutes ago been released from prison on bail. She had enough problems of her own without adding mine to the list. But desperation washed away my good sense. Who better to catch a thief than another thief? She could help me stop the kids and return for her court hearing, leaving me with the bail money and more blueberries to sell.

Alex Norse had called me for a reason—and now, I had a way to save the farm.

I switched on the truck's ignition and said, "They're called the Blueberry Bandits, and you're going to help me bring them down."

FIVE

Though I kept the house in a state of cleanliness that would work as the "after" shot in a cleaning commercial, it had been so long since I'd had a guest that it made me feel like a bad host to not have something prepared. Was she hungry? All I had in the fridge was old coffee grounds, blueberries, and a half dozen eggs. I'd have to remember to get the extra shampoo and conditioner from my bathroom cabinet and bring them downstairs, along with clean pajamas and maybe some towels in case she was allergic to the cotton ones already in the guest bathroom. All Alex seemed to have was a plastic bag containing the papers Officer Heathman had made her sign and a cell phone.

What would Alex have done if I hadn't picked her up? Hitched a ride on the freeway? Stolen a vehicle from a nearby parking lot? Broken into a house to get some cash? A shudder ran through me—from both fear and rage. The justice system had left Alex, someone who clearly needed help, to fend for herself. I clutched my phone with reverence, grateful for the lifeline this tiny piece of plastic had provided.

"Watch your step," I said when we reached the porch. "The bottom one is broken. One of those classic 'I dropped a paint can' incidents."

She complied despite my rambling nonsense.

When I opened the front door, Juno tore down the stairs. She barked and jumped, excited that I'd brought someone home.

"This is Juno. She's the neighbor's, but occasionally she stays here," I said, relieved when Alex started petting the border collie.

After five seconds, Juno trusted Alex enough to roll over and get belly pets.

With Juno on our heels, I showed Alex the house, switching on the lights as I moved from room to room. She took in the house silently, occasionally rubbing her wrists where the handcuffs had left a faint red line. I added lotion to my growing list of things she'd need.

The guest bedroom was warm, so I opened the window, apologizing for the lack of air-conditioning. "There's a decent breeze most nights, and it's got the best view in the house." *If you like blueberry fields,* I added to myself.

What the space lacked in air circulation, it made up for in privacy. Located just off the kitchen, the bathroom was directly across the hall, so she'd have it to herself. I never had company over, so the back half of the first floor would be all hers. In fact, besides Juno and Wade—the latter of whom I begrudgingly let inside on occasion to fix things—Alex was the only person I'd had in the house for the last three years.

Guests posed too much of a risk.

All I had left of my mom were the things she'd touched, so I loved her possessions the way I'd loved her. Her pictures and paintings, though valueless, held immense sentimental worth to me. I couldn't risk exposing the inside of the house to anyone, because everything—from the dishes to the furniture to the faded curtains—was a memory I clung to with both hands.

Of course, I didn't tell Alex any of this. My apprehension might scare her off, and I didn't want her to be afraid to touch something. Though, for some reason, my anxiety hadn't spiked when she entered the house or when she sat on the guest bed and wrinkled the blanket. Her presence felt natural, as though the room had always belonged to her.

Alex stared at the pictures hanging above the dresser. My mom had called it her "beach room," decorating it with items we'd collected from years of vacationing on the East Coast. Alex examined a photograph of the two of us standing in the ocean, my mother's arms wrapped around me as I smiled. I'd been ten when that photo was taken, but I remembered the surf crashing into our ankles as we walked the shoreline. I still smiled when I dusted that photograph, recalling our trips to the beach with fondness.

"Have you ever been to the Outer Banks?" I asked.

"Where's that?"

"North Carolina."

She shook her head and turned away. *Okay, then.* I cleared my throat and finished the tour, leading her to the guest bathroom.

"I have one upstairs, so this will be all yours." I demonstrated how to twist on the finicky showerhead and showed her the toiletries under the sink. She followed me back into the guest bedroom, where Juno jumped onto the twin bed. Alex's eyes remained expectant.

The house must be really underwhelming, I thought, then said, "So that's everything." I held my hands out like I'd said *Ta-da.*

"What are the house rules?"

"What?" I must've misheard; I didn't have rules for guests.

"Like no smoking or drinking or going upstairs. Stuff like that."

My childhood sleepovers, though few in number, had never included a list of prohibitions. "Where are you staying that there are rules?"

I regretted the question the moment I asked it. She looked like the deer I often caught munching on blueberry bushes after they'd hopped the fence. A single shout sent them fleeing back to the woods.

She spoke to the floor. "Well, I, um . . . Well, at foster homes, the parents normally had rules about what we could or couldn't do in their house."

"You've lived in a foster home?" Shock clouded my voice, and her head ducked lower.

"Not anymore," she mumbled.

I wanted to ask her follow-up questions all night, but in our limited time together, I'd discovered she was rather quiet—not entirely unlike me, in that regard. So I didn't press her, no matter how much I wanted to. Like the deer, I had the distinct impression Alex would flee at the first loud sound.

"I don't have any rules." I fought to keep my voice casual. "But if you smoke, perhaps do it on the porch."

She nodded, looking relieved. When the awkward silence grew to be too much, I retreated upstairs to get the list of items I'd mentally tallied. I set a basket full of things, including a set of my favorite pajamas and a hairbrush, on her bed.

"Yell if you need anything, but you're welcome to whatever you can find."

She looked around the room. "I won't need anything."

Her dismissive tone sent me toward the door. Message received: She needed some space.

"Come on, Juno." I patted my outer thigh. "Come on, girl."

Juno lifted her head in response, then set it back down on Alex's bed.

"Come on." I hit my leg again, awkwardly hovering in the doorway, but Juno rolled onto her side, making it clear she had no intention of leaving the bed.

Since when did Juno prefer this room? "Are you okay with her staying in here?"

Alex shrugged as if she didn't care, but as I closed the door behind me, she reached out and scratched Juno's head, a small smile on her lips.

Heading upstairs, I crossed my fingers that Alex wouldn't be gone in the morning, along with half my things, although I had nothing to steal but pie plates and the bucket of seashells on her dresser—both of which were more valuable than my television. Since it had been purchased in the early months of 2001, she'd need a forklift to get the television to the driveway.

Perhaps going to bed way past my usual time, or the stress of last night's adventure, had caught up to me, but my eyes wouldn't close. A glass of tea would settle my nerves, but I feared Alex would think I was hovering. So I did what everyone does when they can't sleep: I lay in bed and scrolled through the internet on my phone.

The mindless scrolling quickly turned serious when I searched for information about foster care children. Articles about the adoption process popped up first, but Alex hadn't intimated she'd been adopted. She'd mentioned *foster homes*, as in plural, and said that she didn't live there anymore.

I refocused my search on teenagers who'd aged out of the foster care system. My heart ached the more I read. No wonder Alex had gotten arrested. Twenty-five percent of these teenagers end up in prison within two years of aging out. Per the articles, if she'd aged out, Alex would be at a much higher risk of teenage pregnancy, having a criminal record, being homeless or human trafficked, and developing substance abuse problems. Was there anything she wasn't more likely to have?

The answer appeared as I scrolled: a high school degree.

My heart shattered as I imagined what Alex had endured.

From the day I was born till the day she died, my mom had been a constant presence in my life. At eighteen, I wouldn't have lasted a week without her help. She'd answered my questions about laundry, the best price for groceries, how long chicken remained edible before I had to freeze it, and a thousand other things I hadn't learned before heading to the University of Chicago.

At Alex's age, I'd also leaned heavily on my mom for emotional support. We spoke every day on the phone, sometimes for hours. With my social anxiety, I didn't have many friends—at least not the kind who wanted to stay home and watch movies on Friday nights. I disliked drinking, loud music, and crowds. Any friends I made slowly drifted out of my life because we wanted different things. Sara-Lynn, my senior-year roommate, had once told me, "The city is wasted on you." Another friend had grown frustrated with my lack of energy and said, rather harshly, that my life was "depressing." Sooner or later, I ended up feeling judged by anyone who got close to me, and I withdrew from people more and more, sticking to less emotionally threatening activities, like academics and my part-time job as an English tutor.

When she died, I lost more than a mother—I lost my best friend.

The hole in my heart, the place I tried to keep my mind from entering, swallowed me into a sea of hopelessness.

Perhaps Alex never had anyone to lose. Was that pain worse than mine? To have an intact heart because no one had claimed any part of it?

My eyes drooped, too well conditioned to close at the first sign of tears. I'd cried myself to sleep countless times, but tonight would be different. I couldn't fall apart.

When tomorrow came, I had to be prepared, well rested, presenting a positive outlook on life. Because Alex was here, in my house, with my mother's cell phone number, and these kinds of things didn't just happen.

For the first time in three years, I had a reason to get out of bed in the morning, and I had no intention of failing both my mother *and* Alex.

Voices drifted up the stairs, stirring me from my sleep. Light under the curtains revealed morning had arrived. Had I left the television on? I pulled the pillow over my head to block out the noise. Then my eyes snapped open.

Alex!

I'd brought Alex home from jail last night, and that noise wasn't coming from the television.

Who was she talking to? Who was at the house? I never had visitors. Tossing on my robe, I darted downstairs, not bothering to tame my wild hair.

My mood soured when I saw Wade in the kitchen, going through the fridge. I had every right to be concerned.

Juno followed his every move, waiting for him to drop something edible.

"So that's when the judge decided I wasn't worth the hassle," Wade said as he pulled out a carton of milk. He opened the top and sniffed.

Shrugging, he reached for a glass from the cabinet. *Not the fancy glasses!* I wouldn't let him drink from my garden hose, let alone my mother's favorite dishware.

Alex laughed at his story.

"What are you doing here?" I entered the kitchen, and both Alex and Wade turned to look at me. Since when did he wake up before noon? I should've warned Alex not to let him in the house. That should've been House Rule Number One. "Don't you have your own kitchen to mess up?"

"Morning, Felicity." He sounded unconcerned with my harsh tone. He pushed himself up and sat on the countertop. "Seems you had an out-of-character and exciting time last night. What with your stealing cars and all . . ."

Blood rushed to my cheeks. Stealing the truck had been out of character, but Wade had no right to judge. This thirty-year-old man-child still partied like it was spring break at Daytona Beach.

"Borrowed it," I said. "The keys are in the glove compartment."

"Lucky I didn't report it stolen."

"Nobody would steal that hunk of metal."

Wade smiled as if my words amused him. He turned back to Alex, who still wore the pajamas I'd laid out for her last night; apparently, the color pink didn't bother her.

"So, like I was saying, you're young and harmless looking. It's going to be easy. All you have to do is tell the judge whatever sob story you can think of. One tear and you'll be golden."

"They're not going to buy it," Alex said. "I've got priors."

Wade snorted and jumped down. "Juvenile priors that are probably off your record by now. When I was sixteen, I lit the opposing football team's bus on fire. Barely got a slap on the wrist. Then, when I was seventeen—"

"We don't need to hear every detail of your deplorable teenage behavior." My voice rose, drowning out his and putting an end to his stories. Alex didn't seem to need any inspiration for getting into trouble.

"Too much fun for you, anyway," Wade said. "But I've got a connection to a lawyer who can help with this shoplifting charge."

Now it was definitely time for him to leave. I snatched the glass of milk from his hand and set it gently in the sink. "We don't want the lawyer who handled your public intoxication charge."

"Hey, that guy was good. Only got forty hours of community service. And he handles everything: DUIs, divorces, botched medical procedures—"

"Absolutely not."

Wade turned to Alex and pointed over his shoulder at me. "You'll have to forgive her. She's usually in bed by nine, so last night was a lot for her."

"Goodbye, Wade." I shoved him out of the kitchen and toward the front door.

"So inhospitable," he said, then called over his shoulder, "It was nice to meet you, Alex!"

I kept my hand pressed to his back until his feet landed on the porch.

Once outside, he turned and lowered his voice. "You know this is a bad idea, right? Don't get me wrong, I'd love to grab some popcorn and watch this train wreck, but bringing home a teenager from jail? You're not equipped to handle this."

I grabbed the side of the door, ready to slam it in his face. How did he know what I could or could not handle? He didn't know anything about me. "Gee, thanks, but you're the last person I'd take advice from. Didn't you get drunk last year and superglue your hands together?"

"Yes, but there was a good reason for that."

"Which was?"

"I can't remember." Wade stuck his head back inside and whistled. "Juno." He whistled again. "Come here, girl."

Paws clattered on the hardwood floor. I scratched Juno behind her ears as she raced outside after her owner. I closed the door, thinking the dog was welcome in my home anytime—but her owner, not so much.

When I returned to the kitchen, my anxiety spiked at Alex's expectant look. My grand plan to impress her had vanished the moment Wade set foot in this house. What would I say to her? Was I doing the right thing by letting her stay here? Nothing had gone according to plan lately, and now a homeless eighteen-year-old sat in my kitchen. She'd need food and clothes and a whole host of items I couldn't afford. With my wider hips and pudgy waistline, Alex would have to wear my old, out-of-style—probably never-in-style—clothes from high school. Blood rushed to my head. My fashion choices had now harmed more than just me.

"Sorry about that," I said, sitting across from her at the kitchen table, trying not to enter full panic mode. *Be cool. Be calm. Take a jab at Wade.* "He's annoying, but his dog is nice."

"Are you still dating him?"

I choked on the air in my lungs. "No." My answer was emphatic. If he'd suggested otherwise, I'd strangle him. I didn't care how cute his dog was. "I've never dated or done anything close to resembling dating Wade."

Alex looked like she didn't believe me. She glanced out the side window toward his house. "He's good-looking."

She wasn't wrong, but I'd never admit that. Not to Wade, or Alex, or anybody.

"Don't bother telling him, because he seems to already know."

"He's better-looking than you described him."

My heart slammed into my throat. I'd mentioned Wade frequently to my mom in the voicemails, almost none of it good. The fact that Alex knew about him from those messages sent my mind into a tailspin. Had she listened to all the messages? How long ago did she get that phone number? If she listened to the messages, then she'd know all my problems and secrets.

I bit my lip, mortified, but Alex gave nothing away.

"So, what's the deal with these Blueberry Bandits?" she asked, playing with the edge of the place mat.

I seized the distraction. "I'll tell you as we eat breakfast." I stood and opened the fridge. I'd been right about its sorry state last night. "We've got eggs, cinnamon, flour, butter, two slices of bread, half a carton of milk, and . . ." I opened the cupboard to the right. Oh! "About two cups of brown sugar." When had I last bought brown sugar? It'd probably been there for over a year—but no matter, because I had all the ingredients necessary to cook a great breakfast. "How about blueberry coffee cake?"

Alex made a face. "Coffee tastes like battery acid."

"There's actually no coffee in coffee cake."

"Dumb name, then."

I set the butter on the counter, her lack of enthusiasm not dampening my excitement. Years had passed since I'd baked for anyone but myself. "Do you want to grab us some berries? Two cups ought to do it." I held out a bowl.

Her eyes widened, and I realized she'd probably never picked fruit straight from the vine before.

"Come on, I'll show you how to pick the best ones." I moved toward the back door and turned the handle.

She mumbled under her breath—something about child labor—but stood and followed me outside.

SIX

Alex crouched to examine Timmy's bucket.

We'd trudged out to the back acre after breakfast because she wanted to examine the "crime scene," as she called it. The bushes, set in organized rows, lay flat against the Ohio earth until they reached the woods and disappeared along the horizon. Not exactly the Rhine, but it had a certain charm.

"Four of them, you said?" Alex asked.

"That's right. Timmy Callaway and three unidentified friends."

"How are they getting onto the property?"

"Climbing the fence."

"So they're relatively athletic?"

"I suppose."

She inspected a bush that had been picked clean. "And they come every Friday night?"

"At midnight," I said. "What's with all the questions?"

"This is what they usually ask."

"Who?" My shoulders dipped in bafflement.

"Detectives in crime shows. They always start at the scene of the crime. Haven't you watched *NCIS*?"

"No."

"*CSI*? *SVU*?"

Now she's just making up acronyms. "I don't watch—"

"If you say *Bones*, this partnership is finished."

"I'm a woman in her late twenties, living alone on an isolated farm. Twenty minutes of any procedural cop show and I won't sleep for a week."

Alex snorted. "Well, lucky for you, I know what I'm doing . . . and I've got plans for little Timmy."

"We can't do anything that makes him ill, injured, or dead," I said quickly. The glee in her tone made me anxious.

"You're ruining all my creativity."

"I'm serious, Alex. We're dealing with children, not murderers from your crime shows. I think the best option is to catch them stealing on video. Then we'll have proof for the sheriff."

"You're bringing Johnny Law into this?" She made it sound like I was a traitor. "Haven't you tried that before?"

"I haven't had proof before. That's where you come in. Between the two of us, we can cover the whole back section of the field."

"If you want this problem taken care of, it's going to take a hell of a lot more than video evidence. We need to scare them off once and for all; otherwise, they're going to keep coming back."

"I don't want anyone to get hurt."

"All I'm saying is, a little poison on the berries and problem solved."

"Alex—"

"Felicity. Wake. Up." She emphasized each word. "No one in town cares about proof. If Timmy steals all your blueberries, you won't have any left to sell. Who benefits if you go bankrupt?" She started walking toward the shed, dirt kicking up as she opened the double doors.

"But that's so . . . diabolical and . . . wrong . . . and . . ." Words became difficult as I trailed after her.

"No, that's motive." Alex examined a shovel, swinging it back and forth as if testing its suitability to whack someone upside the head. "And the stronger the motive, the more dedicated the criminal. You're lucky you found me when you did."

Lucky? Found her? *She called me!*

Alex scraped the shovel on the concrete floor. "If you wanted someone to stand around and take pictures, you brought the wrong girl home from jail."

That much was true. From what I could tell, she had both feet on the gas pedal as she drove directly toward a brick wall. She was either going to break through or crash in a fiery spectacle—there was no in-between with her.

I had less faith we'd survive the crash, but perhaps Alex was onto something. At the bakery, Cheryl had basically said Timmy could steal whatever he wanted—my business be damned. How could it be larceny when they considered the farm to be rightfully theirs? It was open season on Lavigne Blueberries, and the Callaways were pushing me toward a going-out-of-business sale.

For all I knew, Cheryl and Jonathan had encouraged Timmy's behavior. At nine years old, he couldn't be trusted to get on a school bus by himself, let alone roam the town at night without supervision.

Relying on the law, asking for help at town meetings—doing the right things—had gotten me nowhere except to the verge of bankruptcy. Another few months of theft and I'd be forced to sell—a decision that only benefited the Callaways. Who else would want an unprofitable blueberry farm in Elswood?

I couldn't let that happen. I wouldn't.

Though my mother had taught me to make smart, responsible choices, to avoid scrutiny at all costs, dire times called for equally dire measures. This was my house, my farm, my property. If I didn't defend it, no one else would.

"Okay," I said, hesitation eroding just enough to entertain Alex and her vast knowledge of criminal behavior. "What's the plan for getting rid of the thieves?"

Her answering smile made me wonder how quickly I'd regret asking that question.

SEVEN

The whole town knew Alex was living at my house within forty-eight hours. When people asked about her, I kept my response short and to the point: She'd come to help with the farm. Not exactly a lie. They didn't need to know she'd been arrested or that I'd paid her bail. Elswood residents were so judgmental that, at the word *jail*, they'd write her off as a criminal without considering any of the circumstances that had led to her arrest. Alex didn't deserve that stigma. "The Elswood Doormat" carried enough shame for the both of us.

Alex, though, didn't tell anybody anything. She kept to herself, something most of the locals figured out when she refused to acknowledge them or respond with a polite hello. I almost insisted on manners, but I wasn't her parent. Just her bail bondsman, as Wade had so charmingly put it yesterday when he dropped off Juno so he could go on an overnight fishing trip.

"What's the holdup?" Alex entered the kitchen. Juno, her new best friend, followed her from room to room. With Alex around, Juno got three walks a day, plus more treats than any veterinarian would've recommended. Even now, when Alex opened the fridge to grab a soda, she tossed a few pieces of broccoli on the floor.

"It's not like we're going to eat it," Alex muttered at my raised eyebrows.

I pulled two slices of cheese from the fridge, admiring the abundance of options stacked on the shelves. It had been months since I'd bought enough food to fill the fridge. My appetite had decreased in proportion to my happiness. But yesterday, I'd dragged Alex to the market to find sustenance, then embarrassed her with my "excessive" number of coupons.

After slapping the cheese onto sandwiches, I placed them in a bag and packed the basket. "All right. Let's get out of here."

To my surprise, Alex had agreed to go on a picnic. She'd responded with a surly "Whatever" at breakfast, which meant *Absolutely, I'd love to* in teenager. With nearly a week until the Friday-night Blueberry Bandits returned, we needed something to occupy our time.

We strolled into town, Alex helping Juno find a stick to carry, and me swinging the basket—with a huge, goofy smile on my face. A picnic. In the summer. In the town square.

Like I used to do with my mom.

We laid a blanket on the grass, ate grilled-chicken sandwiches, and people-watched, one of my favorite Elswood activities. Juno chewed on her stick, oblivious to the rest of the world.

"Wait for it," I said, watching Janelle approach Hilda on the sidewalk. "Wait for it . . ."

Alex craned her neck to get a better view as both ladies kept their heads down, until at the very last second, Janelle gave Hilda a tight smile, unable to be rude to a neighbor in public.

"There. That's how it's done. The two of them haven't spoken in years. Not since Hilda won Best Christmas Cookie at the tree-lighting ceremony four years ago."

Alex looked lost. "Why not say something?"

"Because our social fabric couldn't handle that many feuds at once. Elswood only has twelve hundred residents, so while everyone knows everyone, that doesn't mean everyone *likes* everyone. When families have lived in the same social circles for generations, blood is bound to turn bad. And unlike a big city, small towns leave a person with nowhere to hide." Enemies couldn't be avoided when you both had the same hairdresser, grocer, accountant, and doctor. "Some feuds go back generations, such as my troubles with the Callaways; others, like Glen and Blair's competing snow-globe stores, have only cropped up in the last few years. Elswood runs on social tenets that keep the town from crumbling into chaos."

Our discussion moved from Janelle and Hilda down the line of shops, restaurants, and service locations. I hit the major conflicts, the ones that had boiled over in some fashion. Alex's interest in town gossip baffled me. Crime and conflict seemed to be her favorite things.

"So, what's his story?" Alex asked as Patrick walked into the post office. Oh, Patrick. Where to begin with that man? He bounced from one shenanigan to the next. But I skipped over the time he accidentally lit his shoe on fire, and settled on a juicier tale.

"He married Leslie LaCroix right out of high school, but she left him two years later . . ." I paused for dramatic effect. "For the history teacher, Mr. Shaw, who is twenty-three years older than her."

"Ewww," Alex said, revulsion mixing with her smile. She reached into her sandwich and pulled out a piece of chicken to give to Juno. "That's disgusting."

"Tell me about it." Mr. Shaw had been my history teacher, too.

"This is the weirdest town on earth," she declared, not looking the least bit upset that she was now living in such a place. "Who would've thought a town of this size would have so many problems?"

"Are you from a city, then?" I picked at the edge of the blanket.

In my short time with Alex, I'd learned that any personal conversations would require me to do the heavy lifting. She was not a sharer, and neither was I, typically. But with Alex, I couldn't help myself.

Who exactly was Alexandra Norse? And why had fate put her in my life?

"I'm from Buffalo," she responded after a long, heart-wrenching pause.

As I'd practiced last night, I kept my response light and casual. Small talk only. No probing or intrusive questions.

"I've never been to Buffalo. All I know is that it gets lots of snow."

"You're not missing much."

"How long did you live there?"

"Till I was fourteen."

"And then your mom moved to Florida?" I hadn't connected the dots between her mom in Florida and how she came to be in foster care in Ohio.

"What do you care?"

An invisible shield came down, separating the two of us though we sat but feet apart on the picnic blanket. Two women, from two completely different worlds—neither of us great at social interaction. Her tone made it clear I'd overstepped. Better to cut my losses and move the conversation toward safer waters, like picking blueberries or Patrick's peanut allergy that had randomly appeared when he was thirty-seven.

But didn't she know I was dying to hear about her life? Where she had lived, where she'd gone to school, if she'd had any crushes, and what she wanted to do in the future? What had caused that pained, wounded look in her eyes—the one that made my soul hurt?

I'd spent the last several days trying to learn more about her, uncovering her affinity for Coca-Cola, crime shows (the more gruesome, the better), and Korean pop music. As an avid reader, I'd tried to bond with her over books, showing her my vast collection of romance novels and taking her to the local library. I'd signed her up for her very own library card, which Alex promptly used to check out two copies of *The Devil Takes You Home*—one for her and one for me. The first chapter had me sleeping with the lights on.

Not exactly the buddy-read I had in mind.

But Alex had successfully dodged all my attempts to learn anything meaningful about her life. And as impressive as her artful avoidance might be, I *needed* answers.

"For starters, it would be nice to know something about the person living in my house."

"Why?" She sounded defensive, and my heart cracked open a little more. Despite knowing all about my life and its many problems from the voicemails on her phone, she didn't trust me. Not yet.

"Because I don't have a lot of people in my life, and I want us to be friends." Internally, I cringed, knowing how pathetic and desperate I sounded. "After my mom . . . Well you know what happened to her." I swallowed. "You're the first person I've let into my house in three years. That's kind of a big deal for me."

Slowly, she leaned back and let her ankles cross in the grass. She scratched Juno's head. Anytime Alex became anxious, she reached for the dog—a comfort mechanism. I recognized the signs. For me, it was cooking—re-creating my mother's recipes, using her dishes, sitting at the kitchen table where she used to sit. I touched the things she'd loved because they were an extension of her, and so long as I had them, she would remain a part of me.

At least Alex wouldn't gain twenty pounds from petting Juno.

"What do you want to know?" Her eyes never left Juno, as if the dog had asked the question instead of me. "I'm not that interesting."

I worked to keep my voice calm, unsure which of my thousand questions to ask first. "How long have you had that phone number?"

"Two and a half years."

"Did you listen to every voicemail?"

"You called me, remember?" Alex said. "And I didn't have much else to do. You were the only person who called."

"What about your mom?"

Alex adjusted her legs so Juno's head fit comfortably on her lap. "She's my biological mother, but I never lived with her. She got pregnant when she was sixteen and dumped me with Ted and Judy."

Alex paused, ruffling Juno's fur, then flattening it out again. Juno lay very still, eyes on Alex's face, as if she, too, could sense the anxious storm brewing inside the teenager. "They went to the same church as Brittany, and when she got pregnant, they offered to take me in. I lived with them for fourteen years, but they were older, and they had to go into a nursing home." She took a deep breath. "Judy died four years ago, and Ted followed about a year after."

"They died?" My heart constricted. She'd lost people she loved, too. "Oh, Alex, I'm so sorry."

My eyes watered, but Alex turned away, not seeing the tears. "They were in their late eighties. It's a little different than what happened to your mom."

"But still . . ." I wanted her to keep talking, to tell me everything about her time in foster care and what happened when she aged out of the system. I was being as nosy as every other person in this town, and I didn't care.

"But nothing. They died, I went into foster care till I was too old, and now I'm here. That's the end of the story. Nothing more to tell."

She stood, grabbing Juno's leash. "Let's head back" was all she said before stepping toward the sidewalk. I quickly folded the blanket, grabbed the basket, and chased after her, worried she wouldn't stop once we reached the house. I'd overstepped; I'd pushed her too far, too fast.

We walked in silence, making my bones hurt. Our relationship hadn't been ready for my probing questions. Her precarious presence in my life could be snapped with one wrong word.

I should've listened to my head, not my heart.

When we reached the house and she headed toward her bedroom, my mouth, with a mind of its own, went rogue again. "Alex," I called out, and she stopped in her doorway. She looked like she wanted to be anywhere but around me. "I know you don't want to talk about it right now, but if you do—"

"I won't."

"But if you change your mind, I'm here, okay? I'm not going anywhere." I think it had been established that I was going nowhere, both literally and metaphorically.

She sighed and said, "I'll see you later." She made it sound more like a question than a statement, giving my overactive brain something to ruminate on for hours and hours until I could twist her words into the worst-case scenario—which meant she'd essentially said *Goodbye.*

She shut her bedroom door with a decisive bang.

I shouldn't have expected so much from Alex. I couldn't expect her to stay here for a couple of nights and instantly trust me with all her secrets. She probably had more emotional baggage than I did, and I had an entire houseful.

My lower back rested against the countertop. I'd shared so much of my life with her through those voicemails, things nobody told their best friends, let alone a complete stranger. She likely associated me with hysterical crying and ranting. Gaining her trust might be harder than dispensing with the Blueberry Bandits.

I'll try again tomorrow, I thought, heading upstairs. And if that didn't work, there was always the next day, and the day after that.

As I'd told Alex: I wasn't going anywhere.

EIGHT

Alex turned the easel to face the couch, revealing the poster board with the elements of her master plan. My heart thudded so fast that I felt dizzy. Five days had passed since I'd gifted Alex carte blanche to solve the Blueberry Bandit problem. I'd regretted the decision within the hour, almost as soon as I remembered that prison was a very real place. This was what I got for making a rash decision and letting my eighteen-year-old roommate take control of this revenge train. Wade was right when he'd said it was going to crash.

"Voilà," Alex said, running her hand over her artwork.

I covered my eyes, separating my fingers to absorb the plan in fragments.

"Will you quit with that?" Alex stepped toward the couch and knocked my hands away from my face. "It's going to be fine. I've thought of everything."

She had drawn arrows from one side of the board to the other, listing the steps. My throat went dry. Why did we need so much food coloring?

"What do you think?" she asked after she ran me through the scheme, start to finish. She put her hands behind her back, admiring the plan she'd worked on for several days.

"How . . ." I struggled to find the right words. I didn't want to insult her efforts. "How did you get a map of the sprinkler system?"

"The garage. You've got tons of stuff in there. You never throw anything away."

"But the floodlights? Why do we need them?"

"It's for dramatic effect, Felicity." She tossed her hands up like I was not understanding something simple. "I heard they do this to prisoners in Guantánamo Bay."

Oh. My. Word.

I managed a long exhale, then focused on Alex, not the plan. Her court date had been scheduled for July 30 at eleven a.m. I'd written it on the calendar and circled it three times so I wouldn't forget. Though that wasn't likely, as it was the only thing *on* the calendar.

Even so, I dreaded each day, growing increasingly uneasy with the thought of her leaving once the judge handed down a sentence and my bail money was returned. I thought of the house—empty and silent, no dishes in the sink, her bedroom unoccupied. She would leave, and then where would I be? *No,* I corrected myself, as I had so many times before. *Where would* Alex *be?*

"It's good," I said in a bright tone, which of course was a lie because the plan wasn't good at all. It wasn't poison, but accepting her second-best idea solely because it didn't involve elements of the death scene from *Romeo and Juliet* set the bar too low.

I didn't have time to dwell on the illegalities. While we waited for the approaching weekend, lots of things had to be done. First, we bought all the blue food coloring, dry Gatorade packets, and Kool-Aid pouches in Northeast Ohio. As Alex had discovered, the house and shed were equipped with a total of four garden hoses, each running from the water tank to drip-line sprinklers that ran throughout the bushes. My nails were caked with mud by the time we detached, then reattached, the hoses, diverting all water lines to one single spot in the blueberry field.

"The fun zone," Alex called it. If her scheme succeeded, nobody would escape from the overpicked back section unscathed.

My mother had put in drip-line sprinklers a decade ago to ensure a constant water supply for the berries in the summer. Blueberries, with their shallow roots, required just the right amount of water. Too much water and the roots would flood; not enough water and they'd dry out like a beached whale.

But we'd held on to the irrigation sprinklers—the ones that shot water in every direction like a grenade.

"It'll be like a water park—only, not the good kind," Alex said, shoving the rusted sprinkler poles into the dirt, creating a twenty-five-foot circle.

Alex guessed that the kids wouldn't return two Fridays in a row now that I'd caught them. "Far too predictable," she'd said. So we pushed the revenge plan to Saturday, hoping we wouldn't miss our opportunity and have to wait another week. Honestly, I'd have been fine if we guessed wrong, but Alex was determined to see her plan work.

And that was how I found myself lying in the dirt on a Saturday night—cold, tired, and getting bitten by mosquitoes. What I wouldn't have given to be in my bed, fast asleep, dreaming of something calm and safe, like the beach on a warm, sunny day.

I pushed the side button on the walkie-talkie. "Alex?"

Static responded, then Alex's voice: "Careful. This channel isn't secure."

I rolled my eyes. The Motorola walkie-talkies were so old they were from Radio Shack. Of course they weren't secure. I'd almost said no to the radios when she found them in the closet, but we needed something to communicate with, because I had to be outside "the fun zone" before she flipped the switch that turned on the sprinklers. Otherwise, I'd be shooting myself in the foot. It would be just like me to fall into my own trap.

"Where are you?" I asked.

"I'm in the woods, in the northeastern quadrant."

What was she talking about? We didn't have quadrants.

"What's wrong, Felicity?" I sensed her smile over the radio waves. While Alex had spent the day counting down the hours till go-time, I'd used my inhaler twice.

"Are you sure this is going to work? What if something happens? What if someone gets hurt?" My what-ifs had been driving her crazy since she'd announced her grand plan.

"Relax before you give yourself a heart attack. It'll be fine. I put enough dye in the water tank that the Smurfs themselves wouldn't know the difference." She sounded confident. If only I could say the same. I'd never done anything like this in my life, let alone to children.

It's water, I reminded myself to stop my finger from hitting the walkie-talkie and calling the whole plan off. *Lots and lots and lots of water.*

The sun had set hours ago. Alex insisted I cover the fields, as I knew them better than anyone, even the children. She waited near the tree line, using the darkness as cover so she could connect the two extension cords and create a waterworks display rivaling the one at the Bellagio Hotel in Las Vegas.

She was to wait for the all-clear signal from me before turning on the sprinklers. After that, the plan was in fate's hands.

My walkie-talkie buzzed. "Any sign of them?"

"Negative," I said.

"What's taking so long?"

"Maybe they got the message after the incident in the bakery?" I suggested without any real conviction. Even if Cheryl had intervened—which she hadn't—those kids would find a way to return. Timmy's face in the bakery had said it all. My tune changed as I pictured his irksome face. "Stay alert. They'll be here any minute."

"Stupid kids are never on time. I'm growing bored over here."

Growing bored? My body hummed with a mixture of anticipation and nervousness. How could she be growing bored at a time like this? "Don't do anything till I tell you to."

The kids made us wait another fifteen minutes, but my straining ears didn't miss their approach. Small, dark figures roamed the edges of the field. Their heads were close together, the universal sign of planning. I made myself tiny, ducking below the bushes so they couldn't see me.

"We've got company," I whispered into the walkie-talkie. My muscles tightened. Hopefully, Alex hadn't fallen asleep out of boredom.

"Excellent. I'm wai—"

She must've moved her finger off the talk button too early.

Four shadows paced through the field, heading right for our trap. But this time they weren't carrying buckets. Metal scraped against metal, sending a shiver down my spine. My worst fear had been realized: hedge clippers.

No! I nearly lurched from my hiding spot when they cut into the bushes, taking off an entire section. Laughing softly, they moved to another bush. Then another. This went beyond picking blueberries without paying; they were deliberately destroying my property. Didn't they know how long it took for blueberry bushes to grow? My grandfather had probably planted the seeds that grew those bushes.

They would pay for this. Alex had been right: Those kids had it coming. I hustled toward the eastern acre, keeping my head low.

"Now," I said into the walkie-talkie when I'd gotten far enough away. She didn't respond. "Now, Alex."

What was taking so long? I'd given her the go-ahead, the very thing she'd been begging for all night.

I glanced at the radio. "Alex?" The green light had turned to a blinking red—the battery was dead. What the hell? I nearly hurled the useless radio to the ground. Why did nothing ever work for me?

I looked over my shoulder at the kids. Another bush fell. I couldn't stand around doing nothing while my business was literally chopped down. More laughter propelled me toward the woods. The longer it took, the more blueberry bushes I'd lose. Two decades to grow, two seconds to destroy. There was a lesson in there somewhere, but I didn't pause to consider it.

I dodged around roots and worked my way toward where I assumed the northeastern quadrant was located. When the bushes were behind me, I spun in every direction, eyes searching for any sign of Alex. It was dark, too dark to see anyone lying in the leaves and moss.

Where is she? Where is she? My heartbeat sputtered. I was not going to be foiled by these kids again.

A silhouette moved in the tree line. "Now! Alex! Now!"

My scream hit the night air like thunder in a storm. The thieves would hear me, but it would be too late for them. They'd stepped into our trap precisely as Alex predicted.

And now they'd face the consequences.

As soon as the words left my mouth, Alex switched on the sprinklers, sending gallons of water straight into the heart of the blueberry field.

My feet faltered as I ran toward her. My hand went to my mouth.

Water shot from the irrigation sprinklers like a fire hose, each pointed at the kids' location. The water struck them from all sides. In the moonlight, I couldn't tell that the liquid was dyed dark blue.

The kids scattered, running in every direction. Someone slipped in the wet mud as they darted for the tree line. I hoped the unfortunate soul was Timmy Callaway, but I couldn't see his face. He cried out and tried unsuccessfully to stand, clothes sopping with water and mud.

The entire bloodbath took five minutes. The kids—some crying, others screaming—fled from the field. When it was over, I wanted to lift Alex onto my shoulders and carry her back to the house like she'd hit a walk-off home run in the World Series.

"Holy shit," I said as Alex switched off the sprinklers. I ran a hand through my hair, unable to contain my energy. "Alex, you destroyed them. You probably made them pee their pants. I almost feel bad for how pathetic they were."

The moonlight made her smirk more pronounced. "You know they're kids, right?"

I was smiling at the onslaught of terror Alex had unleashed upon unsuspecting children, and I didn't feel guilty. Quite the opposite. I felt good for the first time in a long while. My smile widened. What was happening to me?

I wrapped my arm around Alex's shoulders, laughing at how well the plan had worked. We trudged through the blue mud back to the house.

So, this is what it's like to win, I thought. *Who knew it would be so awesome?*

NINE

I woke early, my body unused to sleeping so well.

Staring at the ceiling, I reconstructed last night's events. There had been kids in the field, hedge clippers—then an onslaught of blue water, followed by a night of celebrating. I vaguely remembered pouring grapefruit juice into champagne flutes and eating chips straight from the bag. I couldn't remember the last time I'd felt that good.

I reached for my phone and started dialing.

Shoot! Stop!

Fumbling with the phone, I ended the call, hoping it hadn't connected.

Breathing heavily, heart pounding with panic, I sat up. My head rested against the bed frame, covers falling to my waist.

I can't call her anymore—not even when I have good news.

A pang of hurt cut through my heart, draining the happiness from my limbs. What did it matter if I'd stopped the Blueberry Bandits if I couldn't tell my mom about the tale? My triumph suddenly felt meaningless, empty, like it had never happened. Other than me, who cared about this victory?

I jumped when the phone lit up, its loud ring blaring in my bedroom. *Shoot, shoot, shoot!*

I worked to keep the tears from affecting my voice. "Alex?"

"The house better be on fire."

"It's nearly six."

"Exactly," she muttered. "Why are you up so early? And more importantly, why are you calling me?"

"It was an accident. You should go back to sleep." She sounded groggy and angry—not a good combination for a teenager.

She muttered what I thought was a curse word; then the line went dead.

After an hour of handpicking berries, I headed inside to make breakfast. Juno greeted me at the back door, tail wagging, ready to go for her morning walk. *After coffee,* I thought, scratching her head. My tired, bloodshot eyes wouldn't last long without caffeine.

Alex was drinking a soda when I entered the kitchen. Normally, she slept in till around ten, door firmly closed, ignoring the world until I woke her and declared it was time for blueberry deliveries.

That unintentional six a.m. wake-up call had achieved a miracle.

She stood directly in front of the side window and didn't turn when I said, "Good morning."

I filled the coffeepot with water and switched on the machine. Still no response. "Alex?" I stepped around the kitchen table. "What are you looking at?"

She reacted to my close proximity, startling a bit. "The view."

What? I didn't have a view—at least, not that way. The blueberry fields could be seen through the back of the kitchen, not the side.

I looked out the window.

Oh! My face flushed. Wade was unloading his truck, moving tackle boxes and fishing poles to his porch. He bent down, then tossed a sleeping bag over the side. By all accounts, this July morning was a scorcher, because he was shirtless.

"Are you serious?" I instinctively stepped away from the window, worried he'd notice us watching. But even as my feet moved, my eyes never left Wade.

"He's got abs." Alex took a sip of Coke. "Great abs."

Wade stacked the fishing poles against the truck. Why did he have to look so good, even when he likely hadn't showered all weekend? I tried to be repulsed, but it wasn't quite working.

The warm morning breeze floated inside, swaying my hair. I came to my senses, clearing my throat to get Alex's attention. It didn't work. I whacked her lightly on the arm. "He's going to catch you staring."

"Don't care," she muttered. "Worth it."

Wade arched his body over the side of the truck to collect another tackle box. He wiped the sweat from his brow as he set it on his porch and returned to retrieve more items from the truck bed.

The coffeepot chimed, but I didn't move. *Coffee can wait,* I determined somewhere in the back of my mind. Caffeine had become unimportant.

"You're sure you don't like him?" she asked.

"Mm-hmm?" I almost hadn't heard her, but the skepticism in her voice demanded an answer. "Yeah, I mean no. I don't like him."

Alex pursed her lips together, fighting a smile. Flustered, I gave up on trying to hide our gaze. If he didn't want people staring, then he shouldn't be parading around shirtless in broad daylight.

"When you two are finished, can you send Juno outside?" Wade called over his shoulder.

We ducked below the windowsill. Alex laughed, but my cheeks warmed with embarrassment. I adjusted my robe and moved to fetch my coffee. I had a lot to accomplish today, and I wasn't going to be distracted by the Neanderthal outside.

After two helpings each of french toast, we left to deliver blueberries. Deliveries were easier with two people, as Alex would run cartons to the bakery while I was in the market. Or Alex would wait outside and sell to people as they walked past.

She ventured up the street with a few cartons for the health food store, hoping Bob would buy the nonorganic produce. Berry snobs were the worst kind of people. With an extra bounce in my step, I wheeled the wagon behind the Elswood Market, which happened to be my best customer. Mary Londergan, Wade's mother, had owned the grocery store for nearly twenty years, and she purchased a significant amount of berries—two wagonloads per week, at least. Without Mary's business, the blueberry farm would go under, leaving me with no way to make ends meet.

Eric, her store manager, normally accepted the deliveries, but today Mary stood behind the store. She put her hand on her hip and looked over the wagon. My weightless feeling disappeared, like someone had dipped my shoes in cement.

"Good morning," I said cheerfully, though I knew Mary didn't care for nonsense like cheer. "Where's Eric this morning?"

"Threw his back out, leaving me in a lurch." No sympathy in her voice or expression. "This is what you're selling these days?" The bite in her tone made it sound like a shout.

"Yes, a dollar a pound. Same as always."

"And how much for the berries you dyed blue with the hose?"

"You heard about that?" How did she know about the Blueberry Bandits already?

"Whole town has heard by now, Felicity. Don't be naive. You turned a bunch of kids blue, one of whom is the mayor's son."

"All I did was water my crops—which, last time I checked, isn't a crime."

Mary could've stopped the theft with one word to Cheryl or Jonathan. But she wouldn't. Mary considered herself to be above petty feuds. If it didn't involve her family, she didn't concern herself with other people's squabbles.

She must've been thinking along those same lines, because she uncrossed her arms and said, "How's my son doing out there on Clementine Lane? His yard still a mess?"

Wade, the human equivalent of an immature squabble, annoyed her to no end. His lifestyle made people question what kind of mother had raised him.

"He just returned from a fishing trip."

Mary rolled her eyes, muttered, "That boy never works," then turned the conversation back to business. "A dollar per pound, then. Eric will pay you at the end of the week."

With nothing else to discuss, Mary turned and walked back inside the store. I exhaled in relief. The less time I spent around Mary and the grocery store, the better off I'd be.

Alex had chosen the gazebo as our rendezvous point. The bulletin board near the sidewalk held an assortment of flyers, signs, and odd ramblings from *The Elswood Gazette*. The blue Founders' Day ads caught my eye, causing sadness to creep into my soul on an otherwise-glorious morning. Those flyers haunted me all through town, day in and day out, a reminder that my mother would never participate again. I pictured her by our blueberry booth, passing out free slices of pie. "Kindness costs nothing," she'd said. "And everyone likes pie."

"What's wrong?" Alex asked, coming to stand beside me. I hadn't heard her approach.

"Nothing." I hastily cleared the emotion from my throat. "Did you manage to sell any berries to the health food store?"

She held out a crisp twenty-dollar bill.

"Nice. You were polite, right? No threatening Bob like last time? The man only has the one toupee, Alex. Ripping it off his head would be downright cruel."

"Bob's cheap. When I burn that rug, he'll have another one pronto. You'll see."

"We need customers. I can't afford to piss everyone off."

Something behind me caught Alex's attention. "Speaking of pissed-off people . . ." she said, voice low.

I turned, and my stomach dropped. Four women, all looking their Sunday best—which meant straight, blond hair with neutral-colored dresses that went to their knees—marched down the walkway. There could be no mistaking where they were headed or their intent when they arrived. Once Mary had revealed that she knew about last night's incident, I'd expected this confrontation. My blood pressure rose with each clack of their heels on the concrete.

Cheryl Callaway led the pack, so her weekly Pilates sessions must have been paying off. I considered complimenting her calf muscles as a distraction so I could grab Alex and flee.

Don't run, don't run.

"Is it me, or do they look murderous?" I whispered to Alex. There was no time for a response as they came within hearing distance. "Good morning, ladies. So nice to see you all. The whole gang, wow, just like high school—but we really must be going . . ." I grabbed the wagon handle, indicating that I was on my way to someplace else. Anywhere else.

"Felicity." Cheryl stopped ten feet from me. She crossed her arms. The other three women—Evelyn, Victoria, and Trisha—crowded behind her, staring menacingly at the two of us. I was shocked they didn't have a bucket of tar and feathers.

"Yes?" I responded sweetly, as if unaware what this could be about.

"Do you have any idea what you've done?"

"Excuse me?"

"You think you can harm our children and get away with it?"

"Um . . ."

Cheryl took a threatening step toward me. "The boys came home crying last night, covered in blue dye. We almost had a coronary. They said you were responsible."

"Um . . ."

"The doctor said it won't fade for days. Days! Their youth-football pictures are tomorrow! How could you do this? How could you harm innocent children?"

"'Innocent'?" Alex snorted, and I nudged her with my elbow.

Cheryl's eyes found Alex, who, unlike me, didn't cower or signal retreat. "And this is the one I've been telling you about." Cheryl turned to the ladies behind her. "The *criminal* Felicity took in and set loose on our children."

Alex seemed pleased by Cheryl's assessment. Branding her a "criminal" only increased her self-esteem, giving Alex the confidence to gleefully say, "Your kids are a bunch of spineless losers. We should've decked them with the shovels and been done with it."

The ladies collectively gasped.

Cheryl put a hand over her heart like Alex's comment had knocked the breath from her lungs. "They're nine."

Alex shrugged. "You're never too young to learn from a shovel to the face."

"Why, you deplorable—"

"Leave her alone, Cheryl." I stepped toward the blondes, partially hiding Alex behind me. Alex would stand in the town square and trade threats all day. She had plenty more insults in that clever brain of hers, but I couldn't let her fight for me, no matter how much I wanted her to. This was my score to settle, even if I lost. "If your kids hadn't snuck onto my property, then maybe they wouldn't look like Smurfs this morning."

"*Your* property?" Cheryl looked outraged. "That land was never yours to begin with."

"My mother left me that farm, and if you think I'm going to let you or that punk you call a son damage it, you're even more delusional than . . . than . . ."

It was at that moment, when everyone's tempers were about to boil over, that Timmy Callaway departed the diner, pastry in hand, searching for his mother.

It would have been comedic, if I hadn't stopped breathing the second I saw him.

"Look at what you did!" Cheryl screamed, clutching Timmy's hand as he came to stand beside her.

Timmy's skin was dyed pale blue from his elbows to his hands and his thighs to his ankles. The worst farmer's tan I'd ever seen. But nothing—and I mean nothing—compared to his face. Splotches of blue ran from his chin to his hairline. And here I'd thought Alex added too much blue powder to the water tank, but she'd gotten the combination just right. Timmy was truly and utterly blue.

I couldn't speak, too stunned for words, but Alex burst out laughing. I nudged her with my elbow again.

Cheryl pursed her lips like she was going to blow out the candles on a birthday cake. "I want you to know, we've all given statements to the sheriff. He's going to be watching the two of you night and day. If anything like this happens again, Rodney will escort both of you to jail."

"We're not the ones dyed blue like a bank robber," Alex said, still laughing.

Cheryl took a step toward her, but I was quicker, fully blocking her path.

Cheryl looked like she wanted to strike me. I'd never been in a fight before. I was surprised when I didn't retreat. Instead, I tried to remember how to make a fist. Thumb on the outside, right?

Cheryl glared at me, but onlookers had stopped to watch the confrontation. If she hit me, there'd be witnesses, which was likely why she settled for narrowing her eyes and saying, "This isn't over. You're not getting away with this."

Straightening her dress sleeve, she squeezed Timmy's hand and hauled him down the sidewalk, not stopping until they'd rounded the corner and disappeared from view. The other blondes followed her like sheep.

"Bye-bye," Alex called after them, waving gleefully. After a moment, she turned to me and said, "Well, that was fun. We should do that every morning."

She opened a blueberry carton and ate a handful, looking rather pleased with herself. My recovery took longer; the foreign sensation of adrenaline didn't leave even after Cheryl had departed the square.

This fight wasn't over; it hadn't been for the past century. The Callaways wouldn't let me get away with publicly embarrassing them, shaming their family—the last thing Jonathan, the five-time Elswood Man of the Year, wanted right before this year's vote. My insult to their perfect reputations would not go unanswered.

I adjusted my grip on the wagon handle. People were watching. We couldn't stand in the center of town like this was *Gangs of New York*. Tales of our showdown had likely already spread from Apricot Avenue to Plum Street, leaving little room for the truth among the gossip.

"Come on, let's head back to the house," I told Alex. "Before Wade takes a shower and turns himself blue."

She laughed again, matching my pace but not my mood as we left the square. "Now, *that* would be funny."

TEN

By Monday morning, news of our confrontation with Cheryl had spread around town. I was surprised to learn that, at one point, I'd slapped her and called her mother a whore. I was equally shocked to learn that Cheryl had tried to pepper-spray Alex before dragging me to the ground by my hair. Lies and exaggerations had grown quicker than the weeds in my garden. The town seemed obsessed with the growing feud, and for the first time, I couldn't wait for football season to start. The games would take some of the attention away from us, and hopefully, we could walk around town without people staring or pointing in our direction.

Cheryl's threat of retaliation had me on edge, and whatever that woman cooked up would be a lot worse than foul names or pepper spray. Though not known for her cleverness, she'd be a formidable adversary because she had the whole town wrapped around her finger.

Sooner or later, that shoe would drop, and I'd have another mess on my hands.

But by Wednesday morning—when Alex and I had returned from our blueberry deliveries—any hope of quietly ending the conflict vanished.

At least twenty people stood by the blueberry shed.

"Since when do we have customers?" Alex asked.

"Never." It had been weeks since anyone stopped by to pick berries, let alone twenty at once. My stated business hours had become obsolete with no customers, but I supposed gossip increased business better than any coupon.

My watch showed eleven a.m. "Alex, can you grab the buckets in the garage?"

After darting inside the house, I snatched the cashbox from its hiding place under the winter gloves in the living room closet. It contained two envelopes of cash, about fifty dollars in assorted bills, and a handful of coins for change.

As soon as I unlocked the shed door, customers approached, in a single-file line that seemed to be growing by the minute. Where were these people coming from? Was it National Blueberry Day and I'd missed the announcement? I'd been so out of touch with the world lately that I didn't notice holidays at all. Were it not for Wade's drunk-Santa party—where everyone dressed as Santa and drank candy cane–flavored vodka until they puked—I'd have completely forgotten about Christmas last December.

"Hi, Robin," I said to the first person in line, waving her inside. She ran the hair salon on the corner of Boysenberry Street. I hadn't gotten a haircut in four years. Maybe it was time for a trim? Or the bangs I'd always wanted but was too scared to try out?

I ran my fingers through my split ends as she asked for one bucket.

Alex, not asking for a color preference, slid a green bucket across the table. "There's a one-hour time limit, or we charge an extra ten dollars per half hour."

"She's joking." I laughed like Alex was being funny. "Take your time, Robin. There's no extra charge."

Alex's scowl pushed her toward the door.

I whacked her on the arm. "Don't frighten the customers."

"You finally have people lining up. You need to charge more."

My mother had charged ten dollars per bucket for the last two decades. Unlike my ancestors, she had an occupation outside of farming. Her high school–teaching salary had covered our major expenses, so she'd been happy to keep the prices low, aiming to break even each year.

Unfortunately, I had no outside income to subsidize the family farm. My mom's cancer diagnosis arrived one year after my college graduation; there'd been no time to establish a career path. Not when my mom and our beloved farm needed all my attention.

It didn't help that farming was expensive and unpredictable.

After a late frost three years ago, nearly four acres of blueberry bushes had to be replanted, an expense that ate up the rest of my mom's life insurance policy and retirement savings. Those acres wouldn't turn a profit for five years—if I was lucky.

With fluctuating produce prices, and no budget to hire seasonal berry pickers, I couldn't sell enough berries to cover the property taxes, irrigation costs, insurance, and equipment maintenance. The farm had operated at a loss for several years, leaving me cash-strapped, as all the money was tied up in the land.

Selling, I'd been told by several accountants, was the only way to stay afloat.

But I couldn't sell an inch. I wouldn't. Even changing her standard business practices felt like a betrayal.

So, for today, ten dollars a bucket was the going rate.

The customers kept coming into the shed. Robin, then Peter and his wife, Allison, who worked as a nurse two towns over. They had three kids with them, and the moment they received their buckets, the children started hitting each other with them. Alex encouraged the battering, loudly rooting for the smallest boy. I frowned, but at least she was engaging with the customers.

The two of us stood in the shed for over an hour, greeting people, exchanging buckets, weighing blueberry containers, and adding cash to the envelope. *A lot* of cash to the envelope. Business hadn't been this good in a single day in—well, since I'd been alive, probably.

"Here you are, Gregor," I said, elated that blueberries had made a comeback on everyone's summer grocery list. "Pick until it's full."

He leaned in, lowered his voice. "Well done, Felicity."

Excuse me? "What?"

"Well done." He touched his nose with one finger, then winked at Alex before departing.

Had Gregor lost his marbles? If he'd been the only person acting strange, I might've been able to ignore his odd remarks, but more people entered the shed, bringing ridiculous comments and questions with them.

"How exactly did you do it?"

"The boys look ridiculous."

"Did Timmy cry?"

"I heard Cheryl is out for blood. Has she stopped by the farm yet?"

"Um . . ." I had no response, but I finally understood why the farm had become popular.

Drama.

Elswood residents were eating up my feud with Cheryl like it was queso at Eli's Mexican restaurant. This sudden display of patronage had nothing to do with me or the blueberries—they wanted to witness Cheryl coming for my head, delighted that she had her sights set on me and not them.

When Susanna stepped inside, I nearly slammed and bolted the door. A member of Cheryl's inner circle, Susanna had been her trusted friend since their high school cheerleading days.

She paid for two buckets but didn't leave the shed.

"What?" I asked, a little too heated, ready to defend my actions against any criticism.

"I heard what you did to those boys. They'd been stealing from you, right?"

Was this a trap? Was she wearing a wire? Paranoia burrowed into my consciousness, but such fears were unfounded. This was Elswood, and Rodney didn't have wires or undercover informants. He didn't have enough money for a police cruiser, so he'd painted the town logo onto his navy truck and mounted a set of police lights to the roof instead.

"If you're here on Cheryl's behalf—"

"I'm not." She held up her hands as if signaling good intent. "I thought it was clever."

"Why, thank you," Alex said, a smug smile on her lips. "I'm glad *somebody* appreciates my efforts."

"Enjoy the blueberries" was all I said before giving her a polite smile. My eyes flicked toward the door, but she didn't take the hint.

"Actually, I was hoping you might help me." She glanced over her shoulder, then lowered her voice. "I'm having a problem with my neighbor. He's a mechanic, and he parks all the cars he's fixing on the street. Sometimes they block my driveway in the morning and I can't get out. Mr. Harris has threatened to fire me if I'm late to work again, but Patrick won't move the vehicles."

"So, call the sheriff." It was the same advice everyone had given me. Fat lot of good that did.

"Rodney and Patrick are friends. Rodney asked him to move the cars, but after a week, Patrick stopped caring and moved them back."

Why was she telling us about this? I barely knew her or Patrick.

"I'd pay you," she continued in response to my silence. "How much do you charge?"

Pay me? "For what?"

"To make it stop. Get rid of his cars, destroy them, burn them, send them to Siberia. I don't know. Whatever you did to the kids, do that to the cars."

"Done," Alex said, just as I responded with a sharp "No way."

Those were my words, but my heart leaped at the chance for extra cash. The electric payment was two months past due. The credit card bills were stacking up, along with Alex's hour-long showers and inability to turn off lights when she left a room. And I didn't know much about lawyers, but I doubted anyone capable of representing her in court accepted payment in baked goods. Those were all decent reasons to take the money and steal a bunch of cars that didn't belong to me. But didn't all criminals have decent reasons for doing bad things? My family name was already associated with theft—and after our standoff with Cheryl, I couldn't afford any more negative press.

"I can't help you, but thanks for stopping by." When Susanna's eyes moved to Alex, my temper snapped. "*We* can't help you."

My voice rang with an authority Susanna couldn't ignore. She quickly left the shed.

"Don't even think about it," I said, reading the silence in the cramped space. Alex and that clever brain of hers were putting together an argument to convince me to commit a crime. "Your court hearing is in a few weeks; you can't be caught doing something illegal while out on bail."

"Nobody else is going to help her."

She tugged at my sense of empathy. Alex knew me better than I'd realized.

No one would help Susanna because her gripe was about Patrick Menke. By the end of the summer, if things went disastrously wrong for all the other Man of the Year candidates, he could be the mayor. Nausea bubbled in my gut when I pictured Elswood under his authority. We'd go bankrupt in a month, having spent all our tax money on sports, alcohol, and used cars. He'd somehow be worse than the corrupt, sinister Jonathan Callaway, who at least took steps to hide his horribleness.

We really needed to expand our choices for mayor beyond the founding families.

Alex bounced on the balls of her feet. "It'll be easy to get rid of the cars. I've already got about ten ideas."

"Your criminal days are behind you."

"You didn't think so when I helped dye those kids blue. I seem to remember celebratory grapefruit juice and pop music blaring. So we do a few more pranks, make some extra cash—"

"A few?"

"With all the problems in this town, we'll be raking in the dough by the end of the month."

Even with felony charges pending, she was too reckless, obsessed with not following the rules. She'd take the money and ask no questions, working her way through this town's squabbles with no remorse.

Until she got caught. "We don't need the money badly enough to risk jail time."

"We're not going to get caught."

"I'm sure you thought that before you got arrested, too."

Her cheeks reddened. "That was different. The cops here don't do anything but eat doughnuts. You complained for months and nothing happened, which is why nothing will happen to us, even if someone alerts the sheriff. And besides, I won't get caught twice. Especially not if I have a lookout."

She had everything planned out—and she almost had me convinced. *Almost.*

As much as I wanted the money, to have customers at the farm once again, even if it was only for the drama, I couldn't disrespect my mother's memory by sullying our good name. Our actions against the Blueberry Bandits had been to save the farm. It was justice. What Susanna wanted was revenge.

A few extra dollars didn't justify the risk.

Not to me, or Alex, or the farm.

ELEVEN

Alex sulked around the house for the next several hours like . . . well, like a teenager. The lawyer, whomever Wade had contacted when I tossed my pride into the ether and asked for help, was due at the house by three that afternoon. With Alex in such a bad mood because I wouldn't let her commit crimes, I spent the better part of the day anxiously scrubbing the house from top to bottom, leaving the entire downstairs with the sharp smell of Pine-Sol.

I showered, taking more care than usual with my hair, before selecting an outfit for Alex. The internet had led me to believe that blue made a person look innocent. So I laid out a light-blue shirt and a navy cardigan. I didn't explain my rationale to her, but nothing was off the table when it came to her upcoming court hearing. She needed all the help she could get.

A pitcher of iced tea took center stage on my wood table, along with several of the good glasses my mother had brought out for special occasions.

"I thought those plates and cups were only for decoration?" Alex asked as I straightened the flowers for a second time.

"Not today."

"Why are we putting on airs for a stupid lawyer?"

I ignored her. I was counting on this lawyer to get Alex out of trouble. First impressions meant everything.

I smoothed my shirt, rethinking its red color, when someone knocked on the door. They were on time, I realized, checking my watch. Already a good sign.

A woman in her mid-thirties with blond hair down to her waist stood on the porch. My hand paused on the doorknob. I'd assumed Wade had contacted his older brother, Sam, who worked for a law firm downtown. How many lawyers did Wade know?

"Felicity?" she said warmly. "I'm Tess, Wade's sister-in-law. May I come inside?"

"Yeah, of course," I said, recovering my manners. I opened the door wider and stepped back. "Sorry, I was expecting Sam."

"My husband doesn't handle criminal cases. The man gets squeamish if he has to handle anything beyond a corporate merger."

My face flushed. I hoped she didn't think I was expecting Sam because he was a man and she was a woman. I wanted to clear up the confusion, but knowing me, I'd make it worse.

I led her into the kitchen, where Alex sat, shoving potato chips into her mouth. Crumbs fell down her shirt and onto the floor.

I took a steadying breath and introduced them.

"Tess, this is Alex. Alex, this is Tess."

Alex didn't acknowledge Tess other than to look at me and say, "I was expecting the queen with all your cleaning today."

I motioned for Tess to take a seat, then lightly whacked Alex on the shoulder. "Stop it," I mouthed, then cleared my throat as Tess studied the two of us from across the table.

"Nice to meet you, Alex." Tess kept her tone professional. "Felicity, I need you to give Alex and me some privacy."

"Oh?" I shot a glance at Alex. She wasn't prepared to have this conversation on her own. Knowing her, she'd tell Tess to get lost the minute my back was turned. "Is that a good idea?"

"Attorney-client privilege won't apply if you're present."

My fingers drummed on the table. Leaving felt wrong. I'd paid Alex's bail and would be paying for Tess's legal services—why shouldn't

I get to participate? But what could I say? I didn't want to mess with this privilege thing.

"Oh, let her stay," Alex mumbled, causing my head to shoot up. "I'll tell her everything anyway."

"If you waive attorney-client privilege, Felicity could be called as a witness to testify about our conversation," Tess said. "Under oath, she'd have no choice but to tell the prosecution everything we discuss. While that is unlikely to happen, you need to know it's a possibility."

Alex gave me a patronizing look. "She'll freak out if she isn't allowed to be here."

"Fine, then." Tess shook her head like we were fools, but withdrew a notebook from her purse and clicked the top of her pen. "I had an interesting chat with the prosecutor this morning. Do you want to tell me what happened on the afternoon of June twenty-seventh?"

"No."

See, this is why I need to be here.

My glare got Alex to say, "The cops said I tried to steal something from the department store."

"What did they say you tried to steal?"

"A necklace. Wasn't even my style."

"And you ran from security, is that correct?"

"When some big dude is running straight at you, you don't stand around waiting to get tackled."

"And the police? They claim you gave them a hard time. Officer Heathman claims you said his 'elevator doesn't go all the way to the top.'" Tess used her fingers to make air quotes. "Is that correct?"

"That he's dumb, or that I said that?"

"Alex," I groaned, placing my hand on my forehead.

"What? They were arresting me, and I hadn't done anything wrong. I was objecting to false imprisonment."

Tess made a note. "So you didn't attempt to take the necklace or any other item from the store?"

"Nope."

I recognized Alex's tone from that night at the police station. She was lying. But it didn't make any sense—why lie to your lawyer?

Tess remained unfazed. "All right, then. Tell me about yourself. What's your full name?"

"Alexandra Norse."

"Middle name?"

"Don't have one."

"Birthday?"

"June twenty-third."

"Age?"

"Eighteen."

"How long have you lived with Felicity?"

"Since the arrest."

"And before that?"

Alex abruptly leaned back in her chair. I smiled in what I hoped was an encouraging way.

"I was in foster care until the end of June; then I turned eighteen. I was staying at a shelter in Cleveland until I figured things out."

Tess took everything in stride, but I felt lightheaded. A homeless shelter? She'd been on her own in the city, sleeping on a cot in a crowded room with strangers. And here I was, worried she wouldn't like her twin mattress because it was a bit too firm.

Alex, a champion of underdogs and nonconformists, deserved so much better. At eighteen, she'd already shown more resilience than most people did in their entire lives.

Though she was on my last nerve, I wanted to hug her. But I resisted, barely, and only because she hated affection. She'd have swatted me away.

I broke into the conversation. "What does this have to do with the shoplifting charge?"

"I'll need to make a deal with the prosecutor, and any mitigating circumstances I can present will help reduce the charges. Alex's age, being homeless, and aging out of the foster care system will go a long way in ensuring she doesn't have to spend time in prison."

I balked. "They would give her prison time for attempted shoplifting? That seems a bit excessive."

Tess didn't stop writing. "Not for someone who tried to steal a diamond necklace."

I rounded on Alex. "You tried to steal a *diamond* necklace? You don't even wear jewelry."

"Allegedly," she shot back. "Who's to say the cops aren't lying? Or the store clerk isn't setting me up?"

"The store's security manager who caught you with the necklace." Tess raised her fingers one by one. "The surveillance footage that clearly shows you reaching over the counter and taking the necklace. The store clerk who told the police she saw you take it. Oh, and the five other witnesses who all saw you either take the necklace or run when security approached you. And that's what the prosecutor's office had on hand when I contacted them. I'm sure they can dig up more evidence, because the department store will fully cooperate."

"I'm still not convinced." Alex folded her arms across her chest, glaring at Tess, but that sounded like more than enough evidence to me.

"What do we do next?" I asked. That seemed to be the only question left. How would we deal with her actions and move on without it destroying her future?

Tess folded her hands on the legal pad. "Hopefully, the prosecutor reduces the charges in exchange for a guilty plea. Then Alex will fulfill the conditions of the plea deal and never, ever do anything like this again," she finished with a pointed glance at Alex.

"I'm not pleading guilty," Alex said.

"Yes, you are," I countered.

"No, and neither of you can make me. That's the law. I get to decide, and I say I'm innocent."

I ignored her. She was being unnecessarily difficult. "After she pleads guilty, what's next?"

Tess spoke as Alex opened her mouth to argue. "A significant fine will have to be paid to the department store as restitution, and to keep them from suing her civilly. I'll negotiate it down, but right now they're asking for five thousand dollars."

Five thousand dollars. My head fell into my hands. How would we come up with that kind of cash? My credit card was already maxed out to cover her bail.

"When she pleads guilty, are you comfortable with Alex staying here for the foreseeable future? The prosecutor will want to know that she's living somewhere stable and with responsible supervision. She'll also need an address for the parole officer, assuming we avoid any prison time."

"Yes," I said before Alex could answer. I didn't have to think about it for a second. Of course she would stay here.

Tess pointed the top of her pen at Alex, but she spoke to me. "And she'll need to get her high school diploma."

"No way," Alex cut in before I could agree on her behalf for a second time. "I'm not doing any of this."

"Alex, calm down. We're going to do whatever it takes to make this go away, and if that means going back to school, then fine. You would've had to go back anyway. What on earth would you do without a high school diploma?"

I didn't get a response because Alex had already stood and was heading for the door. I chased after her, but she slammed the front door behind her. She marched through the yard and toward the street.

I turned back to Tess, who was putting her legal pad in her purse. "I think that she . . . needed some fresh air."

Tess gave me a sympathetic look. "She's right in that I can't accept a plea deal on her behalf. She's going to have to agree. I'll proceed with the prosecutor, but having her enrolled in high school and showing that she's making positive steps to turn her life around will go a long way."

"She's not a bad person," I said, rushing to Alex's defense. "She hasn't been given a fair shake in life."

"Oh, I know. Trust me. I've seen worse crimes." She slipped her purse over her shoulder. "I'll get the court date pushed back to buy you some time."

"You can do that?"

Tess smiled at my awed tone. "When my client's out on bail, I'll postpone until the prosecutor practically begs me to get this case off her plate. That's when we'll have the most leverage in negotiations."

I reached for my checkbook. Perhaps I could pay her in installments like a hospital? "How much do I owe you?"

"That's not necessary." She waved her hand at the checkbook. "I'm doing this as a favor."

What favor? I hadn't asked her for a favor.

Like any good lawyer, she anticipated my question before I could get the words out. "Wade promised to settle up later this month by redoing our pool deck."

He'd never mentioned this to me. "I'd prefer to pay you."

She smiled conspiratorially. "I'd prefer to have the new deck. Besides, I promised Wade that I wouldn't take your money when you offered. A deal is a deal."

I didn't know what to say. Now I'd have to thank Wade for his help. Honestly, I'd prefer to pay her than admit he'd done a decent thing for me.

Tess moved to the door, hand pausing on the handle. "Do your best to convince her to plead guilty. I've known this prosecutor for quite a while. She's not a complete asshole. I can get the charges reduced, but Alex will need to give me something to work with."

"I'll get her to come around." I meant it. I'd get Alex to stop shooting herself in the foot if it was the last thing I did.

TWELVE

I waited on the couch for Alex to return. I had a whole speech planned, starting with how sometimes life didn't go as expected and ending with a sob story about how I'd once handed in a college essay two hours late and it turned out okay. One shoplifting incident wouldn't derail her future. She'd been doing so well here. Alex could turn things around if she gave herself half a chance to be happy.

When it grew dark outside, I ceased giving her time and space. I called her cell phone, stomach wrenching as I dialed the number. How convenient that I had the number memorized. She didn't answer.

So I waited ten minutes and called again. I repeated this pattern while I stress-ate lasagna on the couch. Where was she? Had she gotten lost? Not likely in Elswood. Four left turns and she'd be right back where she started.

Maybe I'd come on too strong today. I shouldn't have pushed her. Was she upset that I wanted her to plead guilty, or did she hate the idea of returning to high school? *It's just high school,* I thought, then realized that maybe the problem wasn't school but staying here with me. Would she want to live somewhere else? I fidgeted with the blanket. Looking after someone had been good for me—I had a reason to get up in the morning beyond blueberries.

What if Alex felt differently?

I picked at the burned cheese on my plate. I was young and healthy, yet sitting on the couch in my pajamas, stuffing my face with lasagna. Even before my mom died, I wasn't what anyone would consider a partygoer. I liked my television, my comfy clothing, and being fast asleep by ten so I'd be well rested the next day. The grief had exacerbated these qualities, and for the last year, I hadn't made an effort to get out of the house and experience the world. But for a cell phone number, Alex and I wouldn't have met, let alone become friends. We were very different people.

I scrolled through my Kindle for a romance novel, needing a distraction from my worries. It was getting late, and I wasn't going to bed until she returned home. I was about to make a selection when my phone buzzed.

"Alex?" I said without glancing at the number. I hadn't realized I was so worried, but my voice sounded anxious. I sat forward on the couch.

"Felicity, it's Wade."

Disappointment washed through me. Not who I wanted to speak to.

"Whatever it is, I don't have time." I wanted to keep the line clear for Alex.

The loud background nearly drowned out his voice. "Well, make time, because your friend is here."

I stopped, finger on the end call button. "Where? At the bar?" Alex was underage. She couldn't be in a bar.

"She's here with a couple of guys." He paused. "You need to come get her."

No shit, Wade. I was already getting up from the couch. The blanket fell to the floor. "Why did it take you so long to call me?"

I heard his exasperation. "I just walked in and noticed she was here. Will you put your book down and come get her before I have to call the cops?"

I hated that he knew me so well. "I'm on my way."

I ended the call and went upstairs to change out of my pajamas. I'd known something was wrong when she didn't return home. Why did nothing good happen after eight o'clock?

I hustled to the bar, ignoring my fear of the dark. My initial research from the night I'd brought Alex home flashed through my mind. The term *human trafficking* blinked in bright-red letters before my eyes.

People who age out of the foster care system are more likely to be human trafficked.

And here I'd been concerned about her criminal record.

The logical part of my brain said that I was overreacting—things like human trafficking didn't happen in Elswood. But I shoved that logic into a drawer and slammed it shut. Terrible things didn't discriminate based on location. Human traffickers, drug dealers, and psychopaths could be anywhere, doing anything, and they didn't introduce themselves as human trash. I walked faster, practically running until I crossed the square and saw the bar's neon sign lighting up the sidewalk.

Wade had bought the place five years ago, turning the quaint restaurant where I ate french toast after church into a smoke-filled bar. It was the only place in town open after ten p.m., except for the twenty-four-hour pharmacy.

Breathing heavily, I entered the bar. Music blared—people had to yell at the person sitting two feet across from them. It was everything I'd imagined and worse. Why on earth would Alex willingly come here? Unless she wanted to develop liver cancer and go deaf at the same time, it wasn't a suitable place.

Irrational anger at Wade swept through me. If someone hurt her, it was because he'd opened up a place for cheap beer and pretzels, and the scum had come crawling into town. Condemning Wade eased my fears. I'd blamed my problems on that man for years, so why stop now?

My scapegoat stood behind the bar, pouring liquid from one bottle into another. A white towel was draped over his shoulder. His eyes found me, and they didn't look pleased. He nodded to the far back corner. "Get her out of here before I lose my liquor license."

I didn't need to be told twice. My eyes locked on Alex, sitting between two grown men whom I'd never seen before. It didn't look like they'd seen a shower before, either. I marched toward them, trying to appear bigger and more intimidating. At least I'd put on jeans, because my heart-patterned pajamas weren't going to get the job done.

I stopped beside the table, putting my hands on its round edge. Glasses, both empty and full, shook with the movement. Alex's eyes widened when she saw me, but I'd already reached across the man seated between us and grabbed her arm.

"Come on, Alex. We're leaving."

"What are you doing here?" Her words sounded sluggish. Her red face, along with the empty glasses directly in front of her, told me she was drunk or headed in that direction. I yanked her sleeve, trying to get her to stand.

"Let go of me." She snatched her sleeve out of my grasp.

The man seated between us looked me over from my shoes to my ponytail.

"What's going on?" he asked, eyes glazed. He ran his hand down my outstretched arm. I fought the urge to recoil.

"She's leaving: That's what's going on." My voice sounded confident—possibly fierce, if I was hearing myself correctly. I didn't know where I was getting this courage from, but I needed it to last a few more minutes. These men worried me. Unlike Alex, who at first glance hadn't looked like a criminal, these men fit the bill. A sleeve of tattoos glinted in the bar's muted lighting as the nearest man reached for his beer.

"What's your name, darling?" His eyes fell to my waist, then lingered on my chest.

"Don't worry about who I am. Worry about the fact that you're buying drinks for an eighteen-year-old." My eyes returned to Alex. "Up. Now. Let's go."

He stood and placed his hand on Alex's shoulder, pinning her to the chair. His touch broke my resolve to leave peacefully. I lifted my foot and kicked him in the groin as hard as I could. "Learn some manners, and keep your hands to yourself."

He buckled over, clutching his crotch. "You bitch!"

With his head lowered, I seized my opportunity. I pulled back my fist and punched him in the face.

Ow, ow! I cradled my hand, jumping twice at the pain in my knuckles. *Cheese on a cracker!*

Swear words rang around the table, and Alex lurched from her chair. "Felicity!"

I suspected that all eyes in the bar were glued to us. We needed to be long gone before someone called the cops and Alex got into more trouble.

As Alex stepped toward me, so did the man's companion. I turned, expecting to get punched or kicked or worse by the broad-shouldered guy, who looked even taller than his friend.

Before he could reach me, another set of shoulders—with a white towel draped over one side—blocked the man's approach. This gave me enough time to grab Alex and pull her behind me.

"Nobody wants any trouble." Wade's voice carried above the music. "You guys are good customers, but you're going to let them leave without another word."

The man's companion took another step toward me. Wade blocked his path, holding out his hand. "Don't fucking test me."

I'd never heard him talk like that before. Not even when I'd dented his bumper a year ago and neglected to tell him about it. He'd shouted through the window that my driving privileges were revoked, but that had lasted all of a week before he relented to my pleas.

"You got her?" Wade didn't turn as he spoke, keeping his eyes on the men in front of him.

"Yeah."

The best I could do for him was leave before things escalated.

Wade reached into his pocket, still not turning toward me. He held his truck keys behind his back, and I took them with shaking fingers.

The keys clanged as I half carried Alex to the door. The cool night air struck my face, and the bubble of fear I'd been suppressing burst. I took a deep breath, doing my best to unlock the passenger door and keep Alex standing.

When I finally got the door open, she buckled over, hands on her knees, and vomited.

I leaned against the truck, my weak stomach twisting. Maybe Wade had been right that first morning: I was not equipped to handle this.

THIRTEEN

I dabbed a washcloth on Alex's cheek. Black eyeliner was smudged under her eyes, making it look like she'd lost a boxing match. Where had she gotten makeup? She hadn't been wearing it when she left the house.

"Stop," she slurred, trying to sit up and avoid my dabbing. Her back was propped against the tub, near the toilet so when she vomited it wouldn't go all over my clean floors. To think the house had smelled like Pine-Sol only a few hours earlier.

She turned away as I dabbed at her eyelid again. "Stop . . . I don't need your help."

I pursed my lips and stood straight. Was she delusional? She absolutely needed my help. I twisted the washcloth over the sink. The water turned cloudy.

I intended to yell at her until I was blue in the face, but it wouldn't do any good tonight. Alex needed to sleep it off. Hopefully, the hangover tomorrow would be punishment enough, but I doubted it. She was eighteen, drunk in a bar with strange men who hadn't looked like they wanted to go home and play Scrabble. What had she been thinking?

I held out my hand when her makeup was mostly removed. That would have to do. "Come on. Let's get you to bed."

I'd deal with the state of the bathroom in the morning. I nudged open her bedroom door with my foot and laid her on the bed. She rolled toward the wall.

"Leave me alone. I don't want your help. You're not my mother or my sister or my friend."

"Do you think I punch strange men in the face for someone who's not my friend?"

"I don't think you punch anyone, ever."

"That's not the point." I wasn't going to get distracted. "You're smart enough to know how incredibly stupid—not to mention dangerous—it is to get drunk around people you don't know, especially in a bar when you're underage. I'm not saying it would've been your fault, but you were just asking for something bad to happen to you."

"Who cares?"

Was she really so blind? "Me! I care!" She jumped like I'd startled her. Maybe if I yelled, she'd finally hear me. I'd done nothing but care about her since we met. How could she think I'd be fine with her getting hurt? I'd be a complete mess if something happened to her, especially if it happened on my watch. I felt responsible for her, and that feeling was only growing stronger as time went on.

I'd promised to save the lecture for when she was sober, but I decided to give her a preview.

"I get it: You're a teenager. You don't understand that your life could be over in an instant, but I know better than anyone that time is finite. And I swear to God, Alex, if something happens to you, I'm never going to recover. So the next time you want to go out and get drunk, you can think about that."

I didn't want to go into detail about how I thought my mother had sent her to me. Some twist of fate had given her the same cell phone number as my mom, and that meant something to me, even if it didn't to her. I knew it was crazy, but at this point I'd ceased caring about sanity.

My voice softened. "I'm your friend, and I don't have many of them. So, for me, try not to put yourself in situations that could go terribly wrong."

"Stop caring, then." She said it like a curse. "Stop bothering me. Stop trying to teach me things. And stop worrying about me. I can take care of myself."

"Sleep it off, Alex. I'll be here in the morning." *Whether you want me to or not,* I added, but only to myself. I pulled the comforter over her shoulders so she wouldn't get cold. She slapped my hand away, and I flinched.

"Of course you'll be here. All you do is mope around the house like a kicked puppy. You don't even try to have fun. You might as well be dead for all the things you do." She spoke toward the wall, but I caught every word. "Your life is pathetic, Felicity. And I'm not going to end up like you."

Her words cut straight to my soul until I forced myself to believe it was the alcohol talking. People said mean things when they were drunk. I put my hand to my chest and took a calming breath so I wouldn't cry. It was a trick I'd learned after my mom died and someone had said something that made me think of her. I disassociated from the pain and focused on my breathing, letting the sadness slip away.

Alex started crying, wrapping her head in her hands as she sobbed. She obviously didn't want me to touch her, but I waited, perched on the side of the bed until she ran out of tears and her breathing evened out.

I placed a bucket on the nightstand in case she had to vomit in the middle of the night, then left the room.

It was late, but I wouldn't be able to sleep, not with every emotion—including sadness, anger, and pity—bubbling inside me. I boiled water for tea, which usually solved everything, but I was unsure it could cure the hole Alex had punched in my chest.

Drunk or not, she had no excuse for treating me so poorly. I'd been nothing but kind and supportive since she called me from jail and asked me to pick her up. I was still waiting on that thank-you she owed me for the ride home, the $3,000 bail, and everything else after.

I'd gotten into a bar fight for her. I'd never so much as flipped anyone off, let alone punched a drunk man with tattoos. I wrapped an ice pack around my knuckles. I hadn't even hit him that hard, but they hurt. At least I'd remembered to keep my thumb outside my fist.

The house was quiet and dark outside the kitchen. Sitting at the table, I drank small sips of tea until the cup was empty. Alex's words tumbled through my mind. Was she right about my life? Was it pathetic? I hadn't done much lately, but I'd been so focused on the farm and keeping my mental health in check that there wasn't time for much else. I was twenty-seven years old. I had responsibilities. I couldn't keep up with the exciting times of an eighteen-year-old.

I didn't know how long I sat at the table, but I didn't move until headlights swept through the side window. A car came and left. Before I could talk myself out of it, I headed outside.

I'd show Alex how non-pathetic I was. I could have fun and do reckless things, too.

The wet grass tickled my ankles as I trudged to his porch. I knocked twice. Juno barked at the noise.

Wade answered the door with a beer in his hand. He'd been home for all of two minutes, and he was already drinking. He looked surprised to see me but didn't say anything. He stepped back, letting me pass inside. Juno's tail wagged as I petted the top of her head. Several plastic barrettes were clipped to her fur—a sign that Wade's nieces had been over earlier in the day. They loved to dress her in sweaters and hats and give her "makeovers" with hair accessories. More than one time, I'd found the ever-patient Juno wearing glittery head- and wristbands reminiscent of an 1980s Jazzercise instructor.

"You feeling okay?"

Wade stared at me with an odd expression. I probably didn't look like my usual self. I didn't feel quite like myself. I'd hit rock bottom after an eighteen-year-old insulted me. Obviously, my self-esteem wasn't high to begin with, but I'd no idea it was that low.

So, what the hell? Why not bring Wade into this mess? I had nothing left to lose.

I wiped my hands on my jeans, then took the beer from his hand. Seeing as I was breaking all the rules, why not drink, too?

"Yup," I lied, taking a sip. Compared to my tea, the beer tasted sour. I took another gulp and wiped my mouth with the back of my hand. *Yuck. Who makes this, an oil refinery?*

"I'm asking 'cause I've never seen you drink before." He paused, then added, "I've never seen you kick a man in the balls before, either."

"Then I guess you don't know me very well." I pointed the mouth of the bottle at him. "You know I'm not what people think. I can have fun. I'm a fun person who does fun things. All the time. And sometimes just for fun."

He hesitated, unsure what to say. "Sure. You're . . . fun."

"I am."

"Fine."

"Fine."

"What are we arguing about?" he asked after a minute.

"I don't know."

Flustered, I took another sip of beer. It wasn't as sour tasting now. Perhaps it would help me forget this whole night. That strategy worked well enough for some people. I'd always thought that avoiding alcohol was helping me and my problems, but maybe it was adding to them. Perhaps a few drinks would do me some good.

Taking another drink, I let my eyes wander over Wade. Why did he have to be so good-looking? Tall and muscular, with unkempt blond hair. He possessed every physical quality I found attractive in a man. And while his personality left a lot to be desired, lately I couldn't find myself as annoyed with him as I used to be. He'd helped me tonight, and more important, he'd helped Alex. And for that, I'd push aside some of our history, even if it was only for a moment.

I stepped closer to him, closer than I'd ever been before. Without thinking, I leaned onto my toes and pressed my lips to his.

Wade didn't hesitate. What I'd intended to be a quick thank-you kiss, he immediately deepened, lifting his hands to the sides of my head and pulling me closer. His hungry lips devoured mine, pushing them slightly apart. He tasted like the beer, only without the sourness. With a mind of their own, my hands wrapped around his waist, feeling the muscles of his back.

When Wade broke off the kiss for air, I came to my senses. He bent down to kiss me again, but I placed my hand on his chest, holding him back.

"What's wrong?" he asked, his forehead touching mine. I felt dizzy, and not because I'd forgotten to breathe for the last few seconds. That had been a much better kiss than I'd anticipated. *He's had tons of practice, though.* I'd watched more than one woman leave his house in the early morning. Way too much practice. The realization steeled my insides. I didn't plan on being one of those girls. Not tonight. Not ever.

There was only so much forgiveness in his actions. Our past—the incident in high school—couldn't be erased quite so easily.

I stepped back, extricating myself from his grasp. "This never happened."

His eyebrows drew together, but his eyes remained on my lips. I'd shown up on his doorstep late at night, and no woman had probably ever said no to that perfect face.

When he tried to close the distance between us, I headed toward the door. "I mean it. This never happened, understood?"

"Sure," he agreed, running a hand through his hair.

"Good night, Wade." I left, taking a long swig of beer as the door closed behind me.

See, Alex? I can be fun, I thought as I ran toward my house.

FOURTEEN

An egg sizzled in the pan.

My swollen knuckles, evidence of my first and last bar fight, protested as I scrambled the yellow-and-white liquid. The pain kept me grounded to this moment, not the problems of last night. Alex's words had cut through my heart, but the last time I'd chosen to block out the pain, it had cost me everything.

My anxiety seized upon the dark thoughts, ruminating on the night my mom died.

The pain, the grief, the heartache—it had been overwhelming. Despite knowing she had terminal cancer for over a year, I hadn't faced her death with dignity. I'd cried and sobbed, so much so that the nurses had to sedate me.

My mother, my best friend, the only person in this world who truly loved me, had died alone in a hospital bed, with her daughter too overcome with grief to say goodbye.

Any final words of love or comfort we would've shared had never been said.

What had my mother wished to tell me at the very end of her life? What wisdom had she never had the chance to impart? Would her words have helped me cope with her death in the days that followed? I'd never know.

Because the pain had been too much for me to bear.

A knock on the front door startled me, causing my hand to slip. My finger caught the underside of the pan. *Ah!* Hopping from foot to foot, I ran my finger under cold water from the faucet.

The knock came again, stronger this time.

Still in my pajamas, I found a stranger on the porch. His black suit and pressed shirt clashed with the rising sun over the treetops. People didn't usually wear dress clothes to pick berries.

"The farm opens at eleven," I said, surprised my voice worked after crying all night. "If you're from out of town, I can recommend a few places to visit until we open."

"Not here to pick berries, ma'am," the man said. "I'm looking for the owner, Felicity Lavigne."

"That's me."

He reached into his suit pocket and withdrew an envelope. "I've been asked to give you this notice. I'm with J&C Enterprises; we've taken over collection services on behalf of the town."

Panic beat in my heart. *Collection services* might be the worst two words I'd ever heard.

The envelope had the Elswood town seal on the front: two robins sitting on a branch.

With Mr. Suit watching me, I broke the seal and removed a single piece of paper.

TAX CERTIFICATE NOTICE

Notice is hereby given that the lands, lots, and parts of lots (known hereafter as "Property") have been returned delinquent by the town treasurer of Elswood, and have been assigned under section 5721.32 of the Revised Code. A tax certificate has been acquired as the first lien against the Property, and an additional interest charge of eighteen percent per annum shall be assessed against the parcel. Failure by owner to pay the overdue twelve thousand, three hundred and fifty-two dollars and redeem the tax certificate may result in foreclosure proceedings against the Property . . .

My hands shook, causing the words to blur, and the longer I read, the less I comprehended. *Property. Tax certificate. Lien. Foreclosure.*

All buzzwords for giving me a heart attack. "I don't . . . What is this?"

"The letter serves as notice that you're in default on your property taxes, and the town has assigned its rights to J&C."

Whoa, whoa, whoa. "You can't do that. Laurel and I had an agreement—she said I could pay in installments and there'd be no penalties," I said, holding back tears. If I could get him to listen, he'd understand this notice, being delinquent on the taxes, was a misunderstanding.

"You have this agreement in writing?"

The thought had never crossed my mind. I'd known Laurel and her family since birth. The woman used to babysit me. "She gave me her word."

"The problem, ma'am, is that the town treasury department has no record of this agreement."

"Laurel will tell you. Call her and ask. I have her number on my phone—"

"Unfortunately, Ms. Montgomery has no further say in this matter. She's been relieved of her position."

"You *fired* her?" Horror caught in my throat. She had three kids in college; she couldn't afford to be out of a job. What would she and Bob do for money?

"*I* didn't do anything, ma'am."

"But—"

"J&C has bought your tax debt, and should you fail to pay off the lien, foreclosure proceedings will be initiated. There's a number you can call at the bottom of the letter."

That was all he said before turning and descending the porch steps. In my shock, I'd forgotten to warn him about the faulty last step. He somehow avoided it anyway.

I stood in the doorway, holding the letter in both hands, not believing the words. *Twelve thousand dollars. Eighteen percent interest. Possible foreclosure.*

Reality sank in slowly, as if my brain could handle only a few parts at a time. Someone had purchased my debt and expected me to pay them in full, or they'd evict me.

They'd take the farm, and there would be no more blueberries.

No Lavigne living on this land.

No place to keep my mother's possessions.

The world tilted, my panic leading to lightheadedness. The farm had survived multiple wars and the Great Depression. Four generations of Lavignes had held on to this property, whether by hook or by crook, and I'd be the one to lose it.

All because some man in a pretentious suit had given me a letter demanding $12,000.

Where the hell would I get $12,000? The credit cards were maxed. The blueberry deliveries brought in barely enough money to buy food. Any spare dime went into farm upkeep. I had no money, no valuables to sell, no occupation to rely on.

Somewhere along the way, it had become too costly to live.

I spun around and slammed the door, then bolted it for good measure.

My eyes traveled across the living room, over the couch to the bookshelf and the mantel, where my mom's ashes sat in a wooden box with a heart burned into the top. Down the hall, I spotted the kitchen table, with its place mats and the fruit bowl she'd kept fully stocked. Her very essence was embedded into this home.

Her clothes, the dishes, the farming equipment—every blueberry—reminded me of her. I'd never part with any of it.

"Felicity?" Her voice dragged me back to reality as she rounded the corner. "Stop slamming doors. Some of us are trying to sleep." She rubbed her temples.

Alex.

I'd promised her a home, a safe place to stay until her court hearing. Without the house, I would lose her, and it would have nothing to do with my pathetic lifestyle or her legal troubles.

"I'm in," was all I said, easing my back away from the door. Selling blueberries would never dig me out of this financial hole. If I wanted to keep the farm *and* Alex, something had to change, immediately. Once the interest on the tax lien started accumulating, I'd never find a way out of debt without selling the property.

I could do this.

I *had* to do this.

Twelve thousand dollars wouldn't magically appear in my bank account.

"What's the plan to get rid of the cars?"

Hungover, it took her a few extra seconds to connect the dots, but when she did, a diabolical smile formed on Alex's lips. "Do you want to hear the felonies or the misdemeanors first?"

"Whatever's going to get the job done."

I needed a paper bag. My breath came out in shallow gasps. We sat in Wade's truck, which we hadn't told him we were taking. Alex had called it *plausible deniability*, and I didn't question it. I'd moved beyond questioning stolen vehicles, far more concerned with what we had in the truck bed than with Wade calling the cops.

We parked two blocks from Susanna's house. I cut the headlights and swept the area for movement. No signs of life. Nothing out of the ordinary. The green light above the radio showed 5:02 a.m.

Alex drummed her fingers on the dashboard. The longer we waited, the more likely we were to get caught. When the sun rose in forty minutes, people would be heading outside to leave for work or walk their dogs. For all my thoughts about protecting the farm and finding happiness, I was having a hard time remembering my name, let alone my motivations for committing this crime.

5:03.

"Felicity, it's now or never," Alex said. "I can't do this on my own, so if you're losing your nerve, you need to—"

"I'm ready," I said, cutting off what was likely to be a great insult. I unbuckled my seat belt. "Five minutes, and we're back in the car. Do you have the number?"

She held up the burner phone. "Ready to go."

Anytime a cell phone was paid for in advance, you knew you were doing something wrong. But if the prepaid minutes didn't do it, the black T-shirts, hats, and gloves would have been good indicators. We looked like criminals, and this time, appearances were not deceiving.

I put the garden shovel through my belt. I'd need both hands free for this venture.

"Let's go," I said, opening my door.

The silence outside penetrated my bones. My breathing threatened to disturb the street's stillness. I shut my door as gently as possible, cringing at the faint noise.

Alex met me behind the truck, grinning from ear to ear. "Child's play," she'd called this at the house. I couldn't fathom what kind of childhood she'd had, but mine never included theft of city property coupled with stolen vehicles.

Susanna lived in the more developed part of town, a few blocks off the square. Here, the driveways were closer together, with a pitch of grass between them. Patrick had parked three cars along the curb, not caring that Susanna's driveway was denied access to the street. *Douchebag,* I thought as we lifted the metal sign from the truck. Why hadn't the sheriff's office enforced any parking ordinances? Blocking a driveway was against the rules. All these vehicles should be ticketed. Not only did Rodney deprive the town of money, he also allowed Patrick to have free rein of the public street. The mayor should fire Rodney for incompetence and corruption, effective immediately.

I grunted and adjusted my grip, seeing the words Do Not Park in the moonlight.

"Quiet," Alex snapped. She was still grinning. "Move faster."

After Susanna had paid us a hundred dollars, we conducted "recon" of the target area, and Alex created three separate courses of action. I picked the tamest one. For Alex, digging up a Do Not Park sign from the center of town was practically legal—though, of course, it wasn't.

Careful not to let the metal frame strike the sidewalk, we maneuvered around the cars and set the sign in Susanna's front yard.

Breathing heavily, I grabbed the shovel from my belt and started digging. The sign needed to stand straight, like a professional had put it in years ago. The metal glinted in the moonlight. My mom had used this very shovel to plant roses and lilies near our mailbox. I tried not to think about how far this garden tool had fallen from grace as I dug into the dirt and made a neat pile.

My heart raced as I excavated, expecting sirens to wake up the neighborhood at any moment.

"Hurry, Felicity."

I glanced up, finding Alex under the streetlight near the sidewalk. She examined Patrick's cars.

"Do you want to help or make comments?"

She didn't answer. Her eyes traveled down Orange Avenue, away from the square.

"Car," she whispered, then waved me toward her. I abandoned my spot and threw myself closer to the street-parked cars. I curled up behind the front wheel. Alex had ducked below the car frame, head inches from the gutter. Headlights flew over top of us. *This is such a bad idea,* I thought, even as the car drove on. *What the hell was I thinking?*

We needed to be quicker now. If that driver had spotted us, someone would investigate. I knew from experience that the sheriff didn't respond to calls right away, but I didn't want to give Rodney a chance to catch us. That would be beyond humiliating.

We lifted the sign upright and stood it in the hole. I packed dirt around the bottom, then tossed a handful of grass on top. I scooped the remaining dirt inside a plastic bag. We couldn't leave evidence of a freshly dug hole—not when the sign had supposedly been there for years.

Clank. Clank. Clank. Alex hovered beside the nearest car.

"What are you doing?" I whispered.

She chuckled, shaking a spray-paint canister.

My eyes narrowed, using the faint moonlight to trace her movements. "Are you seriously drawing penises on the cars?"

"Well, I'm not going to *not* draw penises on them. What fun would that be?"

I grabbed her shirtsleeve. There was no time for childish vandalism.

We ran back to the truck and climbed inside. The truck's musty odor, smelling faintly of Wade and his gym bag, made me feel safe. I exhaled loudly, grateful I could make noise again.

"Are we good?"

"Almost." Alex picked up the cell phone. She pressed a few buttons and put it on speaker.

"Travis Towing," someone answered.

"Hello? Young man?" Alex said in a cringeworthy old-lady voice. I clasped my hand over my mouth to keep from laughing.

"Can I help you?"

"Yes, young sir. We need a tow truck on Orange Avenue in Elswood, Ohio. There is a problem. The cars are everywhere. I tried to push them, but I've fallen, and I can't get up."

I whacked her on the arm.

She took a breath, biting her lip to keep the laughter out of her voice. "Young sir? Are you on your way? I'll keep calling back if you don't send someone out here in thirty minutes or less."

The man sighed. "Yeah, we'll send someone. What's your name, ma'am?"

"My name is Cheryl Callaway." Alex ended the call, smiling triumphantly. "Now we're good. Hit it, Felicity."

FIFTEEN

After the car debacle, Alex gave our illegal and fledgling business a name: Revenge Incorporated. She considered herself the founder and CEO, a dedicated owner who worked all hours of the day, soliciting requests from locals in the blueberry shed.

Correction: my *dead mother's* blueberry shed.

On Sunday alone, we got five cash offers. Church seemed to be a great place to think about stabbing a neighbor in the back. Who would've thought this town had so many problems the sheriff wasn't solving? Melinda needed her upstairs neighbor to stop stomping above her bedroom every night. Jackson said that Greg had cut in line at the grocery store, so he felt that Greg shouldn't be allowed groceries anymore. William sobbed, telling Alex and me about an incident with his parrot and how his younger brother, Roger, had purposely taught the bird to say, "Will's a loser."

They were petty grievances, but over time little insults added up—to the point where someone would pay good money for revenge.

That was where we came in. All cash. No guarantees. No refunds.

"Revenge Incorporated: where money truly does buy happiness," Alex said as she counted the $150 Regina had paid us to sabotage Mick's tomato bushes.

Her enthusiasm was equally matched by my anxiety. What if we got caught? What if we got arrested? What if we died in prison? Escalating worries kept me up at night, but I didn't have the heart to pull the plug on the venture. Not only did we need the money, but my business partner didn't need my approval to drum up customers. She could run Revenge Incorporated on her own.

And if Alex conducted the business without me, she'd get carried away and commit a real crime, something beyond a prank. She had no qualms about causing real, lasting damage. If she burned down a building, Rodney would be forced to forgo his beauty sleep and investigate.

Therefore, Revenge Incorporated had limits—my very own liability shield.

"No hurting anyone," I said after Greg paid us $200 to sabotage the spin studio that woke him up every morning with rock music. "No permanent damage, illness, or injuries."

Alex accepted my terms without argument. "I'll only destroy their property, reputations, and will to live."

I should learn to choose my words more carefully. "And we're never messing with the grocery store."

Alex raised an eyebrow. "Because Wade's mom owns it?"

"No," I said, voice rising so she would take my words seriously. "Because Mary has no sympathy for anyone who commits even the tiniest infraction. She once petitioned the town council to take away Claudine's driver's license after she forgot to use her blinker before making a right turn into her own driveway. She fined Ashley five hundred dollars for flying a kite in the park without the proper permit. Ashley's seven years old. Can you imagine what she'd do to us if we vandalized her store? She'd probably execute us in the town square like this is the early 1600s."

Alex rolled her eyes.

"Promise me you'll leave the market alone."

"Wh—"

"Promise me, or Revenge Incorporated goes under and we return everyone's money."

"Jeez, okay. I won't mess with the grocery store."

"Or the bakery," I added, thinking of the elderly Philomena. "Or Mike and Noreen, who own the bookstore." They'd been giving me free books on Christmas and my birthday since I was ten. "And absolutely no teachers. They deal with children and teenagers all day; they don't need to return home to more antics."

"Does that leave anyone in town?"

"Glen," I suggested with a shrug.

Alex opened her mouth to protest, but the shed door swung back and Edith entered. With blueberry customers only interested in booking revenge services, seeing Edith, the seventy-eight-year-old former librarian, made me relax. Finally, a *real* customer whom I didn't have to suppress my morals for. I highly doubted she wished to solicit illegal activity.

I handed her a bucket for free. My mom had never charged Edith for blueberries in the three decades I'd been alive. Perhaps if the revenge business kept up, we could offer a senior citizen discount—free blueberries for everyone over seventy.

"Can I have two buckets, dear?" Edith asked Alex, holding out her hand. "One for me and one for Charlie."

I quickly cut in, handing Edith another bucket. "Let me know if you need anything. I'll be right here in the shed."

She smiled and slowly made her way to the door. I'd find a reason to check on her in ten minutes; her hip replacement from last year still caused her pain, and I didn't trust her body to cooperate in the heat.

Frustration radiated off Alex. "You can't give everything away for free. This is why you have no money."

I ignored her and filled out a receipt, happy this transaction was only for blueberries—the first legitimate, albeit free, business in several days. *Maybe I should frame it?* With Alex around, it could be the last of its kind.

"I take it she's also on your Do Not Harm list?"

I nodded, and she tossed her arms in the air like I was the most ridiculous person she'd ever encountered. "And who the hell is Charlie? Her grandson?"

"Her dog. Charlie passed away six years ago. She was really attached to him."

"She got a bucket for her dead *dog*?"

Some people did weirder things for dead loved ones. Edith was getting older, and she had no children or family living in the area. If she wanted to believe Charlie was still with her, who the hell was I to judge what brought her peace? I probably would've grabbed an extra bucket for my mom, too.

When I was younger, Edith had taught me to sew. The lessons seemed useless at the time, but now I hadn't bought new clothes in years because Edith had taught me to mend them myself. "A lost art," my mom had called it. She'd paid Edith in blueberry pies, eating a slice with her as I played with an energetic terrier named Charlie. Over the years, there had been a few Charlies in Edith's life—always a terrier, though some were better behaved than others.

"You guys having a sale or something?"

I looked up as Wade stepped into the shed, then immediately back down, stacking the receipts into a pile. Juno ducked under the table to greet Alex.

"Woke me up with all the racket over here," Wade said, putting his sunglasses on top of his head.

"It's one in the afternoon." My voice came out an octave higher than it should've. We hadn't spoken since I'd kissed him several nights ago. I'd never been more grateful for his irregular work hours. The one time I'd noticed him in his yard after delivering blueberries, I'd run into the house, leaving the wagon near the front steps, only retrieving it after he'd gone inside.

"How much for a bucket?" he asked.

"Since when do you pay for things?" Alex responded.

"Do you want my money or not?"

"Twenty dollars," Alex said. "Cash only. No refunds."

Her sales pitch needed work.

"The sign says ten," he countered.

"Sign's outdated. It's National Blueberry Day."

"Never heard of it."

"Pick whatever you want, Wade. It's on the house," I said. The man mowed my lawn every week, removed leaves from the rain gutters, shoveled the driveway, and let me repeatedly borrow his truck. He'd earned some free blueberries.

I was aware of his eyes on me as I worked. *His* blue *eyes,* I thought, cheeks growing warm. I should've been more prepared for awkwardness after kissing Wade Londergan. It was to be expected.

"Did you guys hear the talk that's been going around town? Patrick had his cars towed a few nights ago."

My pen stopped moving.

"Yeah, we heard," Alex said. "What about it?"

"Curious timing, is all. First, I see Susanna over here; then my truck goes missing two nights later, only to reappear with dirt in the back. Rumor has it, someone dug up a street sign and moved it."

"Weird." Alex tossed the bucket at him. "One-hour time limit."

Wade leaned over the table, crossing into my personal space. "Service around here has really slipped. I think you need to make some changes."

"I'll get right on that." I swallowed to suppress the fluttering in my stomach.

He smiled, then drummed his fingers on the table, like he was looking for an excuse to stay in the shed. "I'll see you around, Felicity. Alex." He nodded in her direction and headed toward the door, swinging the bucket in front of him. He whistled, and Juno took off after him like he was the greatest person in the world.

When he was gone, I looked up from the receipts. A crisp twenty-dollar bill sat on the table in front of me.

"What was that about?"

"No idea." I flushed, detesting the feeling.

"You're a terrible liar."

Why did my face have to reveal everything? No sense in hiding it, I supposed. Wade would probably tell her to embarrass me. "We kissed. Once."

"And?" Alex asked like I was being purposefully obtuse. "How was it?"

Amazing. Heart stopping. Wonderful.

"It's Wade," I said, like that should answer everything for her.

"So?" Alex said. "He's hot and he's into you. Always has been."

"He's into every woman in town."

She smiled at me like a proud mother.

"Get back to work," I snapped, my voice harsher than it should've been. "We need to check on people in the fields."

"Check on them? They can either pick blueberries or they can't. Nothing I can do to help if it's the second."

"Alex—"

"All right, all right, we'll check on them. They probably want to ask about Revenge Incorporated anyway. But don't worry, I'll leave Wade in your capable hands."

I never should've told her about the kiss. I'd never hear the end of it.

SIXTEEN

Our target was the Snow Globe Emporium.

The small tourist trap occupied the building between the diner and the photography studio. As we approached the shop, Alex gave me the usual pep talk. After weeks of antics, I still needed the encouragement. The disaster at the car wash, where I'd tripped over the hose and fell face-first onto the concrete, came to mind.

"We'll be in and out in twenty minutes. We don't need a repeat of the antique store," she concluded.

"That wasn't my fault."

"I found you organizing the chairs."

My skin prickled as I remembered the furniture in disarray. "Everything was stacked to the ceiling with no order. If she decluttered the walkways, the store would flow—"

"You need to get a handle on your OCD," Alex interrupted.

I grimaced at her insult but didn't disagree. Besides, there was no time for an argument about my mental health issues. The streetlamps flickered, the only source of light as it neared midnight. It was go-time.

"Do you have the pictures?" Alex's tone was all business.

I checked my pocket for the twentieth time. The paper crinkled. My sole job involved transporting the pictures Alex had printed out this afternoon. Per usual, she handled everything else, not trusting me to act under pressure. "Nerves of soggy oatmeal," she'd said three nights ago in Simon's Clock Shop after an owl hooted outside and I dropped the brass clock in fright.

Alex, however, had shown no fear, diligently moving from clock to clock, creating havoc with every turn. Time in Elswood might never be standardized again.

Alex led us down the narrow alley behind Main Street, where a row of shops had back entrances enclosed by a high fence. I twisted away from the trash bins, careful not to let my jacket touch the foul-smelling containers. *Yuck.*

She used her flashlight to locate the shop's door handle. "See? Glen never locks up." Her smug voice cut through the night air as she pushed the door wide open. "Why not put a neon sign in the window saying *Welcome, Thieves*. If you ask me, we're doing Glen a favor. Next time someone breaks into his store, they might not have your morals."

How could she joke at a time like this? I was one loud noise from having a heart attack. I'd never done anything remotely against the rules for twenty-seven years, and now revenge had overtaken my life. Even as we picked and delivered blueberries, we studied the town map and walked up and down the streets until we were qualified to be the next city planners. My heel had a blister that wouldn't pop, I hadn't gotten a full night's sleep in ages, and my therapist had increased my antianxiety medication to twice its normal dose.

But I was finally well paid. We'd made over three thousand untaxed dollars in four weeks.

With a fifty-fifty split of Revenge Inc.'s profits, and in conjunction with Alex's returned bail money, I'd have the property lien paid off before the interest rate could bury me. Alex had been right: Crime pays.

So when Blair had asked us to hit the rival snow globe shop, I'd barely batted an eye, seeing nothing but dollar signs.

"It's got to be tonight," Blair had said, holding out $200, the going rate for small-time, no-property-damage jobs. A typical breaking-and-entering scheme—or B and E, as Alex called it, using the proper criminal lingo—took a few hours of planning and one night to accomplish. The homes, shops, and farms in Elswood had lackluster security, baffling me beyond reason. Who didn't lock their doors when they left the house? I triple-checked mine. But Nancy had left her windows wide open last week when we broke inside to paint Pick Up Your Dog's Poop on her living room wall. The brown paint had smudged in certain spots, but Alex thought the "client" would be happy with the results.

We'd taken advantage of the small-town, no-crime-happens-here mindset—thriving even as people became more aware of Revenge Incorporated. A stroll through the square had people glancing at us like we were either rock stars or the devil, depending on the person and the day.

"Since you want it done tonight, it's a rush job," Alex had told Blair, taking the cash and counting the bills. "For any requests with less than twenty-four hours' notice, we charge double."

Alex insisted on being the prime negotiator. She drove a harder bargain, and seeing as we were conducting illegal activity, I wanted to squeeze every possible penny out of the clients to make the risk worth the reward.

Blair protested for a full minute, but eventually forked over the extra cash.

Alex had started brainstorming pranks from the moment Blair departed the shed. She had several ideas, but like always, I made the final decision, keeping the damage limited to a misdemeanor.

Inside the Snow Globe Emporium, I handed Alex her share of the papers. She ran the flashlight over the pictures and laughed quietly. "I actually think these will be an improvement on his current merchandise." She laughed again.

Yes, who wanted to look at their family when they could have a lovely color portrait of dictator Kim Jong Un in their snow globe?

White glitter swirled inside the glass as I unscrewed the plastic bottom. I slid the picture into position, noting how out of place the leader of North Korea looked with a Disney World background. I shook the snow globe, admiring that the prank was simple, yet effective. Alex was too clever for her own good.

"Jeez, how many does he have?" Alex asked after a few minutes. We only had a hundred Kim Jong Uns, but there were shelves and shelves of snow globes.

Alex had taken the section near the front windows, while I hovered in the back.

"He can't be making much money. There's no way these are more popular than blueberries," she said, sliding a globe back onto a shelf.

A light flashed outside the front window.

"What was that?" she asked, retreating to come stand beside me near the checkout counter. We ducked as someone moved on the sidewalk. I waited, ears straining, unable to hear anything above my thumping heartbeat.

Another light shone outside. Someone peered through the window.

Fear trapped the scream in my throat.

Oh no, oh no, oh no.

Alex tapped my shoulder, getting my attention, then pointed behind her. Her movements made no sense. What did she want?

She pointed again, more urgently this time.

I raised both arms in puzzlement. She yanked my shirtsleeve hard. "Let's go," she whispered. She tiptoed toward the back exit, quiet as a shadow.

With the flashlight turned off, I didn't notice the shelf to my right. My elbow knocked into the wood, and a snow globe crashed to the floor, sending liquid and glitter across the linoleum.

"Run!" I said, giving up the ruse of being quiet.

The front door burst open as my foot disappeared through the back entrance.

Moonlight barely lit the alleyway. I looked behind me. Any moment, someone would enter the alley and we'd be caught. We'd never make it to the end of the alley without being seen.

We're not going to make it.

Which left me with one option.

"Quick," I said, lacing my fingers together. I bent down so Alex would have a step. "Climb over the fence!"

Alex, picking up on my intentions, placed her boot in my hand, and I heaved her upward, using every bit of strength I possessed. She climbed to the top and swung a leg over the metal bar.

"Head straight home," I said before running farther down the alley. I wouldn't be able to climb the fence quickly enough—if I could climb it at all. During the dreaded rope climb from my elementary school days, my feet had never left the gymnasium floor.

The chain-link fence rattled, and I assumed Alex had made it to the other side.

Trapped, I dodged behind the metal trash cans, throwing myself into a week's worth of garbage. The back door of Glen's shop banged open.

"Freeze!" Rodney yelled. "Police!"

A swath of light ran over the area, narrowly avoiding my ducked head. I pulled my feet to my chest, making myself as small as possible. Fear squeezed my throat, blocking out the putrid smell of decomposing eggs in the trash.

Rodney's footsteps clattered on the pavement. I held my breath as he drew closer. If he walked down the alley, he'd spot me mixed in with the trash bags. At least Alex had escaped. I exhaled, relieved she wouldn't get caught and arrested again.

"Where are they?" another voice called out. I knew that voice, though it was out of place in the dark alleyway. *Jonathan Callaway.*

Why was the mayor here?

"They must have hopped the fence. It was shaking when I got out here."

More footsteps approached. They seemed to stop only a few feet from me.

Don't move, don't move, don't move.

As soon as I thought it, every muscle in my body had an overwhelming urge to stretch.

"So, you let them get away? We had one chance to trap them by paying Blair to request their services. *One.* Now Felicity will never leave the house." Jonathan didn't sound angry; he sounded furious. "We should've gone inside sooner, not waited on the sidewalk so they could slip away. What is the town paying you for other than to drink coffee and let criminals escape?" His tone made me embarrassed for Rodney's police skills. Jonathan shouldn't shame him so harshly to his face.

"I can't enter a store without permission; there has to be probable cause," Rodney said. "I'm doing everything I can."

"Is that so? Because you didn't bother questioning her when she assaulted my son."

"Those kids were on her property late at night, stealing blueberries. Can't get an arrest warrant for that, which is precisely what I told your wife."

Their shadows danced on the ground, pacing back and forth like slithering snakes.

"They're making the town look like a criminal haven, and you're sitting on your ass. Voting for the Man of the Year takes place in five weeks—the town won't accept a one thousand percent crime increase on my watch," Jonathan snarled. "Felicity is making a mockery of you and your entire department."

"My department is three people!" Something scattered across the concrete. Rodney must've kicked a stone. "Even if I catch her, Felicity is in her late twenties without so much as a speeding ticket. No judge will give her more than a slap on the wrist."

"Maybe so, but her *friend* is a different story." I practically heard Jonathan's smile. "How many times must we tell you that catching the teenager is the top priority. Felicity is nothing without her delinquent sidekick."

I drew in a breath, then slapped my hand over my mouth. He was going after Alex! How dare he! I almost jumped up and confronted him on the spot. He couldn't do that. She was only eighteen years old. If the Callaways wanted to blame someone, it should be me.

"Your top priority—no, your *only* priority—is getting rid of the teenager. Without her, Felicity's business will crumble."

"And we'll be protecting the town from her crime spree," Rodney added.

"They are one and the same. This town will be better off without Felicity Lavigne. There's no room in Elswood for thieves—not anymore."

The smell of rotten eggs didn't compare to Jonathan's decaying soul.

Consumed with anger, I didn't notice that the conversation in the alley had ended. Their footsteps grew distant and a door closed, leaving me in overwhelming silence until the wind skated through the alley and rustled the trash bags.

I counted to a thousand, not sure how long I should wait before risking the long walk home. Would they be waiting for me in the street? Or did they think I'd already hopped the fence? When I reached a thousand, my nerves remained agitated, so I counted back to zero by threes, and only when a rat scampered across the pavement did I abandon my hiding spot and run in the opposite direction.

The dark streets showed no sign of Rodney or Jonathan. Smelling like spoiled milk, with sweat stains running down the back of my T-shirt, I refused to turn on my flashlight until I reached the unlit country roads.

My fear of the dark tempered my rage, my mind preoccupied with getting home and taking a shower as quickly as possible. There were probably roaches in that alley.

The front door had barely opened when a pair of arms wrapped around my shoulders.

"Alex?" I asked, making sure the stress of the evening hadn't caused me to hallucinate.

"I thought they caught you."

I fought the impulse to smile. Since I'd met her in the police station, I'd wanted to hug her. In the weeks since, I'd given her space, knowing she didn't like physical affection. But now, I wrapped my arms around her, realizing this was the first time I'd hugged anyone since my mom died.

The whole night suddenly seemed worth it. "It's fine. I'm fine. Everything's fine."

The last thing I wanted was Alex worrying about me, though I should have anticipated her anxiousness when I didn't return home right away. What would she think other than that I'd been arrested?

I tightened my arms. I'd forgotten what it was like to have someone care about whether I made it home.

Before I could continue reassuring her, Alex released me. She cleared her throat and straightened the hem of her T-shirt. "How did you get away? When I hopped the fence, I thought you were done for."

"Hid in the trash behind the diner."

"So *that's* what the smell is."

She tried to steer the conversation to lighter grounds, but I noticed her red, puffy eyes and the scratchiness in her voice. Didn't she know I was the queen of tears and anxiety? I could spot the signs of an emotional breakdown better than anyone.

Something hissed in the kitchen. "Are you making tea?"

"Is that illegal or something?"

I pursed my lips, fighting off another smile. I'd taught her well.

The kettle rattled on the stovetop as we made our way to the kitchen.

"Can't believe that oaf of a sheriff almost caught us." Alex poured the steaming water into cups; tea bags rested on the side. "Can you imagine what that would've done to my reputation?" She shuddered as if bugs were crawling across her arms. "I'd never be able to show my face in this town again."

A run-in with the sheriff while vandalizing a store should've made me want to stay inside for the next year. We'd been lucky to escape without having our mug shots printed in *The Elswood Gazette*. It'd be foolish to do anything illegal for the next several months. Forget Alex's reputation—her future could be in jeopardy, and the Callaways would get exactly what they wanted: Alex in prison and me alone and friendless once more.

All the rage and resentment I'd suppressed for the last several years—all the stolen blueberries, the unkind words about my sanity, the whispers as I dragged my wagon through town—bubbled through my thoughts. I'd been miserable since my mother died, but all that paled in comparison to losing Alex or the farm, two things I couldn't live without.

The Callaways had left me with no choice but to fight back. I didn't want to just *win* this feud; I wanted to *destroy* them. I'd sink their reputations so far into the ground they'd need an oil rig to drill for signs of decency.

Nobody threatened Alex. *Nobody.*

"You know that prank you wanted to use for the ice-cream parlor, but I said it was too dangerous?"

"Operation Murder Mystery?" Alex sat up straight in her chair. "I believe you called it 'deplorable,' 'immoral,' and said over your dead body would we ever do it."

That was the one. "How do you think it would fare against Cheryl's catering company?"

SEVENTEEN

"We need something else for Operation Murder Mystery," Alex said.

I stopped flipping through television channels. We were leaving for the catering company in a matter of hours—as soon as the town fell into a deep sleep after their Sunday dinners.

"What else is there? You got the chalk yesterday." She'd made me drive the truck forty minutes away to buy it. I'd had to fill up Wade's gas tank, something I'd never done before. Somehow I'd found an extra twenty dollars in my pocket. Another thing that had never happened before.

Alex sat next to me on the couch. "I was at Wade's place this afternoon—you know, soaking up that sweet air-conditioning." She sighed with fondness. "And I saw yellow crime scene tape from the Elswood Sheriff's Department in his closet. It'll add so much to the plan if we can get our hands on that tape."

What was she doing in his closet? She shouldn't be over there at all, but I'd given up trying to stop their friendship from growing. It was a lost cause. I ate a handful of popcorn, settling on a romantic comedy I'd seen a hundred times, knowing it would keep me awake until after midnight. "So go ask him for it."

"He won't give it to me."

"Sure he will." Wade seemed to adore her—much more than me, anyway.

"He won't. I already asked him."

This might be the first time she didn't just take it anyway. "Bummer."

"He'd give it to you," she said, sitting up straighter. "If you asked, I'm sure he'd give you the tape."

"If you couldn't get him to cough it up, then I won't be able to."

Alex snatched the popcorn from my lap.

"Hey!"

"Stop playing dumb." Her voice turned serious. "He obviously likes you."

"*Likes* me? Is this high school?" I laughed at the thought.

"It's not funny."

"Yes, it is." Why was she so mad about my reaction? Jeez, she'd grown more attached to him than I realized.

"He's a good guy, and you never give him the time of day. You just fight with him, even after he fixed the fence when I accidentally backed the truck into it."

I cringed. The dent in his truck's bumper would probably never be repaired. He hadn't been pleasant after that, threatening to never let us use his truck again. But he'd relented the next day after Alex baked him a blueberry pie.

It was the first time she'd apologized to anyone. It was a sweet moment, even if it happened with Wade. It bothered me how attached she was to him, because he was attractive, but maybe, despite our actions, she was growing more mature. She didn't steal from him, took responsibility for damaging his property, and apologized. That guilty-plea deal didn't seem so far-fetched after all.

But of all the people in Elswood, why did she respect the one person I never would?

"I appreciate that you think Wade isn't a total loser, but the two of us . . ." I shook my head. "It's not going to happen. He doesn't like me." I needed to let her down easy. Her hopes and dreams for my romantic future would be as lost as Micaela's house keys, which we'd thrown into the river. That ought to stop her from stomping all night long on the apartment below her.

"Why not? How can you be sure?"

I groaned. Why oh why was she doing this to me? I never wanted to discuss Wade with anyone, ever. I'd never be with him, no matter how friendly, generous, or kind he appeared to be. It would be impossible at this point. I'd have to hit my head and get amnesia like a damn soap opera character to ever be romantically linked to Wade Londergan.

"There was an incident when we were in high school. Wade was a popular football player, and every girl in school had a crush on him, it seemed—including me."

"And?" She waited eagerly, not understanding that the story didn't end well.

"And he turned me down. Simple. He didn't like me." I crossed my fingers behind my back, praying she wouldn't ask any follow-up questions. That was as close to the truth as I could make the story without dying of embarrassment.

"You're not in high school anymore. I don't see why he couldn't like you now."

"Maybe I don't like him, Alex. Maybe that's the problem."

She bit her lip, trying to come up with a counterargument.

"Can we not talk about it anymore?" I asked, snatching the popcorn back while she was distracted.

"Oh, we're going to talk about it. Probably for a long time. But first I need you to march over there and get the tape."

"We need it that badly?"

"Operation Murder Mystery won't work without it," she insisted, reclaiming the popcorn once again. "And be nice to him while you're at it. We'll need the truck in a few days."

For Alex, that settled the matter. But she wasn't the one who had to put on her tennis shoes and walk over to his house. Out of loyalty to her, I did what she'd asked. When it didn't work, I hoped she'd understand what I'd known for a decade: Wade Londergan absolutely did not like me.

When Wade answered his door, he looked surprised. "Oh, hey."

"Wade."

"What are you doing here?"

Goose bumps prickled my arm. "It's polite to invite the person on your porch inside."

He rolled his eyes but stepped back so I could squeeze past him. He led me to the kitchen, where several pieces of bread sat directly on the counter next to sliced cheddar cheese. So this was what Wade ate for dinner. How inspiring. I'd started teaching Alex to cook from one of my mom's recipe books. She didn't approve of my methods, often tossing in random ingredients or adding more or less of something. "The recipe's there for a reason," I'd admonished after she added too much cooking wine to the chicken marsala. I had to add twice the vegetables to soak up the extra liquid and salvage the dish.

I sat on the kitchen stool, twisting back and forth as he haphazardly stacked cheese on top of the bread. I couldn't help but notice the freckles on the bridge of his nose, prominent from his days in the sun. Or how the dimples on his cheeks appeared when he smiled his big all-American smile that only he could pull off and not look like he was trying too hard.

"Did you come over here to watch me cook, or was something on your mind?"

I took a deep breath, composing myself to ask for another favor, but he put the sandwich on the skillet, and I rushed to correct him.

"You can't do that," I said, jumping up. "Are you a savage? You have to butter the outside if you want the bread to cook right." I snagged the sandwich from the stovetop. "It's Grilled Cheese 101."

"I always eat them like this. And then I put a handful of potato chips on top of the gooey cheese."

I shook my head, tuning him out. I didn't find butter in his fridge—another black mark against his name. Who the hell didn't have butter?

I settled for mayonnaise.

When I placed the bread back onto the pan, it sizzled. "You can thank me later."

"Enough comments about my cooking. What do you want?"

I reclaimed the stool and folded my hands in front of me. "Alex claims you have crime scene tape. I want to borrow it."

He leaned against the counter. "What for?"

"None of your business."

"As it's my tape, it's entirely my business. I'm assuming it's for another one of your adventures. Like the incident at the warehouse on Guava Street."

"Alex has been talking too much."

"Felicity, the entire town is talking about it. Now, I know Rodney isn't a hard worker, but sooner or later he's going to come knocking on your door."

"I can handle Rodney." Since when was Wade so concerned about following the rules? He wasn't exactly an upstanding citizen who used crosswalks and obeyed speed limits.

"You need to flip it," I said.

"What?"

"Your sandwich is burning. Flip it."

Cursing, he used his fingers to turn over the sandwich. Somehow he managed to burn both sides before removing it. He put it on a paper plate and tossed a handful of potato chips between the bread and the cheesy center. He lifted the sandwich to his mouth, then paused. "Want half?"

I didn't have time for this. I needed to get the tape and go over the plan a few more times with Alex. This wasn't going to be like the snow globe incident. This time we'd have two exit strategies and a cover story. So I cut to the chase. "What do you want in exchange for the tape?"

Wade never did anything that wouldn't benefit him in return.

He smiled again, and my stomach clenched. Why did he have to do that?

"Well, the talk around town is that you two are on quite a roll. Anyone can pay you for petty crimes and you'll do it, no questions asked."

Oh, there had been questions. I'd made Alex reject several cash offers that she pouted about later, but there was no way I was letting her get into too much trouble. And now with the Callaways trying to set us up, we'd need to vet all our customers for duplicity and loyalty to the mayor.

"You want us to do something for you?" Who did Wade have a beef with besides me?

"If I wanted to do something, I wouldn't need to hire the two of you; I'd handle it myself. No, I want a promise from you. If I give you the tape, no matter what—no matter how much money you're offered—you can't do anything to me. No pranks on me or my property, including the bar. Agreed?"

Was he scared of us? I doubted Alex would have struck out against Wade—not after our last conversation, where she'd defended him like this white knight. The three of us over here on Clementine Lane were, as Alex had put it, the Elswood Outcasts, and messing with a fellow member of the club was strictly forbidden. Though Wade hardly qualified as an "outcast," seeing as his house parties drew bigger crowds than most high school sporting events, I made no outright objection to his inclusion. Since Revenge Incorporated started, I'd learned to pick my battles with Alex.

Besides, I was almost sure Wade was helping her come up with some of our pranks. He'd lived in this town his entire life and owned a bar, a place where people said more than they should. How else would Alex uncover that Glen didn't lock his shop's back door? Or that Sandy stayed with her mother in Wellington every Tuesday night so she could drink at her book club? He'd likely conveyed inside knowledge so Alex could exploit it.

But what was his angle? What was he getting in return for helping us?

He could've made this exact deal with Alex and saved me the trip over here.

"You give me the tape and we'll leave you alone."

There was no point in fighting it. I'd never been able to say no to him. That had always been my problem.

He took another bite of his sandwich, washing it down with beer. I studied the way his smile disappeared into the side of his face as he chewed. My insides clenched once more when I remembered how his perfectly proportioned lips had felt against my own. *Stop it, Felicity!*

EIGHTEEN

Lying face up on the concrete sidewalk, I marveled at how the sky held no clouds. Not a single wisp of cover for Operation Murder Mystery. Moonlight shone over us like the spotlight on a stage performer—only we didn't need any witnesses for this performance. Though Alex had assured me multiple times that no security cameras covered the sidewalk outside Cheryl's storefront, that wouldn't prevent someone from walking by and glimpsing Revenge Incorporated in action.

We needed to be quick and quiet.

"Are you done yet?"

"You can't rush perfection," Alex whispered from somewhere near my feet. "Great art takes time."

"You're confusing art with vandalism again."

I lifted my shoulders from the ground, trying to get a glimpse of her "art."

She smacked my leg. "Don't move. You'll wreck it."

I lay back on the cold concrete, one arm straight out, the other above my head as Alex circled around me. My limbs ached, urging me to change position, but I held still. We had no time to start over. The blood capsules had already been spilled.

"Done," Alex whispered, putting the white chalk in a Ziploc bag. She held out her hand. "Careful not to smudge it."

Delicately, I found my feet and looked over her handiwork.

"Oh my gosh." My hand covered my mouth. "You might be right: This *is* a work of art." The sidewalk looked like the opening scene to one of those procedural cop shows she loved. Alex's gift for detail was as amazing as it was horrifying. How many true-crime episodes did she have to have watched in order to replicate a murder scene? I bent to examine the white tennis shoe and the smudge of red paint on the laces.

"Don't touch anything," she hissed, lurching forward to grab my shoulder. "They might dust for fingerprints."

"Rodney doesn't know how to find fingerprints."

"A good criminal takes no chances. Now, come on, we need to vanish like thieves in the night." Clearly having more fun than a toddler at Disney World, she pulled me under the police tape, looped her arm through mine, and led me away from the scene of the crime.

Not until my alarm went off a few hours later did I realize we might have taken this revenge scheme a bit too far.

Alex had never been so eager to deliver blueberries. With Juno at her side, she walked ahead of the wagon, urging me to pick up the pace. At one point she snapped her fingers like an impatient dance instructor. "What is the holdup? I've seen nursing-home residents walk faster than you."

"They probably weren't hauling thirty pounds of blueberries across town."

Alex slowed long enough to open a carton. She popped a handful of berries in her mouth. "There, now it's lighter."

She skipped ahead, humming a song I didn't recognize. Juno's tail swished back and forth like windshield wipers in a downpour, responding to Alex's excitement.

In truth, my pace had slowed the closer we got to town. Thinking of what we'd done last night—the scandal it would cause—made each step reverberate up my spine with anxiousness. What if we'd been seen? Identified? Alex had insisted that no cameras were pointed at the patch of sidewalk in front of the catering company, but how did she know for sure?

Not deviating from our established routine, we made our first delivery to the bakery. Only, I'd never seen the eatery so empty at this time of day. Everyone must've ordered their muffins and coffee to go. Philomena handed me cash, her lips pursed with disapproval.

"This is amazing." Alex swung Juno's leash like a jump rope, the two of them bouncing in unison after we delivered a majority of the cartons to the market. Our next stop, the ice-cream parlor, would take us straight past the crime scene.

"Remember what I told you at the house." I'd given her specific instructions to let me do all the talking. There was little hope she'd stick to the plan, but I'd tried. "Stop skipping, and at least try to look normal."

Alex turned her smile into a pout and hunched her shoulders. "Better?" She still sounded like a kid on the first day of summer vacation.

I squeezed the wagon handle as we walked toward the crowd.

Whispers swirled. A few people muttered, but everyone seemed to be collectively holding their breath. I tried to look interested as we approached, as if I didn't already know what they were staring at.

"Morning, Paula," I said to the better of the two hairdressers in town. "What's going on?" I raised myself on tiptoes to sell the lie.

"Rebecca found the body when she was out walking. Gave her quite a scare." Paula winked, and my insides tightened.

"They found a dead body?" Alex asked, reaching to pet Juno's head.

"Just the outline, dear. No one knows who moved the body."

You're looking at the body, Paula. Because, of course, Alex had insisted on being the artist.

"Maybe somebody jumped from the roof because of Cheryl's cooking," Alex suggested.

"Maybe." Paula winked again, then turned her attention toward the sidewalk when a shriek thundered up the street.

"What do you mean, I can't open the store?" Cheryl yelled. "Tear this tape down, Rodney, so I can get back to work. I have orders that need to go out. It's Sydney Haskall's fortieth birthday!"

The crowd parted, giving us easy access to the front, almost as if they wanted to force a confrontation between Cheryl and me. Our feigning-innocence routine, while necessary to avoid vandalism charges, had fooled no one.

My fingers skimmed the yellow police tape that sectioned off the entire front entrance to Crown Catering.

The fake crime scene looked more gruesome in the daylight.

The white body outline was surrounded by yellow evidence markers and an old pair of tennis shoes. Men's size 11, to be exact. But where Alex's creativity had really shined was with the blood capsules. She'd painted a bloody trail from the body outline to the catering company's door as if the person had been inside before collapsing on the concrete. At the bottom of the white door, written in fake blood, were the words CHERYL C DID IT.

"Best twenty bucks I've ever spent," Alex had said as she used her fingers to paint the door. "As soon as we get home, I'm ordering more."

Cheryl pointed a finger at Rodney, who had bent down to study the chalk outline once again. "Do you really think someone died here?"

"No, but we have to be sure. There's blood and evidence markers." He rubbed his round head, looking stumped. This was way beyond the purview of the former football player, even one who had attended *the* Ohio State University. Perhaps he needed a real sheriff to assist him with this fake crime. "That tape came from our police station. I had it custom made three years ago."

"Told you," Alex whispered in my ear. "Totally necessary."

I gave her a stern look, silencing her.

My attention returned to Cheryl, who hovered over Rodney as he stood.

"You can't be serious. This is obviously a prank—and a dumb one, at that."

"Until we can be sure, I have to take every precaution, Mrs. Callaway. I'm sorry, but those are the rules." Rodney pointed toward the street corner. "We tried to pull the video footage from the security camera, but it must've lost power last night."

I stopped breathing. There *was* a security camera on this street. Alex had been wrong.

We'd been very, very lucky that it didn't work.

"We don't need the video. Everyone already knows *she* did this." Cheryl took a step toward me, her face blotched with red. "Arrest her. Now. Or you'll be fired before noon."

My knees locked so I couldn't run.

The crowd watched, eyes ping-ponging between the two of us. Excitement sizzled in the morning heat. A showdown between Cheryl Callaway and Felicity Lavigne—what could be better on an otherwise-boring Monday?

My stomach lurched with panic, but my voice remained calm. "Arrest me for what?" I nodded toward the door behind her. "According to the blood, you're the murderer."

Cheryl stopped right in front of me. "I know this was you; don't try to deny it. You and your *friend*." She looked threateningly at Alex, who couldn't have looked any more bored with this woman and her drama. "There might not be proof, but I'm going to make you pay for this. First my kid, now my business."

"Careful, Cheryl, you wouldn't want to threaten someone in public," I said. She took a step back, eyes looking from face to face, as if she'd forgotten about the crowd due to her rage. "And good luck with this . . ." I gestured casually at her storefront, unsure where this newfound confidence had come from, but grabbing it with both hands and holding on for dear life. "I sure hope business doesn't suffer. I know what rumors can do to sales."

"Actually, it's already on Yelp," Alex announced, holding her phone out to read from the screen to the onlookers.

"Don't do business here. The cops shut the place down due to an unsolved murder."

"Crown Catering? More like Coffin *Catering."* Alex snorted at her own joke.

"One star—there was a bloody finger in my tomato soup."

She paused to glance over at Cheryl. "Those were verified customers, too."

Alex had written over fifteen negative reviews, all from fake accounts, tanking Cheryl's 4.7-star rating to a dismal 3.1. From murder to undercooked chicken to poor customer service, she'd ruined the business in a matter of minutes. With the internet, it had been almost too easy.

I'd never been more grateful that Lavigne Blueberries had no online presence.

Cheryl's face had turned so red, steam should've been coming out her ears. "Shut your mouth, you lying, good-for-nothing brat." Her finger jabbed threateningly at Alex. "You're going to wish you'd never set foot in this town."

Juno started barking protectively, her eyes on Cheryl.

"Get her, Juno," Alex said. "Get the mean lady."

A flash came from my left, and all eyes shifted to Herman and his outdated camera. He must've bought that contraption in the '70s.

Herman pushed up his glasses and pulled a pocket-size notebook out of his bag. "Would anyone like to comment on the murder?"

He might as well have shouted *The Cleveland Browns just won the Super Bowl.*

Chaos ensued. The crowd pushed toward Herman, their hands in the air. I could barely hear myself think over the shouting.

When someone bumped into me, I stepped toward Cheryl and seized my opportunity to speak only to her. "If you ever so much as say Alex's name again, I'll tell everyone you gave Blair that spare four hundred dollars. I think Glen will care that you sacrificed his shop to settle your score with me." I dug the knife deeper into her front; stabbing her in the back would've been too easy. "In fact, I think *everyone* will care."

Her eyes grew round with shock. Now she'd be questioning everything. How did I know about Blair? Had her friend snitched? Could she trust no one in this town? When Cheryl's eyes took in the crowd, I gathered that it had become quite small to her. Perhaps she didn't have as firm a grip on the town and its people as she'd led herself to believe.

Her reputation, and that of her husband, would be as tarnished as mine if the truth came out. I'd never known Glen to let anything go, especially where his precious snow globes were concerned. If the Callaways wanted to pretend they were the perfect family, with the perfect life, sabotaging a town shop would sling mud all over their windows. I'd drag her and her husband with me to the depths of social pariahdom until Jonathan Callaway had to relinquish his Elswood Man of the Year title and resign from public office.

A smug smile tugged at the corner of my mouth.

This time, I got to be the one who walked away with the upper hand.

When I entered the deserted ice-cream parlor, Alex was already leaning against the counter, smiling wider than a stretched bungee cord. Juno lay by her feet. "I think they know."

"Know what?"

Alex tapped the silver bell on the counter. "That you, Felicity Lavigne, are no longer the Elswood Doormat."

NINETEEN

The Elswood Gazette ran a special edition to cover the crime story, getting it printed by noon. The headline read Murder in Elswood? The front page had a shot of the crime scene, with Cheryl's outraged face in the background. Herman had mentioned the catering company by name twice, and although the article declared the crime a prank, the words *murder*, *crime scene*, and *blood* would be forever linked to her business.

Alex had purchased three copies of the *Gazette*, stashing one in her bedroom, displaying the second prominently on the coffee table, and sticking the third on the front of the refrigerator like she'd received an A+ on a school assignment. She took great pride in her work.

So when I built up the courage to question her methods over dinner, she naturally became defensive.

"I didn't say there were no security cameras." Alex set her fork down with a clank. "I said there were no security cameras *covering* that section of the sidewalk."

"But how could you possibly know that?" What kind of criminal had I gone into business with? Avoiding security cameras went far beyond committing a prank. Based on what I'd seen in movies and TV shows, only hardened criminals knew how to do such things.

"What does it matter?" Alex said. "The important thing is, I had us covered. Voilà! No video evidence of you creating a fake crime scene." She waved her hands in exasperation. "You're welcome, by the way."

"That's not an answer." How had she turned off the camera without anyone noticing? Without *me* noticing? She'd been at home all day leading up to the prank; I would know, because other than my trip to Wade's house, I'd been home all day, too. According to *The Elswood Gazette*, the security camera went down at 1:00 a.m.—a full hour before we'd arrived at the scene.

"If you knew about the security cameras in downtown Elswood, how did it slip your mind to check for cameras at the department store?" Tess had said the cameras caught Alex stealing the diamond necklace.

Alex froze.

Waiting for an answer, I almost missed the sound of crunching gravel outside.

Light fanned through the front windows, making me stand and abandon my argument. Flashing red and blue lights, the universal sign of trouble, lit up the driveway.

"Open up!" Rodney knocked on the front door. The knock rang with authority, signaling that he was not to be ignored.

"Perfect," Alex said, cracking her knuckles. "Time for round two."

I grabbed her arm, preventing her from answering the door. "Don't you dare."

"Well, someone has to answer it, and I don't think he's here to pick blueberries." She smirked, and my instincts told me to keep her as far away from the man on the porch as possible.

He knocked again. "Open the door, Felicity! Now!"

"Promise me you won't say a word," I said to Alex. "Promise me that you'll let me handle this."

She bit her lip, mulling over my frantic plea as if deciding which pair of socks to wear. "Only if you agree to stop asking me questions for the rest of the night."

"Deal," I snapped, unsure how this had turned into a negotiation. I'd never gotten Alex to reveal anything she didn't want to anyway.

I paused, hand on the doorknob, and gathered my courage. Being questioned by the police would be an experience worthy of a journal entry.

I opened the door. "Rodney," I said as calmly as I could manage. He stood a few paces behind the threshold, looking every inch of 6'3" and 230 pounds. "Unfortunately, the blueberry fields close to self-picking at six p.m. You'll have to come back tomorrow. We open at eleven."

"Not here for blueberries, as you damn well know. I need to speak with you about the recent string of criminal activity in town."

"Oh? I didn't realize you investigated crimes in Elswood."

He didn't laugh at my joke, but Alex did.

"Where were you between midnight and three a.m. last night?" he asked.

I rested my hand on the doorknob, ready to shut it if things got too heated. According to the internet, he couldn't enter the house without probable cause or a warrant. "Right here, at my house."

"Can anyone vouch for that?"

Alex, standing directly behind me, loudly cleared her throat. I stepped on her toes, imploring her to remain silent. I should've prohibited all sounds and laughter in our bargain. Leave it to Alex to find a loophole.

Rodney kept his eyes on me. "Anyone besides a known criminal and liar?"

He must've received quite the threat from Mayor Callaway to get him out here after dark. *Good.* His looming presence on my porch meant the Callaways were scared, so much so they'd sent their lackey to threaten me.

"You know, Rodney, we were eating dinner. So if you could come back at another time—or preferably, not at all—that would be great." I moved to close the door, but he tossed his hand out, keeping the door wide open.

"I know the two of you created the body outline. Just like I know that you opened the pigpen on the Mathews' farm and got Patrick's cars towed."

"Let go of my door."

"We're going to be watching you, night and day. For as long as it takes to prove you and your friend are responsible."

"Watch away." I narrowed my eyes at his hand, still holding the front door open. "But unless you have a warrant, get off my porch."

Clucking his tongue, Rodney released the door. He moseyed down the porch stairs, stepping hard on the last one until the wood splintered more.

He turned to tip his hat at me before getting inside his truck. I slammed the door, locked it, and pressed my back against the wood—as if that would keep him out forever. I breathed deep, calming my anger. Rodney and his threats wouldn't rattle me. Not anymore. I didn't fear him or his badge. If he wanted to follow me around town, then so be it. He'd find nothing to use against us, because I wouldn't give him the satisfaction. If he was smart, he'd learn from the Callaways' mistakes and leave me alone.

Alex peered out the window.

"Don't do anything unless I say so," I warned her in the sternest voice I possessed. "I mean it. Nothing. He's not catching us."

After a moment, she nodded, clearly understanding that I'd never been more serious in my life.

The town provided us with a police escort everywhere we went. At first, it was odd having Rodney or one of his volunteer deputies follow us around in their cars, going everywhere we went or parked on the curb in front of the house, but after the third day, I'd grown used to it. On my way to get a haircut, I left a fresh cup of coffee for Rodney on the hood of his truck. Watching me run errands was probably putting him to sleep.

Eventually, they'd grow bored and leave us alone. Or they'd run out of money, resources, or people. Only three of them worked in that police station, and whatever Callaway had promised wouldn't be worth the rotating twelve-hour shifts.

But after a full week of no revenge antics, I grew jumpy, restless for something—anything—to do. People still came by the blueberry farm, but berries didn't pay well enough to pull me out of debt.

Because of Jonathan and his *dogs*, I had to stay inside, twiddling my thumbs, wasting precious time to earn cash and save my property.

I wanted to pull my hair out at the thought of them being all smug over how they'd put an end to Felicity Lavigne's crime spree.

Then, when I thought things couldn't get worse, Jason, Rodney's second-in-command, knocked on the front door and asked to use the bathroom.

"But, Felicity, I really have to go," he whined when I said no. Other than Alex and Juno, nobody was allowed inside this house, especially not the sheriff's deputy.

"Not without a warrant."

"Felicity—"

"Go ask Wade."

He bounced from foot to foot on the porch. "He left an hour ago."

I sighed, taking pity on this puppy dog of a man. "Wade leaves his back door unlocked. The bathroom is down the hall on the right."

He'd already descended half the porch steps when he yelled "Thanks" over his shoulder.

"And let Juno out while you're over there!"

"Will do." Jason dashed toward Wade's house without a backward glance.

"Such a joke," I muttered, forehead resting on the doorframe. Why did Jason get to enter Wade's house without permission, but when Alex and I committed the same offense, it was considered a crime? I supposed the need to pee made criminals of us all.

But Wade wouldn't mind the intrusion. It wasn't like Jason could make the place any messier. Picturing the state of Wade's bathroom made me shudder, and I swiftly shut the door to block out the image of a sink filled with toothpaste and hair gel that hadn't been cleaned in months.

"Who was that?" Alex asked from the kitchen table. She had her feet propped up on a chair as she decorated a new sign for the blueberry shed. A marker slid across the cardboard. Not only had she raised the price per bucket to fifteen dollars, but she'd also imposed a hefty "self-picking fee," plus a one-hour time limit.

The only place she'd be hanging this sign was her bedroom.

"Jason," I responded.

"The one with the pimples?"

"No, that's Harry. Jason's the one who switches his car lights on when it gets dark outside." Such a crack team Rodney had assembled. "Stop, you can't write that."

"Is it too obvious?" she asked, admiring her handiwork. In small print at the very bottom, she'd written SUPPLEMENTARY SERVICES AVAILABLE UPON REQUEST FOR AN ADDITIONAL FEE. ASK FOR ALEX, FOUNDER AND CEO OF LAVIGNE BLUEBERRIES SUBSIDIARY, REVENGE INCORPORATED.

"We can't advertise Revenge Incorporated on a sign; it's supposed to be a secret. Have you forgotten about the cops watching us night and day?"

She snorted. "They don't even carry service weapons. What are they going to do, yell at us?" She pretended to shiver, then added a small trademark symbol beside the name *Revenge Incorporated.* "I'd be surprised if Rodney can read, let alone recite the Miranda rights."

She had me there. And these were the people keeping us inside, depriving us of much-needed money? What a joke. I'd been relegated to the sidelines by a sheriff and two deputies—one of whom had abandoned his post to use the bathroom. We should've used his absence to escape the house and commit a revenge prank. We had several schemes in the works, but thanks to our escorts, we couldn't do anything without risking detection. They'd catch us in the act, and the Callaways would get exactly what they wanted.

But that didn't mean we had to make this quite so easy on them.

"Alex," I said before she could find tape to hang the poster outside on the shed, "what would you say if I suggested we pull a prank today?"

"That it's about damn time. This town isn't going to destroy itself. Who's the target?"

I bit my bottom lip. "The police."

She froze, but her eyes snapped to mine as if searching for a sign that my words were a joke. "The police?" she asked quietly. "You want to pull a prank on Rodney?"

Just a small one. "Is that a problem?"

I'd never seen her smile so big, not even when I'd told her she could execute Operation Murder Mystery. "We can spray-paint their cars—no, that's not good enough. Let's vandalize the police station. Or we could steal Rodney's phone and rename all his contacts as Dunkin' Donuts. Ugh, I can't think—too many possibilities." She rubbed her temples.

When it came to pranks, Alex had an infinite number of ideas, but I had only one—and I knew it would be perfect.

"We're going to flood the police scanner and make them do actual work."

Nothing hurt people like forcing them to do their jobs.

Alex opened her mouth, closed it, then opened it again. "That's diabolical."

Her tone had me backtracking. "Too much?" Was messing with Rodney and his two bumbling fools a mistake? If Alex was questioning the plan, I'd clearly gone too far.

"No, it's genius." She put her hand over her heart. "I'm just so proud of you. Coming up with a revenge plan against the police, not caring about the consequences—my girl's growing up." She pretended to dab at the emotion in her eyes.

"Pull yourself together," I said, not entirely displeased with her assessment. Pranking the police would be the icing on an already-delicious cake. Served them right for harassing us night and day. And the plan had been entirely my idea. "We've got work to do."

TWENTY

Operation Midnight Hustle kicked off once Jason returned to his vehicle. Alex and I made a show of pulling the empty wagon into town, doing our best to look suspicious as his 2005 Ford rolled behind us at two miles an hour. Jason switched his hazard lights on and started waving cars past.

"We should've asked for a ride," Alex said when country music spilled from the car's rolled-down windows. "Would've been iconic to have the sheriff's deputy literally drive us into town so we could commit a revenge mission."

"We need to be seen," I said. "By as many people as possible."

"Wasted opportunity," she muttered, kicking a stone across the pavement.

Ten minutes later, we arrived at the square, and people crowded the sidewalks on this idyllic Saturday afternoon—some carrying shopping bags, others strolling past the gazebo. An elderly couple sat on a bench, eating ice cream.

We parked the wagon in the middle of the square, where everyone could see us. My anxiety spiked to unhealthy levels; I hated being the center of attention. My cheeks burned and my movements became stiff—I was well aware that Elswood residents had paused their busy day to stop and stare at the pair of us. In the last few weeks, we'd become the town's main attraction.

"Take out your notepad and start sketching," I said, adjusting my sunglasses atop my head.

"Sketch what?"

"Anything. Everything. Make it look like you're casing the town and about to pull a bank heist." I gestured toward the bank, then pointed across the square at the bakery. Onlookers seemed to follow my movements with precision, holding their breaths.

Behind us, Jason clicked on his police radio and whispered something into the microphone.

I consulted the notepad, ignoring Alex's depiction of Jason sucking his thumb, and nodded my approval, then whipped out the binoculars from my purse and zeroed in on the post office. The lens passed over Paula's stricken face before she darted behind the magazine stand.

"Can't believe people are falling for this." Alex continued to dramatically scratch on the paper. "Don't they have any respect for my criminal skills? I'd never conduct a revenge mission in the middle of town in broad daylight."

I doubted that anyone underestimated Alex's pranking abilities. In a little over a month, she'd turned this quiet middle-of-nowhere town into a petty-crime haven.

But Elswood residents had observed my shortcomings for three decades. They'd have no trouble believing I was the worst criminal in the world—so bad, in fact, that I'd plan a crime in the town square, with fifty people watching my every move.

Smugness bubbled in my gut. They'd underestimated me.

"Ready for phase two?" I handed Alex a twenty-dollar bill.

She held the paper up in line with the sun as if examining its authenticity—or its ability to pass as legitimate cash. "I'll swing through the alley," she said. "You head straight to the hardware store."

"We'll regroup in ten. Do your best to look suspicious."

Alex snorted and began walking away. She looked over her shoulder three times to ensure Jason was watching. Then she started running.

"What the . . . ?" Jason sputtered, eyes darting between my position by the gazebo and Alex, who had disappeared behind the library. The problem seemed to click in his brain a second later, because he shouted, "Wait! You can't do that!"

Taking the bait, he chased after Alex, leaving me free to hit Wilkinson's Hardware.

The store's air-conditioning raised goose bumps on my arms.

The salesclerk, Ian, looked startled when I approached the checkout counter. "Would you please tell me where you keep the paint?"

He blinked. "Paint? For what?"

"Business," I said, my sarcastic tone adding the unspoken thought, *As in, none of yours.*

"A-aisle three."

"Thank you," I said sweetly, then strode away, leaving a line of customers dumbfounded.

Wilkinson's had a decent selection—all the basic colors. *Two cans ought to do it,* I thought, selecting blue and yellow. *Let the Ohio State fans stew on this.*

Ten minutes later, laden with a paint can in each hand, a grocery bag containing nails, a hammer, and a heavy drop cloth, I made my exit. The wagon shook as I dropped the cans onto the metal frame with a bang.

Pulling the wagon through town, I let people get a good long look, hoping their imaginations would run wild. What were Alex and I doing with University of Michigan–colored paint, a hammer, and nails? *Getting an early jump on Christmas shopping for Wade,* I thought with a smile.

Alex darted into view, carrying a lamp from the antique store. The cord trailed behind her on the sidewalk, as did a blotched-faced Jason.

"It's the best I could do for twenty bucks," she said, dumping the lamp into the wagon.

We wound our way through the ever-growing crowd of people.

"We'll come back after dark," I told her a little too loudly, putting the sprinkles on this sundae of success. "Around midnight."

Someone gasped. Brian took off down the alley. Jason switched his radio back on.

We'd lit the fuse. Now all we had to do was wait for the powder keg to explode.

And explode it did. Around eleven o'clock, the calls started coming over the police scanner—one after another—all claiming that something strange was happening at their stores or homes.

Paula said she'd heard a suspicious noise out back.

Tammy wanted Rodney to check on the diner.

Brian insisted he'd seen Alex on the corner of Plum and Apple. "I think she's carrying a light bulb," he said.

The Elswood Police Department was having an uncharacteristically busy night.

Alex laughed as we sat on the front porch, drinking Diet Coke out of the fancy glasses. Juno lay at Alex's feet, a tennis ball tucked under her head for safekeeping.

The police scanner buzzed. "10-23, boss," Jason responded. "I'm near the corner of Apple and Boysen. Over."

"Any sign of them?" Rodney asked.

"Last three reported sightings were dead ends. But we did find Hilda's cat, Mr. Whiskers, in the bushes near the fire hydrant on Lemon Street."

"I'm not asking about the damn cat," Rodney said. I pursed my lips to stop from laughing at the stress in his voice. "Let me know when you've got something useful. Until then, stay off the radio."

"Roger, boss. 10-79," Jason responded.

"10-79 is a bomb threat."

"Oops. I can't see the code sheet so well in the dark. 10 . . . something."

Rodney sounded beyond annoyed. "Harry, tell me you've got eyes on the targets."

"Negative. No sign of Felicity or Alex."

Alex turned the scanner's volume up like her favorite pop song had come on. "Only you could come up with a non-prank prank."

"They'll be looking for us all night."

Our glasses clinked in cheers.

Tastes like success, I thought, taking a sip. *And rebellion.* The whole town currently lived in fear of my every move. I'd gone from a social outcast sobbing into a voicemail every night to a complete badass who messed with the police. To keep my reputation thriving, I'd have to capitalize on this victory as soon as possible. My fingers tapped the side of the wineglass. What should I do next?

My eyes drifted to the house across the street. Light shone through the kitchen windows.

My moral compass started spinning, landing solidly on one person.

Alex and Juno disappeared into her bedroom, and the moment her door closed, I darted upstairs. Under a pile of old jeans in my closet sat a bag of clothing I hadn't worn since returning to this house four years ago. There had been no reason to wear lingerie since then. But with my confidence at an all-time high, it was now or never.

I set the black lacy underwear and bra on the bed while I took a hot shower and shaved my legs. I blew out my hair, taking extra care to make it appear natural, as if I'd always had this slight curl at the ends that framed my face.

My eyebrows needed plucking, and my skin was in serious need of exfoliation. Once the stubborn hairs above my lip had been disposed of, I dabbed my face with concealer. Not too much, but enough to hide the bags under my eyes. After a quick touch of mascara, it was time for some lip gloss. I made a kissing motion, evenly spreading the pink over my cracked lips. It tasted of strawberries and summer. I'd bought the gloss during a beach vacation when I was thirteen.

Still works, I thought with a smile, testing the pink color against my eye shadow.

My heartbeat spiked to an unhealthy level as I slipped on the lingerie. I pulled the underwear up to my hips, noticing the material was tighter than it used to be. I fought with the bra strap until it fastened behind my back. My boobs poured out the top, and I pushed them back inside as if admonishing them. If I'd been planning this for longer than an evening, I'd have gone shopping for something new to mark the occasion, but alas, this was the best I could do on short notice. At least Revenge Incorporated had taught me how to improvise.

A freestanding mirror stood in the corner of my bedroom. I twisted and turned, and for the first time, my eyes didn't focus on the layer of fat that had accumulated around my waist or the pudginess of my thighs.

I looked good. *No,* I corrected myself, *I look fucking amazing.*

I paired the lacy, somewhat-itchy underwear with my darkest jeans, the ones that hugged my butt a little too tightly, and a blue halter top.

I tiptoed through the house so as not to wake Alex, and switched off the TV. Unlike me, she was a heavy sleeper, but I took no chances. Tonight's crime needed no witnesses—not even my trusted business associate. With fumbling fingers, I slipped on my flats and headed outside.

I knocked softly on his door. What would I say when he answered? I had no moves, no charm that made men take an interest in me. In college, I'd waited for the guy to make the first move, not risking rejection. I was hesitant, shy, and a little too self-conscious than was good for my mental health.

But that had changed in the last month. Tonight I was Felicity Lavigne, Elswood supermodel.

And Wade Londergan, the guy I'd had a crush on since I bought this lip gloss, had better be ready.

TWENTY-ONE

Wade's eyes widened when he opened the door, taking in my outfit. He tried to smooth his expression, but intrigue lingered on his face. I nearly patted myself on the back for how great I looked. A supermodel, indeed.

He glanced over my shoulder. "Still got a groupie?"

Rodney's navy truck idled by the mailbox. He'd shown up thirty minutes ago, engine revving, no doubt trying to reclaim some of his dignity after realizing Alex and I had never left the house tonight. "Yeah, he's a big fan."

He waved at the truck parked out front. "What's up, man?"

Rodney honked the horn. *Old football buddies,* I thought darkly as I ducked past Wade and snuck inside. *Figures.*

Wade looked me over again, this time in a more calculating fashion. I could practically see the wheels turning in his head, wondering why I was at his place so late and dressed in anything other than sweatpants.

"I don't think this is a good idea," he said before I had a chance to make it to the living room.

My heart constricted. *Oh no, is he turning me down?* Not again.

Nausea twisted my stomach. My pride would never recover. I'd have to move to another continent this time. Maybe Alex would enjoy the Arctic Circle. I'd heard it was nice there a few times a year.

"I can't distract Rodney while you and Alex go somewhere and do something that I definitely don't know about." He winked, then smiled ruefully. "It's too reckless. You guys should wait until the heat dies down."

Oh. He thought I wanted help ditching the cops. That was a first. "We're not doing anything tonight."

"You're not?" His eyes lingered on my tight-fitting shirt. He looked confused. No, he looked hot. Really, really hot, in that casual way I'd tried so hard to accomplish. Wade had perfected it, with his blond hair going in every direction and his gray T-shirt slightly askew so I could see the top of his collarbone.

"Alex is fast asleep."

I walked uninvited into his living room. Eventually, his feet remembered how to move, but instead of joining me on the couch, he went to the kitchen. "Do you want something to drink?"

Uh . . . I didn't have a go-to alcoholic beverage. I said the first thing that popped into my head: "Do you know how to make a margarita?"

He turned, hand on the fridge handle, and looked at me. "Have you forgotten that I'm a bartender?"

"Oh, right."

He muttered under his breath, pulling various bottles out of the fridge and setting them on the counter.

Not a minute later, he returned to the living room, a glass in one hand and a beer bottle in the other. I took a hesitant sip. It tasted good. Better than good. He'd put sugar instead of salt around the rim.

I drained the margarita in a couple of gulps. He eyed me curiously from the other end of the couch, leaving too much space between us.

The glass clanked on the coffee table as I discarded it. The living room was quiet, as he didn't have the television on. Perhaps he'd been heading to bed when I invited myself inside. If he'd done this to me, I would've kicked him out and slammed the door. It was way past my usual bedtime, though lately, I hadn't been keeping regular sleep hours.

The awkwardness in the room grew to an uncomfortable level. I didn't know how to start the conversation. I'd never mastered the subtle art of flirting. What would I say besides *Wade, let's have sex*?

But I couldn't sit here silently forever.

I flipped my hair over my shoulder and adjusted my body on the couch so I could cross my legs. I misjudged the depth of the cushion and scooted too far, falling off-balance. My butt slid off the couch and I tumbled to the carpet.

"Ahhh!" I screeched, throwing my hands out. Somehow I avoided a collision with the chipped and stained coffee table.

"What the hell?" Wade moved closer, reaching his hands out to help me. "I only put one shot of tequila in that drink."

One bloody shot and I'd already fallen to the floor.

I sat up before he could touch me. "I think your couch moved."

I think your couch moved? What was wrong with me? *So much for looking attractive,* I thought as I crawled back onto the couch like an idiot.

He took a sip of his beer, looking me over. A thought seemed to occur to him.

"I don't mean to get involved in your business, but have you and Alex been smoking pot? You're acting weird."

"I'm not acting weird."

"Yeah, because you do this all the time." His tone turned conspiratorial. "I'm not going to tell the authorities. That's not my style. I just think the two of you should share."

"We're. Not. Doing. Drugs." Anger made me emphasize each word.

"Hell, I don't know what goes on in those blueberry fields. You've got all that land, and no one would notice if you grew a bit of pot."

I ran a hand through my hair. Why were we discussing marijuana in his living room? This wasn't how I'd envisioned the night going.

Part of me wanted to wait for him to make the first move. What did Wade Londergan say to all the women that made them disregard their self-worth? The lines were probably rehearsed and very well researched. Unfortunately, that didn't seem to be on his mind tonight. I'd have to initiate this, because he clearly wasn't picking up on my signals.

I scooted closer to him and leaned my head against his shoulder. He didn't move, just sat there, body rippling with surprise. Then, after a long pause, he slowly reached his arm around my shoulder, pulling me closer. That was progress. *Courage, Felicity.*

I tilted my head back, twisting until my front brushed against his side. Before I could think, I lifted my leg and maneuvered it over his waist until I was partially straddling him. I'd meant for him to lean down, but the moment I saw his jawline, I went for it, leaning up and pulling his head toward mine.

It was a hard, passionate kiss that made my stomach flip. His beer bottle clanked onto the floor and his other hand went to my cheek, fingers eventually twisting in my hair. I breathed raggedly as he leaned down and started kissing my neck.

I'd forgotten he was such a great kisser.

My hand crept under the hem of his shirt, but I couldn't lift it, as I was sitting on top of it. He didn't loosen his hold on me, so I couldn't lean away and dispose of the garment, which smelled like freshly cut grass and aftershave.

His hand was still tangled in my hair when I pulled away, breaking his hold on my lower back. I stood, dragging him with me by the front of his shirt. There could be no mistaking my intention as I sauntered backward toward the hallway. But we didn't get very far.

His lips found mine, and I fell back against the wall. A picture frame rattled. He pressed his hips into my stomach. I tried to lift his shirt again.

He grabbed my hands, pulling back to look at my face. "You're not drunk, are you?"

"I only had one margarita." I sounded breathless. I wasn't drunk, but definitely intoxicated by his presence.

"Just checking." His forehead rested against mine. "I didn't plan for this to happen or anything." He took a deep breath, trying to compose himself. "Not that I'm complaining. I've thought about it more than once. I . . ." He pulled away until his eyes locked on mine as I waited, heart pounding, back flat against the wall as he towered over me. He stroked my cheek with his thumb. He seemed to settle on something. "I don't want to mess this up."

I wrapped both hands around his neck and brought his lips to mine, kissing him hard. That seemed to resolve his hesitation.

I yelped in surprise as my feet left the ground. He grabbed under my thighs, carrying me with my ankles locked behind his back. He made it seem like I weighed no more than a pound, though I knew that wasn't true.

I vaguely heard a door open behind me. His lips never left mine until he gently set me on the bed. He put his hands under my arms and scooted me back until I was in the middle of the sheets, head resting on a pillow, with his body above me.

Though I hadn't had sex in four years, I felt sure of myself. I didn't worry about the roundness of my hips, or how I always tried to cover up my arms because at an eighth-grade dance, Becky Lucas had told me they jiggled. My mind suddenly didn't care, and from the way Wade kissed me, he didn't mind, either.

Tonight I was a sex goddess, and Wade was lucky to be in the same bed with me. Even if he was far more experienced, I didn't care, for I'd done things recently I'd never done before. I felt confident for the first time in my life, and I wasn't going to waste the moment by not having sex with Wade.

He rolled to my right to kick off his shoes. I seized my opportunity and straddled his waist, bending down to kiss him.

Fluidly, as if I'd practiced the move a thousand times, I pulled my shirt over my head, letting it whip my hair to one side. Then I lifted the hem of his shirt, drawing it up his chest. He leaned forward so I could pull it over his head.

Finally, I thought, discarding it unceremoniously on the floor.

I'd seen Wade shirtless plenty of times in the yard or on a hot summer day when he drank a beer on his porch. He always looked good. But there was something different about seeing his upper body up close. I poked his ribs, studying the muscles. They were better than I'd imagined.

Wade leaned forward to kiss me, but I didn't meet him halfway. "How often do you work out?"

His eyebrows furrowed. Even that was hot. After a second, he answered, his voice sounding rough, "Almost every day."

He kissed my neck, leaving a trail of kisses down to my collarbone. A tingling sensation floated all the way to my fingers. *Whoa.*

But I couldn't be distracted from his abs—they were too magnificent. "Do you just do sit-ups the whole time?"

He laughed softly against the hollow of my throat. "Felicity," he whispered, then kissed me again. "Concentrate. My abs aren't going anywhere."

I smiled and drew his mouth to mine once again.

TWENTY-TWO

When I woke, the room was dark. I blinked and tried to figure out how long I'd dozed off for. Couldn't have been long. I still felt breathless, and sweat had beaded near my temples.

I stretched and rolled over, finding Wade flat on his back, snoring softly. I'd thought we'd be awkward—ridiculous, even—when we had sex. With him being so experienced and me being, well . . . me. I'd anticipated our bodies going in different directions, never quite syncing enough to find a rhythm.

Somehow the opposite had happened. We hadn't needed to find a rhythm, because we had it from the moment we started kissing. He'd kissed me roughly, holding me close, but was surprisingly gentle with his touch. His hands had glided along my skin like they'd traced the same route a thousand times before. And I'd fit into place beside him, my hands pulling him closer than I could possibly hold him. I'd nearly drowned in sensations, the rest of the world forgotten while our pulses melded together.

It would've been easy to go back to sleep. To curl up beside him, close my eyes, and let the morning light wake us in a few hours. I was already matching my breaths to his faint snores.

But that hadn't been the plan. Even as the mattress threatened to swallow me, begging me to stay, I tossed the sheet back and slipped off the bed. Our clothing was scattered on the floor. With no light, I used my sense of touch to find my underwear and jeans.

As I pulled on my pants, I lost my balance and knocked into the dresser. My hip bone caught the corner. "Ow!"

Wade stirred, reaching his hand across the mattress. "What are you doing? Come back to bed," he mumbled.

I searched for my bra, finding it on the other side of the room. I clasped it behind my back as Wade opened his eyes. He wore a lazy smile. "The clothing is going to make it harder to have sex again." Then he waved his hand in my direction as if no longer concerned. "Never mind. I'll make it work."

"I'm sure you would have."

He yawned like a lion. "Where are you going?"

"My place."

"It's late, just stay here. I'm tired, and I don't want to walk you home."

What a gentleman. "I think I can manage the fifty feet from your door to mine."

Catching my tone, he sat up and leaned on his elbow. He ran a hand through his hair, tousling it more. "What's wrong?"

"Nothing."

"Then why are you sneaking off in the middle of the night like a teenager?"

I found my shirt under his pants. How had it ended up near the bathroom door? "I'm not 'sneaking off.' I'm going home and going to bed."

There was a pause. "What are you doing Wednesday?"

I didn't answer. Just pulled my shirt over my head.

Wade continued, no longer sounding tired, "I work tomorrow and Tuesday, but I thought we could grab dinner."

"Why?"

"'Cause dinner's typically what happens on a date."

"That's not necessary."

"Why not?" There was an edge to his voice. "I want to take you on a date. What's the big deal?"

"Have you ever been on a date, Wade? I don't think you'd like it."

"Of course I've been on a date, just not with you—which is why I'm asking. I don't want to mess this up."

"There's nothing to mess up. We're fine."

"Then why are you leaving?"

"Because I'm tired and I want to get to bed. It's not rocket science."

"Felicity," he said, sitting up to get a better look at me, "what's going on? You don't sound like yourself."

"I told you once that you didn't know me very well."

"I know you're not the kind of girl who has one-night stands."

"Well, you're wrong, Wade, because that's all this is." I headed toward the bedroom door. "I'll see you around."

"Wait."

Out of the corner of my eye, I saw him leap out of bed. He chased after me into the hallway, but I didn't stop. I didn't look back. "Felicity, wait! What did I do?"

I grabbed my shoes and ran outside barefoot. The door slammed behind me with a frightening bang. The sound hit me so hard that I fell to my knees in the grass. The cool air swept through my hair. Fortunately, I didn't see the navy truck. Apparently, Rodney had trusted that I'd be staying in for the rest of the night.

I rushed to my feet, wishing I could move my house closer. I stepped onto the porch, forgetting about the broken first step. "Ahhh!" I cried out as my bare foot fell straight through the wood, slicing the skin in several spots. I hopped, pulling my foot free, and launched myself onto the porch before I could make any more noise and wake Alex. I tiptoed upstairs, not worried about my dirty feet as I crawled into bed. Sheets could be washed. The scrapes would heal. But memories could haunt a person forever.

Exhaustion became my only advantage.

I stared at the ceiling, fighting to keep the feeling in my gut—the one screaming that I'd made a huge mistake—from taking over.

A loud banging noise floated upstairs. I rolled over. The alarm clock showed that it was 7:00 a.m. I groaned. What was Alex doing? Normally, I couldn't get her up and moving before ten.

"Alex, stop it!" I shouted and rolled back over. I was in no mood for this. Whatever she was doing could wait a few hours. The banging continued. The whole house seemed to be shaking. "Alex!"

Half asleep, I grabbed my robe from behind the door and went downstairs to stop the madness. I gingerly stepped around the couch and toward the front door, where the sound grew louder.

Wade knelt near the bottom porch step, toolbox by his side, as he hammered the wood into place.

"What are you doing?" I covered my ears as he hit the step again. If he whacked any harder, the house was going to collapse.

He wiped the sweat from his forehead but didn't look at me. "Fixing your step."

"I can see that, but maybe you could come back at a normal hour." Like at one in the afternoon. How was he not tired? I'd left his house only a few hours ago.

He didn't acknowledge my words beyond continuing to assault the porch. Each bang made my eardrums hurt. I wanted to go back inside and sleep for a few more days.

"I think you've got it nailed in there."

He stopped and glanced up at me. His dark look made me take a step back.

"Wade—" I started, but he interrupted me.

"We had a deal, Felicity." He stood. "I gave you the tape for your prank against Cheryl, and you left me alone. That was the agreement." He pointed at the ground for added emphasis. "We had a deal."

"I remember."

"Then how do you explain last night?" He shook his head in disgust, like he didn't want to look at me. "I lay awake thinking that I'd done something wrong, until I realized that last night was nothing more for you than an opportunity to get back at me for what happened in high school."

"Don't you dare bring that up," I hissed, taking a step closer to him as if I were going to fight him. He should know better. It was our unspoken rule that we'd never speak of that incident. That was how we'd kept relative peace between us for the past four years.

His voice rose, and if we had neighbors, I'd be concerned about waking them. "I'm not that bright, but it took about an hour after you left to connect the dots. You should feel proud of yourself. You got me. You knew I liked you so you had sex with me, then tossed me out like trash. Well done, Felicity."

"Perhaps now you know how every woman in town feels after you sleep with them and ditch them the next morning."

"You don't give a damn about the other women in town. This is about you. It's about what I did to you when we were teenagers."

"What you did deserved far worse than what you got."

"So you *were* trying to hurt me."

"Get off my porch, Wade." I turned to go back inside. I wouldn't feel guilty. I had told myself that a hundred times last night. I wouldn't feel any remorse for what I did.

He called after me, "It was one night like, ten years ago. I really would've thought you'd be over it by now."

"Is that what you thought?" I spun around to face him. "You had, what, one bad hour where you thought a woman wasn't interested in you? I had four miserable years of high school because of you. I didn't go to prom because of you. I didn't go to homecoming or school events because the girls mocked me mercilessly. It might've been better if you'd left town, but of course you stuck around because you had nowhere else to go. Then you moved in next door and made everything worse!"

He had the good sense to look repentant as I shouted, but then he muttered, "I was seventeen. I did stupid things. We all did."

"I didn't. Not like that."

"Well, we can't all be perfect like you, Felicity. Some of us are trying to have interesting lives, and with that comes a few mistakes."

"It wasn't a mistake. You did it intentionally!"

"I was a teenager. What's your excuse? You're twenty-seven years old and running around town vandalizing stores and stealing cars." He paused, eyes meeting mine. "Is this something your mom would be proud of?"

There was nothing else to say except, "Fuck you, Wade."

He'd gone too far by bringing my dead mother into the conversation. "Don't you ever speak about my mom. And as for what I did to you, she wouldn't have cared. She hated you, because that's what mothers do when their daughters come home in tears and can't get out of bed for a week. If she were here, she'd be applauding."

He grabbed his toolbox from the ground. "The step is fixed. Have a great life, Felicity."

"I didn't need you to fix it, Wade. And I certainly didn't ask you to."

I walked inside and slammed the door. My chest rose, and I put my hand over my heart to steady it. I had never been so angry in my life. I felt as though the ground were shaking and the paintings and photographs would fall from the walls any second.

Alex stood by the couch in my baggy pajamas. She'd heard everything. There was no way she could've slept through that.

"You had sex with Wade?"

"Alex, not now." I didn't want to have this discussion. Not now, and not with her. She wouldn't understand. Nobody would understand.

"Did you?"

"Yes."

"But you said you didn't like him."

"I don't."

"Then how could you do that if you weren't serious about him? You know he's practically in love with you."

I snorted. *Not anymore.* "It's complicated, which is why I don't want to date him."

"But you wanted to sleep with him and kick him to the curb the next morning?"

"Yes," I answered honestly. I dug my fingernails into my palms to keep from feeling guilty. "And he deserved it. I'm not going to feel bad because Wade can't handle his feelings."

Her eyes widened like she'd never seen me before. Which maybe she hadn't. At least, not this side of me.

"But he comes over all the time. He lets you borrow his truck, he fixes everything we break, he helped dig up the sprinkler system when we had a leak two weeks ago. You can't do this to him."

I understood how the situation looked to her. It killed me that she thought I'd done something wrong. "He . . . he only does those things because he feels guilty. It's not about him liking me; it's about him not liking himself."

"And you handled it by hurting him? How is that fair?"

"I don't have to explain myself to you. Or Wade. Or anyone in this town. I'm done acting like it's okay for everyone to treat me like crap and ignore me when I complain. Why can't I do what I want? Everyone else seems to be able to."

"But it's Wade," she said. "He's not like everyone else."

"He's exactly like everyone else! You can't see it because you're eighteen and he's attractive and has that bad-boy attitude. You're not the first person to fall for his act."

"What if it wasn't an act?"

I held up my hands. Tears brimmed in my eyes, threatening to spill over, and I didn't want her to see them. "I don't want to fight about this. I had a long night, and I'm going to back bed."

"Felicity!" Alex called out as I ran up the stairs. "Felicity!"

TWENTY-THREE

High school had been an excruciating time. My experience wasn't unique. It was expected that those four years would be bumpy and awkward, and everyone had to get through them.

But not everyone had to endure four years with their mother as an algebra teacher, who was universally considered by the male student population to be "hot." It didn't help matters that I was decidedly less than attractive—or, in the eloquent words of Danielle Herbert, "Why is your mother so pretty and you're so ugly?" I wished I had an answer for her. All I could glean from my frizzy hair, short frame, and pudgy waistline was that the gods had hated me.

And on a rainy Thursday my sophomore year—September 28, to be exact—I found out how deeply that hatred ran . . .

The bell rang for sixth period, and I hustled to my locker. A red homecoming banner covered the wall above it, a constant reminder that once again I would not be attending the dance that Saturday. *Oh well,* I thought, swapping my biology textbook out for my geometry workbook. I already had Saturday's movie picked out anyway. There was nothing that my couch, television, and popcorn couldn't fix.

As was my routine, I put on lip gloss between fifth and sixth period, smacking my lips together as I headed to Mrs. Byrne's classroom. As per school policies, I couldn't be taught by my mother, which was unfortunate because Mrs. Byrne wasn't nearly as good of a math teacher. She was strict and a hard grader. Showing your work didn't count unless the answer was completely correct—the bane of every math student.

But unlike everyone else who justifiably felt their spirits drop the moment they entered the classroom, sixth period was my favorite hour of the day. First, I had an undiscovered knack for geometry. Second, I had been assigned a seat in the back row of the classroom, where I could hide and avoid everyone unless called upon. Third, and most important, a seventeen-year-old named Wade Londergan occupied the seat directly in front of me.

I was already seated when the senior quarterback walked into the room just before the second bell. He let his gym bag slide down his arm before he crashed into the chair. He smiled casually at Shelby Glensen, whom he'd dated for a week last year before moving on to Wendy Stells, the current captain of the cheerleading squad. That relationship had lasted for a record-breaking five weeks for Wade, but he'd broken up with her during the summer, as he didn't want to be tied down during his upcoming senior football season.

Staring at the back of his head for the first three weeks of school hadn't been our only interaction. No, no, no. On August 29, the fourth day of school, he had turned around in his seat and asked, "Do you have a pen?"

"Uh . . ." I'd sputtered, seeing only his bright-blue eyes. I hadn't answered quickly enough before three other people offered him several choices. Drat! He'd turned around without a second glance, but the interaction was significant enough to merit an entire page in my journal that night. I'd cursed my slow brain while noting that he'd chosen the blue pen over the black and green options. *Blue like his eyes.*

Then, on another occasion—September 6, the day after Labor Day—he'd said, "Hey, Felicia," to me before sitting down. I didn't even mind that he'd messed up my name. Close enough. I couldn't expect more from the guy who routinely bragged about having a 2.6 GPA. Ohio regulations stated that students must maintain a 2.5 GPA to be eligible for participation in after-school activities.

Mrs. Byrne spoke at the chalkboard, drawing a myriad of shapes and angles. I took diligent notes as Wade tapped his fingers on his desk, looking like he wanted to be doing anything else. A note was passed to him from Evan, one of Wade's friends who followed him everywhere. Wade chuckled under his breath and put the note in his pocket. Several people had turned in their seats to look at him, excitement etched across their faces.

Mrs. Byrne noticed the distraction. "And what, in the equation, is C squared, Mr. Londergan?"

Wade straightened in his chair. I could tell he had no clue.

"Sixty-four," I whispered from behind him. I didn't know what had come over me. I'd never really spoken to him before, much less given him the answer to a question when he hadn't asked. But it didn't take a genius to realize he was going to get it wrong. Often he threw out the number 4, his football-jersey number, and didn't worry about being incorrect.

"Sixty-four," Wade said, sounding as confident as ever.

Mrs. Byrne's lips pushed together, but she moved on without a follow-up.

"Nice," Shelby whispered, twirling her hair with her finger. I was surprised that the entire room didn't break out in applause. He'd never answered correctly before.

Wade shrugged like he was naturally a genius but didn't want any attention for it.

I ducked down, hoping to go unnoticed for the rest of the class.

When the bell rang, I collected my books, ready to move quickly to the gymnasium. I had exactly four minutes to make it all the way to the locker room so I could change for the one class I was in danger of getting a B in.

As was my custom, I said a silent prayer that we were not playing dodgeball in gym that day.

"Felicity," Wade said, standing beside my desk. I shouldn't have known his voice so well. I paused, arms full of books, and looked up at him. I wasn't sure he knew my actual name until that moment. My heart soared with nervousness, especially as his friends, the ones who usually waited for him so they could follow him around, were all standing by the classroom door. They were huddled in a group, heads together and whispering. Shelby laughed, then someone shushed her. Their eyes were on Wade, who for some reason was only looking at me.

"Yes?" I was encouraged by his smile. His perfect all-American smile that had never been reserved for me. I pushed my glasses farther up my nose.

"Walk with me to my next class." He didn't give me a chance to say no.

I trailed after him, praying that my feet wouldn't get tangled and embarrass me.

We were heading in the opposite direction of the gym, but I didn't say anything. I followed him blindly and without complaint, like everyone else. People called out to him as we walked, giving him high fives and smiling at him. I'd never received as much attention from anyone in my life as he did during that two-minute walk to his locker. It wasn't presumptuous that the dance committee had already written his name on the homecoming-king plaque.

So why was he talking to me? The school's shy straight-A student, who'd founded the three-member French club?

"Do you need help with your geometry homework?" I crossed my fingers, hoping he did. That would be amazing. I'd have to tell my mom that I couldn't help her with the farm that evening, but she'd understand. It was Wade Londergan, after all. I probably would've missed my own birthday party if he asked me to. But luckily, I wasn't turning sixteen until January.

He shook his head as if not understanding the logic of my question. "I've got a solid D."

He was getting a D? That was terrible. Even trying a little bit, he should be getting a C. "Yeah, the Pythagorean theorem is difficult to understand," I lied. I didn't want him to feel bad about himself.

"What's the python theorem?"

"Pythagorean," I corrected automatically. Mrs. Byrne had said it like fifty times yesterday, and we'd had a quiz on it today. "It's what we went over in class today." Somehow his question made me wonder if I'd misremembered the last sixty minutes. Had I been daydreaming again?

He shrugged, unconcerned. "Whatever."

He stopped at his locker. His friends waited about fifteen feet away. They seemed to be watching us, but I ignored them. Everyone stared at Wade, even me.

My attention was drawn to the inside of his locker. Books were stacked in no order, loose papers crumpled at the bottom, and there were protein-bar wrappers falling onto the floor. The only item that seemed to be in the right place was his letterman jacket, which had been neatly placed on the hook.

"So, I was wondering," he began, turning to look at me, "if you're busy this Saturday."

My mind went blank for a full second. Wade was wondering about me? About my plans? I thought I'd misheard, so I didn't answer, letting the words sink in until I was confident I had them correct.

"This Saturday is homecoming," I said. I couldn't help him with geometry when he was at the dance. He must have forgotten. *2.6 GPA,* I reminded myself. "Maybe next weekend we could study."

He snorted like the idea was absurd. "I don't study." He crammed his textbook into the only available space, clearly not worrying about turning it in at the end of the year with crinkled pages. "I want you to go to the dance with me."

He said this casually, like it wasn't the most significant thing to ever happen in my life.

But significant or not, I wasn't prepared to attend the dance. It was two days away, and I didn't have a dress, shoes, or any idea how to tame my frizzy hair. And now I was expected to go with Wade Londergan, where everyone in the school would be staring at me, wondering how I had secured this coveted invitation. The attention alone made me so nervous I wanted to vomit.

The smart thing would've been to decline. It was too much, too fast. I needed my inhaler. But then he grinned down at me, that perfect all-American smile.

I accepted immediately. There had never been a chance I'd say no.

In my haste to get to gym class, I'd missed the laughter erupting in the hallway behind me. And it would take until Saturday night, in a blue dress my mother could barely afford, when I found him under the bleachers kissing Shelby Glensen, for me to realize the whole thing had been a joke.

I took a deep breath; the sobs made it difficult to speak. "I was so embarrassed—I didn't know what to do other than run away."

Alex hugged me on the bed, wrapping her arms around me until I calmed down. As my breathing steadied, I heard her saying "It's okay" over and over again. Pain shot through me as I was once again crying over Wade Londergan. Only this time, Alex had to comfort me instead of my mom.

Alex had knocked on my bedroom door for ten minutes before finally coming inside and refusing to leave until I told her everything. Her worries weren't irrational. I'd been this upset another time in my life—the one-year anniversary of my mom's death. Alex was probably replaying those voicemails in her head, remembering how I'd almost given up. I didn't want to worry her. Upsetting Alex went against everything I stood for. But I also wanted her to stay. I didn't want to be alone.

The situation was made worse when I remembered the good things Wade had done for me since I moved home to take care of my dying mother. He'd been sweet some days—letting me use his truck, bringing his dog over so I'd have company, fixing the porch light for the seventh time after I let it run constantly because I was afraid of the dark. He'd tried to make up for his actions when he was seventeen, and that had only made things worse. I'd felt embarrassment when he was nice to me, even shame as I found myself liking him more and more.

But deep down, I'd never forgiven him.

I'd lacked confidence to initiate anything until Alex showed up and completely upended my life. One prank after another, my confidence meter had risen until it reached Destroy Wade Londergan levels.

His assumptions this morning were correct: I'd meant to hurt him. From the moment Alex had demanded that I retrieve the crime scene tape and I learned he liked me, I'd thought about what it would be like to hurt him the way he'd hurt me.

And now, I was crying because, as it turned out, I was no better than seventeen-year-old Wade Londergan.

My mother would be ashamed of me.

TWENTY-FOUR

Headlights flashed into the kitchen, and laughter floated through our open windows.

Alex slammed the window shut so hard the glass shook. "Every damn night!" she yelled, glaring at me in my pajamas. "When are you going to let me handle this?"

She didn't say his name. It was an unspoken rule the two of us had abided by. He didn't exist anymore. Only he did, and every night this week, there had been evidence of that.

"Don't you dare," I said, pointing a finger in her direction. She was not going to tell our nonexistent neighbor that he was getting on our nerves. I wouldn't give him the satisfaction.

He knew what he was doing, throwing a party every night since *it* had happened. And these were not his usual parties. They were louder and wilder. The house shook, as he must have put the bass on his porch and directed the sound at the side of my house.

Night after night we had to listen to rock music and shouting, followed each morning by a string of women leaving his house. He made no effort to hide it, knowing I was stuck. I couldn't call the cops to shut down his parties, and I couldn't ask him to stop, either. So we were left without adequate sleep, our sanity slowly slipping away like my hopes and dreams.

"We could kill him," Alex suggested, sitting on the couch with a can of Coke. The rock music started up, drifting through the windows we couldn't keep closed because it was too hot inside the house without air-conditioning. "I'll get the poison, and you grab the shovel. We'll bury him in the back field, where no one will ever find him."

I yawned and closed my eyes, trying to ignore the noise. "Don't do anything, Alex." I didn't want him to think I cared or that his immature behavior bothered me in the slightest. I'd made Alex go along with this plan, though I knew it was killing her to not fight back.

"Can't we at least take his truck and drive it into a lake? Lake Erie isn't far. And while we're at it, we could dump his body off a pier."

"No."

"Then I'll find this Shelby Glensen and take her down, too."

"I think she lives in Seattle now." Someone had told me she'd gotten divorced and lived with her aunt in Washington. I hadn't paid much attention. When your mom was dying of cancer, Shelby Glensen and her divorce didn't hold much intrigue.

"I wish *I* lived in Seattle," Alex muttered. "Please, Felicity. The earplugs don't work. I'm going mad."

"No."

She groaned and lay down on the couch, squishing two pillows against her head.

Sooner or later, I'd break and do something about the noise, but it wouldn't be tonight. I hadn't been pushed far enough yet. We were in for another long, sleepless night.

Maybe she was right. Perhaps living somewhere else wasn't the worst idea in the world.

But that would mean selling the house and the farm. My body vibrated with anxious energy. What would I do with all my mom's things? How would I transport everything? Who would get the farm? What would they do with it?

No, no, no.

Moving wasn't an option. Not now, not ever. We'd have to make do with our current sleepless circumstances. Which meant finding better earplugs or learning to sleep with Switchfoot blaring at all hours of the night.

He'd picked that band on purpose. When Wade got mad, he went all in.

After a week of wallowing, I had no choice but to put on real clothes and leave the house, setting out for the one event on my calendar that couldn't be ignored: the final Elswood Founders' Day preparation meeting.

With all Revenge Incorporated activity on hold, the upcoming Founders' Day Festival needed to bring in some serious dough—like three thousand dollars' worth. Otherwise, all the scheming and revenge would have been for nothing.

I'd only avoided the town for eight days, but the atmosphere had a bite to it. Even as I passed the construction workers repaving the sidewalks, the noise didn't push the uneasiness from my bones. It clung to me, a cold, unwelcoming feeling on an otherwise-humid July afternoon.

Slightly shaken, I arrived at city hall by 2:50 p.m. to get a decent seat in the back row.

The last official Elswood Founders' Day meeting occurred exactly twenty-one days from opening day. All the local business owners attended to receive their booth locations. The event brought tourists from all over Ohio to our little town, celebrating the finest goods and services we could provide.

My mom had loved the festival, and I'd be damned if I didn't at least set up a table and sell cartons of Lavigne Blueberries. The family tradition would remain intact.

But unlike in past years, where the seats had been arranged in organized rows, chairs were scattered across the conference room in an odd formation, nobody sitting near anyone else. The heavy, tense atmosphere made me look at the ceiling for signs of rain. I hardly breathed for fear of disturbing the unsettling quiet.

Natalie glared at Roger. Kim refused to look straight ahead, angling her body away from Michelle, who sat two seats in front of her. The Elswood Council, a group comprised solely of women from the founding families, had seats on an elevated platform at the front. They lorded over us commoners. Mary Londergan scanned the room, her eyes finding mine. I looked behind me to see who or what she was staring at with such hostility. There was nothing there but the wall.

The only person who looked mildly happy was Cheryl Callaway, who switched on her microphone at precisely 3:00 p.m. Because heaven forbid she had to shout or strain her precious vocal cords. "Hello, hello, everyone. As you know, the Elswood Founders' Day Festival is three weeks away. You've all been working hard to prepare, but we're in the final stretch and need everyone's full participation." Her overly sweet voice grated against my headache. It physically pained me to sit this close to her. She pursed her lips to hide a smile so at odds with the room's tense atmosphere. "Now, I know there have been concerns about the state of the town. Lots of you have reached out to complain about the recent uptick in criminal activity. Before we begin tonight's final planning session, I wanted to give each and every one of you a chance to speak your minds."

Oh no.

A public platform for airing grievances? That was the last thing someone like me, the person who had been sabotaging half the town, needed.

Cheryl pointed at her dear friend Evelyn, who promptly stood and said, "I don't feel safe in this town anymore. There have been too many break-ins, too many thefts, and"—she let her voice hitch—"I don't think the festival should go on if we're not able to root out the problem. It's too dangerous."

No one in the room missed how her eyes flicked to me at the word *problem*.

Cheryl nodded, thanking Evelyn for her obviously rehearsed speech. "You're so brave for speaking out on behalf of all of Elswood,"

Cheryl said, hand over her heart. Then she called on her next-door neighbor, Lucas Helm.

He took off his hat, looking crestfallen. "After a decade of participation, I also am not going to partake if the culprit isn't apprehended."

Cheryl looked down the row of festival directors. "I'm sensing a pattern. Maybe we should cancel? Try again next year?"

The effect of her words was immediate.

"Shut down the festival?" Glen cried. "That's preposterous. I'm already in debt. Who is going to pay Simone back for that time I hit her mailbox with my car? I need to sell more snow globes."

"And what about my lemonade stand?" Francine asked from the left side of the room. "I think I should be able to sell my drinks at the festival. It's not fair."

One after the other, they all stood and decried Cheryl's idea to shut down the Founders' Day celebration. There was simply no way the local business owners would allow the festival to be shut down. Capitalism, as Cheryl well knew, would dictate the response to her question.

Which meant something had to be done about "the problem."

"Safety is the top priority," Cheryl said. "I'm sorry, but we can't allow anyone to get hurt."

They'd shut down the festival because of Revenge Incorporated? The Founders' Day Festival was an annual tradition that hadn't stopped for tornado warnings, sewage spills, or that time Glen gave everyone food poisoning after making homemade jam.

But a few towed cars had everyone panicking?

From the front of the room, Cheryl sent a cunning smile in my direction.

Oh, that bitch. She intended to cause a public panic, sending the wolves straight for me. This was precisely why I didn't like leaving the house.

As if on cue, the calls for my head echoed in the conference room.

"Kick Felicity out!" Simone stood and pointed a finger at me. "She's the problem. Without her, none of this would've happened."

"They're the criminals, not us."

"Ever since that Alex girl came to town, they've ruined everything."

Victoria's head popped up in response to Cheryl's nod. "My kid is afraid to sleep at night because that witch dyed him blue."

"Down with Felicity!" Glen chanted. He bunched his hands into fists and pounded the air. "Down with Felicity!"

Shouts rang out, a buzz of hatred directed at my soul. It felt like the entire town hated me. But conflict had existed in Elswood for generations, bad blood turning darker with each new decade. Had everyone forgotten that they had come to my blueberry shed and demanded help? We'd only done what they asked.

Cheryl, looking as if cheerleading had officially been declared a real sport, cut into the mayhem. "Motion to ban Lavigne Blueberries from this year's festival."

"Seconded," at least five people responded.

My outrage caught in my throat, squeezing the air from my body. They couldn't ban my family's blueberry business from participating. We'd contributed for decades. My mother had donated countless hours to festival preparation, had baked pies, and had run the medical tent when Allison took a smoke break. She loved this festival. Some of my favorite childhood memories were made as Josette Lavigne worked her magic, making everyone feel welcome and appreciated.

No one in city hall came to my defense. Cheryl called for a vote, and the result was unanimous. I'd attended enough town meetings to know these people never agreed on anything. Not the zoning regulations, or the color of the street signs, or the proper way to slice watermelon at town events (cubed had won by a slim margin).

The only thing they seemed to agree on was banning me from the festival.

It took a minute for the earth to stabilize under my feet. I stood, and every face turned toward me, expectant. Defending my actions should've been easy. These people had paid for a service and then complained when it was rendered. Hypocrites. All of them.

Fight back, Felicity. Fight back!

I opened my mouth, but no words passed my lips. I ran from the room, leaving my name and reputation undefended.

Luckily, my feet instinctively knew the way home because my brain was too inundated with self-loathing and humiliation to be of much navigational use.

Yelling reached me before I saw the house, snapping me from my dark thoughts. *What now?*

"You're such an asshole!" Alex screamed. I rounded the corner and saw her throw something at Wade's truck. It splattered against the windshield. Wade pointed the garden hose at her and sent a stream of water into her stomach.

"You're going to wreck the paint!"

"After the paint, I'm going to slash your tires!"

I ambled toward them, too tired to get involved, as Alex threw another egg at his truck. Good thing most people in town had backyard chicken coops, resulting in fairly cheap eggs at the farmers' market. If she'd been throwing pork chops, I might've intervened.

He chased her around the truck bed. "Fucking stop!"

He aimed the hose, and water struck her in the face. She stepped back, lifting her arms to deflect the assault.

"Stop it!"

Wade didn't relent, but turned as I approached the house. "Will you get her away from me?"

It was the first time he'd spoken to me in over a week. His harsh tone cut straight through my flesh and into my heart. I almost flinched. Almost. His tone was practically friendly compared to what I'd endured at the Founders' Day meeting.

Ignoring the arguing pair, I trudged onto the porch, letting the house feel every ounce of my weight. Alex could act as she pleased. I'd done all I could to suppress her rage, but Wade's loud, obnoxious parties demanded a response. She threw another egg at him, aiming for his face.

And to think they'd been friends only a week ago. Now they were fighting in the yard.

Wade's string of cuss words followed me into the house and floated through the open windows as I sat at the kitchen table. I rested my head against the back of the chair.

My body had no energy, no fight left in it. In one summer, I'd broken everything.

For the first time in four decades, Lavigne Blueberries would not participate in the Founders' Day Festival. I'd been counting on that extra income to make up for our recent decline in Revenge Incorporated antics.

I glanced across the kitchen, then out the window at the blueberry field. If I didn't get that money, I'd have to sell, and all this—everything I had left of my mother—would be gone.

My ancestors had stolen this land, given our family a chance of success, but as always, I'd managed to ruin everything—even an already-disgraced family name.

TWENTY-FIVE

"They can't kick you out of the festival because of a few pranks," Alex said.

I'd told her about the city hall incident, how Cheryl had all but run me through with a sword as she took away our festival slot. The town could have their games, competitions, and fried food; all I wanted was a small table to sell blueberries with my family name on the sign. I wanted to be included.

"The vote was unanimous," I said. "Even Mary, the woman who never gets involved in squabbles, voted to exile me." The town had basically sentenced me to life on a deserted island, like Napoleon Bonaparte.

And like with Napoleon's banishment, my world shrank to the size of a blueberry. People stopped coming to the farm, not interested in blueberries or revenge. Other than the bakery, the town businesses called one by one to cancel any future deliveries, leaving me with almost no income. No one wanted to be seen partnering with me—not if it meant getting on Cheryl's *and* Mary's bad sides.

Soon the house and all its furnishings would have to be sold, whether I could mentally handle it or not. Without a serious influx of cash, the property taxes would go unpaid, and someone would buy the land and tear down every last memory I had of my mother.

I'd cried in the shower so Alex wouldn't have to witness my shame.

When I worked up the courage to scour the house for valuables, seeking anything of worth to sell, I found nothing to part with. The items, priceless to me, held little financial value. Unfortunately, we couldn't fill our stomachs with sentiment.

Finding a job was the next logical step, but no one would hire me in this area after Revenge Incorporated. I also had no work experience outside of blueberry farming—a skill that didn't transfer well to high-paying positions. My college English degree, which had seemed like a great idea at the time, didn't actually qualify me to do anything. I should've studied business or engineering.

At the end of the day, it didn't matter, because working full-time meant abandoning the blueberry farm—which would defeat the purpose of getting a regular-paying job in the first place.

So we rationed. Alex and I measured our toothpaste, didn't buy meat unless it was on sale due to immediate expiration, and only used electricity when necessary. She seemed to understand our dire financial circumstances, not complaining about having to light candles once the sun set. "At least they smell good," she'd said, blowing out a match two nights ago. "And they have an eerie vibe that makes me think this place is haunted. A win-win."

This place is *haunted,* I'd wanted to reply. *Just not by ghosts.*

Searching for a legal way to pay off my debt and keep the farm had proven pointless. So much so that when Alex entered the kitchen with a backpack slung over her shoulders, I immediately panicked, thinking she'd taken another revenge job.

"What are you doing?" Anytime she left the house after dark, I got nervous.

She bit her lip, hesitating in a very un-Alex-like fashion. "It's time for me to go."

"Everything's closed, and you're not going back to the bar."

I added the last bit as a joke, though the comment held no real humor. The only good thing about fighting with our neighbor was that he'd kick her out straightaway.

"I have to leave."

Leave? The word echoed in my head.

"It was nice of you to let me live here for a bit, but I've already stayed longer than I should have." She hoisted her backpack higher onto her shoulder, as if signaling her resolve. "I'll let you know when I land someplace."

The world tilted. That was it? Just like that, she was going to leave me in this empty house with no one? And she'd let me know where she landed? "But . . . where are you going to go? What about your court date?" I didn't mention the bail money. If she left, then she might as well burn the money, because I'd be beyond consolation.

"I don't want to be your problem anymore."

"We're friends. I want to help you."

"You can't even help yourself, Felicity. You don't have enough money to pay the bills, let alone carry me and my baggage."

I stood from the kitchen chair as she headed toward the living room. This was not happening. She couldn't leave. Not after everything we'd been through.

I grabbed her arm, making her turn and face me. Her eyes were anxious but determined. She didn't want to leave, but she had her mind made up. *Why?* Nearly thirty years of insecurity led me to believe that her departure was my fault. Did I say the wrong thing? Did I offend her?

"Whatever it is, we'll figure it out." My voice shook, decreasing the believability of my next comment. "Everything will be fine."

"You're going to lose the farm. I can't let you do that for me. When I leave, you can blame me for Revenge Incorporated, and the business owners will forgive you. There's a chance you can still get into the festival and make some cash—but only if I leave right now."

If choosing between the festival or Alex, I was picking Alex every single time. No question. How did she not know that by now?

"Things weren't great before you got here. It was always heading this direction, even before you arrived." I didn't want her thinking any of this was her fault or that I blamed her for our revenge antics. "Just because we're having a hard time doesn't mean you have to leave. I know you're trying to help, but if you leave, it'll make everything worse."

I tried to take the backpack from her shoulders.

She stepped away, knocking my hand down. "I lied to you. I lied to you about everything."

I froze.

Alex looked around the living room, then toward the kitchen, then at the ceiling. Everywhere but at me. "I stole the necklace."

That was her big concern? The stupid necklace? The moment we met in the police station, I'd known she was guilty. But I'd never thought less of her. She was homeless, for goodness' sake. What was she supposed to do, starve on the streets? "I know you stole it, and guess what? I don't care."

"You don't understand. That's not what I lied about." She took a deep breath. "I stole the necklace so that I'd get caught." Tears streaked down her face. "Felicity, I . . ." She searched for the words as I felt the temperature in the room drop. "I planned the entire thing to manipulate you, long before I left foster care. I knew after the first voicemail that you were desperate for someone—anyone—to be in your life. I knew you'd feel obligated to come get me from the police station."

"You stole a necklace so I'd help you?"

Alex looked small—fragile, even—but my instinct to comfort her faded when she said, "I stole the necklace so I could rob you."

Her words knocked into me like a punch to the gut.

"I'm sorry," she said, stepping toward me. "I learned all about you from the voicemails, and I knew you'd help me because of your mom. I knew you'd offer to take me in, and then I was going to take—"

"Stop." I held up my hand.

"I was jealous of you. At least you had a mother to miss. And I knew you were almost suicidal, so I thought you might not call the cops when things went missing. If I stole from you, I had a better shot of getting away and starting over."

"Stop!" Every word she said made the pain worse. My hand shook when I raised it to my forehead. The thought of losing anything that had once belonged to my mother made me want to vomit. Alex stepped toward me, but now it was my turn to move away. She dropped her hand, thinking better of trying to comfort me. I crossed my arms over my chest. Perhaps we weren't friends, after all. Friends didn't steal from each other.

Was I really so pathetic that I hadn't seen an eighteen-year-old was manipulating me? I'd been so desperate for her to like me, so desperate to have a friend, that I'd ignored what was right in front of my eyes.

She headed to the door, but before leaving, she turned and said, "I'm sorry, Felicity. I'll leave and you won't have to worry about me anymore. I'm so sorry, for all of it."

The door swung closed. She was gone.

As quickly as Alex had come into my life, she left it. Only, the hole in my heart felt bigger, wider, fresh, like I'd moved too quickly and the stitches had torn loose from my flesh.

I sank to the floor, cradling my chest as I cried. I was going to be alone forever. I had truly lost everyone. First my mom, then Alex, and even Wade. I rubbed under my eyes with the back of my hand and took deep breaths. Why did I deserve to lose everyone I loved? What great crime had I committed that the universe saw fit to punish me for with unending loneliness?

The more I caught my breath and slowed the sobs, the more I noticed the silence surrounding me. The house was quiet. Empty. I felt the change in my bones.

Either because I was unable to help myself or because I wanted to rip through the pain as quickly as possible, I walked to the guest bedroom and switched on the light.

The room looked exactly as it had before Alex arrived. She'd even made the bed, something she was adamant about never doing. I'd teased her about how the blankets were revolting against her, not understanding how anyone could sleep when the comforter and sheets were twisted in every direction and falling on the floor.

Alex had been messy, there was no doubt about it. She was sarcastic, bad-tempered, constantly toeing the line between fun and recklessness until the line moved into danger territory. She'd come into my life like a tornado, sweeping everything into her funnel and casting things into chaos. But she'd also been warm, and kind, and she'd looked after me even when I made mistakes. She never judged me the way others had.

I remembered her hugging me, never leaving my side as I'd cried after the incident with Wade. She made us pancakes the next morning. She hadn't followed the recipe, and they fell apart before leaving the pan, but it was the thought that counted.

Those weren't the actions of someone who wanted to hurt me. Maybe her intent had been to steal from me, but no eighteen-year-old looks after someone like that unless they cared.

Solace washed over me. Alex cared a little bit. I knew she did.

I lay on the bed, placing my head on the pillow. Something crinkled.

Under the pillow, I found an envelope with a piece of paper and her cell phone inside. I twisted the plastic phone in my hands. How would I contact her without calling her phone? She was gone, and I'd never find her.

Feeling sick at the thought of never seeing or hearing from her again, I unfolded the paper.

It had two words written on it: *Thank you.*

I ran a hand through my hair. What was I doing? She was eighteen with nowhere to go. So, she'd set me up. Knowing me, I'd have forgiven her for stealing all my possessions, including the television and the ancient stereo. I was a sucker for a good sob story, and one look at Alex, and I'd have folded like my rusted beach chair. Alex had been right: I never would have pressed charges against her.

I glanced out the window. It was dark outside, and she was alone on the streets. Though I was mad—really, really mad—I couldn't give up on her.

I headed to the front door, running outside as fast as my flip-flops would allow. She couldn't have gotten far. Nothing in town was open. Without a cell phone, she couldn't call an Uber or a Lyft. She had one option: the bus stop.

Twenty minutes had passed since she left, but those buses never ran on time. I could still catch her.

I headed straight toward the town square. A bus stop stood near the northwest intersection of Plum Street and Main. My breath came in gasps as I darted across the winding country roads and up the poorly lit streets. I rounded the corner, breathless, with sweat on my forehead. I was prepared to yell across the grass as loudly as possible, shouting for Alex to come home.

Flashing blue and red lights lit up the square like a Christmas tree.

I ran forward, knowing deep in my gut that Alex was involved. Who else could find trouble in Elswood on a Tuesday night? My flip-flops made me trip on the sidewalk as I approached the car with lights mounted on top.

Glass covered the sidewalk outside the grocery store; it crunched under my feet. Someone had broken the store's window.

"Jason?"

The sheriff's deputy turned and stopped writing on his notepad. He clutched me under my elbow. Did he know I was about to collapse? He walked me to the back of his car, a sympathetic look on his face.

At least he didn't sound pleased when he told me. "She's being booked at the police station. Rodney arrested her about five minutes ago."

TWENTY-SIX

The Elswood Sheriff's Office wasn't so much a police station, but a basement room in city hall. The main space had three desks, a coffee machine, and several filing cabinets along the far wall. The office could have belonged to a failing high school–newspaper staff. But Elswood didn't require a dedicated or experienced police force, much less an expensive police headquarters. There were so few crimes in the area that anything more than one sheriff and two deputies would have been excessive.

"Good evening, Felicity." Rodney held up his hand, halting my progress into the room.

I looked around wildly. "Where is she?"

"In the interrogation room. Caught her myself."

I crossed my arms, giving him a skeptical look. "Doing what?"

"Breaking into the market. Mary's on her way over."

That was not good. But I couldn't let Rodney know I was worried. "Congratulations. This must be the first time you've ever caught anyone. And look at that, you caught an eighteen-year-old girl." I mockingly clapped twice for him. "Well done. I'm sure the FBI will call any minute and ask you to join their supersecret task force against teenage girls in small towns who are ruining America."

Behind me, Jason snorted into his coffee.

Rodney looked like he wanted to punch me. "Make all the jokes you want, but I got her. There's nothing funny about that."

No, there wasn't. I could beat up on Rodney all night, but that wouldn't help Alex. I was confident that Jesus could walk through the door and it still wouldn't be enough to save her.

"I want to see her."

"She's being booked. You can talk to her when we're done."

"When will that be?"

"Several hours." Rodney paused, taking a sip of coffee. "Maybe a day or two. I'm a slow typer."

"Oh, come on, Rodney. You're not going to keep her here for days. Let me see her."

"I've got forty-eight hours before I have to do anything. And seeing as Alex is an adult and you're not her lawyer, I don't have to let you see her." He started walking away from me, but turned and added, "Who knows, maybe a few days in lockup facing burglary charges will loosen her tongue and we'll find out if she had any accomplices."

Alex ratting on me was the least of my worries. She was not going to talk, least of all to Rodney. I'd tried to get her to open up to me for weeks with little success. Rodney would die of old age before she told him anything he wanted to know.

I sat in a chair near the door, resting my head on the wall. Rodney would leave soon to get his beauty sleep, and when he did, I might be able to convince Jason to let me see her.

My eyes grew heavy, and I yawned. Why did Alex always get into trouble in the middle of the night? Was a burglary during brunch too much to ask for?

Despite the exhaustion, my eyes snapped open when she arrived. I instantly felt the judgment coming off her, the kind I used to get in church when I wore jeans to Sunday Mass. Condemned straight to hell.

Mary Londergan.

"Where is she?" Mary headed straight for Rodney. "Where is the brat who broke my window?"

Rodney stood at his desk upon her approach. "We have her in lockup. I need to take your statement."

I sat up straight, feet clacking against the linoleum floor.

The movement drew Mary's attention like a cat catching sight of an unsuspecting bird through the window. "Give me a minute, Rodney."

He didn't question her as she marched toward me. *Oh, fuck.* I wanted to sink straight through the floor. We were doomed. And there was no way Tess would defend Alex against her mother-in-law. I'd have to get another lawyer, and that would be costly.

Mary stopped in front of me. For a short woman, she seemed like a giant. "You should be ashamed of yourself, Felicity."

"Mary—"

"You brought this girl to town and set her loose. She should've been in jail long before tonight."

I squared my shoulders and deflected. "Maybe it was a misunderstanding."

She shook her head in bafflement. "A misunderstanding? A misunderstanding is when you go to the store and buy the wrong kind of toothpaste even though your husband, for some unknown reason, will only use Crest. I had to come out here in the middle of the night after someone smashed in my store window with a brick, and you think that's a misunderstanding?" She seemed beyond words for a second. "And all of this happens a few days after your blueberry booth is banned from this year's festival. You really want to go with 'misunderstanding'?"

"Well . . ." I began, but I didn't have anything better to add.

"For all I know, you put her up to it."

Just the opposite. I'd told Alex the grocery store was off-limits. "Look—"

"You send that brat anywhere near my store again and I'll—"

"Hey!" I shouted, finally getting a word in. "Whatever happened tonight wasn't good, and I don't have the full story yet, but I'm not going to sit here while you bad-mouth Alex."

Mary ignored my outburst. "So, it wasn't enough to ruin the entire town—you had to come after me, too?"

"Oh, like your family is perfect," I spat, thinking of Wade and all the trouble he'd caused. "I seem to remember something about a sixteen-year-old quarterback lighting a bus on fire. Where was his punishment? Perhaps if Alex played football, she wouldn't face any consequences, either."

I stood, arms folded over my chest, breathing heavily. I'd never argued so long with Mary, but I had nothing to lose. If Alex was going down, I might as well go with her.

Mary eyed me suspiciously. "How do you know about the bus incident?"

I did a double take. Wade had told Alex that tidbit of information the morning after she'd arrived. I'd kicked him out swiftly after that, wishing to shield Alex from his troublemaking ideas. Fat lot of good that did me. "I know all sorts of things. You might not be aware, but I have ears everywhere in this town."

"Yeah, right. You have one blond gossip, and from the rumors floating around, the two of you are doing more than talking."

I pursed my lips and glared over Mary's shoulder at Rodney. Of course—he'd watched me enter Wade's house and not come out. Naturally, the entire town had known within a matter of hours that Felicity Lavigne had succumbed to the charms of Wade Londergan. I wondered what they would think if they knew the whole story, that I'd made him succumb to me and not the other way around. But I kept this information to myself because I didn't think it would help my case with Mary if she knew I'd purposely hurt her youngest son.

Mary took a deep breath, looking me over. Her posture softened by a fraction. She looked like she wanted to seriously injure me but not kill me.

"I might be willing to make a deal."

"A deal?" Had I misheard her? Since when did she compromise? The woman was as tough as anyone I'd ever met and a stickler for the rules.

"You want me to drop the charges against that girl, then you'll have to do something for me in return. You deliver, and I'll tell Rodney that I'm redecorating the store and asked Alex to start demolition on the window."

"What do you want?" I knew I wouldn't like the answer, but with Alex's future on the line, there was very little I wouldn't do. I crossed my fingers, hoping it wouldn't be impossible. Free blueberries for life? Did she want the farm? The house?

"I want Wade to ask me."

I uncrossed my fingers. "Wade?" What did he have to do with this?

"You get my son to come here and ask me to let her off the hook, and I'll do it."

So she *did* want something impossible. "Mary, I don't know what you've heard, but Wade and I don't have a relationship where I can ask him for things. I have no influence over him. In fact, I'm fairly certain he hates me as much as everyone else does."

"Not my problem. You tell my son he has to come to five weekly dinners, and in exchange, I'll let Alex off the hook."

"I'm telling you, it's not going to happen."

"So be it." She shrugged. "I'll give you an hour before I tell Rodney that I'm pressing charges, and your teenage friend can deal with the consequences of her actions."

TWENTY-SEVEN

"Hey, you've reached Wade. Leave a message."

I ended the call. I'd heard the same voicemail four times as I ran from the police station to the bar. Why wasn't he answering? In my haste, I'd tripped over the front of my shoe again. I kicked off my flip-flops and carried them as I ran past the florist shop. *It's because he can see who's calling and he hates you,* I realized. That was going to be a problem.

The bar was crowded and loud. Scarlet- and gray-uniformed players were on the televisions, but unlike everyone else, I ignored the game and scanned the bar for its owner.

"Oh, hey, Felicity," Rachel, a server, said. She had a platter of fries and chicken tenders surrounded by beers on a tray. She looked surprised to see me. I probably looked terrible—frantic, even—with bare feet, blotched cheeks, and watery eyes. "What's going on?"

"Have you seen Wade?"

"He was behind the bar." She craned her neck, looking across the room at the counter. "He might've left for the night, though. He's having a party at his place after the game. You should stop by."

I ignored her last comment. He couldn't be at home. I'd never make it in time without a car, and I didn't know how to steal one. I twisted around, searching every face in the crowded room. Something must've happened in the game, because people cheered, throwing their arms into the air at the same time.

I had the opposite reaction as hope seeped from my body like blood from a wound. My legs collapsed into a booth. I rested my forehead on the table and ran through my dwindling options.

The table was sticky, but I didn't care. What was I going to do? I called Wade for the fifth time. I knew it was useless. He wasn't answering because he hated me. Our fight had been disastrous. Even if I had gotten hold of him, he'd have turned me down. What hurt the most was that I'd been counting on him for years. Wade, though incredibly annoying, had become a sort of friend, a person who was at least there when I needed him, even if he laughed at my ridiculousness the entire time.

I choked out a sob. Other than Alex, I had no one else. And now I was going to let her down, all because I'd been holding on to a grudge since I was fifteen.

Resigned to my fate, I stood and walked toward the door. According to my watch, I had thirty minutes to meet Mary's deadline, and the house was too far away to reach, make my plea, and drag Wade to the police station. It wasn't going to work, but I had to at least try.

When my hand was on the door handle, I heard him—or, I thought I heard him. Maybe my mind was playing tricks on me. I turned, and relief flooded through me.

Before I knew what I was doing, I yelled, "Wade!" across the room. People turned to look at me, the woman interrupting their precious sports game. At the noise, Wade's eyes found me by the door. Initially, he looked surprised—maybe even confused—but then his glance turned dark as he returned his attention to the box in his hands.

I hadn't spoken to him in weeks, had even avoided him when he took his trash out, but now I crossed the bar in ten steps and stood right in front of him.

"She wants to have dinner with you!" I blurted out with no context.

"What?" He set the box behind the bar, then straightened. "Who are you talking about?"

I tried again. "Your mother wants to have dinner with you. Five times. And you have to do it."

"And she sent *you* to ask me?"

The words still weren't coming out right. I'd been so focused on finding him that I hadn't given much thought to what I'd say when I finally did. I sputtered as everyone in the bar looked on, listening intently. I had a feeling we had become more entertaining than the game.

"Lovers' spat," Glen muttered to Evan over his glass of beer.

"We're not lovers!" I yelled down the counter.

"Don't get mad at me because your boy is uncontrollable." Glen looked like he wanted to laugh, until I took a step toward him. He gulped and glanced back at the television. Before I could confront him, somebody grabbed my arm and yanked me away.

Wade led me through a swinging door and into a back room. Boxes, crates, and bottles lined the shelves. It was quieter back here.

He released my arm. "What the fuck is going on?"

"You know I didn't understand before. I thought if I worked hard and kept my head down, everything would be fine. I might not be rich, but I didn't care about that. I thought that competence and decency would win the day."

Wade looked at me like I had lost my mind. But it was the opposite. I'd figured things out tonight—the reason why I'd gotten nowhere in this town and my business was failing. "I have no pull, Wade. None. Even in this little hick town, it's all about who you know and what you have to hold over them. And I've got *nothing*."

"What are you talking about? What pull?"

"The favors and the backroom deals. It might not be the Mafia, but the principles are the same. 'I'll help you, but only if you give me something in return.'"

He took a deep breath and looked like he was trying hard not to lose his temper with my ramblings. I cut him off before he could. "Alex and I got into a fight, and she left."

"What?" He stepped toward me. "When?"

"A few hours ago." My hand shook as I ran it through my hair. "Wade, she got arrested."

He tossed his hands in the air. "Why didn't you lead with that? Instead, you're spewing this nonsense about pull and favors and several other things that I'm not following."

"She got arrested and it's bad. Like really, really bad. And I need a favor from you. Your mom said she'd drop the charges if you ask her to."

"What does my mom have to do with it?"

My insides clenched as I anticipated his reaction. "Alex may have thrown a brick through the grocery store window and then tried to rob it." I bit my lip, then added, "Allegedly."

He seemed to be at a loss for words. He turned, then turned back around before coming to a halt in front of me and saying, in a deathly quiet voice, "What the hell, Felicity? How could you let her do that?"

I cringed, wishing he'd yelled. "You know how Mary is. She'll probably petition the judge to give Alex the death penalty."

"She said she'd drop the charges if you agreed to have five weekly dinners with her." I continued before he could say no: "I realize you have no reason to help me after what I did. I hurt you, and we're not speaking, and that . . . that sucks. I ruined everything, and I don't expect your forgiveness. But this isn't for me; it's for Alex. And no matter what happened with the two of us, I thought you liked Alex."

He took a deep breath, not answering my plea for help. For a fraction of a second, I thought I saw his anger thaw. But I wasn't sure. This favor was asking a lot of him. Wade didn't have the best relationship with his mother. Though he lived less than two miles from her, she never came to his house, and he never spoke about her. It might take a lot to convince him, but I wasn't above begging. I wasn't above pleading with him for whatever he wanted, so long as he saved Alex. That was all that mattered to me.

"She doesn't have anyone but me, Wade. She's alone, and people have cast her off her entire life. I'm not going to do that to her. I can't. I won't."

I took a step toward him, gauging his resolve. My lip trembled as I fought back tears. "I'll do anything you want. Anything. But you have to come to the police station in the next twenty minutes and tell your mom that you'll do it. Please. *Please.*"

He stared at me for a long moment, his jaw tense.

"Please, Wade. I'll never ask you for anything again. Please."

His eyes settled on mine before he looked away and muttered "Fine" at the floor. "If you stop begging, then I'll do it."

I leaped into the air. I raised my arms and hugged him around his neck.

"Thank you," I gushed into his shoulder. I waited until, after a long pause, he gave in and wrapped his arm around my back.

I released him quickly after that and shooed him toward the door. "Let's go, let's go. I don't have all night."

"Don't push your luck," he said, but he started moving. He paused, hand on the doorknob, and turned to face me. "I do have one condition, though."

Of course he did. I put my hand on my hip and waited, wondering what on earth the mind of Wade Londergan had dreamed up. He'd probably ask for unlimited favors or servitude for life.

"What's the condition?"

He smiled at the mixture of anger and hesitancy in my voice. "If you think I'm going to these dinners alone, you're sorely mistaken."

TWENTY-EIGHT

I'd left the lights on in my haste to find Alex, which made the house feel welcoming as I collapsed into a kitchen chair. I wanted to sit for a while and process everything that had happened in the last few hours.

Alex sat across from me. She hadn't said a word since we left the police station. I didn't think she knew what to say, and quite honestly, I was at a loss for words myself.

We sat for a while, listening to nothing but the hum of cicadas coming through the open windows. Alex stared at the table, and I searched for divine intervention in the kitchen, a place that held so many memories for me. The house creaked in response to my silent pleas for help. This was the chair my mother had sat in every evening for dinner. She would've had some profound words of wisdom to change Alex's life and make everything better. Unfortunately, Alex was stuck with me tonight, and I had no idea where to begin.

"It's getting late, Felicity. Are you going to start the lecture or what?"

"You want to be a smart-ass, or do you want to continue living here?" My tone cut across the table, and she sat back against her chair. My mother would've been patient and kind, spoken softly about all the havoc Alex had created tonight. But I couldn't do it anymore. It was time for some tough love—for both of us. I'd have to stand my ground and finally get Alex to understand that she couldn't destroy everything the moment she got upset. I exhaled, steadying myself, fully aware that I was more likely to cry than yell at her.

"First, you call me from jail in the middle of the night. No thank-you. No *Hey, Felicity, I realize I don't know you, but thanks for posting my bail, especially because you have no money.*"

She pursed her lips at my imitation of her voice. Whether from amusement or offense, I couldn't say.

"And then I let you live here, even though your intent was to *rob* me. I teach you how to cook, how to fold clothes so they don't get wrinkled, and I pay you under the table to help me with the blueberry farm. I even let you earn some extra cash doing the thing you love most: stirring up trouble around town. I defended you. I put aside my grievances with Wade to get you a lawyer, and all I asked in return was what?"

I raised my eyebrow, waiting for her to answer.

"Don't mess with the grocery store," she mumbled at the table.

"That's right," I said much louder. "Don't mess with the fucking grocery store."

"I was defending you. Mary had it coming after the festival bullshit."

"Well, you defended me with a brick through her window. How did that work out?"

"I messed up," Alex said, eyes sweeping across the kitchen.

"You're damn right you messed up. And now I'm going to have to pay for it in spades, because I had to eat crow and beg Wade to help us."

"So, this is about Wade getting involved? I messed up, but I did it in a way that inconvenienced your feud with Wade, so you're pissed?"

"No, Alex. This is about my complete helplessness as I watch you throw your life away!" I took a deep breath, steadying my temper. I placed my palms flat against the table on either side of the place mat. "I can almost understand the grocery store incident. Almost. Because I believe you were trying—in your misguided, insanely loyal way—to help me. But what I can't understand is why you would leave with no money, no place to go, and no way for me to contact you. 'Cause I've got to tell you, that hurt." My voice broke at the end, ruining my tough-love persona. "You scared the shit out of me tonight."

"I was helping you. You don't need me here, destroying everything. I thought if I left, everyone in town would forgive you."

"Alex, for such an intelligent person, how could you think for one second that I would put my relationship with the town ahead of you?"

She shifted in her chair. "You're just saying that because of the stupid cell phone number."

Oh, Alex. Was she ever going to understand? "Whether my mom put you in my life, or it was fate, or some random one-in-a-billion chance, I got to meet you. And because of that, I got to know you—and the more I did, the more I liked you." I let the words sink in before adding, "We're family. Just because we both made mistakes doesn't change that."

She took a deep breath, her lower lip shaking ever so slightly. "I screwed up, but I didn't know what else to do."

"*We* screwed up. You weren't out there vandalizing cars alone."

At least she was showing remorse. With Alex, that was a decent start, but I needed more tonight. "From this moment on, we're done messing with people. No more revenge. No more schemes. No more sneaking around at night. And definitely no more property damage. It's over. Going forward, we're doing things the right way." I leaned forward so my elbows were on the table, bracing myself for her reaction. "And you're pleading guilty to the shoplifting charge."

"No way. That's not fair!"

"It's nonnegotiable, Alex. If you want to live in my house, you're going to take responsibility for stealing the necklace. You'll plead guilty, avoid jail time, and we'll move on."

"I don't want to," Alex said, looking anywhere but at me. "And they can't prove I took it."

Why couldn't she see that the prosecutor had more than enough evidence to convict her? Tess had laid everything out at this very table. Alex wasn't thinking clearly about this, which was why we'd gone in circles about it for weeks. But tonight I was putting my foot down. It was the best thing for her. I couldn't give in solely out of fear that she'd leave if I didn't go along with her plans. That wasn't fair. Not to me, and certainly not to Alex—who, despite her grumblings, needed someone to knock some sense into her.

I kept it simple. "Did you take the necklace?"

"It wasn't my fault. The security—"

"*Did* you take the necklace?" I repeated louder. She wasn't weaseling her way out of this one.

She crossed her arms over her chest, then looked at the wall before muttering, "I already told you I did."

"Then what are we arguing about?" I dipped my shoulders in bafflement. "It doesn't matter if they can prove it or if you had the best reason in the world. You stole something that didn't belong to you. It was wrong, and you're too smart not to know that."

She didn't respond, but at least she wasn't arguing with me about it.

"You'll call Tess in the morning?"

She glared at the wall, but eventually nodded. *Ha!* I thought, wanting to celebrate. I had finally done it. Eight weeks, two arrests, and a string of criminal activity later, and I'd gotten her to plead guilty. At this rate, I'd have her in college by the time she turned forty.

"Why are you smiling?" she asked.

"Because you agreed." I made no attempt to conceal my elation. "And because my tough-love speech worked. I'd been doubting myself even as I said it."

Alex snorted. "Tough love? More like you freaked out for the last five minutes and I agreed to shut you up."

"Whatever you want to believe." There was no diminishing my success.

She drummed her fingers on the table. "Did you really ask Wade for help?"

My smile faded as I remembered my dash to the bar. My feet ached from running barefoot on the pavement. "Yes. Worst night ever, but I got it done."

It was her turn to smile. "I knew he liked you."

"He made me beg. Now I have to go to five Londergan family dinners with him."

"Like a date?"

"No," I said immediately. At least, I didn't think so. The dinners were with his family, and that didn't count as a date. Did it? I blinked. That was a problem I'd sort out tomorrow. I still had something on my mind that I needed to discuss with her.

"I have one question, and then we'll put it to rest forever." I hesitated, unsure how to ask, but I had to know. Every part of me had to know. "Were you really going to steal from me?"

Her admission that she'd intended to rob me would hang over us until we addressed it. Unlike the old Felicity, I wasn't burying this in the backyard with my fingers crossed that it would magically sprout blueberries.

Alex rubbed her forehead. She looked ashamed. Guilty. "Yes."

The breath left my lungs. I'd desperately clung to the fantasy that she'd been lying about stealing from me, hoping it would anger me and I'd let her leave without a second thought. I bit my lip, unsure what to say.

She broke the heavy silence. "A couple years ago, after Ted and Judy passed away, I went to see my birth mother in Florida."

My head shot up, sadness and humiliation replaced by intrigue. She never spoke about her birth mother unless I pressed for information, and even then, I'd barely get more than a grunt or a shrug. I returned my gaze to the table, feigning disinterest so she wouldn't get embarrassed and cease talking.

"Ted gave me her address before he died, so I went to Orlando, thinking Britney might take me in after she learned that my adopted parents had passed away." Her voice caught as she hesitated. "It didn't go well."

Her eyes wandered toward the back window and stayed there, replaying something in her mind. The silence lasted so long I worried she'd never tell me.

"What happened?" I asked, so quietly that I wasn't sure she heard.

"I knocked on the door, and she wouldn't let me inside. She screamed at me, told me to leave, said that I was trespassing." Alex ran a hand through her hair. "I didn't know what to do. I had nowhere to go, and I'd spent all my money on the bus ticket. I smashed in her car windows. The cops arrested me for trespassing, property damage, and threatening Britney, her husband, and their two sons. Since I was a minor, they sent me back to my foster family in Ohio."

My heart felt like it had dropped through my stomach and straight to the floor. How could anyone turn her away? I certainly couldn't. My eyes watered as I searched for something to say. I wanted nothing more than to take this pain from her shoulders and carry it for her. No eighteen-year-old should feel unwanted or unloved, especially not someone as loyal as Alex.

A tear slipped down my cheek, and I brushed it away before she could see. "Alex, I had no idea—"

"It's fine," she snapped. "I don't want to talk about it other than to say, the day I got back to Ohio, my foster parent, Janelle, bought me a new cell phone. I'd ditched mine in a trash can at the bus station so they couldn't track me down. And that night, I got a voicemail from you, something about selling your car because you were worried about driving it off a cliff or into the lake and killing yourself."

Oh no. I replayed that voicemail in my head. The sobs and my shaking voice that distorted half my words as I told my mom about how close I was to giving up. Not the best first impression. Alex must have thought I was insane.

"You were struggling, but you'd promised your mom that you'd find a way to be happy again. It was clear that you loved her, and she had loved you, and I grew jealous. The more voicemails I listened to, the more jealous I became, curious and fascinated by you and your daily squabbles, but also upset that you had a mother to miss and mine didn't even want me inside her house."

"So why didn't you do it? Why didn't you rob me?"

"Well, like I said, I was curious about you and the town. I wanted to see it for myself, and when I showed up . . ." She stopped talking to catch her breath. "I felt safe here. I'm not used to people treating me so well or putting up with my attitude. Normally, they ignore me or let me dig my own grave. Instead, you picked up a shovel and started digging, too."

That, I did. My hands should've been covered in blisters. "We dug ourselves into quite a hole."

"It was fun, though." Her voice hadn't quite returned to normal as she shrugged, trying to distract me from asking any further questions about her past.

I took the bait, appreciative that she had shared so much with me. "We had a better run than I expected."

"Remember Cheryl's face when we dyed her son blue?"

"Or Rodney trying to solve the fake murder?"

Alex snorted. "I thought the vein in his forehead was going to burst. It's a wonder the man doesn't drown every time it rains."

I smiled, shoulders relaxing. As the tension left my body, exhaustion took its place. It was well past midnight, and I yawned, covering my mouth with the back of my hand. Alex seized the opportunity to head to her bedroom and avoid further conversation.

But she didn't move fast enough.

"Alex," I called after her. She paused in the doorway. "What happened with your birth mom . . ." I hesitated, searching for the right words. "That had nothing to do with you. Those are her mistakes, not yours."

"She didn't want *me*, Felicity."

"It's hard to understand, but one day you'll realize that it's her loss. You did everything you could to have a relationship with her, and if she doesn't want to be in your life, then she's the one who has to live with that."

I stood and turned off the kitchen lights, listening to Alex mutter, "Whatever," as she closed her bedroom door. And just like that, she was back to being the Alex I'd come to know: emotionally withdrawn and unwilling to accept that she was a wonderful person.

Calm washed over me as I headed upstairs, knowing that she was safe in her bedroom. After a day with more ups and downs than a Cedar Point roller coaster, that was all I really needed. For the first time, I went to sleep truly believing that when I woke up, Alex would still be here.

TWENTY-NINE

My mom had enjoyed dressing up. Nice shirts, well-fitting jeans, or a dress with a complementary necklace to tie the outfit together. Three years after her death and I still didn't have the heart to donate a single piece of her clothing. Her twenty pairs of boots stared at me as I slung hangers aside, roaming her closet. Even dead, the woman had better dress sense than I did.

I settled on her red shirt and a black cardigan. Nice, but not fancy, and they would pair well with jeans. When Wade had told me to be ready at six, he'd said, "Look good." I didn't know whether he was being his usual annoying self or Mary would kick me out of her house if I didn't wear a dress. But if it was Wade's plan to stress me out, then mission accomplished. Making a woman fret about her outfit equated to psychological torture.

I dabbed my face with concealer, attempting to hide the dark bags under my eyes, still present from those nights I hadn't slept, thanks to Wade's parties. The thought made my cheeks flush, giving them some color. I savored the anger, knowing it would serve me better than nervousness.

When I'd finished applying my mascara, there was a knock at the front door. He was five minutes late! I'd been counting on him being at least fifteen minutes behind schedule. Why was he trying to be dependable all of a sudden?

Alex answered the door.

Sweat broke out on my forehead, threatening to ruin my makeup. Why was I so nervous? I ran a comb through my hair, snagging it painfully in my haste.

Alex came up the stairs and paused in my doorway. "Your future husband is here."

My face flushed again. "You should be the last person making jokes." I set the comb down a little too hard. I opened my lipstick drawer and flung around several different colors; they all looked the same. "I feel like I'm serving your prison sentence for you. If I had any sense, I'd be making you sit through a two-hour dinner with Mary."

Alex stepped closer. "Use this one." She pulled a tube of lip gloss from the drawer and set it on the desk. "And unfortunately, Wade isn't in love with me, so this is something only you can do."

"You owe me," I said darkly, but didn't mean it. She'd called Tess yesterday morning and explained that she was willing to take a plea deal. She didn't sound happy about it, but at least she'd made the call. I wasn't sure I had the guts to follow through on my threat to kick her out.

I smacked my lips together, admiring the gloss. Anything darker would've been too much with my simple makeup. "Tell Wade I'll be down in a minute."

She left me and my nerves alone. It wasn't just that I was having dinner with Wade—or that I'd have to converse with people for hours, which I hadn't done in so long—but rather, that everyone was going to hate me. I was already socially awkward. It didn't bode well that I'd pissed off the town matriarch and now had to sit at her dinner table and smile. I glanced longingly at my bed on my way out the door.

Alex laughed at something on the television as I descended the stairs. Juno bounded forward to greet me, paws clattering on the floor.

Wade stood behind the couch. He'd found the doughnuts in the kitchen. Could he ever come to my house and not help himself to the food? Especially when we were going to his parents' house for dinner immediately after?

He had on a simple pair of jeans and a green T-shirt that had a hole in one of the sleeves. *Look good,* he'd said. The man was truly trying to torture me.

He held a white box in one hand, the other leaned against the back of the couch.

"You look nice." He stepped away from the couch, shoving the remainder of the doughnut in his mouth. "You ready?" he asked as he chewed.

"Let's get this over with."

"Don't blame me; I didn't try to rob the store." He leaned over the back of the couch and mussed Alex's hair.

"Allegedly," Alex said. She brought a spoon laden with ice cream to her mouth, but held the bowl up as Juno attempted to shove her nose into the dessert. "I think there's been an elaborate conspiracy to frame me."

I tossed on my cardigan and walked closer to the couch so I could get Alex's attention. "Call me if you need me."

"Why would I need you?"

We had discussed Alex calling with a medical emergency if I texted her the code word: *flamingo*. She smiled maliciously before noticing that I was about to freak out. She quickly amended her question. "I mean, my stomach is acting funky, but hopefully I'll be okay."

Neither of us is going to be an actress, I thought as she took another bite of ice cream. And to think, this was the girl I'd trusted to evade police questioning when we sabotaged half the town.

With no more reasons to stall, I followed Wade toward the door. He held it open with one hand, letting me pass through first. The white box smelled like something fried was inside. My stomach growled.

"Have fun," Alex called from the couch, twisting around to watch us leave. "And have her home by ten!"

Wade chuckled as he closed the door.

The fifteen-minute walk to his parents' house was straight through the square and onto Peach Street—the ritzy part of town, if we had one. The houses there had manicured lawns as well as pools in their backyards. The Londergans owned a two-story house with a wide front porch. There was a swing to the right of the door. White columns stood on each side of the entrance, making it look like the house of a statesman.

I paused on the top step, turning to stare at Wade, who had stopped with his boot on the lowest stair. He looked like he was about to cross a fraying rope bridge over a canyon.

"What's wrong?"

"You know, I was thinking . . . Alex is young. She'll be fine if she has to go to prison for a few years. She'll bounce back."

"Wade," I said, retreating a few steps so we were the same height, "come on."

"Just give me a minute."

"Why are you freaking out?"

He took a deep breath. He tested the step with his foot but still didn't move. "I have to see my mother."

I'd never seen him nervous before. It was entertaining. But I suppressed my glee as I said, "It won't be that bad."

He gave me a skeptical look. I tapped my foot on the step. I didn't point out that we were already late. I held out my hand, palm up. "If knives are drawn, I'll protect you."

"Good in a knife fight, are you?" He took my hand and joined me near the front door.

"Don't act so surprised. I've done things."

"Oh, I know," he said, turning so I could see his smirk. "That's what got us into this mess."

With a deep sigh, he knocked on the door.

Wade's father answered. My interactions with Jeff had been limited—his construction company didn't cross paths with the blueberry farm like Mary's business did—but he'd always come across as a kind, jovial man. Tonight he had his blue dress shirt tucked into his pants, making his stomach more pronounced. His face roamed from me to Wade and then back again before he spoke. "Really?"

Wade shrugged like a child caught doing something he wasn't supposed to but didn't care enough about the consequences to stop. "What's the big deal? There's always enough food."

Jeff sighed. "Come on in, Felicity."

When his father departed the foyer, leaving us to close the door, I punched Wade's arm.

"You didn't tell them I was coming?" I hissed, trying to keep my voice low. "What's wrong with you?"

"If I had told her you were coming, she would have said no, and I need a buffer."

"A buffer for what?"

"Her disappointment." He ran a hand through his hair, messing it up more. "You're the only person she's more disappointed in than me right now. It's perfect. She'll focus on you, leaving me free to escape should things get too heated."

I bristled, ready to snap at him, but he took my hand and led me through the foyer. The smell of roast chicken grew more pronounced as we moved into the living room. Wade's brothers sat on the couch, watching the news.

"Only twenty-nine minutes late," Ben, the oldest brother, said. "Mom will be pleasantly surprised." His eyes took me in as I stood awkwardly at Wade's side. "Oh, and you brought a guest. Two for two, Wade."

Wade acted like his brother hadn't spoken. "Felicity, you know, Ben, right? And that's Sam."

I knew Ben, but had rarely spoken to him for more than a few minutes. He was the local doctor and split his practice between a building near the square and working shifts at the hospital in Avon. He and his wife, Lauren, lived two streets over from here. Sometimes they would bring their three daughters—Katelyn, Bethany, and Willa—to the blueberry farm. Though I suspected it was more to see the state of Wade's house, which Ben enjoyed commenting on, than to pick blueberries.

I'd never met Sam, but if he was smart enough to marry Tess, whom I'd come to adore, then he must not be a total loser.

"Hello." I waved awkwardly.

Both brothers nodded politely in response, and my nervousness grew exponentially. Should I say something else? Should I make a joke? I tried to think of something funny that would be at Wade's expense. His brothers beat me to it.

"Onion rings?" Ben asked, inclining his head toward the box in Wade's hand.

"Yeah."

"What an idiot." Sam shook his head in brotherly disapproval. We moved farther into the house, coming to a stop in a kitchen that had magnificent French doors leading outside to a patio. An in-ground pool sat beyond the outdoor furniture.

Mary, Jeff, and Lauren stood around the marble island. Glasses of red wine had been poured. Jeff took his and left the room before we were fully inside. He sent a sympathetic glance in my direction before disappearing around the corner.

"Mom." Wade kissed his mother on the cheek. She took him in with discerning eyes but made no comment as he opened the fridge and grabbed two beers. I declined when he gestured toward me with a bottle. The last thing I needed was alcohol.

"Felicity." Mary finally acknowledged my presence.

"Thank you for having me for dinner, Mary. Your house is beautiful." My mother hadn't raised me to be impolite, no matter whom I was talking to.

Behind the counter, Lauren gave me an encouraging smile. I was about to address her when a loud shriek erupted behind me.

"Waaaaaaade!" A girl with long brown hair ran into the kitchen. Bethany, I thought, the oldest daughter who was around seven years old.

Her sisters came running behind her, shorter legs not carrying them as fast. They had a stethoscope and one of those hammers a doctor bangs against your knee.

Wade smiled as they bolted toward him. "Oh, good, the monsters are here."

"I'm not a monster," Bethany shouted, but she was smiling from ear to ear.

"He's sick!" Kate pointed a finger at him. She looked at her sisters for support in her assessment. Her hair had been jaggedly chopped across her forehead, making me wonder if she or one of her sisters had cut it.

"He needs the hospital," Bethany said. Willa dropped her stethoscope in her excitement.

Mary eyed them with impatience. "We're having dinner in five minutes."

"A local hospital, then," Lauren responded, cutting across Mary's harsh glance. "Go ahead, girls. He's looking a bit pale."

I was shocked when Wade shrugged, taking a sip of beer before allowing himself to be led from the room by his nieces. "All right, but don't tell your dad, or he'll bill my insurance."

"What's that?" Kate asked, pulling at his arm.

"Something he doesn't have," Ben shouted from the living room.

With Wade gone, I was awkwardly left in the kitchen. I considered offering to help cook, but that would probably offend Mary. I settled for helping Lauren set the table in the dining room.

"Sorry about the chaos. With Halloween coming up, we're encouraging the girls to be something other than princesses this year," she said.

I set a plate on the far end. "Cinderella?"

"Elsa," she responded. "Always Elsa. She's cool and all, but I want them to try something else. Ben had the stethoscopes already, so . . ."

"No, I think that's great. And they've got the perfect patient, because I doubt Wade has been to the doctor in years. They'll find tons of things wrong with him."

She glanced toward the kitchen, then lowered her voice. "I think Mary's upset because the girls took him away before she could comment on his shirt."

"He doesn't come over here much, huh?"

"Almost never. We're in for a fun evening."

I grew anxious once the table was set and Lauren fetched the girls.

When Mary took a seat at the end of the table, I retreated to the opposite side, sitting to Jeff's left. Wade slid into the chair on my other side. He had a pink Band-Aid on his arm.

"What's the diagnosis, girls?" Lauren asked, pulling Willa into a chair beside her. "Is he going to make it?"

Bethany, whom I understood to be the boldest of the group and the lead doctor, spoke up. "He's got the flu. But we gave him a shot, so he'll survive."

"A shot of what?" Ben asked. "Flu shots are given to prevent infection, not after."

He stopped talking when he saw the look Lauren was giving him.

"It was a special shot," Kate said, missing the exchange between her parents.

To my right, Jeff started filling my wineglass.

"Oh, none for me, thanks." I didn't want to waste his wine. The bottle looked expensive.

He kept pouring. "Trust me. It will help." His devilish smile reminded me of Wade's. Maybe this was where he got it from. "Besides, congratulations are in order." He pulled the bottle away with a flourish. "On selling the farm."

I nearly knocked the wineglass over. "What?" My hands shook. "What are you talking about? I didn't sell anything."

Jeff looked confused. "I saw the construction plans a week ago . . . for your lot."

I couldn't afford the ice cream Alex was currently eating, let alone construction for the farm. I felt faint. "You're mistaken."

"I could've sworn it was your place. Not many spots in town with blueberry bushes."

The mere thought of not owning the farm made me spiral. I had to get out of here. I had to run home and lock the front door and tell Alex to barricade all the windows. No one was getting my house or the blueberry farm. I'd die before I relinquished my control over that property.

"Who gave you those plans?" I asked Jeff, but Wade turned to me, trying to draw me into his spat with Sam, clearly not reading the anxiety on my face.

"Did you know that Sam peed his bed when he was thirteen?"

Jeff rolled his eyes. Wade's immaturity knew no bounds—not even at his parents' dinner table.

Sam pointed a fork at Wade's head. "I was eight, and I'd just watched *Halloween*."

"You were at least twelve," Wade insisted.

"Well, now your story's changing," Sam said, eyes lighting up at the potential for a counterargument. "So why should anyone believe you?"

"Knock it off, boys," Jeff said, eyeing Mary with caution. "No fighting at the dinner table."

Their squabble slipped beneath my conscious thought, as I was still focused on what Jeff had said about selling the farm. Why would he think I'd sold my house? Someone could offer me a billion dollars and I'd still never sell an acre. Per the tax certificate letter from J&C, I still had time to pay off the lien before they initiated foreclosure proceedings.

Jeff was mistaken: That was the only logical conclusion. He could've seen the plans for any number of farms in Elswood. Half the town dabbled in growing fruits or vegetables on their property. He probably didn't know the difference between a peach tree and a blueberry bush.

"Bed wetter," Wade slipped in, getting the last word, completely oblivious to my panic attack. Bethany and Kate laughed at their uncle's expense. Now I understood why they liked Wade so much. He and his nieces were all at the same maturity level.

"So nice you could join us, Wade," Mary said, silencing Sam's retort.

Jeff nudged me with his elbow and picked up his wineglass. I did the same, trusting the man to his ways. He knew the routine better than I did.

"Even if it took a two-month crime spree and a broken window to get you to walk a mile to your mother's house for dinner," Mary said.

"My work hours don't leave a lot of time for dinner parties."

Ben rolled his eyes, but Mary narrowed hers. "How is that bar of yours?"

"It's still there. You thinking of stopping by for happy hour? We've got two-for-one shots on Mondays and Wednesdays."

Mary looked ashamed. "I'm shocked the health inspector hasn't shut it down."

"They tried, but the lady lost the paperwork."

Lauren laughed until Mary gave a look that silenced her. I took another sip of wine, steeling my nerves.

"I like the bar," I chimed in. Holding a wineglass made me feel like a true adult with opinions. "It's got a certain charm to it."

"We all know your taste is flawed, Felicity," Mary said.

"What's that supposed to mean?"

Wade stared down at his plate, suddenly fascinated with the heap of chicken and potatoes he'd assembled.

"Only that your taste in friends leaves something to be desired."

Jeff stirred beside me. "Mary, we agreed we weren't going to discuss it."

"No, you *suggested* that we shouldn't discuss it, but this is my house, and I'll discuss whatever I want." Mary turned from Jeff to me, not quite done with her rant. "Do you have any idea how much trouble you've caused, Felicity? You deserved to lose your festival slot. The council should've gone one step further and banned your criminal friend from the town once and for all."

Her words knocked the breath from my lungs.

"Mom!" Wade set his beer on the table with a thud. "We haven't even started dinner yet. Save the eternal damnation for dessert."

"That girl tried to steal from me," Mary said. "Broke the window to my store and cost me several hundred dollars in repairs. I'll speak about her however I want."

"No, you won't," I said, matching her tone. "Not in front of me." Anxiety over losing the farm, coupled with my anger over Mary's insults, made me bold. "If the choice is between Alex and that elitist, embarrassing Founders' Day Festival—it's going to be Alex every single time."

"You sound like your mother," Mary said. "It would've been just like Josette to take in a teenager who had problems with the law."

The corners of my mouth twitched upward. "That might be the nicest compliment anyone's ever given me."

She hadn't said it to be nice, but warmth flooded my body. Mary was right: My mom would've taken Alex in and defended her, no matter the consequences to her own reputation.

Despite the tense atmosphere around the table, I found myself thinking about my mom and her compassion and generosity—two qualities that defined her life, two qualities she'd tried to instill in me.

When Brenna Walsh hadn't invited me to her birthday party in the fourth grade, my mom said I still had to be nice to her.

"But I invited everyone to my birthday party," I'd said through tears. "It's not fair." My mom didn't understand that everyone else was going to get to go to the bowling alley and eat cake.

Everyone except me.

"Sometimes the best thing you can do is continue to be kind even when someone disappoints you. I don't want you to give up on people, Felicity." My mom had put her hand under my chin, raising it. "Because you, my dear girl, have so much love in your heart. And one day, that love is going to change lives."

Despite the entire Londergan family looking in my direction, a tear trickled down my cheek. Wade squeezed my knee under the table.

"Does anyone want an onion ring?" he interjected, taking the attention off me. He held up the box, grease seeping through the bottom and onto the polished wood table. Sam shook his head, and Ben grabbed Kate's arm as she reached for one.

"No takers?"

Mary's eyes narrowed as Wade set the box on a white dinner plate between the asparagus and homemade dinner rolls.

Grateful for the distraction, I took an onion ring and put it on my plate. Solidarity. Somehow Wade and I were in this nightmare together. He smiled as I ripped the fried vegetable in half. It was greasy, but much better than the baked yams. Maybe the extra calories would give me enough energy to go another round with Mary.

THIRTY

"Only four dinners to go," Wade said as he shut the door behind us. He looked shorter than when we'd begun the evening three hours ago.

"I don't know if my self-esteem will survive four more dinners. By the time we finished passing around the mashed potatoes, Mary had already carved out my heart to serve next week."

He laughed without humor, then gently yanked my sleeve. "Come with me. I've got a cure for that."

The sky had turned almost black, but streetlamps lit the way as we walked through the town square. Wade disappeared inside the ice-cream shop, then reappeared with two cones. We made our way to the gazebo and watched cars pass as we ate our dessert.

Wade stretched out, crossing his ankles in front of him.

"What's the deal with the onion rings?"

He smiled my favorite devilish smile. "Mary doesn't approve of anything bar related."

"Why not?"

"I was supposed to take over the construction business from my dad, but I nixed that idea after a few days of manual labor." He gestured in the general direction of his parents' house. I liked that he didn't have huge ambitions or a demanding job. He was content with his bar—happy, even, living the life he wanted. I smiled warmly, knowing he couldn't see my expression in the dark. "She's upset she can't control my every move."

"I don't think that's true. She wouldn't have traded Alex's freedom for your presence if she didn't love you and want to spend more time with you. Sometimes it's nice to be needed." That was how I felt about Alex. There were days after my mom died when I didn't shower, eat, or get out of bed. But after Alex had called and needed me to do something, to be somewhere, things had changed. I had a reason to get up and start the day because Alex needed me, whether she wanted to admit it or not. And in return, I'd needed her, too. "Mary wants to spend time with you because you're her kid. I'd give anything to have dinner with my mom one more time. Or think of Alex, whose mother gave her up for adoption."

He tensed beside me on the bench. "I shouldn't have complained."

"Relax," I said. My goal hadn't been to guilt-trip him. "I'm just saying you could let some of her comments slide because you still have a mom. But I get it. Mary's no picnic."

I finished the last of my ice-cream cone. Wade had finished minutes before me, having bitten straight into the cold dessert like a savage.

"Unlike your mom, who was probably the nicest person in town," Wade said.

I looked around the gazebo. "She used to love sitting in the square and watching the sunset. After she died, I tried to donate money and get a bench named after her, but all of them had sponsors already." I bit my lip, not wanting to think about that time of my life. I tried to lighten the conversation. "Did you have her in class?"

"Algebra, sophomore year. Got a C plus."

"Really? You did that well?"

"She was an easy grader." He ran a hand through his hair. "And of course, I had her before the homecoming incident. I imagine she would've graded a bit harder after that."

"Well, she did pop champagne after you tore your ACL."

He turned to look at me. "Did she really?"

"She didn't say anything about you, but the day after your injury, she came home with a bottle, and we drank it out of teacups." I smiled at the memory. We'd toasted to karma. Wade Londergan had been the only person my mother couldn't stand. What would she think about me sitting on this bench with him after having dinner at his parents' house?

"I suppose I deserved that," he muttered. "One of the worst days of my life, when that tore during practice. Stupid Grady Wellser tackled me from behind during a drill." His hand went to his leg as if the pain was still there. "But what I did to you was way worse than a torn ligament."

My first thought was to act like it was no big deal. Like I had magically gotten over it. But I knew I wouldn't fool him. That dance had stood between us for years, and we wouldn't get beyond it without addressing some uncomfortable truths.

I looked at the ground when I spoke. "If you think your mother messed with my self-esteem, you have no idea what something like that does to a fifteen-year-old girl who hadn't even been kissed yet."

He flinched. "I'm sorry. I was so used to people giving me whatever I wanted, whenever I wanted it, because of football. It took me a long time to realize how terribly I acted."

So I was finally getting my apology. Twelve years later.

"At least you have an excuse. You were a teenager. I was twenty-seven when I decided to hurt you."

"Yeah, well . . . like I said, I deserved it."

"It was still wrong, Wade. I shouldn't have done it. And then you came through for me with Alex, even after some of the things I said the next day." I knew what I needed to say, even if it took me a second to build up to it. "Thank you for that."

"Five dinners isn't exactly torture. I think I can handle it."

"But it's not easy for you, and I appreciate it. I owe you for what happened with Alex."

"Can we call it even? I can't keep track of who owes who for what. You may not remember, but I wasn't the brightest guy in high school."

"2.6 GPA."

He laughed loudly. "It went up, actually. Graduated with a 2.84."

"What an accomplishment."

He sat back against the bench, draping one arm around my shoulders.

"So, are we friends now?" I asked after a moment.

"Friends?"

"You know, like no more throwing loud parties to piss me off, no more half-dressed women leaving in the morning, and—"

"No more stealing my truck or egging it, or yelling that I'm an asshole . . ."

"Well, maybe not in public," I countered.

He squeezed my shoulder once. "I'm game if you are."

"Then we're friends."

"Fine."

"Fine." I couldn't help grinning. It felt significant, past regrets mended and closed up so that I could move on. One down and about two hundred to go before this town accepted me again. I hoped everyone would be as forgiving as Wade.

We split up at the end of our street as he went toward his house and I went toward mine. I waited on the porch, hand on the doorknob, till he reached his door and turned back. I waved at his smile, then went inside, feeling better than I had in weeks.

"How did it go?" Alex asked from the couch. She had her feet propped up on the footstool. Had she moved since I left?

"Well . . ." I sat down beside her. "We're friends with Wade again."

She smiled. "Good." Then she cleared her throat and tried to act like she didn't care. "'Cause we're out of eggs." Her focus returned to the cop show on TV. From the music, I surmised that the hero was closing in on the murderer. Most episodes ended with a neat bow—a rectified wrong. The predictability was comforting, but life had more nuance than good versus evil, cop versus killer.

"Hey, Alex," I said, drawing her attention away from the show. She was going to think I was crazy. She looked at me expectantly while I searched for a way to explain. "You remember the night you went to

Wade's bar, when you told me that I didn't do anything for myself and that's why I was so obsessed with you?"

She swallowed. "Yeah . . . and I'm really sorry about that. I was drunk."

"I'm not mad—mainly because you were right. I was clinging to helping you because I couldn't help myself, but . . . there's something I want . . . there's something I want to *do*."

The plan had cemented itself over dinner—one last chance to get everything I wanted.

To keep the family tradition alive.

To live up to my mother's expectations.

To save the farm from foreclosure.

To be brave and stand up for myself.

Alex turned the television off. "Are you going to spit it out before next year?"

I looked at my palm. The words had faded, but the sentiment remained, as if the ink had been an invisible tattoo. *Don't run.*

"I want to be the Elswood Man of the Year."

THIRTY-ONE

"'The Elswood Man of the Year—or the EMOTY, as it's commonly referred to—is a competition that includes four events, ranging from fine arts to athletic talent, to charitable contributions. EMOTY candidates must participate in all four competitions, which account for fifty percent of their total score. The additional fifty percent comes from Elswood-resident votes. The candidate who earns the most points will serve as the Elswood mayor for the next twelve months.'" Alex sat at the kitchen counter. Papers covered the granite surface. "So to become the mayor of this ridiculous town, you have to win all these competitions, and people still have to vote for you?"

I understood her frustration. The Elswood Man of the Year wasn't an easy competition.

Most participants began planning the moment last year's winner was announced. There were a lot of hands to shake, people to impress, and charity events to host. Though Jonathan Callaway had won for the past five years, that didn't mean everyone else was out of the running. Rodney had eyed the coveted prize for years, as well as Joseph Wilkinson, the man who claimed his family had been in town the longest. Wilkinson owned and operated the local hardware store, and used it to schmooze everyone he could.

It'd be difficult to make up enough ground to win in less than three weeks—nearly impossible, especially for someone with my reputation. But that was what I'd thought about Alex getting out of trouble, and a miracle had been delivered because Wade was a terrible son. Maybe luck would find me twice . . .

"It says you have to throw a charity party. How are we going to throw a party? We have no money, no friends, and no prospects of having either anytime soon. *We're* the charity, Felicity."

I stood over her, scanning the page about entrance qualifications. *Any resident of Elswood, Ohio, living within city limits for at least three years can be nominated to participate by a member of the Elswood council.*

Having a Y chromosome was not required—just preferred, apparently. Even as I felt relief, my eyes caught the words *Elswood council.* Five women, each from the founding families, chose an EMOTY participant. They almost exclusively nominated a fellow family member, ensuring the town's leadership remained a member of the privileged few. The competition was designed to be elitist, to show off the contributions of the top-tier families while the peasants watched.

Cheryl had nominated Jonathan for the last eight years. Lydia Wilkinson nominated her grandfather, and Margo, with no other male relatives, had no choice but to nominate her cousin, Patrick. Last year, Patrick hosted such a horrendous charity party that the charity had to pay money to settle the lawsuit that ensued. He was a town embarrassment, but at least he had a proper last name. The same couldn't be said for me.

"Um . . . Felicity. We have a problem," Alex said, regaining my attention. "Okay, we have many problems, but how will we get enough people to vote for you? I like being outcasts, but it's not exactly going to win you any votes. And neither will Revenge Incorporated, may it rest in peace." She looked at the ceiling and made the sign of the cross.

"We'll win people over, one person at a time."

"We don't have time. The voting happens in sixteen days."

"Then we'll divide and conquer. You're in charge of the charity party. Figure out what we have to do, and start planning." I paused, not sure this needed to be said, but I added it anyway. "Every EMOTY candidate supports the high school football team or the athletic program, which earmarks the money for the football team. I was thinking we'd pick a different charity to support."

"I'll try to come up with something," she muttered, then placed her forehead directly on the countertop.

So dramatic, I thought, but I didn't have time to reassure her that everything would be fine; there was too much to do. I grabbed my purse.

"Where are you going?"

"I need to convince a council member to nominate me." I made it sound simple, but it was probably my biggest EMOTY challenge. It wouldn't matter if I couldn't throw a football, create a work of art, or drive a tractor in the derby. Not if I couldn't enter the competition.

The market looked the same as ever, except a single windowpane had a fresh coat of paint. Most people wouldn't notice, but I did. It was a glaring reason for why my EMOTY ambitions would fail right out of the gate. But I had to try. I took a deep breath and went inside, my first time since Alex's incident.

I pulled the nomination paperwork from my purse. Of the five people on the council, only one hadn't chosen an EMOTY participant yet.

I stood in the back of the line and waited my turn to approach the checkout counter.

"Do you have a minute, Mary?" I asked when I got to the front. She was ringing people up, something I hadn't seen her do in years. Jessica must be sick.

Mary looked up, saw it was me, and sighed in exasperation. "What now?"

Off to a great start. I shuffled the papers in my hands. "I wanted to speak to you about the Founders' Day Festival."

"Your booth was removed from the festival for a reason. You almost got the entire thing shut down. There are people waiting, so either buy something or move along."

Jeez. I grabbed a pack of gum from the shelf next to the conveyor belt. I'd read once that the items near the checkout counter were more expensive on purpose. I put the gum on the belt and let it slowly move toward Mary as I spoke, buying myself time.

"It's not about my booth—though if you'd reconsider, I wouldn't complain. Actually, I was hoping you'd nominate me for the Elswood Man of the Year competition."

Mary nearly dropped the gum as she scanned it. "You can't be serious."

"I am."

"Why on earth would I nominate you?"

I'd spent the entire walk to the grocery store ruminating on this question, but I still didn't have an answer. I had more enemies in town than the rival high school football coach. I wasn't welcome in the diner, the ice-cream parlor, the spin studio, anywhere the Callaways had set foot, or at town events. At this point, Glen would've made a better EMOTY candidate. Mary had no reason to help me with this. She'd be better off choosing Ben, Sam, or her husband, Jeff, again. They'd all be respectable choices.

She put the gum in a bag, and I snatched another pack from the shelf to buy more time.

"It's a charity event. Are you really going to say no to charity?"

I'd anticipated her next question, and once again was well aware that I should've had an answer. "What charity are you representing?"

I cringed as I said, "Haven't decided yet."

"Is this a joke to you?"

"No," I insisted at once. "I'm very serious about winning the competition. I have a lot to make up for in this town, and this seemed like a great way to start."

"And you decided that, almost two weeks out, you'd enter the most prestigious town event that you have no chance of winning?"

"Well, when you put it like that, it doesn't look so good, but—"

"If you won, you'd be the mayor."

I swallowed. Yes. That part-time job would fall to me, but I intended to take the position seriously should I be selected. "If Callaway can manage to do it, then so can I." She didn't look convinced, so I spoke to my qualifications. "I'm a small-business owner who has a vested interest in the town's success. I'm incredibly frugal and wouldn't waste money on unnecessary expenses, so taxes wouldn't increase. I also know everyone, and while they may not all like me at the moment, I'm well aware of everyone's history. I could successfully navigate all the squabbles and issues." The more I thought about governing the town, the more appealing it became. Stable income, with time for the farm and an opportunity to right the town's wrongs. So much good could be done if someone other than Jonathan Callaway had the authority to enact ordinances and enforce the rules. "I'd end corruption and restore law and order."

"You?" Mary choked, either from shock or a repressed laugh. "You? Felicity Lavigne, the leader of that deplorable revenge business, are going to restore law and order to Elswood? In what world would anyone believe that?"

My newfound reputation for trouble would be a problem. "I—"

"It's the *Man* of the Year Award, Felicity."

I sent three more packs of gum her way. "There's nothing in the rules that says the winner has to be a man. With three granddaughters, don't you want to help me overcome this sexist tradition?"

"I don't want to help you do anything."

Normally, this would be the moment when I gave up. She wasn't going to help me. She had already done enough by dropping the charges against Alex and accepting me at her dinner table, though I suspected her Midwestern manners had demanded the second.

But I wanted this. Somewhere in heaven, my mom was telling me not to give up. I had to at least try, for both of us, and my first challenge was Mary. If I could convince her to forgive me—well, at least *sponsor* me—it would be the first domino in my path to victory.

Don't run.

I passed her another pack of gum, then went for it, nothing left to lose. "I'm sorry about what happened with Alex and the market. I should've apologized the moment I saw you in the sheriff's office, but I was scared and upset. I needed to defend Alex, even though she'd done something wrong. She's my family, and she thought she was defending me when she vandalized the window. But that's no excuse for what she did. If you give me some time, we will pay for the window and the labor costs to repair it."

It was the apology I'd never gotten from the Callaways or the other parents whose children vandalized and stole from my blueberry farm. I knew how upset I was about that and how angry Mary must've been at Alex. Unlike the parents of the Blueberry Bandits, I'd apologize and make amends. I'd be better than they were. My mother had raised me to be an honest, good person, and though I hadn't lived up to her expectations these last two months, I intended to start trying.

Mary looked me over, scanning the gum and setting it aside. The checkout line wrapped around the counter and into the cereal aisle, but nobody voiced any irritation. I wasn't the only person terrified of Mary Londergan.

"Does Wade know you're asking?"

I shook my head. "He has nothing to do with this. It's my thing, and I'd appreciate it if we kept it that way."

She paused for a moment, as if seeing me for the first time. I thought I saw something like respect in her eyes, but it was so fleeting I couldn't be sure. Then she held out her hand. "Give me your nomination papers."

I handed them across the counter, practically jumping. Elation ran from my head to my toes. The impossible had happened: I'd worn down Mary Londergan. I almost asked the next person in line to take a picture and document the moment as she signed and dated the form.

"I don't intend for my participant to lose. You'll be representing the Londergan name, after all."

"I'll do my best."

"Then I suggest you get my son involved." She handed the forms back to me. "You're going to need help with the football toss. That boy has an attitude that would make a saint slap him, but he can throw one hell of a spiral."

"I'll see if he'll help."

I didn't sound hopeful, but she pursed her lips like she already knew the outcome. She passed me the bag of gum. "That'll be $45.50."

For gum? Was it that everlasting Willy Wonka kind? I couldn't afford that. But I was so overcome with relief that she'd agreed to sponsor me that my fingers dug through my purse for my credit card.

Mary swiped the card and gave me a receipt. I hovered by the counter, looking over the charges.

"Out of curiosity," I asked as she turned to the customer behind me, who had been waiting far too long. "What's your return policy?"

"Goodbye, Felicity."

Mary's tone made me head straight for the door.

THIRTY-TWO

The sun peeked over the clouds, but Emerald Lane looked as asleep as its inhabitants. The manicured grass and flower beds set me on edge. Places like this, where the owners projected a perfect life by paying others to labor on their behalf, made me uncomfortable. The landscaping fees alone would cost several hundred dollars per month.

I pressed the doorbell several times, the way an impatient driver honks in traffic. My dramatic plan—the grand announcement of my entrance into the town's most prestigious competition—wouldn't resonate unless I saw their faces when they learned the news.

Because I'd pieced things together since the Londergan family dinner.

Jeff had barely spoken to me, but I knew precisely who had drawn up those construction plans: J&C Enterprises.

I kicked myself for not figuring it out sooner. Only one person had the means and motive to reassign the tax lien against my property, and his initials didn't stand for Jesus Christ. That knowledge had led me to Emerald Lane at six in the morning, ready to toss the challenge flag into the air and settle this score once and for all.

Jonathan opened the front door still wearing his pajamas. Cheryl hovered behind him, and I tried with all my might to forever remember what she looked like without makeup or hair products. I should've snapped a picture of her disheveled appearance.

"Here," I said, unceremoniously handing Jonathan Callaway a bucket of blueberries. I'd picked them fresh that morning. Two handfuls. No more, no less. "That should get you started."

He balked. "What are you talking about? What are you doing at my house?"

Oh, so he didn't like people showing up announced on his property. Hypocrite—maybe he should've kept better control of his kid.

"You're interested in the blueberry business, right?" I gave them no opportunity to respond. "Well, this should get you started. Grind the berries down and harvest the seeds. You may need to freeze them for three months or so, and then blend using plenty of water. That'll make it easier to get the pulp. Plant the seeds in acidic soil, but don't give them too much sunlight. In another few months, they'll be big enough to plant in the ground outside. In four to five years, you'll have blueberry bushes." I turned as if to leave but paused and held up a finger. "And don't forget to water them, but not too much. You don't want to flood the roots. It's a delicate balance. I'm sure you'll master it in a next decade or so."

Cheryl peered into the bucket like she expected to see snakes. "Why would we want to plant blueberry bushes?"

"Not sure—but then again, I'm not the one trying to buy a blueberry farm."

Their eyes widened in unison. *Yes, I uncovered your plan,* I thought smugly. It may have been revealed through sheer dumb luck, but I knew the Callaways' intentions all the same.

"That's the same amount of seeds my family had when they started Lavigne Blueberries a century ago. Debt repaid."

I brushed my palms against each other as if wiping away all the residue of our feud.

Jonathan stepped onto the porch, looking tempted to launch the bucket at my head. "Why start our own farm when we can have yours? I'll give you three, four months tops before you have to sell that house and all its land . . . We've got first dibs due to the tax lien."

His tone irked me. "Have you ever grown blueberries, Jonathan?"

He looked puzzled and I took that as a no.

"It's hard work. I don't think you'd like it." The Callaways—never ones for manual labor. "That's why the land was transferred to my family in the first place."

"Your family stole it."

"No," I said, shaking my head. "Your family *lost* the land—the same way you're going to lose your fancy position and all the benefits you've reaped for the last half decade." I descended the porch steps, then turned, as if something had slipped my mind earlier. "Oh. And, Jonathan, when I win the Elswood Man of the Year competition, the first thing I'm going to do is reinstate Laurel as town treasurer and restore the payment deal we had for my property taxes." I tossed a blueberry into my mouth and chewed. "And there's not going to be a damn thing you can do about it, because we both know that reassigning the lien to J&C—clever name, by the way—wasn't legal."

I stalked off into the dawn, ready to pull off my best and final revenge scheme.

For the next week, Alex and I did nothing but plan for the Founders' Day Festival. We talked about the competition from the moment we woke till the moment we went to bed. Last night, Alex had fallen asleep at the kitchen table going over prices for food and drinks at our still-unplanned charity event.

Turned out, nobody in town wanted to donate food or support us. The festival directors may have accepted my nomination packet—begrudgingly, because they didn't want to oppose Mary—but there was a big difference between tolerance and support. The latter was going to take a while.

"They told me I had to pay twice the usual fee," Alex muttered, eating her mashed potatoes. "Something about being a liability. Like I would destroy a stupid tent." She paused, then smiled. "Though

I probably will now. We'll see how good Jake's tents are when they have no tops."

"Alex," I grumbled, thoroughly exhausted, "we talked about this. We're not doing anything illegal, immoral, or unethical to win." I had been adamant that we do this the right way, even if it meant losing. I had to set a better example for her, the way my mother had for me.

"Just a couple slices to the fabric. Maybe I'll take all his cables and ropes and tie them in a big knot like the wires of a child's PlayStation console."

"We don't need a tent anyway." I crossed my fingers, hoping that it wouldn't rain that night. Bad luck had to end at some point, right? I changed the subject before Alex could protest my decision. "Did you pick a charity yet?"

"Can't come up with anything. Nothing seems good enough. I know you said that I couldn't support the Elswood High School football team, but what about their rivals?"

"We want people to vote *for* us, not hate us forever."

Alex stabbed a fork into her chicken. "Fine, then. I think bats are endangered. We'll support them, and maybe in the future one of them will bite Jake on the head as he's putting up one of his dumb tents."

"That's the spirit." I let the bat comment go, hoping she wasn't serious. I checked my watch, leg shaking under the table. Ten minutes after three. I couldn't stall anymore. EMOTY planning would have to wait.

"I'm heading outside. Why don't you take a break and watch television or something?" I hoped she wouldn't watch from the window. I didn't need an audience.

"Can't," she said. "Too much to do. Those bats aren't going to save themselves." She smiled wickedly. "Say hello to Wade for me."

I ignored the comment, listening to her laugh as I went outside to meet Wade. I had the capacity for only one troublemaker at a time.

Beyond Wade's back porch sat a hundred feet of grass before the yard disappeared into the woods. I'd put on my sneakers and tied my hair back, and was ready to learn about a sport I'd avoided my entire life. But apparently, throwing a football was essential to being considered a man in Elswood. I couldn't avoid it any longer.

Wade had tied a tire to a tree branch—or had it always been there? We measured off twenty-five feet from the tire, and I marked the spot with a flip-flop.

He had five footballs by his feet and one in his hands. "Have you ever thrown a ball before? Outside of gym class, I mean."

He was already aggravating me. "Yes. I played softball for three years." I'd been on the Purple Team, but I didn't add that.

"Really?" There was a pause. "What position did you play?"

"Shortstop."

He didn't fall for it. "What position did you actually play?"

"Fine. Right field."

Everyone knew that was code for *worst player on the team*. The coaches had placed me in right field hoping that nobody would hit the ball in my direction. I, too, had hoped that the ball would avoid my coverage zone. Sports weren't my thing, but my mom had wanted me to try everything, even if it scared me.

Wade handed me a football.

Why was it shaped so weird? I examined the oblong leather ball, not knowing the first thing about how to hold it.

"All right, Dan Marino, throw the football straight through the tire."

"Who's Dan Marino?"

"Don't worry about it, just throw the ball."

I gripped the football like I didn't want to be touching it. "You haven't told me how."

"I need to see what I'm starting with."

"Wade . . ."

"Throw it."

"Fine." I pulled my arm back and threw the ball. It soared about twenty feet and hit the ground. It was a testament to how seriously

Wade took the sport that he didn't laugh. Something told me that wasn't a good start.

I bit my lip, waiting for his reaction.

"That was a joke, right? That was you trying to be funny?"

"Wade!" I wished I had faked how terrible that throw was, but it was very, very real. "It was my first time."

"Okay," he said slowly. Measured. Calm. What was with him? "Well, that was terrible. I think we need to manage expectations of how well you're going to do at the football toss."

"I don't need to win; I just don't want to embarrass myself."

"Oh, don't worry—you're not going to win."

I took a deep breath to rein in my temper. I had never expected to win the football toss. There were four other participants all vying for the EMOTY Award, and unsurprisingly, all of them had played football in high school. Two of them, Rodney and Jonathan, had played in college. Winning was out of the question, but my goal was to get one toss through the target zone. Just one. I didn't think I was asking too much.

Though Wade's reaction shook my confidence.

"Are you going to make comments, or teach me how to throw?"

He stepped closer to me, eyebrows coming together as he looked me over.

"Turn toward me, feet shoulder-width apart."

I shuffled my feet. Evidently, I didn't do it right, because he bent down and moved my feet for me.

"You're so pushy."

I rested my hand on his shoulder to steady myself.

"That's your stance. Now . . ." He picked up another football. "See the laces? You have to put your fingers in the right position to throw it properly. If the ball is going all over the place, then it's not going to make it through the circular target."

He adjusted my fingers, spreading them between the white laces. I dropped the ball twice before I learned to tilt my palm back and balance it.

"Throw it again."

I twisted, turning my shoulder so I could bring the ball back, remembering those years of softball I had blocked out. I stepped forward and threw it at the tire. It sailed farther this time but was still too low. It bounced on the grass a few times before stopping.

"Pitiful."

"I'd like to see you throw it through the tire. If you're going to ask me to do it, you should be able to."

He gave me that devilish smile, reached down, and picked up a football. He turned, repositioned his feet quickly, and threw. The ball went straight through the tire as easily as if the opening had been the size of a house.

My pride deflated. I'd thought that was going to get him off my back, but now I had only made things worse.

"Twenty bucks says you can't do it twice."

He muttered something under his breath that I didn't catch, and threw another football. It sailed through the tire. Then he threw another, then another. He was in his element, relaxed and calm, but I could see the excitement in his stance. He tossed the football like he was the greatest player in the world. He was that Dan Arino person.

"Show-off," I muttered as we collected the footballs from the yard. I had little doubt that if he were competing in the cherished football toss, he'd wipe the floor with the other guys. He threw like he knew what he was doing—no hesitation, no second-guessing, all instinct.

"Do you think that if you hadn't gotten hurt, you would've played in college?"

He set the footballs on the ground next to me. "Who knows? My dad thought so, but I don't think I would've made it in college."

"Why not?"

"Can you see me trying to keep up in college classes?" He smiled at the thought, then shook his head. "But this isn't about me. You're the quarterback now."

My breathing picked up as he moved to stand behind me. He ran his hand down my arm before lifting it over my shoulder and holding it in position.

When he spoke, his mouth was right by my ear. "You need to throw it hard, like I'm standing directly across from you and you want to hit me in the face."

"I can imagine that."

He chuckled, and his breath tickled the back of my neck. I almost dropped the football again. "As this arm comes forward"—he moved his arm, dragging mine with his—"you have to follow through, shifting your weight to your left foot."

He tapped my left thigh before pulling me forward to show me how to follow through. "Understand?"

"Huh?" I asked, unsure what he had said. All I could think about was his left hand traveling from my thigh over my hip and resting on my waist.

He laughed near my ear. I turned and saw his face only inches from mine. He knew what he was doing. *Bastard.* I pursed my lips. "Are you going to take this seriously?"

"I'm not the one with my mind in the gutter." He still hadn't removed his hand from my waist. *Not fair,* I wanted to say, but I was determined to learn how to throw this oddly shaped ball through the tire. To do so, I'd need him to stop distracting me.

I shook his hand off my body and tried to ignore him. Gripping the football tightly, I pictured Wade's head across from me, right in the middle of the tire. Then I threw.

I missed, but it was closer that time. It ricocheted off the rubber and landed in the grass.

"Better. There might be a hint of athletic talent in you, after all," Wade observed, moving to stand across from me. There was still humor in his face, but his eyes had turned serious. "Again."

I threw the football until my arm ached, probably another fifty times. I rubbed my shoulder as Wade assessed my chances. I'd gotten better over the past hour, but I was nowhere near competition-ready. The ball had somehow found its way through the tire twice, bouncing in each time. "Luck," Wade had said. "Sheer dumb luck."

I couldn't disagree, but luck was better than nothing. I decided to take it as a victory, jumping in excitement each time the ball wobbled through the tire.

Wade didn't look nearly as enthusiastic. "People get really into the football toss. Screaming, cheering, booing . . . they will do their best to distract you. Are you going to be able to handle that and still throw the ball?"

"Yes," I said, wiggling my arm so the muscles wouldn't cramp.

He leaned closer. "I only ask because you seemed a bit distracted earlier . . ."

"Oh, did I? I wonder whose fault that was?" I grabbed a football and threw it at him. Of course he caught it before it could strike his stomach. He laughed as I stalked home, my hatred for this sport completely justified.

THIRTY-THREE

"Attention, ladies and gentlemen!" Mayor Callaway stood in the gazebo. The crowd, already several hundred strong, looked on. "It's my pleasure and honor, as your esteemed mayor, to welcome you to the Elswood Founders' Day Festival!" The loud cheering rang in my ears.

"Why are people so happy? It's nine in the morning," Alex muttered beside me. Our tempers were running high. I hadn't slept last night due to nervousness, and Alex, well . . . she hated crowds, and sunshine, and seeing other people happy. So we were all out of sorts at the opening of the festival entrance, waiting for the mayor to do his job and cut the red ribbon running across the front. Of course, he was making a show of it, going on about the town's history and why Elswood was the best place in America. I rolled my eyes. These people hadn't come here to listen to him prattle on about the town's founding; they wanted fried food and carnival games. Glen had worn his elastic waistband shorts for a reason.

"And while I hope all of you enjoy the festival, I would like to especially wish all my fellow EMOTY competitors good luck." He paused, looking over the crowd. "Well, except one of them."

"Hey!" Alex shouted as my face turned red. It didn't take a genius to realize he was calling me out.

Using normal-size scissors, Callaway cut the ribbon, and people stormed inside the entrance. Having no choice but to walk with the crowd or get bowled over, Alex and I made our way to the first EMOTY competition: the art auction.

The arts and crafts tent had been a favorite of mine as a kid. Stations were scattered inside, selling items and teaching kids how to make soap and jewelry, as well as paint and play an assortment of drums. A spaghetti necklace I'd made at the age of seven still hung across the corner of a mirror in my mom's bedroom. While each EMOTY contestant had to create and auction off an artistic project, I couldn't part with that noodle masterpiece, so I clutched a painting from second grade. Two decades later, I didn't know what the painting depicted, but Alex said to claim it was "abstract" if anyone asked.

I sat onstage with my fellow contestants. Occasionally, my shoulder bumped Patrick's.

"What's your art project?" I asked, trying to make conversation.

He pointed to a table across the stage.

"You built a table?" I couldn't keep the astonishment from my voice. Since when did Patrick do anything impressive? I'd counted on beating him easily in this competition. My second-grade painting, which I thought came across as cute, would be overshadowed.

Patrick puffed up his chest. "Pretty much. I didn't build it, but I glued beer-bottle caps on top. If you squint, it looks like the state of Florida."

"Lovely," I said, hoping to end any further communication between us. I should've let Alex draw more penises on his cars.

A crowd formed under the tent. I wrung my hands, trying to ease the nervousness turning in my gut. Being onstage, the center of attention, sent my anxiety spiking.

Margo claimed the microphone stand. She introduced the contestants, who all received cheers, except for when she sighed and said, "And that's Felicity." She waved her hand at me as if I were an afterthought. Polite, but admittedly quiet, applause followed my name.

Rodney presented his art project first, explaining that he'd spent the entire year handcrafting a chair. *Bullshit.* I'd seen that very chair in Amelia's Antique Shop a few weeks ago when I vandalized it. Alex had sat on it when she adjusted all the price tags on the furniture.

"Let's start the bidding at a hundred dollars!"

It sold for $150. That was $149 more than Alex had written on the blue sticker attached to its leg. Rodney's chair was followed by Patrick's vaguely pornographic table. It fetched a respectable $85.

Mayor Callaway received cheers and well-wishes when he took control of the microphone and called Timmy onstage. As I slumped in my chair, hand to my forehead, people bid on the father-son pair to sing "Take Me Out to the Ball Game."

How did that qualify as art? And why did someone bid $200 for it? They couldn't even keep it. They sang the worst rendition of the song I'd ever heard. Timmy forgot the words halfway through, but nobody laughed at the nine-year-old.

My only solace came from thinking about how embarrassing this would be for Timmy when he grew older. Somebody should upload a video of it to the internet. No, with my luck, the video would go viral by tomorrow morning.

I started hyperventilating as Wilkinson showed off an impressive desk he'd constructed from cherry wood. The town seal had been burned into the top. As with every year I'd been alive, Wilkinson earned the highest bid of the day, $350, which of course I had to follow with my painting. Did they choose this presentation order on purpose to make me look bad?

My feet shuffled toward center stage. I held out my painting.

"What's it a painting of?" Margo asked, taking the paper. She squinted and turned the painting in every direction.

Her guess was as good as mine. "It's an abstract."

She stared at the squiggly lines for a few more seconds, then shrugged. "Let's start the bidding at fifty dollars."

Way too high, Margo. I had nowhere to go but down, and I was going to sink like the *Titanic.*

"Do I hear fifty dollars?"

I'd made Alex promise not to bid, not wanting her to spend money on my elementary school artwork. I had plenty of clay pots, necklaces, and drawings she could have for free. She'd less than politely declined, telling me that I wasn't meant to be an artist, no matter what my mom had said.

The silent crowd seemed to agree with her.

"Uh, forty dollars?" Margo asked.

The audience remained silent. No bids. Nothing. Zero. None.

My ears burned with embarrassment.

"Twenty dollars?"

Oh no, oh no, oh no. Humiliation sank into my stomach. Nobody was going to bid on my artwork. I wished for the fortitude to stand defiantly on the stage, unconcerned with their opinions of me, but I'd never been someone capable of withstanding criticism. A single slight, something as minor as another driver honking at me, would strike my soul and deeply affect me for hours. This crowd of disapproving spectators directly hit my self-esteem.

"I'll take it for a dollar," Glen said, biting into a turkey leg wrapped in bacon. He spoke with his mouth full, juice dripping onto his chin. "Never had any fancy artwork before."

Before I could object, Margo yelled, "Sold!"

My soul seemed to leave my body like blood seeping from a wound. The thought of my painting, my precious second-grade painting, being in Glen's possession made me want to vomit. Unbidden tears wet my cheeks. I dashed off the stage. Laughter and boos rang out, sounding harsher in the enclosed tent space.

The tears didn't stop until I was home, in my kitchen, with a blanket around my shoulders and a warm cup of tea in my hands.

"The people in this town don't appreciate good art," Alex said, sitting across from me. She had caught up to me before I made it through the festival exit. "Pablo Picasso could've been on that stage and they would've booed him."

Her attempt to lift my spirits, while touching, did little to placate me. And she knew it. Alex always discerned my mood before I said a word. For all her many talents, her perceptiveness ranked near the top.

I clutched the blanket tighter around my shoulders. She leaned forward in her chair, elbows on the table. "I'm thinking we put something in the water supply. This time we won't just dye the kids blue—we'll get the whole town. Or I've got this idea that involves poison ivy—"

"No," I interrupted her before she could continue. "I told you, no more of that."

"They started it. We have to do something."

She stood and paced the length of the kitchen. Her footsteps calmed my apprehension because I still had one person in my corner. "I appreciate the sentiment, but I meant it when I said we were doing this the right way." I couldn't say I wasn't tempted to go along with her plans to temporarily make myself feel better. But deep down, I knew revenge wouldn't solve anything.

This competition wasn't about the town, or the votes, or the events that I would surely lose. The EMOTY meant putting myself out there for the world to see—even if that meant criticism. For so long, I'd been quiet, afraid, and unwilling to risk anything. But not anymore. I'd see this competition through to the bitter end.

Because I was done running away from the things that scared me.

The art auction had been a disaster because it was a gimmick—I'd taken the easy road, choosing an elementary school painting over rolling up my sleeves and doing the work to win.

People noticed effort, or lack thereof. They'd want a mayor with fortitude, someone who could make hard decisions and solve problems. To earn their votes, I'd need to show them how hard I'd work as their mayor. No more choosing the easy way out, or quick fixes, or disingenuous behavior. That had never been my style anyway.

If I was going to fix my reputation, make my mom proud, and keep the farm from foreclosure, I'd have to eat some humble pie.

I smiled, thinking that pie was exactly where I should start.

The smell of baked blueberries and sugar drifted through the house. I lifted the pie dish from atop the oven, where I'd set it to cool, and headed toward the door. As I passed Alex's bedroom, I stopped and said, "I'll be back in an hour or so. If you're hungry, there's leftover hamburgers in the fridge."

She was on her bed, scrolling through her phone. "Where are you going?"

"Somewhere I should've gone a while ago." I didn't say more than that. Alex might not understand, but this was something I had to do.

"Whatever," she said, sitting up and grabbing her backpack.

Now it was my turn to ask. Anytime Alex left the house after six p.m., I got nervous. "Where are *you* going?"

"Bingo starts in twenty minutes."

"Bingo?" I asked, laughing. Oh, I needed that laugh. It had been a horrible, rotten day, but the thought of Alex sitting with a bunch of middle-aged and senior Elswood residents, hovered over multiple cards and randomly shouting "Bingo!" was too much for me to handle. Like any proper Midwestern town, bingo was expected at any carnival, fair, or festival, but it wasn't something I'd pictured Alex doing.

"You're going to play bingo? Are you in your mid-sixties with four grandchildren?"

"Shut up." She smiled at how hard I was laughing. "I think of it as gambling."

"Have fun," I said, still amused as she went to the door. I followed her outside, a huge smile on my face. I planned to tease her about this for quite a while.

My next stop was Wade's house. He, too, inquired about the blueberry pie's destination, but I kept it from his reach. "Can I borrow your dog?"

"In exchange for the pie? Absolutely."

"You're not getting the pie, Wade."

He stopped trying to snag the dish from my hand. "What do you need Juno for? Alex already walked her three times today."

"There's someone who could use a little canine company." I didn't want to say more than that. I wasn't doing this for attention or to win back the love of the town. I wasn't even doing it for my mother, though I knew she'd approve. This one was for me.

The quiet ten-minute walk into town, with the copper sun hovering at the horizon, brought me into the present. My lungs filled with fresh air. It was a perfect evening. I almost didn't want to knock on Edith's front door, hating to be inside on a night like this.

But with a leash in one hand and a pie in the other, I hit the wood several times with my elbow. Edith answered, surprise etched across her lined face. "Felicity?" Her eyes found Juno through the screen door, and she said, "Why, hello there, sweetheart."

Juno's tail wagged in response to her high-pitched voice.

"Juno and I were wondering if you wanted some dessert?"

Edith adjusted her pink robe. The sun was setting, but it wasn't after eight yet. I'd made an effort to get over there before she went to sleep. "It's blueberry," I said, holding up the dish.

Edith smiled and held the screen door open. She petted Juno as we entered.

"I thought we could cut a slice for Charlie, too," I said. "Do you have any pictures of him?"

THIRTY-FOUR

"Alex, what's this?" I held up the pink T-shirt, twisting it to see the front and back. We needed to leave for the football toss in five minutes.

"Your football-toss uniform," she muttered like it was obvious. "Someone called last week asking about the color and what number you wanted."

"And you just happened to pick the number four?"

"I thought that was your favorite number," she said innocently. A little too innocently.

"No, but it does happen to be Wade's. It's his old jersey number."

"Oh, I didn't realize." She turned away to hide her grin.

"Alex . . ."

"It's a number, Felicity. All the other participants had an old football number they were using, and seeing as I couldn't track down a jersey number from your Purple Team softball days, I picked the number four. It's no big deal." She handed me a water bottle. "Now, if you and Wade see this as a sign and get together, that wouldn't be a big deal, either."

I took a sip of water, shaking my head at her absurdity. I must've told her a hundred times we were just friends.

My stomach dropped when we walked through the festival grounds toward the football toss. The crowd was five people deep, all standing on tiptoes to see into the roped-off space before them. Didn't these people have anything better to do?

Alex followed me to the front, and I ducked under the rope. Five targets stood across from us—tall, inflatable maroon targets with holes cut into the center. The holes were roughly the same size as the middle of a tire.

"Felicity! Felicity!"

I turned. Lauren and Ben were standing behind the rope. Between them were the girls, each wearing a pink shirt with white lettering. When I approached them, I read the shirts.

ELSWOOD (WO)MAN OF THE YEAR

The girls waved at me. Willa jumped excitedly, her cotton candy nearly falling to the ground.

"Turn around, turn around," Lauren told the girls. A large **#4** was printed on the back. I looked pointedly at Alex. Her feigning-innocence routine was up.

She shrugged, unashamed. "Okay, so there may have been some coordination with the jersey number."

I returned my attention to the girls. It meant a lot that there would be friendly faces in the crowd. This day was already better than the art contest. But I didn't share in their enthusiasm. Expectations had to be managed for my upcoming performance.

"Greet your fans later. It's time to focus." Wade purposely shoved into Ben as he ducked under the rope. "If you're going to wear that number, there are expectations of success."

"He's referring to Brett Favre," Ben said to the girls.

"Who's that?" Kate asked.

"A very successful quarterback."

Wade's jaw clenched, but he ignored them, grabbing my arm and leading me a few steps away. He pulled a football from the bin. I would have a total of sixty seconds to throw as many footballs as I could through the circle.

Wade placed the football in my hand, spreading my fingers across the laces. "Remember, aim and throw. It's simple: Aim and throw."

I nodded, trying to pump myself up. The loudspeakers were blasting Kip Moore, so that helped. Should I stretch? Jog in place to loosen up my muscles? I looked around at my opponents to copy their pregame routines.

Immediately to my left was the mayor, in a navy University of Akron jersey. He didn't look the least bit nervous. Last year, he threw seventeen footballs through the target. I hadn't attended the spectacle, but that was the rumor around town.

Next came Joseph, and then Patrick, who wore a ridiculous headband that only accentuated his receding hairline. He was doing high-knee jumps but looked like an idiot. My eyes traveled past Patrick and found Rodney on the far end. There was no mistaking his scarlet-and-gray OSU jersey. He tossed a few footballs, letting the crowd cheer him on.

Wade snapped his fingers, reclaiming my attention. "It's going to be fine," he said. I looked behind him, where Mary and Jeff had joined the group. This was not going to be fine. I was going to embarrass myself, at a charity game where people were eating fried dough on sticks and barn animals were a hundred feet away.

"What if I don't get any footballs through the target?" I whispered. I ran a hand through my hair, messing up my ponytail and not caring. I had bigger concerns than how I looked.

"You will." The corners of his mouth twitched as he looked me over. I knew that smile; my stomach fluttered. "Do you need some help getting into the correct throwing position?"

I flushed, remembering that day in the yard. "Control yourself. There are children present."

Wade winked and my stomach dropped. Oh man, this was not good. My legs felt like Jell-O, and I forgot for a second what football was.

The sun beat down on me as the loudspeakers cut the music and Margo's voice rang out. "Ladies and gentlemen, please welcome our five

Man of the Year candidates as they compete in their second event: the Elswood Football Toss!"

The crowd roared. I covered my ears. People took this way too seriously. If I didn't have to participate, I wouldn't have been caught dead at a football toss. Now, that fried-dough stand was a different matter . . .

Margo introduced each of the candidates again, the loudest cheers coming for Rodney and the mayor. I didn't cringe at the boos that came after my name; that was expected. But even among the boos came a couple of cheers. I turned to see Lauren, Ben, Jeff, Alex, and Wade's nieces cheering for me. Mary clapped twice, then abruptly stopped. My heart swelled with gratitude.

"Let's go, Felicity!" Lauren yelled, encouraging the girls to clap, which they did. I smiled at them in their pink shirts, trying not to think about how I was going to fail spectacularly.

"Focus," Wade said, standing right behind the rope. "Left foot back an inch."

I followed his directions, nervous that everyone was watching. The crowd might have cheered for the others, but all eyes seemed to be on me. Shoulder to shoulder, everyone moved to get a better glimpse of the only female participant.

I breathed deeply, trying to ignore the taunts that were being hurled in my direction. Whoever said there was no such thing as bad press hadn't pissed off an entire town in Ohio. They couldn't have hated me more if I'd been wearing a University of Michigan jersey.

It had been so much easier with just Wade, me, and the tire swing. My mind wandered back to Wade's hands on my waist, his lips at my ear, and the feel of his chest against my back. Abruptly, I jerked, trying to dispel the sensation of his hand roaming down my arm.

The loud buzzer pulled me from my daze. Sixty seconds. People screamed—whether it was for or against me, I couldn't tell. I was so nervous that I tossed the first football wide by about ten feet. It hit the mayor's target instead.

Laughter erupted through the crowd.

My second toss was closer, but still two feet below the target. My third toss sailed wide again. The clock ticked, and my hands shook.

"Slow down!" Wade yelled above the crowd. "It's fine. Slow down."

I pictured Wade standing across from me and threw the ball to him. It hit the red target but didn't go in the hole. I tossed another, and the football struck the outside rim of the circle but bounced outward. I groaned. Why couldn't that have gone in?

In my anger, I looked down the line. Next to me, the mayor sent two footballs straight through his target. My spirits deflated.

Thirty seconds left.

"Aim and throw! Aim and throw!"

I grabbed another football, adjusting my fingers as Wade had taught me. I took a deep breath and threw it, pretending that the center of the target was the mayor's face. The moment I let go, I knew it would be close. My breath caught when the football bounced into the side of the circle, then disappeared. Yes! I jumped, hands in the air, celebrating as the crowd cheered behind me. Maybe they didn't hate me so much, after all.

I twisted around to smile at my cheering section, but Wade pointed straight ahead. "Keep going!"

Quickly, I grabbed another football and threw it. Then another and another. All told, I got two footballs through the circle before the buzzer sounded.

I smiled triumphantly, though I'd no doubt done the worst of all the participants. But I didn't care. And neither, it seemed, did the crowd.

I raised my arms in victory, and the roar nearly knocked me over. Dang, no wonder Wade had liked this feeling so much. *This must be what it's like to be an athlete.*

Whack!

Something hard hit the side of my face. I fell to the ground, clutching my cheekbone, where the football had struck me.

My knees collided with the grass, and my vision spotted around the edges. I couldn't make much sense of what was happening. I felt someone's hands on me, trying to get my attention, but all I could hear was Wade shouting.

"What the fuck, Callaway!"

"It slipped."

"Alex, no, get back!" Wade yelled.

Alex? Oh gosh, what was happening?

"Felicity, can you hear me?" a closer voice asked. Ben sounded calm, even as the shouting continued around us. Wade unleashed a tirade of swear words. I hoped his mother wasn't listening.

"Is she okay?" a voice squeaked.

"He hurt her, Daddy."

"We'll help her!"

"No, girls, get back. Give her some air. Lauren, will you grab them?"

Fingers gently touched the side of my face. I winced.

"I don't think it's broken," Ben said. I blinked, and he turned to get someone's attention. "We need an ice pack."

"I'm okay," I said, registering what had happened: Jonathan Callaway had thrown a football at my head when he realized the crowd had turned in my favor. The sharp pain seemed to grow worse. I lifted my fingers to examine my cheek and make sure it was still there.

"Felicity, can you sit up?" Wade's voice inspired me to move. He looked relieved as he hovered next to Ben.

"What's the date?" Ben asked.

"August twenty-fifth."

"What's your address?"

"1 Clementine Lane."

"Who's the mayor?"

"Jonathan Callaway," I said with disgust. That jerk had tossed a football at my head. It was bad enough that he and his wife were sabotaging my business to steal the farm, but now they were physically injuring me.

"Can you count back from ten?" Ben asked.

"Why are we playing fifty questions?" Wade cut in with impatience.

"I'm making sure she doesn't have a concussion." Ben's eyes flicked to Wade with annoyance. "But I think she's all right." Ben took something from a person behind him with a thank-you. He placed the ice pack on my face. The cold, along with the pressure, made me jump.

"Give me that," Wade said, snatching the cold compress from Ben. "Don't need a medical degree for an ice pack."

Ben shook his head, but stood and left my field of vision. Wade moved closer, pressing the ice pack to my face as I sat in the grass. I lifted my hand, holding his as he put it on my face.

I vaguely worried that everyone was staring at me. Only, there seemed to be someone missing.

"Where's Alex?" She should have been hovering, and in a worse mood than Wade. My heart raced and I tried to stand, hoping she hadn't done something to get herself into trouble. If she knew Callaway was responsible for hurting me, I doubted anyone could restrain her.

Wade pushed my shoulder down, keeping me seated. "She's fine. Mary's got her. I'm pretty sure the two of them scared the mayor all the way to Michigan."

"Maybe the wolverines will get him."

"Fingers crossed."

The initial shock had worn off, and I was feeling better. I wiggled my jaw; it hurt, but the searing pain had faded. I was going to be fine.

With that realization came an idea.

"Get my doctors, Wade."

He sat back on his heels and looked slightly offended. "Is it getting worse? Do you need Ben?"

I smiled, then stopped when it made my cheek hurt even more. He was so sensitive about his older siblings. "No, Wade. My doc*tors*." I emphasized the plural, and it clicked in his head.

He removed his hand from my shoulder so he could turn and yell, "Bethany!" He chuckled with relief. "We're going to need a full assessment, Doc. Get your team ready."

THIRTY-FIVE

We took the long way toward the fried food, stopping once so Wade could play a game where he threw a baseball at a bunch of bottles. He won a stuffed bear, and Willa cried when he offered it to me instead of her. And so, with empty hands, I waved goodbye to Ben, Lauren, and the girls.

"They like you," Wade noted as his family disappeared around the corner.

"You sound almost upset about that."

"I'm not used to spending so much time with them." He put his arm around my shoulders as we walked. I almost rebuffed him because we were in public, but I realized it was Wade. Hopefully, people wouldn't think anything of it.

"I'll see you guys later." Alex turned to leave, too.

"Where are you going?" We hadn't eaten any junk food yet. I'd promised to show her the fried-food mile and the ice-cream stand that had cones made out of funnel cakes.

"Your charity event isn't going to plan itself."

"Since when are you responsible? Planning can wait for an afternoon."

"Not when the party is tomorrow."

"Can I get a hint?"

Her silence over the party worried me. She hadn't told me anything for the last week.

"It's a surprise." She smiled, and it only made my suspicions grow.

"At least tell me what charity you picked."

"What part of *surprise* don't you understand? Honestly, you might have a concussion, after all."

She departed, leaving me with Wade, which I suspected was the real reason for her sudden sense of responsibility. She pushed the two of us together at every opportunity. I glanced up at Wade, drawing slightly away from his body to see his face. I blinked twice, pretending the sunlight had affected my vision. With those blue eyes, Wade didn't need any help from Alex. "Do you know what she's planning?"

He shrugged, pursing his lips together. He knew. He absolutely knew. Alex wouldn't keep anything from Wade.

"Tell me." It sounded like the demand it was.

"I'm not risking Alex's wrath. She told me that if I spilled her secret, she'd make sure I never spoke again."

That sounded like Alex. Before I could start pouting, he drew me closer, causing my feet to shuffle to keep up with his longer stride. "Let's get you a turkey leg, Marino. To celebrate your football success."

"I came in last place and got a football thrown in my face." I brought my hand to my cheek as I spoke, gently probing the bruise. The sting had been replaced by a dull ache. "Not exactly a performance worthy of a celebration."

"So what you're saying is, you need alcohol? I think they put beer in the corn dog batter."

I shook my head in exasperation, but let him lead me toward the food stands, adding, "What do you mean 'you think'? You know full well Vanessa puts beer in everything."

After three corn dogs, plus the half I gave up on in favor of the fried Oreos, Wade thought he felt a slight buzz. They didn't call it beer-battered for nothing. We sat at a picnic table and consumed more calories than we'd need for a week.

But with a stomachache, sugar rush, and a bruised cheekbone, we called it a day when the sun began to set. I'd had enough excitement for a month, but still had the charity party and a tractor derby to win. I couldn't wait to crawl into my bed and get a good night's sleep.

The sun was a deep copper when we reached our street. Unlike after the dinner with his parents, Wade didn't veer toward his house, but took the porch steps two at a time till he was standing beside my front door.

"You're quiet."

"Hmm," I responded, unsure what to say. "I'm worried about whatever Alex is cooking up. I shouldn't have given her free rein to plan the party."

"She'll be fine. She knows how important this is to you." He stepped closer. "Alex is lucky to have you."

"Thanks." I tried to take a step back, but my feet betrayed me, listening to my heart rather than my head. "Not just for the compliment, but for everything. Helping me with the football toss, saving Alex when she was arrested, putting up with your mom, who I know you have a hard time being around. It means a lot to me. I don't know what I'd do if we weren't friends."

His smile faltered for half a heartbeat. "I didn't do all those things just out of friendship." He paced to the other side of the porch, then back toward me, running a hand through his already-disheveled blond hair. "I've tried to tell you a few different times—"

Oh no. "Wade—"

"Just let me get this out. It seems like something I should say at the airport, like right before you get on a plane, but you don't travel anywhere and . . ." He laughed nervously. "And even if you did, I probably wouldn't say it right. I've been trying to show you for a while now, and the message isn't getting through the way I want it to." He ceased his pacing so that he was standing right in front of me. "With our history, I think it's best to come right out and say it."

"Wade—"

"I *like* you, Felicity. As more than a neighbor, or a friend, or the guy whose truck you borrow and ding the shit out of. You're smart and you're . . . you're funny, not to mention beautiful, and when we're not fighting about whatever stupid thing I did that day, I like being around you. I think we should be together."

I took several steadying breaths. Part of me wanted to reach up and pull his mouth to mine, kissing him until everything else faded away. It would be easy to be with Wade, the man I'd been attracted to since I was a teenager. And here he was on my porch, telling me everything I'd waited so long for a guy—*for him*—to say. I almost couldn't believe it when I said, "Wade, we can't do this. I can't do this."

"What? Why?"

My heart clenched. I didn't want to hurt him. Why did I always have to hurt him? "I can't be with you because . . ." The words caught in my throat. I didn't want to say it out loud, but I had to finally acknowledge what the two of us would never get past. "She didn't like you."

"Who?" He thought about it for a moment. "Your mother? This is about your mom?"

I rushed to explain. "I don't think I can be with someone she didn't like. It feels wrong. I need some time to figure this out."

"You know my mom isn't your biggest fan, either, and I'm willing to overlook it." He continued pacing. "We're like Romeo and Juliet—disapproving families, but they live happily ever after."

"They both die at the end." If he wanted to impress me with his knowledge of Shakespeare, then he needed to actually read the play. But that was an argument for another time. "Your mom dislikes me because every time she sees me, Mary is reminded that she didn't teach her son right from wrong when you were a teenager."

"I'm not that guy anymore. I've changed. If your mom met me today, she wouldn't even recognize me. Hell, your mom probably wouldn't even recognize *you* after the last few months. You've changed more than me at this point."

"I'm just . . . I'm not comfortable dating someone she didn't approve of."

"Felicity, I can't win here. Your mom's dead. Even if I wanted to apologize to her, I can't do it."

"I know. That's the problem."

Wade clasped his hands behind his head. "So that's it? You won't move on. Everything has to stay exactly as it was when she died."

"I . . . I . . ." What could I say? Any changes felt like I lost her even more. Like she was sand slipping through the floorboards of a beach house. Each step knocked more sand away—sand I couldn't recover. "Yes."

"If that's the case, how do you explain Alex?"

"What?"

"I thought you were getting better when you brought her home. I thought it was a sign that maybe you were ready to move on. For years, you didn't let anyone in that house. You barely let me inside to fix your heater, and that was only because you were about to freeze to death. So how do you explain bringing home a random teenager and letting her live with you in your mother's house?"

"You wouldn't understand."

"Try again."

"Alex wasn't some random teenager," I said, searching for the right words. "My mother sent her to me—or, at the time, I thought she did. I still think that, actually, no matter what Alex says."

"What in the world are you talking about?"

"She has my mom's cell phone number. When my mom died, I didn't keep the number, and from time to time, I called it. Checked in. Complained. Cried. I left voicemails on the phone, and the night before I met Alex, I'd been complaining about failing to catch the blueberry thieves. Then Alex called me from my mother's number asking for help."

I doubted he understood. I barely understood and I'd lived it. Eventually, the silence grew to be too much. "Say something, Wade."

"You brought a stranger to your house because of a cell phone number?"

"Yeah."

"A stranger who had committed several crimes?"

"Yeah."

"And you really think your dead mother had a hand in this?"

"All I know is that things were different with Alex. I felt like my mom had put us together because we needed each other. It was easier with her."

"So if I had a different cell phone number, we'd be together right now?"

"You're making it sound crazy, but it's not."

"Oh, no, it's plenty crazy." He turned toward his house, running a hand over the stubble on his jawline.

I stepped toward him. "I'm not ready, Wade. I need more time."

"If you don't like me, you should just say it."

"I do like you, but . . ." I didn't know how to finish that sentence. There was nothing I could say to him that would make this right. I couldn't lie and say I didn't have feelings for him, but I also couldn't say that we should be together. "Why can't we be friends for now? I don't want to lose you."

Ashamed, I started crying. I wrapped my hands around my torso. I so badly wanted to tell him what he wanted to hear. I wanted to hold him, kiss him, tell him that we would try. Hurting him caused me pain. But I couldn't. I just couldn't.

"I'm sorry," I cried out. "I'm so sorry, Wade."

His demeanor softened at my tears. He reached out and ran his hand through the ends of my hair. A sad smile crept to his lips. "Me too." He sounded like he meant it.

"But we can be friends, right?" The desperation in my voice was easy to hear. "Please, Wade, promise me we can still be friends." Besides Alex, he was the only friend I had.

He nodded once, and my panic subsided to just below hyperventilation.

"Good," I said, overcome with relief. I wiped my cheeks with the back of my hand. But even as I stopped panicking, he gently detangled himself from my grasp, wished me good night, and left me alone on the porch.

He walked home and disappeared inside his house. I gripped my hair, wanting to yank it from my head. I wanted to scream. I wanted to shout until the whole world listened to me, until my brain finally listened to me.

Why couldn't I let her go? Why did my grief have me trapped inside my head? I'd broken Wade's heart all because I was too weak to overcome my phobia of the future. I stomped hard on the porch, putting all my anger and frustration into the house that had become my prison. I wanted to let it go. I *needed* to let it go.

I made a noise that I didn't recognize before I clamped my hand over my mouth to suppress the sound. The last thing I wanted was for my neighbor to rush over, thinking I was being murdered.

But the rage had to go somewhere.

I kicked the spindle that held a section of the porch railing up. I kicked the wood again and again, not caring about the pain in my foot, putting all my weight into stomping. I wasn't crying, but only because I was breathing so hard my body wouldn't let me.

Five more kicks, and *bang!* The wood splintered, my foot shooting through the center.

Ow, ow, ow!

I jumped, clutching my foot. The front door opened.

Alex's eyes widened as I stood frozen on the porch, gripping my hurt foot. She looked at the broken porch spindle, then back at me. "Felicity?" Her tone made me think she was frightened. "What's wrong?"

The tears started flowing again. She took my arm, guiding me inside the house. I limped, wincing at the pain in my foot.

"Everything," I said in answer to her question as she shut the door.

I had broken everything.

THIRTY-SIX

I didn't have time to fall apart. It was Thursday, and I had to throw a charity party in twelve hours, which was unfortunate because I'd sat out every party since my mother died. I didn't celebrate Thanksgiving or Christmas, and I certainly didn't kiss anyone on New Year's Eve because for the past three years I'd been fast asleep by 10:00 p.m. I'd become every bit the hermit everyone had always assumed I was.

Those were the days, I thought as I got into the shower and began worrying about today's celebrations. When I'd signed up for the EMOTY competition, the charity event seemed like an abstract concept, not something I'd actually have to host. I'd made up my mind three times over the past week to cancel the entire thing, but couldn't get the words out. Alex had been diligently planning the party, telling me how great it was going to be. Every time she mentioned it, my stomach turned queasy. But she was so excited, and she rarely showed enthusiasm for anything legal, so I had no choice but to let the party go on.

A breeze came through my bedroom window when I got out of the shower and got dressed. I went to the kitchen to make a cup of coffee, trying to avoid thinking about the incident last night. Alex had gotten me some ice for my foot, which, in addition to my face, had also turned black and blue. She'd hovered over my bed until I calmed down, only leaving once my tears had stopped.

"I'm so stupid," I said, limping down the stairs. All I did was create a bigger mess to clean up. I ate my egg sandwich and ruminated over how I'd fix the porch. With my luck, that spindle was integral to the house's foundation, and I'd have to dish out thousands to fix it. Even now, when I sat at the kitchen table, the house seemed slightly tilted.

Alex spoke to someone in the yard. I went to the window and saw Jeff Londergan standing beside a truck filled to the brim with various materials and a handful of guys from his construction crew.

Alex gestured with her hands. "I want it to go from the porch to the bushes."

Jeff moved to achieve a better vantage point. "In a square?"

"Yeah, but not too far over here, because that's where Wade's setting up the bar."

My stomach clenched at his name. I took a deep breath, moving away from the window, desperately trying to keep myself together. I drank my coffee and scrolled through my phone, pretending I had something to do other than anxiously pace and break out in stress hives.

Alex came inside, face flushed. She straightened her shoulders as her eyes glanced over me, assessing my mood. She'd checked on me twice last night; I'd heard the stairs creak outside my bedroom door.

She didn't say anything as she grabbed a Pop-Tart and put it in the toaster. She bounced from one foot to the other, watching the timer impatiently.

I hated to dampen her enthusiasm, but it was for the best. There were five charity parties tonight, and people were unlikely to attend ours. She may have noticed that I wasn't the most popular person in town. "Don't stress about the party. It's okay if it's not perfect. The few people who show up won't mind."

"People are going to come. You're such a worrier."

I wished I could share her confidence, but the last time I'd had a party at the house, I was nine, and the only kids who came had parents in the PTA with my mom. Obligation was a heavy motivator, and it didn't make for the most fun party. I'd hidden in my room after the first hour, and my mom had to deliver a slice of birthday cake to my door.

"Be prepared to eat leftovers for the next month or so."

"Felicity, I've got this. You were in charge of the football toss and the art auction and everything else, but this is my thing, and I'm going to do a way better job than you did at any of those."

"Hey!"

"All you have to do is make the pies, wear the costume, and try to mingle without crying or curling into the fetal position."

I let the insult go unchallenged, mind already occupied. "Costume?"

She grabbed her Pop-Tart and put it on a paper towel. "It's no big deal."

"Is everyone supposed to wear a costume?"

"No, just us."

"Alex—"

"The whole night is going to go smoothly. Just have the blueberry pies ready. Three of them. No reason why we can't get some promotion for the business out of this."

A honk came from outside. *Who's here now?* "Got to run," she said, heading toward the door, taking a bite and spilling crumbs on the clean floor. "Everything is going to be fine. Don't freak out."

After several deep breaths, I stood and took out the glass mixing bowl. What could Alex need with three blueberry pies? She hadn't asked me to cook anything else. Three pies wouldn't sustain the hundred people she was expecting.

But at least she'd given me something to do. I focused on preparing the desserts, reading the recipe twice even though I knew it by heart. My mom had gotten the recipe from her grandmother, who had once operated the bakery in town. My mom had added a few tweaks to the original, though. Her hastily written instructions ran down the right side.

I scooped flour into the measuring cup and used a knife to swipe away the excess, but baking didn't calm me as it usually did. I was too keyed up, nervous about tonight and still emotionally spiraling from yesterday's travesties. When it came time to make the filling, I accidentally added an extra cup of sugar.

I listened to the commotion outside as I rolled out the pie crust, careful to leave pockets of butter in the pastry dough. Alex had the construction crew working hard. They were hauling and hammering until my temples hurt. Swear words flew like leaves in a storm, most of them coming from Alex.

Curiosity bubbled under my rib cage. What were they building out there? I let the pie crusts set in the fridge for a few hours, choosing to read a book over going outside to see what all the fuss was about. My anxiety would only get worse if I saw the damage. Better to stay inside, baking, and pretending the rest of the world didn't exist.

I hopped around the kitchen, careful to keep my foot from bearing too much weight. When the oven dinged, I put the pies inside. There was nothing left to do but wait and see if they turned out half as good as my mother's.

"Alex, I'm not wearing this."

She admired herself in my bedroom mirror, twisting to see every angle. "It's part of the theme."

"I didn't realize this party was the sequel to *The Shawshank Redemption*." I tossed the material on the bed. "I didn't even dress up for Halloween as a kid."

"If you don't wear it, we won't raise as much money through the auction." She turned from the mirror to give me her innocent expression. I knew that look well. She always got her way when she tried to look harmless. Mainly because I was a pushover.

But I drew the line at wearing orange jumpsuits.

"No way."

"It's for charity, Felicity. Between the jumpsuit and your bruised cheek, we'll raise a fortune."

"No."

She took a deep breath like she was arguing with a child. "Tess is stopping by any minute to go over the details of my plea bargain before the party. Put the outfit on and meet me downstairs."

And with that, she left my bedroom. I sputtered, not sure how I'd lost the argument. I cursed as I put on the jumpsuit that Alex had conveniently written my name on. *Ugh.* And to think there was a time when I'd found her clever. If I had any sense, I'd refuse to be bullied by an eighteen-year-old who depended on me for food and shelter.

Instead, I adjusted the sleeves and looked in the mirror. *Kill me now.*

Alex had printed off flyers last week and put them up around town. The vague advertisements stated that the party began at 7:00 p.m. Elswood residents were not the kind of people who showed up late in order to be cool. If the invitation said seven, they'd be here at seven. Assuming anyone came at all.

The Callaways would throw their annual Elswood High School Football Benefit Dinner, which cost attendees $200 per plate. Their dinner started promptly at 5:00 p.m. so everyone could head over to Rodney's tailgate party for cheap beer and flag football at 7:30 p.m. That would leave very few people to attend our humble event.

A knock on the front door sent me downstairs. Alex opened it, and I hovered behind her as Tess stepped inside, dressed in a short navy dress with nude heels. She looked us over and rolled her eyes. "My job is to keep you out of orange jumpsuits, and you guys are wearing them willingly."

"Just preparing for the inevitable," Alex said. "It's not like you went to Harvard Law School."

"It's for the party," I said, giving Alex a severe look. My face felt warm.

I followed them into the kitchen, but Tess turned and said, "This discussion's just for Alex and me. I'm not letting her waive attorney-client privilege this time. With a plea deal, there are more sensitive matters that need to be addressed."

"Oh." I stopped in my tracks and glanced at Alex.

She shrugged and muttered, “Lawyers.”

I wanted to provide emotional support but also keep Alex on her best behavior. With me out of earshot, who would rein her in and ensure she pled guilty? I considered myself Alex’s moral compass at times, and occasionally she needed more than a gentle reminder which direction north was.

“She’ll be fine,” Tess said, sensing my hesitation. She took a seat at the kitchen table. “In theory, everything has been worked out. We’ll be about thirty minutes.”

Begrudgingly, I prepared to leave, but not before I turned to Alex and said, “Behave.”

“Whatever.” She took a seat across from Tess. I left the kitchen, resisting the urge to stand behind the wall and eavesdrop. That wouldn’t be fair. I’d trust Tess to handle Alex. Surely in her profession she’d encountered more difficult clients than my eighteen-year-old roommate.

I retreated to my bed, opened my Kindle, and tried not to think about what was happening in my kitchen.

THIRTY-SEVEN

I'd reread the same paragraph five times, not retaining a word of it, when Alex stomped up the stairs. She knocked once on the door. "Only five years in prison," she announced, coming to sit on the bed.

"Don't mess with me."

She smiled at the harshness in my voice. "I still have to go in front of the judge, but the prosecutor's recommending two years of probation and a hundred and fifty hours of community service. Tess thinks the judge will go for it."

Relief coursed through me. No jail time. Community service. Probation. The best we could've hoped for. Even if the party turned out to be a total disaster, I wouldn't care, because this was a good day. Alex and her future were more important than whatever happened tonight. I didn't have the heart to ask about high school. I'd get her enrolled whether it was court ordered or not.

But there was another item she didn't mention. "And the fine?"

I set the Kindle on the nightstand, preparing for the worst. Her hesitation only increased my fears. Why wasn't she saying anything?

"It's . . . substantial. The department store is pissed that I hit the security guard."

I closed my eyes, pleading with the universe that it wasn't too outrageous. "How much?"

"A little over three thousand."

Not great, but better than the five grand they'd originally wanted. "Once the bail money is returned, we'll put it toward the fine."

"What about the rest of the property taxes? We need that money to keep the house."

"Your future is more important than a house." *Even this one.* "If I win the EMOTY and become mayor, we'll have a stable income for the next year. If you continue to help with the blueberry field, we could make it work."

"It's too risky. You could lose—"

"I've already decided."

The house and all its possessions paled in comparison to Alex's health and happiness. I'd known this since she tried to rob the grocery store, when she'd left and the home's emptiness had threatened to swallow me. I couldn't live without having her in my life.

"Thanks," she muttered, eyes not leaving the comforter and cheeks turning pink. Her gratitude would've appeared underwhelming to most people, but for Alex, accepting help from anyone caused her to grow self-conscious and embarrassed. She didn't think she was worth it, but I knew differently. I'd spend my last dime to help her, the same way my mother would've given up everything she had for me. That was what people did when they loved someone unconditionally.

She searched the room for a distraction and found the clock on the nightstand. "We need to get moving. Our guests will be arriving any minute. I left a paper bag on the table downstairs. When you're done hyperventilating, come outside and greet your guests."

"Very funny," I said, but the paper bag was a decent idea.

It was 7:15 by the time I gathered enough courage to leave my bedroom. I couldn't hide inside forever. I took the trash to the curb, determined to make the trip outdoors serve a purpose. Music drifted toward me as I slammed the lid shut. I headed to the backyard, prepared to tell Alex that I looked ridiculous and was changing after she took one photo. Rounding the side of the house, I stopped dead.

Holy cow.

This was not my backyard. At least, not the backyard I remembered. A solid-wood dance floor ran from the back porch to the blueberry bushes. Soft blue lights hung from the trees and were woven into the bushes, breaking against the backdrop of a russet evening sky. Platters of food lay across two long tables, which ended next to a bar. Rachel twisted the cap off a bottle, then poured liquid into a row of glasses.

But what really surprised me were the people—at least eighty stood in my backyard.

"Do you like it?" Alex asked, coming to stand beside me. She had a glass of something bubbly in her hand.

"How did you do this?" There was awe in my voice.

"You really like it?" She jumped a fraction of an inch.

"Alex, who wouldn't like this?" My eyes swept over the crowd, growing watery at the sight. It wasn't just that I liked it—my mom would've *loved* it. Seeing her backyard filled with people enjoying themselves, eating, dancing, and laughing. And all this for charity. She would've been thrilled.

"Why are you crying?"

"I'm overwhelmed," I said. "It's awesome."

Alex beamed. "And that's just the beginning. Wait until you see what we're auctioning off." She took a smug sip of her champagne. She'd earned it, but there was no chance I'd let her drink alcohol at this event. The whole town knew she was underage.

I snatched the plastic flute from her hands.

"Thanks," I said in response to her outraged look. I didn't bust her on it, but said, "Stick to soda tonight."

We walked toward the buffet. My stomach grumbled, but I had about fifty people to speak with before I made it to the table. One after the other, they came up to me, wishing me well, laughing, and making small talk. There were so many people, including children, whom the Callaways didn't allow at their precious football dinner. As I spoke with Erin about her apple stand, more people came down the side path.

"You going to drink that champagne or carry it around all night?"

My heart sputtered at his voice. I turned with a mixture of a scowl and smile that I reserved only for him. Wade wore a blue-checkered shirt and dark jeans. I tucked a strand of hair behind my ear, feeling awkward. What would I say to him after last night? I hadn't emotionally prepared myself for another encounter—at least not this soon.

He raised his eyebrow when I didn't answer his question.

"I caught Alex with it. Champagne's not my favorite."

"Thought so." He took the champagne from my hand and replaced it with a shorter glass. "It's a margarita," he said, smiling at my inquiring look.

Smooth, Wade. Very smooth.

I took a sip, noticing that he'd remembered to put sugar on the rim. It tasted as good as it had the night we slept together.

"I'm surprised you came," I said, breaking the silence between us.

"There's free food a hundred feet from my porch. I'm not going to ignore that."

"Makes sense." I took another sip, trying to overlook the fluttering sensation in my stomach. I didn't need alcohol when I was around Wade. "I'm glad you came, though."

"Yeah?"

"I was afraid you'd ignore me."

"We're friends, right? This is what friends do." He leaned forward and whispered conspiratorially, "And don't tell anyone, but I'm trying to be more mature."

"Oh?" I chuckled at the thought. Wade? Mature? Those two words didn't go together.

"Laugh all you want, but I'm not the one wearing a prison jumpsuit."

"Another one of Alex's bright ideas." I pulled at my collar, trying to loosen it. "Zero idea what she's going for other than pit stains from the sweat."

Wade pinched his lips together, biting back his amusement.

"What's that look for?"

"Oh, nothing. You'll figure it out eventually."

I stopped fidgeting. "Tell me what you know. Right now."

He rolled his eyes at my tone, then nodded toward a table between the bar and the buffet. "Go have a look."

I marched toward the table that was getting a bunch of foot traffic due to its location. My blueberry pies were on display.

The sign said Bid on a Pie.

People were eagerly writing on three pieces of paper, each upping the other's bid.

It was a silent auction, but that wasn't the problem. When I stepped closer, I noticed the sign had smaller letters written beneath: To Smash in Your Favorite Criminal's Face.

THIRTY-EIGHT

My muscles tensed in preparation for Wade's laughter. After last night's incident, he deserved to find amusement in my humiliation. But the laughter never came, and I didn't think it was because he'd made progress on that maturity declaration.

I turned, and he was staring at the table without the faintest trace of humor.

"Where is she?" Wade's eyes glanced over the dance floor and toward the buffet line. "Alex! Alex!"

She popped up like he'd summoned her. "Yes?" Her innocent voice.

Oh no. What else had she done besides sign me up to get a blueberry pie smashed into my face?

Wade snatched a piece of paper from the table. "This has my name on it."

"Does it?"

"Don't play dumb with me. You said that you were doing an auction for people to pie you and Felicity in the face. You said nothing about them bidding on me."

"Huh?" Alex took the paper from him. She pretended to read over the words. "Must have been a mix-up." She checked all three sheets. "But look at that—you're winning."

He wrenched the paper from her hands. People took several steps away from the table, likely in response to the tension radiating off him. "This isn't happening."

"It's for charity, Wade."

"That's not going to work on me the way it does with Felicity."

"Hey!" I crossed my arms with indignation.

"I'm not doing this," Wade said to Alex, ignoring my outburst. "Find someone else."

"People have already pledged money. It would be rude to withdraw now."

"You should've thought of that before entering my name without asking!"

His tone made me jump into the conversation. "Is it really a big deal? Go home, change your shirt, and it'll be fine. It's just some pie."

Wade's shoulders remained tense, but his tone softened when he spoke to me. "You're actually going through with this?"

Now I was trapped. I couldn't say no, because then he wouldn't have to participate, either, and I'd already said it wasn't a big deal. Of course, saying yes meant that Alex got her way and I had to endure humiliation as an enemy paid money to shove a blueberry pie in my face. Either way, not good, but the chances of Alex letting me out of this weren't high anyway.

I squared my shoulders. "Yup. And so are you. The three of us are in this together."

"There." Alex sounded satisfied, like she knew my words would settle the matter. Wade glared at her and, after a moment, walked away, head shaking in anger.

"You should have asked him," I admonished her when he was out of earshot. "You should have asked me, too."

"You both would've said no. And we need Wade to participate. He'll bring in the big bucks." She glanced around the dance floor and the tables. "We needed to draw a crowd if you're going to win this thing."

I followed her gaze. There were over a hundred people in my backyard. No doubt all of them were willing to pay money to hit me in the face with a pie. "If smashing a pie into my face is the only reason people came, then it's not really a victory."

"You have to give the people what they want, Felicity. That's the first rule of success." She eyed the glass in my hand. "So drink up and prepare yourself, because the auction ends in one hour."

With that, she stepped away, leaving me next to the auction table. Glen hovered over the sheet with my name on it. "Do you guys take credit cards?" he asked.

"Credit card, personal check, a bucket of IOUs—whatever, Glen."

He shrugged, looking stumped, then upped his own bid from $1,100 to $1,200.

It's for charity, I thought, walking away from the table. *Damn, Wade was right: That excuse really does work on me.*

The sun had set, but the soft lights running across the blueberry bushes and over the dance floor illuminated the backyard like stars. Edith and I ate dessert, watching Alex threaten people so they'd donate more money. She was easy to spot—a bright-orange dot flittering around the backyard.

"She reminds me of your mother," Edith said, eyeing Alex over her cake. "She's very spirited."

"Hardly," I said, wondering if Edith's memory was going. "My mother never would've gotten arrested for shoplifting." Or broken into antique stores or clock shops, or vandalized a series of homes and cars. Edith didn't need the full list to know that Josette Lavigne had been an upstanding Elswood citizen. She'd never broken the law, not even to jaywalk across an empty street.

Edith took a bite of cake, mouth turning down. "Maybe not shoplifting, but she did light the gazebo on fire."

I dropped my fork. "What?"

"Took two fire departments to put out the blaze. They had to completely rebuild it."

"Edith, you're joking," I said, seeing no trace of humor in her wrinkled face. "There's no way my mom did that." Set the gazebo ablaze? Preposterous. Even Alex wouldn't have gone that far.

"It was in the papers and everything. Josette Lavigne: Fire Queen."

She smiled at my shocked expression. "Your grandparents were livid. They told her to go to college out of state so the heat would die down."

"'Fire Queen'?" I sputtered, unsure where to begin with my questions.

Alex tossed herself into the seat next to mine. "Threatening people is hard work." She glanced between Edith and me. "What are you guys talking about?"

"Nothing," I said, but a second later Edith chimed in with "Gazebo fires."

"Gazebo fires? Cool." Alex took a bite of my cake, three-fourths of it frosting. "Too bad nobody paid us to do that. Think of the message that would've sent to the town."

Edith's eyes crinkled. "Well, nobody paid her mother, either, but she still did it."

"Edith!"

The old lady shrugged, seeming to have too much fun with my reaction to look ashamed.

Alex looked at me with indignation. "You never told me your mom was cool."

"I . . . I didn't know." That was the truth. "And define *cool*, because setting things on fire is arson, not something to be imitated."

Edith reached for my hand on the table and squeezed it. "She grew out of her rebellious ways eventually."

"I wish I'd met her," Alex said, probably because she thought my mom would've given her some great revenge ideas. Burning down the

Elswood gazebo took conviction. I never would've let Alex do anything that symbolic.

Edith, always one to ruminate on the past, seized Alex's statement and began telling her about some of my mother's younger exploits. I half listened, not entirely sure we were discussing the same woman. Josette sounded like a badass. The mother I knew never would've cut off Simone's ponytail or popped all the school's soccer balls with a screwdriver.

I blushed, listening to Edith say that my mom had once had a nose ring. I'd need photographic proof before I believed it, but Alex was all ears.

"She's my hero," Alex said.

I groaned. I'd counted on Edith being above the revenge antics, and here she was, giving Alex the Josette Lavigne playbook. "She was never like that with me."

Edith smiled knowingly. "That's what happens—people grow up. They learn from their mistakes, and they try to help their kids avoid making the same ones."

My eyes moved to the dance floor, where Wade was dancing with his nieces.

He spun Bethany until she almost fell, and then he caught her. *People do grow up,* I thought, looking him over. Wade hadn't been a bastion of manners or good behavior, but he'd turned out all right. Better than all right, in my humble opinion. I glanced from Wade to Tess, who was dancing with Sam; then to Mary, whom I realized had donated all this food after one bite of the yams. The entire Londergan family had shown up to support me.

My chest expanded with sentiment, looking at all the people in my backyard. People laughing, smiling, and dancing. They didn't look like they were waiting around to see something bad happen to me. Perhaps not everyone in Elswood hated me as much as I'd thought. They did choose my party over the mayor's and Rodney's. That had to mean something.

"We'll continue this at another time, Edith." Alex popped up, interrupting my musings. "It's time for pie."

Alex, delighted at my reaction, took my hand and dragged me toward the auction table. Why was she excited about getting assaulted with a dessert? My feet followed her, no longer taking direction from my brain, which was still ruminating on the possibility that my mother had been a troublemaker—or at least not perfect.

Wade met us at the table. He checked the papers. "After all the shit you two pulled, how am I in the lead?"

Alex laughed as I checked the sheets. Alex was in third place with a $1,400 bid. I'd come in second at $1,950. But Wade's $3,400 bid was unlikely to be caught in the remaining ten minutes.

"Did you guys rig this?" he asked.

I tapped his sheet with my index finger. "I told you, we're done with that. This is legit."

"People really hate you," Alex said, like it was wonderful. I skimmed his sheet. The names were 90 percent women, all repeatedly outbidding each other.

"Jesus, even my mother bid," Wade said, staring at his list again. This time I laughed along with Alex. I gave him a sympathetic look, but then let Alex drag me onto the dance floor before the music died down. Several women pushed Wade aside so they could keep bidding.

When the time came for the grand event, Jeff placed three chairs in the center of the dance floor. I sat in the middle, and Wade took the seat to my left, grumbling, "I can't believe I'm doing this." Alex stood in front of us with a microphone she'd found. She cleared her throat.

"Can I have your attention?" She sounded nervous addressing the ever-growing crowd. It seemed like the entire town had shown up. When a few people continued to chat by the bar, Alex yelled, "Everyone shut up!"

I put my hand to my forehead, hoping they got the message before she yelled at them again. They had no idea whom they were messing with. When Alex thought something was important, she threw everything she had into it. The success of this party was evidence of that. I could never have done anything like it. Now, if only I could get her to channel that focus into something more productive, like school or her future.

"This evening is incredibly important, and not just because Wade is about to get pie shoved in his face." I smiled in his direction as several women cheered loudly, causing Alex to pause for a few seconds. Her voice grew more confident after the cheers. "A couple of months ago, I was homeless, with no one to turn to and nowhere to go, until Felicity took me in. And even though she had every reason to kick me out or tell me to get lost, she didn't. I've been looking for a way to repay her ever since."

I put my hand over my chest, steadying myself.

"I told Felicity that we were supporting endangered bats, but all proceeds from tonight are going to the Josette Lavigne Charity Foundation, a nonprofit that's been set up in her mother's name."

My heart stopped.

"The foundation will provide funding and mentors for local foster care children who have aged out of the system."

"Did you know about this?" I asked Wade, harsher than I'd intended because of the emotion in my throat.

He leaned in so I could hear over the applause. "We all helped out a bit—especially Tess, who did the legal work to set up the charity." My eyes brimmed with tears. It was hands down the nicest thing anyone had ever done for me. "But the idea was all Alex's."

"Can everyone join me in raising a glass to Felicity and Josette Lavigne—the first who is my best friend, and the second who by all accounts was the best mother in the world."

Cheers and toasts rang out among the crowd, but I wasn't listening. I'd already stood and wrapped Alex in a bone-crushing hug.

"Thank you." I squeezed her tighter.

I felt her shrug. "It's no big deal."

"It's a *very, very* big deal." I released her, not wanting to embarrass her further with my tears or displays of public affection. But she needed to know how much this meant to me. "Thank you, Alex."

Unable to stop myself, I reached out to hug her again. She ducked back, holding up a hand to stop any further attention. "It's not too late to save the bats."

"Just accept that you did a wonderful thing for me."

"Whatever." Alex took her seat at the far end. Smiling, I reclaimed mine, suddenly less concerned about the auction and pies. The lights over the blueberry field shone brightly as Jeff took over the microphone and revealed tonight's winners.

Before I knew it, Hilda had upturned a pie into Alex's face, and dark blue ran down her cheeks. The dish fell away, leaving Alex covered in blueberry sauce. I laughed, trying to ignore the mess. I would've laid a tarp under the chairs if I'd known.

The cheers were deafening as Ben, the highest bidder of the night, collected the second pie. He smiled at his younger brother, savoring the moment.

"You donated five thousand dollars for this?" Wade asked, disbelief etched into every word.

"It's for a good cause, and you've had it coming for years."

I would've thought Wade had caught a lucky break with his brother over the multiple women who had come closer to watch. But Ben pushed the pie hard, much harder than Tammy had, right into Wade's face. And he didn't stop there. Ben slid the plate until every drop of blueberry was either in Wade's face, hair, or running down what was probably his only dress shirt.

The clapping didn't stop, even as Jeff announced the winner for my pie. I took a deep breath and closed my eyes as someone pushed the baked good into the side of my face, then dragged it on top of my hair. The sensation gave me goose bumps.

Blueberries dripped onto my shoulders and to the ground.

People clapped and cheered as the three of us stood and bowed. Wade shook his head like a wet dog, sending berries in every direction. I dodged backward, laughing, and without thinking, licked my lips. The sweet, familiar blueberries had never tasted better.

THIRTY-NINE

The next morning, I slept in, exhausted from the party. It had been a long time—years, even—since I'd been to a party, especially one that lasted until after midnight. Living next door to Wade and his constant stream of loud, wild celebrations had not rubbed off on me.

I rolled out of bed and stretched, glad that today was the final day of EMOTY competitions. In six hours, as soon as I crossed the finish line of the tractor race, this competition would be over. The people of Elswood would vote, and win or lose, I was proud of myself for finishing. I'd worked hard, done things like throw a party—and a football—and allowed myself to be the center of attention. All things I would've never thought I'd have the courage to do.

Alex was banging around in the kitchen when I went downstairs.

"Morning," I said with a yawn. The milk carton sat by the sink, along with eggshells. "What are you making?"

She handed me a plate of french toast and a cup of coffee. She knew me so well.

After claiming my seat at the kitchen table, I poured a generous amount of syrup over the bread. I needed the calories as an energy boost after last night. "I think the party was a success." My fork broke off a piece, and I took a bite. She'd gone too heavy on the cinnamon, but otherwise it tasted great. "You did a good job."

She'd done an *excellent* job. The party was a smashing success, but I kept my compliments low-key, knowing that anything more would cause her to emotionally shut down. She couldn't take a compliment even if it was inside one of Patrick's cars.

"You're going to win." She added more syrup to her plate. "The pie-smashing put us over the top."

I didn't want her to be disappointed if the voting didn't go our way, though. If truth be told, I was partly trying to keep my own expectations in check. I pictured Jonathan's and Cheryl's faces when I held that trophy above my head and paraded it through town. I'd put it in the back of the wagon and take it on long walks through the square, shouting loudly that I'd won and they'd lost. I knew I was supposed to be humble and gracious in victory, but I wanted to shove it in their faces until they cried.

I took a sip of coffee, daydreaming about my victory laps, knowing full well I'd never actually take them. Oh, but I wanted to.

After breakfast, we lounged around the house until midmorning. The tractor derby took place on the Hendersons' field across town. Bleachers had been set up for Founders' Day activities, only this time, instead of parading around overgrown vegetables and livestock before the crowd, we'd be driving tractors as fast as we could. The first participant to complete five laps around the hay-bale course would win. Elswood residents treated the derby like the Daytona 500.

I pulled my pink jersey over my head and put my hair up. I planned to stick toward the back. My goal was to finish; I wasn't going to win. I could barely drive a car, and had failed my driving test twice before I'd cried and the driving instructor took pity on me.

I smiled in the bedroom mirror, looking over my outfit. I'd come a long way these last few months. Win or lose, I was taking Alex out to dinner and then celebrating with a rom-com marathon on the couch for the rest of the weekend.

I was halfway down the stairs when Alex screamed. *"Felicity! Felicity!"*

It was the kind of scream that made me jump down the rest of the stairs. I sprinted outside as she yelled, leaving the front door wide open.

"FELICITY!"

"Alex!" I ran toward her. She was crouching by the side of the road. What was wrong? Was she hurt? I was out of breath but ready to help her. My heart stopped when I saw what she was crouching over. *Oh no, oh no.*

Juno.

Alex's words came out in a rush, and I struggled to catch them all. "I was walking her. I tried to pull her back, but she was too far away from me and the car . . . the car . . ."

I knelt on the gravel. Juno whimpered and Alex cradled her head.

"I couldn't pull the leash back . . ." Alex's words cut off in a heart-wrenching sob.

Juno whimpered again, as if Alex's sob had doubled her pain. Juno squirmed closer to Alex, who only sobbed harder.

A plan. We need a plan. One second bled into the next until, for the first time in my life, I knew exactly what to do.

"Keep her as still as possible," I said, looking over my shoulder.

Wade's truck was gone. He must've already left for the tractor derby. I stepped into the road. One benefit of living in a small town: When someone stood in the middle of the street, cars stopped. I waited, heart beating frantically for someone to drive by.

Come on, come on, I thought. If no one came soon, I'd have to carry Juno to the vet's office. If Sean was even working today. Everyone would be at the tractor derby.

I shook my head, dispelling the panic. *One thing at a time.*

When a navy truck shot around the corner, I held up my hands and waved frantically. The truck stopped beside me, and the window came down.

"What's going on?" Rodney called out.

"We need help. It's the dog." I pointed wildly over my shoulder.

He looked past me toward the ground where Alex held Juno. "Shit." He put the truck in park, right in the middle of the road, and got out.

It took a minute to carefully lift Juno inside the truck. I sat in the back with Alex, who was having a hard time breathing. I clutched her as she held Juno.

Gravel kicked out from the tires as Rodney drove toward the vet's office. He clicked on his police radio. "Jason. Jason, come in."

Static responded before someone said, "What's up, boss?"

"I need you to get Sean Quinn from the stands. Tell him there's an emergency."

"What's wrong?"

Alex sobbed harder, and I was grateful Rodney didn't go into detail. "Tell Sean to get to his office right away. I'll meet him there."

The radio static clicked off.

"And get Wade," I choked out from the back seat. "Tell him to get Wade."

Rodney switched on his radio once again.

Tap. Tap. Tap.

The three of us—Wade, Alex, and I—were the only people in the waiting room. We sat in chairs that, once the shock had worn off, dug into our backs and, no matter how much we moved, never provided a comfy spot. I had thought I'd spent my last day sitting helplessly in a bland room, waiting for a medical professional to tell me what was happening. I hated feeling powerless, but this time I wasn't alone. I didn't know if that made me feel better or worse. I would've done anything to spare Alex from this pain.

Tap. Tap. Tap. Wade's boot struck the floor, his knee bouncing. He wasn't used to sitting still. I resisted the urge to reach out and put my hand on his knee to stop the movement. *Tap. Tap. Tap.* He was coping as best as he could.

I pulled at the hem of my pink shirt. When Wade had first arrived at the animal clinic, he told me to take his truck and go to the tractor derby. "You can still make it," he'd said.

I hadn't dignified his words with a response. For me, the EMOTY competition had ended the moment Alex shouted my name.

When Sean entered the waiting room, I sat up straight, feet on the floor, hands folded on my lap. He swiped his gray hair back from his forehead. He looked calm and collected—but not friendly.

The doctor who had confirmed my mother's cancer diagnosis had worn the same expression.

I bit the inside of my cheek, bracing for bad news.

Sean looked at the three of us; then his eyes focused on Wade. "You have one hell of a dog. It's a miracle she's held on for this long."

"When can I see her?" Wade stood. The chair scraped loudly against the tiled floor.

"She'll need surgery, if that's what you decide. Her front leg is broken in several places, and the MRI showed internal bleeding, so I can't . . . I can't promise that she'll walk again or that the surgery will—"

"Then we'll carry her," Alex said. She hadn't spoken since we arrived at the vet's office. "She doesn't need to walk if I carry her."

Sean once again addressed Wade. "It's your decision. I can try to repair the damage to her leg and stop the bleeding, assuming she makes it long enough for me to open her up—but given the potential for complications, we're looking at a long, expensive recovery."

"Do the surgery," Wade said with no hesitation. "I don't care what it costs. I want to try to save her."

Sean nodded. "You can come back and see her before I start in case she—"

"We're coming," I interjected so he wouldn't finish that sentence. Juno would survive. She had to—the alternative was too terrible to even think, let alone voice aloud.

I stood and turned, wondering why Alex hadn't already shoved Sean out of the way to get to Juno. But she hadn't moved from her chair. Her eyes flicked to the door, then to me, as if gauging whether she'd make it outside before I could grab her.

"Don't," I said, not risking any sudden movements, not even when she stood and took a step toward the door. She looked ready to run and never come back. "Alex. Don't leave."

Her eyes glanced toward the door once more.

"Juno needs you right now." Running from the pain had cost me the chance to say goodbye to my mom. Alex couldn't make the same mistake. I wouldn't let her. She wouldn't live each day with guilt and regret—the unknown clawing at her every waking moment. "I know it's hard, but we need to be strong for Juno." I held out my hand.

She retreated another step. "It's my fault. It's all my fault."

"It was an accident."

"She's hurt because of me." Tears ran down her cheeks. "She's gonna die because of me."

"No," I said, to both her statement and her intention to leave. "She's going to survive this."

"You don't know that."

No, I didn't. Having never been to veterinarian school, I had a very tenuous understanding of Juno's medical issues. But I had hope, and hope didn't require certainty or a fancy degree. The feeling had evaded me for three years, but now it coursed through my blood, each heartbeat making it stronger. I believed Juno would live. And I believed enough for the two of us.

"I need you to trust me, Alex." I took a single step toward her, hand still outstretched. "Can you do that?"

Her puffy, red eyes widened. For Alex, trust had to be earned. She'd never give it away lightly. She'd learned to rely on herself, her instincts, her survival mechanisms—and trusting another person contradicted her life experience. Had I done enough over the past three months to chip away at the distrust in her heart?

Her lower lip quivered as she searched my face. If all my suffering, all my loneliness and despair, had led me to this moment to ensure Alex stayed, then the pain was worth it. She'd regret leaving and not believing in Juno's strength—in *her* strength.

"Don't run," I whispered.

Tears dropped onto her cheeks, but slowly her hand, as if she was still deciding, moved toward mine. *Come on, Alex,* I thought, not daring to breathe. *Come on.*

When our palms touched, the tension in my chest unraveled. The earth, which seemed to have shaken for years, snapped into place beneath me.

Without a word, I led her from the waiting room, unsure what fate would greet us on the other side but knowing we were strong enough to face it.

FORTY

"Careful, Wade," I said, knowing he would be, but feeling so overwhelmed with concern that I reminded him anyway. I'd driven his truck at five miles per hour from the vet's office to the house, unwilling to risk hitting any bumps or potholes. We had precious cargo with us, after all.

Gently, Wade scooped Juno into his arms and lifted her from the truck. "That's my good girl," he said softly, cradling her against his chest. She looked so small. The pain medication made her groggy, and for the first time, her tail didn't wag when she entered my house.

"I've got everything set up in the living room." I pointed toward the spot where the coffee table used to sit. "Careful, Wade. Watch the couch."

"I'm being careful, Felicity. Jeez." His words had no bite, not when he'd been up all night with Juno after her surgery. He'd sat in a chair, never leaving her sight. He'd been unable to leave her even when Sean said pet owners couldn't stay at the vet office overnight. Wade had ignored him, and when Sean opened his mouth to insist, I'd said, "As long as Juno's here, one of us will be, too." I'd pointed to the floor for added emphasis. "If you have a problem with that, you'll have to call the police and have us escorted out in handcuffs."

Sean had muttered under his breath about insurance liabilities, but acquiesced all the same.

I maneuvered around the couch to supervise Wade as he set Juno on her bed.

My morning had been busy, a welcome distraction from the anxiousness that made my hands shake. I'd picked up all of Juno's prescriptions and her new dog food, then went to Wade's house to grab her water bowl; her favorite stuffed toy, which she enjoyed tearing apart only for me to sew it back together; and her bed, which I washed. Twice. Wade probably did laundry every couple of months, and I worried about bacteria accumulating on the fabric.

Another reason I'd insisted on Juno recovering at my house.

Wade kneeled next to Juno, scratching her head inside the plastic cone around her neck. Her eyes blinked slowly, but other than that, she didn't move. *My poor baby,* I thought, tears pricking at my eyes.

"She gets pain meds every four hours," I said, not letting myself dwell on anything negative. I had to keep moving or my mental state would collapse, and then I'd be no good to anybody. "Those are in this bottle." I held up the orange container. "Her antibiotics, which she gets twice a day with food, are in this bottle." The pills rattled when I showed him. "I've got water in her bowl, and food ready as soon as she shows the slightest interest in eating. Sean said we should try to get her to eat by this evening. Her stomach may get upset, so I also have towels and cleaning wipes in case she gets sick." I'd arranged all of Juno's recovery items on the table, placing things that we needed to use frequently near the front. "Here's her stuffie," I added, letting Wade put the elephant beside her.

Wade rubbed his forehead. "Is there anything you didn't get?"

"No." My preparation had been more thorough than a skydiver packing a parachute. I'd thought of everything. No stone had been left unturned or expense spared. I'd even programmed all the emergency numbers into my phone. "I bought enough food to last us a week, so we don't need to leave the house."

"And Alex?"

My confidence crumbled. I didn't have *that* situation under control. Not yet. "She hasn't left her room since I brought her home last night." She'd exited the truck, then walked straight into her bedroom and slammed the door. All my attempts to coax her out had been in vain. Between Juno and Alex, we had our hands full.

"I'll make us something to eat." I stood, the restlessness in my legs overcoming the relief of Juno being home. "You should take a nap before you keel over." I lifted the blanket from the chair and set it on the couch. Someone needed to be with Juno at all times, not only to watch for signs of medical complications, but also because dogs preferred to die alone.

Don't think about that, I chastised myself before departing for the kitchen. *Keep it together. Only positive thoughts.*

If I allowed any darkness to linger, the hopeful spell I'd woven around my heart would break. The storm writhing inside me would strike land, consuming my thoughts. *What if Juno doesn't make it? What if she never walks again? What if Alex never forgives herself?*

Cars whipped around that corner without a backward glance all the time. This incident could've happened to anyone. But it would be impossible to convince Alex of that.

What if her life turns out like mine?

Panic clawed at the barrier between my thoughts and my emotions. I couldn't breathe.

Half swallowed by the storm, I gripped the counter until my knuckles turned white. No matter what, I couldn't fall apart—not now. Not when they needed me most.

"She'll be okay," I whispered to myself. "It will all be okay."

Wade snored softly on the couch as I made lunch. Pots and pans clattered, sounds that would've usually driven Alex from her room only so she could tell me to quiet down. But her door remained firmly closed.

Cooking kept me busy, so I made grilled cheese sandwiches with three different kinds of cheese (using butter to toast the bread), chicken wraps with bacon and ranch dressing, macaroni salad, potato wedges, and, for dessert, blueberry muffins with a generous helping of sugar on top. The cooking only stopped once I'd used all the mixing bowls and had to wash them.

With the smell of blueberries floating through the house, I opened the windows and pinned back the curtains. Light and fresh air worked miracles. For too long, I'd shut myself in a dark, closed-off house, and my mental and physical health had suffered for it.

Despite the tense situation, when Wade entered the kitchen after his nap, I smiled at his hair sticking up in every direction. Exhaustion made his face look boyish, a side of him I'd never really seen. Because even in high school, his height and broad shoulders had made him seem like an adult.

He rubbed his shoulder as he looked me over. I'd showered, dressed, and put on waterproof mascara. I was ready.

"Coffee, water, soda, or orange juice?" I had all the options poured and waiting.

"Surprise me."

I set the orange juice in front of him. Vitamin C seemed like an important thing. He eyed the counter with curiosity as he took a drink.

"Did you cook all of that while I was sleeping?"

"I didn't know what you'd want."

"I'll eat pretty much anything." He took another sip. "Give me whatever you don't want. I'm not that hungry anyway."

I set a grilled cheese sandwich on a plate but caught sight of the clock on the microwave. Alex needed rest, but her continued absence had me on edge. I knocked on her door. "Alex? Alex, it's time for lunch." I knocked again, then put my ear to the door, hearing nothing on the other side. "I made those chicken wraps you like."

No answer.

Back in the kitchen, Wade had stacked three sandwiches on his plate. So much for not being hungry.

"She hasn't come out of her room all day." I claimed the seat across from him. "She never misses a meal." Before living with me, she'd never had chicken paprikash, or perogies, or corned beef. The sauerkraut balls had been a big swing and a miss, but for the most part, she loved my cooking, and I loved sharing those meals with her.

Sadness must've shown on my face, because Wade set down his sandwich. "Give her time. She's not a big talker."

He had a point. No one would call Alex *verbose*, and she'd hate to lean on anyone for help. But I thought we'd moved past some of her emotionally withdrawn tendencies. After her second arrest, she'd told me the truth about her birth mother, an immense moment in our friendship. Then she'd trusted me at the vet's office with Juno. I'd never forget her big, tearful eyes searching mine for help, and the relief I'd felt once she stayed to tough out the situation.

Why shut me out now? All I wanted to do was help.

Wade lifted the sandwich to his mouth, then paused. "You got any chips?"

I wanted to say no, that putting those crunchy potatoes on my perfect, delicious, gooey-yet-crispy grilled cheese sandwich was an affront to me, my family, and this house, but I'd prepared for everything—even Wade's frat-boy taste buds.

"In the cupboard next to the fridge."

"Perfect."

Alex never would've desecrated my cooking with potato chips; my best friend had much better taste. My eyes floated to her bedroom door. Half of me wanted to tell Wade to take the door down, but the other half knew that pushing Alex never ended well—for anybody.

She needs to come out on her own. Until then, all I could do was wait.

FORTY-ONE

The four of us settled into a routine over the next several days. Despite Edith, Mary, Lauren, and Sam dropping off baked goods, cards, and dog treats, I continued to anxiously cook enough food for ten people. Wade slept on the couch, watching over Juno and eating whatever I put in front of him. As Juno grew stronger and after Sean had said we were out of the woods, Wade started complaining that my ancient television didn't get cable. Apparently, he needed three different ESPN channels, at a minimum. I forgave his gripes after he fixed the broken porch spindle, glad he didn't ask how it had snapped.

Alex remained in her room, door shut, not speaking. Other than using the bathroom or snatching the food I left outside her door, she stayed away from us, unwilling to talk even when Wade's nieces came over with hand-decorated GET WELL, JUNO cards, which we set near her dog bed.

Juno had licked Kate's hand, but other than that, she didn't move.

Four days after the accident, after going upstairs to change into my pajamas—the flannel ones that were two sizes too big and comfy as hell (I'd moved beyond trying to impress Wade with my sleepwear)—I found Wade on the phone in the living room.

A female voice came through the phone, then Wade, upon seeing me, quickly said, "I have to go." He ended the call.

The tension in his voice made me appraise Juno, who lounged on her bed, head leaning on the stuffed elephant like a pillow. Apart from the white cast on her leg, she looked comfortable. "What's wrong?" My heart constricted, waiting for whatever had Wade agitated.

"Nothing. Don't worry about it."

"Just tell me." Didn't he know I'd worry incessantly until he gave me every last detail?

He sat back on the couch and grabbed the remote. "It's nothing, really. They messed up the order at the bar, that's all."

My shoulders slumped with relief. *Juno's fine. Alex is fine.* The bar's inventory was nothing to start hyperventilating about. "You should go fix it. I'll sleep on the couch until you get back."

"I'm not leaving because Rachel ordered too much tequila and no bourbon."

"I can handle things for a few hours on my own." I crossed my arms. "We're going to need that bar to pay off the vet bills." At least one of us should have steady employment.

"Are you sure?"

My shoulders straightened at his lack of confidence in me. "Carry Juno outside to go potty before you leave."

He sighed but found his feet.

"And before you come back, stop by your place to take a shower," I added, causing him to roll his eyes.

After he'd asked three more times if we'd be okay, my irritation finally pushed him out the door. I curled up on the couch, pulling the blanket to my chest. The cotton smelled faintly of Wade, but I had no impulse to wash it. My hand fell over the side to lie on Juno's back. I petted her absentmindedly, a painful ache piercing my heart. The pain pills made her lethargic, and I missed my high-energy, always-happy, sweet Juno.

I'd first met Juno a month after my mom passed away, while watering the berries near the side of the house. Juno had dashed across the backyard, ears straight back, looking like she'd never been so happy in her life. She came right up to me, totally trusting, and licked my hand. Her wagging tail had pulled a smile from someplace deep inside me.

I'd been using the high-pitched voice I reserved only for babies and animals when Wade came into view.

"Is she yours?" I'd asked him. We hadn't spoken since high school. I'd seen him outside a few times but had done everything in my power to avoid him. Talking to anyone had been difficult, least of all to my high school nemesis.

"I thought we could use some joy around here," Wade had said, bending down to pet her, too. He didn't comment on the tears in my eyes.

He'd started dropping Juno off at my house more and more, claiming he needed someone to watch her while he went to work. Eventually, he'd asked if she could stay overnight when he went fishing. Juno started to feel like *our* dog, though he took care of the expenses and walks, while I reminded him frequently to feed her.

Juno's presence had been the first good thing to happen since my mom's death.

The storm I'd held at bay, the dark thoughts twisting in my mind, broke through. I sobbed on the couch. "I love you so much," I gasped, not sure if I was speaking to Juno or my mom's ashes on the mantel. I'd come so far in these last few months, but in an instant, as quick as a speeding car, my world broke again. Fear constricted my heart. Juno's accident had reminded me of what loss could feel like, how very fragile life was. We were all teetering on the ledge. One step, one mistake, one miscalculation—that's all it would take to lose another soul I cared about.

Whether it be Juno or Wade or Alex, could I survive another loss?

I did not know.

The voice sounded far away. "Felicity." A hand shook my shoulder. "Felicity, wake up."

I groaned, then rubbed my eyes, trying to dispel the exhaustion. I'd fallen asleep crying again. My body ached, a physical manifestation of my stress.

"Where is she?" In the dark living room, I could barely see Wade's face.

"Hmm?"

"Juno." He pointed at the empty dog bed by the couch. "Where is she?"

Instinct took over, and I tossed aside my blanket, standing so quickly the room spun. "She was right there a minute ago." How long had I been asleep? Where could she have gone? All the doors had been shut. No one had come into the house.

Dogs prefer to die alone.

"Juno," I called out before making kissing noises. "Juno. Come here, girl."

A high-pitched whine came from across the house. The sound had me nearly sprinting to the kitchen, not stopping to turn the lights on. Wade followed so closely behind me that I thought he'd step on my heels.

I rounded the corner, heart beating frantically, then stopped dead.

Juno lay on the floor. Her white cast scraped on the wood as she scooted closer to the bedroom door. She whined again.

Wade moved to step around me, but I grabbed his torso, halting him. "Wait," I said.

She scratched at the wood with her uninjured paw. Her whining grew louder until she let out a feeble bark.

My hands tightened their hold on Wade's T-shirt. *Open the door, Alex.*

Juno put her nose at the very bottom of the door, as if trying to slip inside through the crack between the door and the floor.

I know you can hear her.

"Open the door," I whispered, so quietly I wasn't sure I'd actually spoken.

Juno barked again, louder this time.

I couldn't breathe. The world tilted, threatening to topple and crush every tendril of hope I'd ever had.

The doorknob twisted, and the smallest space appeared between the door and the wall. I leaned forward on my tiptoes in anticipation, willing, hoping, praying, that the door would open wider.

A hand poked into the hallway. Juno let out a squeak as Alex petted the top of her head. Her tail swished back and forth on the floor.

After what seemed like a lifetime, the bedroom door opened wide, spilling light into the kitchen. Juno, as if sensing she only had a mere moment, scooted herself inside the room, disappearing from view.

Releasing my hold on Wade, I stumbled forward, peering around the doorframe. The bright light made me squint.

Alex sat on the floor with Juno in her lap. She'd wrapped her hands around Juno's head, hugging her tightly. Juno wiggled until she could lick the tears on Alex's face.

Wade bumped into my shoulder when he stopped beside me. I squeezed his hand; he tightened his fingers in response, an unspoken conversation between the two of us.

Did Alex know we were standing in the doorway? Or was she so focused on Juno that she didn't care?

Juno settled down long enough that Alex could kiss the top of her head. "I'm sorry," Alex said. "I'm so, so sorry."

The two of them lay on the floor, intertwined, like they never wanted to be separated again.

Slowly, without making a sound, Wade and I retreated into the kitchen.

His smile provoked mine, and we stood grinning like idiots in the dark. I bowed my forehead against his chest. He wrapped his arms around me, engulfing me in his strong, sturdy frame. An immediate feeling of comfort washed through me. I breathed in tune with the rise and fall of his chest, relaxing for the first time in days.

When the floor felt solid under my feet once more, I tugged him toward the living room. He started to stop by the couch, but I didn't release his hand. Walking backward, I led him to the stairs.

He followed, confused but obliging, until I released his arm at the top of the second floor. I opened my bedroom door and went inside. I left the door wide open. He hesitated in the hallway.

He could come in or sleep on the couch. The choice was his.

Without thinking, I pulled my pajama shirt over my head.

It didn't take long for him to choose the bedroom.

FORTY-TWO

I'd never had a man in my bedroom before. We lay facing each other, heads sharing a pillow. He smoothed my hair, a subtle smile on his lips. "Are you okay?"

I nodded, knowing what he was referring to, then said, "Kind of cold."

Something had happened to the blankets. I couldn't remember how the comforter and sheets had ended up on the floor, but at some point they'd disappeared. Not that I'd noticed much. For a few minutes there, the house could've been on fire and I wouldn't have stopped kissing him.

He stood up and handed me his T-shirt from the floor. I slipped it on as he wrapped the comforter around me. He pulled on a pair of sweatpants before crawling back into bed. I covered him with half the blanket as he scooted closer to me.

I reached over to his waistband and gently pulled. "Those are going to make it more difficult for round two."

"Oh, I can figure it out." He kissed my forehead and I grinned. Luckily, he remained shirtless, so I could continue admiring his abs.

He put one arm behind his head and gazed at the ceiling. "What happens now?" he asked.

"We go to sleep, and then I make breakfast in the morning. I'm thinking quiche with blueberries on the side."

Even in the dark, I could see him roll his eyes. "You know what I meant."

I snuggled closer to him till my head was on his chest and took a deep breath. I felt calm—even peaceful—with his arms around me. I smiled, listening to his heartbeat. I wished my mom could've met this version of Wade—the solid, dependable person who looked after me and made me smile even when things were at an all-time low. She would've liked him.

After almost losing Juno, my thoughts had changed. I'd gone from wanting to protect the farm, the house, and my mother's items at all costs to facing the realization that my world had expanded beyond Josette Lavigne. Looking after Alex and Juno had preoccupied all my thoughts, snapping me out of my normal coping mechanisms. I'd relied on myself, not my mother's memories, to hold my life together.

My mom would want me to be happy, and Wade, despite our complex history, made me so. Alex had been right this entire time. "If the offer is still good, I'm ready for that date now."

There was a pause. A long pause. Immediately, I read into it and started backtracking.

"Or not," I said. My heart raced as vulnerability took over. He still didn't answer. Maybe I was pushing my luck with him. This was Wade Londergan, after all. Elswood's notorious womanizer. I shouldn't be having this conversation with him right now. Not when I wasn't wearing pants. "If you want to sleep on the couch tomorrow, that's fine. This doesn't have to be a whole thing. I need to focus on Alex anyway, so anything we do will have to wait until I get her up and moving."

I tried to scoot away, but he tightened his hold, keeping me tucked between his arm and his chest.

I looked up to see his face. He was biting his lip, trying not to laugh.

"Are you messing with me?"

"You've turned me down twice. Let me have a minute to listen to you babble."

"Jerk," I muttered through the smile plastered on my face. "I might have turned you down twice, but we've also had sex twice."

"You're forgiven," he said quickly, kissing the top of my head. "And I think I'll stay in this bed until you kick me out."

"You know staying comes with expectations, right?"

"Like what?"

I leaned on my elbow and started the conversation no guy wanted to have. "Well, first there's Alex. She's not going anywhere. At least not for a few years. If we're together, then you have to be on board with her, because as much as I like you, she's my top priority."

"I've always been on board with Alex. You're forgetting that I'm the one who taught her how to cut electrical lines without killing herself, unplugged the security camera before you guys vandalized Cheryl's storefront, and used my one 'Get Out of Jail Free' card with Mary on Alex's release."

I sat up straighter. So *he* was responsible for the incident with the security camera. No wonder Alex had been so evasive when I questioned her about it; she was protecting Wade from my judgment. "How did you manage to turn off a security camera?"

He smirked. "My bar is on that corner. They installed the camera after Glen got drunk and peed on a car—remember? Herman ran a full page on how the bar had corrupted Elswood residents and the dangers of alcohol." Wade rolled his eyes. "When Jason set up the camera, he decided to plug it into an outlet on my property. All I had to do was unplug it when I left for the night, then plug it back in the next morning. Voilà. You're welcome."

He sounded like Alex, so smug over foiling the police. I had to put a stop to all this right now—for everyone's sake. "Well, no more encouraging illegal activity or helping her evade cameras. Alex and I are operating strictly aboveboard now. We've had enough close calls with the law to last a lifetime."

"It's not like we got caught."

I narrowed my eyes.

"Fine." He crossed his fingers in a sarcastic fashion. "Nothing illegal from this moment on."

"Third," I started, but stopped when he groaned and put a pillow over his head. "Third," I repeated, grabbing the pillow and tossing it on the floor. I wanted to see his face for this one. "No other women."

"Don't you trust me?" I couldn't tell if he was teasing or not.

"You wouldn't be in my bed right now if I didn't trust you. But I want you to know it's a deal-breaker for me going forward."

"Done," he said, like he had no qualms about it. "I'm not interested in anyone else."

"'Cause you've already slept with them?"

He snorted. "No, because I like you, and when I like something, I tend to stick with it."

"Oh, like sit-ups."

"Exactly."

I eyed him suspiciously for a moment, waiting for him to change his mind. His acceptance had come easier than I expected. But when he didn't say anything, I moved on to my next point.

"Fourth," I said as he tossed his hands in the air with exasperation. "Just listen," I snapped. I wanted him—like really, really wanted him—in my life. But I wasn't going to risk ruining our friendship if we didn't have a future. My sights were set on the next steps.

"If we do this, then we're really doing it, Wade. If you don't think you want a future with me, say so now, because you were right the other day when you said that I wasn't the kind of woman who had one-night stands. I've already wasted three years of my life, and I'm not wasting any more time. One day I'm going to want to get married and have kids, and if that's not possible for you, then we might as well not even start."

His body had tensed right around the *m* word, then became immobile when I mentioned kids. I threw him a bone. "I'm saying in the future. Like in a few years down the line, if we're still together. I just want to make sure you understand that I'm not dating strictly for fun anymore."

He bit his lip but didn't answer. He waited a long time. An entire car commercial could've played before his face cleared of confusion.

"All right," he said slowly. "In the future, I could see that. One day."

I grinned at him. When he didn't bolt for the door, I figured he must really like me. Satisfied, I rested my head back on his chest.

"Is that everything?" he asked cautiously. His fingers traced across my shoulder.

"For now."

"So I answered correctly? We're dating?"

"If you want to date, let's date."

"Fine, we're dating."

"Fine."

My tone provoked his devilish smile, the one that made my heart hammer and all sense of reason disappear. He rolled over, grabbing my waist and pulling me closer to him. His lips found mine, and suddenly, I wasn't tired anymore. A few moments later, I discovered he wasn't being overconfident when he'd said he could work around the clothing.

FORTY-THREE

Wade and I stayed awake until the early morning. Sunlight broke through the windows, but I remained in bed, drifting in and out. Occasionally, I'd forget he was sleeping beside me and kick or whack him when I rolled over. Good thing he was sturdy.

I had a difficult time believing last night wasn't a dream. My stomach tightened at the sight of Wade Londergan in my bed, sleeping next to me. *He's kind of my boyfriend now.* The last few weeks had been wild, but nothing could've prepared me for a romantic relationship with Wade. I'd have to break out my high school journals and add a footnote.

The sound of feet on the stairs disturbed the quiet morning.

"This isn't fair!" Alex stormed into my bedroom. She was in her pajamas, eyes red and puffy. Her hair was a tangled mess.

"What's not fair?" I clutched my chest from the scare she'd given me. I glanced quickly at Wade, who had his back to me, appearing to not have woken up at all, though I didn't see how that was possible.

She made no mention of him occupying my bed. My cheeks burned, but at least I wouldn't have to tell her we were together. His shirtless presence in my bed said it for me.

Alex held up the local newspaper. Even without my contacts I saw what she was referencing. *Oh no.* I'd chucked that paper on the kitchen counter, intending to throw it in the trash. Wade and his abdominal muscles had distracted me.

"They can't do this to you. You won. Everyone knows it."

"Alex, honey. It's just the Man of the Year competition. It doesn't matter."

I knew I'd lose when I didn't show up for the tractor derby. Every EMOTY competitor had to attend all four competitions, and since I didn't make it, I'd become ineligible to win. I hadn't been on the ballot after getting disqualified.

"But they should have to revote." She paced the open space by the bed. "We should demand they include you this time. It's not your fault you couldn't go."

"Alex, it's fine that I didn't win. I haven't given it a second thought. There's always next year." Jonathan Callaway had won for the sixth time, but I had more important things in my life than revenge and jealousy—like Wade, Juno, and Alex. I didn't need to win the EMOTY to feel successful. "Please don't worry about it."

"No," she snapped. "It's not fair. They don't get to win after what they did to you. They'll take the farm and I'll . . ." She ran a hand through her tangled hair. I thought she was going to rip it out. "I won't let them. I'll . . . I'll . . ." Her knees shook. "Why don't we ever get to win, Felicity?"

I threw the covers off and grabbed her around the waist before she collapsed. Wade rolled over the moment he felt me leave the bed.

"It's all right." I held her up. Wade started, like he was going to stand and help, but I waved my hand. I had her. Alex was my responsibility.

"It's my fault. It's all my fault." Her sobs made it difficult to understand her words.

"No, sweetie, it's not." I wrapped my arms around her and led her downstairs. Juno waited at the bottom of the steps, her leg at an awkward angle due to the cast. She barked, and Alex started crying harder. Juno whined, then crouched on the floor.

"Let's go potty, Juno," Wade said, practically running down the stairs. He scooped up his dog to take her outside—and hopefully find a T-shirt.

I maneuvered Alex onto her bed and stroked her hair, trying my best to calm her. She couldn't keep all these emotions bottled up.

"I should've been paying better attention," Alex sobbed. "She ran into the road before I could get a hold of her. I didn't see the car until it was too late."

"It could've happened to any of us."

"But it happened to me! Why does everything bad always happen to me?" She started coughing. I lifted her so she had to sit up.

"Deep breaths," I said. "Deep breaths."

She coughed until she could say, "She loved me from the moment I met her. Do you remember? She slept on my bed that first night."

I nodded.

"And she got hurt because of me."

"I know you always believe the worst about yourself, Alex, but this was not your fault. And Juno's getting better. She's walking and barking. The vet said with time, she will probably make a full recovery."

Alex didn't wait for me to finish before she said, "And then I had to go and ruin your Man of the Year Award after we worked so hard."

"I told you, I'm not upset about that."

"But I ruined it. I ruin everything. You were going to win, and they took it away from you because of me. You're going to lose the house and the farm and all your mom's things."

"We'll figure something out."

"I'm so sorry. So, so sorry."

How would I make her understand? "If I had put the competition before you, my mother would've haunted me for the rest of my life. This house is worth nothing if you're not okay."

Had the situation been reversed, Alex would've forfeited the competition, too.

"Shhh." I held her tightly, rubbing soothing circles across her back. "It's going to be okay."

"When?" she asked. "When does it become okay, because it feels like my heart has a hole in it."

"There's no timeline. I wish there was, but we all process things at our own pace." I rested my cheek against her hair. "Healing isn't something you can force."

"Did it get better with your mom?"

"It did. Eventually. And you're a big part of that. I need you, Alex. I need you to take care of yourself." I met her eyes, imploring her to understand how important she was to me. I'd never survive without my best friend. "For me, okay? And for Juno."

Above her bed, the four beach pictures had been accentuated by my second-grade abstract painting. When had she gotten that? She must've bought it from Glen after my meltdown. Not many people would've done that, even for a friend. I squeezed her tighter, emotions causing my heart to swell. How had I gotten so lucky as to have her in my life?

My eyes drifted to the top-right photograph, where my mom smiled on a pier. The blue sea shone behind her. She'd loved the beach more than anyplace else on earth.

My chest rose and fell as I contemplated saying it aloud. Would it make things worse?

No, I decided almost immediately. My mother had never made anything worse.

I pulled away slightly so I could see Alex's face as I asked, "How do you feel about a road trip?"

FORTY-FOUR

Two weeks later, as soon as Sean gave the all clear for Juno to travel, we packed the truck and hit the road. I connected my phone to the stereo and set our ten-hour course. I knew the drive well. Every summer, my mother would pack the car and we'd drive east until we ran into the ocean. She'd stare at the blue sea, curly hair blowing in the wind, totally in awe.

I owed it to her to scatter her ashes in a place she loved so dearly.

With the truck windows rolled down, my hair flew in every direction. Wade drove, one hand on the wheel and the other around my shoulders. Alex looked out the passenger-side window, quiet and sullen. Juno had a comfy spot on the floor by our feet, her dog bed wrapped around her like a protective burrito shell.

At a rest stop near Richmond, I forced Alex to eat lunch. I'd bought four cheeseburgers and a mess of fries.

"I thought you didn't approve of fast food?"

"Anything goes on a road trip. That's part of the fun."

She dipped her hand into the bag and withdrew a couple of fries. "Are you sure this is a good idea?"

My eyes flicked to the box of ashes beside me.

There was a time, not long ago, when I would've hesitated. I'd needed my mom with me at all times, and that included her ashes. But things had changed these last few months. With Juno's accident came the realization that life was fleeting, every second precious and a wonder. I wouldn't miss the opportunity to see the ocean again, to show Alex the sand and shore where we used to walk. The tide had rolled in and taken away our footsteps, but with Alex I could make new marks in the sand. "I think it's going to help."

"Long drive just to cry at a bunch of waves."

I took a bite of my cheeseburger. "Have you ever seen the ocean?"

"I've seen pictures."

Pictures didn't do the ocean justice. There was nothing like standing on the shore, staring across the vast sea and realizing just how tiny and insignificant you were in comparison to the world. The sea was humbling and magnificent at the same time.

Wade returned to the truck with Juno, who could walk but had started to love being carried from place to place like a baby. Wade and Alex indulged her more than the vet recommended, but I didn't have it in my heart to chastise them.

"We ready to go?" he said, gently placing Juno in the vehicle. We climbed in after her, and Alex let Juno lay across her lap and mine. I held the bag of fries away from Juno's prowling nose and handed Wade a burger. I'd never seen someone eat so much beef jerky, but I knew he'd still be hungry.

We skipped down the East Coast, through small towns no one had ever heard of. I was pleased to say that Wade and I only got into one fight about directions. He took a right when I clearly meant the *next* right, and we lost about forty-five minutes, thanks to his inability to read my mind.

"Keep driving that way."

He'd peered at the highway as we came to a fork. "That doesn't help me."

"Stay on the road and go south."

"Felicity, I don't know which way is south!"

"That way."

He'd snatched the phone from my hands to see for himself as the GPS loudly rerouted again. Wade probably would've yelled, but a small laugh from the person on my right made the anger vanish from his face.

Alex laughed. Just when I thought she'd never make that sound again.

I ducked my head into Wade's side so she wouldn't see the tears in my eyes. Getting lost didn't matter; we'd make it to the coast eventually. So long as everyone in this truck was safe and happy, I'd never worry about lost time again.

My heartbeat increased the closer we got. I recognized the buildings and the streets and the trees. Every once in a while, I could see the ocean in the space between houses. My mom had preferred this section of the beach because the homes were smaller, unlike the flashy rentals to the north. She'd always found solace in the ordinary.

I disconnected my phone, no longer needing the directions.

I pointed to the turnoff, feeling faint as Wade parked the truck. Overhead, the sun started dropping behind us, spilling pink and yellow across the horizon like a paintbrush sweeping across a canvas.

"Alex." I gently shook her awake. She'd closed her eyes an hour ago, head against the window. "Alex, we're here."

The sign on the walkway leading down to the sand made it clear that dogs were prohibited, and the beach closed at sundown—which, by the looks of the sky, was minutes away. When I pointed this out, Alex said, "That's dumb," at the same time Wade said, "Who cares?"

Rebels, both of them. If I wasn't careful, they'd start to rub off on me.

The thought had me smiling when we reached the sand.

Holding the box of my mom's ashes, I kicked off my tennis shoes. I wiggled my toes, breathing deep in the warm sea air. The ocean roared as waves splashed onto the sandbar.

"What do you think?" I asked Alex, bending down to grab a few seashells to add to the collection in her bedroom.

She looked out across the horizon. "It's perfect." She cleared her throat and looked down. "It's fine. Whatever."

"Come on," I said, tugging her shirtsleeve. "Let's go to the pier."

"Do you want me to wait here?" Wade asked, holding Juno back from running straight into the water and ruining her cast. "While the two of you say goodbye?"

The box felt heavier in my hands. "Not a chance." Wade and Juno were as much a part of this journey as Alex and me.

He smiled, then lifted Juno up so her head was tucked over his shoulder. "Lead the way, then."

The wooden pier stretched from the sand into the water. Fishermen were packing up their tackle boxes, poles leaning against the side. Wade took a long look at their things, clearly wishing he'd brought his own fishing gear. On each plank, sand rubbed against the soles of my feet as I walked, eyes on the horizon, trying not to think about what would happen when we reached the end.

The deep blue stretched for what seemed like endless miles. A sob caught in my throat. Returning to this spot hit me harder than I'd anticipated. My fingers tightened on the box.

We stood at the end of the pier—Alex on my right, Wade and Juno on my left.

"I . . . don't know what to say." I used the crook of my elbow to wipe away my tears, unwilling to relinquish the box in my hands. The ten-hour drive should've given me plenty to time to prepare a eulogy. "Here lies Josette Lavigne . . . my mother . . . my friend . . ." The words choked in my throat. Nothing I said would do her justice, the same way a photograph would never encapsulate the magnificence of the ocean. Some things were simply impossible to describe.

"I can go first," Wade offered. He inhaled, then set Juno on the pier. "My mom used to make me stock the shelves when I got in trouble as a kid, so that was pretty often. But anytime I had to work at the store, a few items—mostly candy bars—went missing. Ms. Lavigne once caught me putting a Snickers in my pocket. I thought she'd bust me. Mary probably would've given her a discount on groceries if she had. Instead, your mom lowered her voice and said, 'You've got good taste.' She slipped me a dollar bill on her way past."

"She's my favorite person," Alex said. "A true icon."

Wade's eyes flicked to the box of ashes, and my heart constricted. Fingers shaking, I opened the lid to my mother's remains. Wade scooped a handful of gray ashes into his palm.

"Thank you for that dollar bill, and thank you for the C-plus in Algebra that I didn't deserve but kept me eligible to play football." He leaned over the railing, then said, "I should've treated your daughter better in high school. I don't intend to make that mistake again. I hope that wherever you are, you can forgive me." His fist opened, and the soft gray specks fell into the sea.

I held back my sob, unable to take my eyes away from the water as the sea swallowed my mother's ashes. I didn't have time to ruminate on Wade's words because Alex had already reached her hand into the box.

"I never got to meet you, but I know you were amazing." Her lower lip quivered. Her eyes flicked to me, then back to the ocean. "I don't know if you're responsible for leading me to Felicity or the blueberry farm, but I'm certain you're the reason Felicity let me stay, even when I messed everything up. I don't know what I would've done if she hadn't helped me." She brought her hand to her lips, whispered, "Thank you for raising the best person I know," then let the ashes cascade into the sea.

My heart melted. "Alex," I said, voice hoarse with emotion.

"Don't," she said, holding up a hand, knowing I was falling apart at her words. *The best person I know.* I'd never be the same after hearing those words. Never.

"I was talking to your mom," she said, then sniffled once to clear the emotion from her face. "Don't make a big deal out of it."

Too late. My arm wrapped around her, pulling her into a hug that she had no choice but to begrudgingly accept. "You are the sweetest, kindest, most loyal friend I've ever had."

Alex sighed—whether from embarrassment, exasperation, or emotion, I didn't know. But we stood for a long moment, in silence, hearing nothing but the waves splashing onto the wood.

Juno bumped her head against my leg, and when I bent to pet her, Alex seized her opportunity to pull back. She used the heels of her hands to wipe away tears. Elbows resting on the pier railing, she stared out to sea.

Sniffling, tears streaming down my face with abandon, I finally knew what I wanted to say to my mom.

I also knew that I didn't want an audience. This conversation was only meant for the two of us. "Would you guys give me a minute?" As much as I wanted Wade, Juno, and Alex by my side, I had to get the words out on my own.

Wade gave me a reassuring smile. "We'll be by the truck when you're done." He squeezed my elbow, then bent to pick up Juno.

I turned to watch them leave the pier. Alex, thinking I was out of earshot, said, "You know if you ever hurt her again, I'm going to dump your ashes in the ocean next, right?"

I didn't hear Wade's response, but it sounded like he was laughing.

"They're a handful," I said to the box of ashes. "But they're family." I exhaled. "Some days I wake up and forget that you're gone. For a brief moment, I think everything is fine and my heart feels whole. Then I remember and . . ." I shook my head, unwilling to end the night with sadness. "I want you to know that I'm not alone anymore, and I'll be okay. I feel almost happy. I don't know if I'll ever be truly happy without you, but I'm working on it." In the dark, I could no longer see her ashes in the box. I closed the lid, realizing I didn't need to relinquish all her essence into the sea. Saying goodbye didn't have to be all or nothing.

"I love you, Mom." I brought my fingertips to my lips and blew a kiss out to sea. "Until we meet again."

With a final look at the ocean, I felt sad about what I'd lost but hopeful for tomorrow. My feet walked along the pier, neither slowly nor quickly, but rather at my own perfect pace.

My favorite misfits stood near the truck.

There would come a time in the not-so-distant future when it would seem perfectly normal for the two of them to be waiting for me. Wade leaned against the vehicle, arms folded across his chest as he spoke to Alex, who gestured emphatically with her hands. They both turned to look at me when I approached. I stopped about fifteen feet away, admiring how incredibly amazing they both were.

Alex noticed me staring and stood up straight. "Are you okay?"

Wade uncrossed his arms when he saw the tears on my face.

"I want you both to know that . . ." My hand covered my heart. "I love you."

EPILOGUE

Ten months later . . .

Alex's high school graduation was at the beginning of June, when the air had turned hot after a brutal Ohio winter. The ceremony took place at the high school football stadium, as it had every year since 1995, when it was built. During my graduation ceremony ten years ago, I'd walked across the stage in that blue sack they called a gown. My oddly shaped hat had slipped off mid-walk, and I was so nervous about tripping that I'd left it on the stage, only retrieving it after the ceremony. I had to fake tossing my hat in the air at the end, missing my vital moment. I'd re-created the hat toss for my mom at home like a dork.

My mother probably had that hat tucked away in the back of a closet somewhere.

"Ouch," Alex said, hand going to her head. "Any more and I won't be able to get it off."

"You'll thank me later." I pushed the bobby pin down, attaching the square hat to her hair. It took fifteen pins till it was sturdy enough for my approval. This hat wasn't going anywhere.

"Bad enough that you're making me go to this; now I'm going to lose all my hair."

Yes, I had made her go to the graduation ceremony. I'd guilt-tripped her until she relented to my pleas. It was an important experience, especially so for Alex, who had worked hard during her extra year. It wasn't easy to return to school, but she toughed it out. Immense pride shot through me.

"Are you crying?"

"No."

"Will you stop? You're freaking me out."

"I'm so proud of you."

"It's the Elswood High School graduation. It's not like I'm heading off to Harvard. I didn't even graduate with honors."

I wiped my cheek with the back of my hand and didn't press the issue. She wouldn't listen anyway. It was hard enough getting her to agree to try college, but in the fall, she'd be attending the local community college. She didn't know what she wanted to major in, but I'd assured her there was plenty of time to figure it out.

At the ripe old age of twenty-eight, I was still figuring that out myself.

"Are you guys ready?" Wade's voice floated through the door. "Any longer and she's going to miss her name being called."

I rolled my eyes. He just wanted us to hurry up so he could get the day over with and take his tie off. The tie was one of the many things I'd forced upon him as he slowly moved more of his belongings into my place. There had been no formal agreement for him to move in, but he lived here now. Last week, he mentioned putting his house up for sale so we could pay Alex's college tuition and add a second car to our collection. Between three people and Alex driving to classes every day, his truck wasn't going to make it.

We left Alex's room and found him in the kitchen eating a leftover hamburger from the bar. He broke off a piece of the burger and tossed it to Juno, who was whining as if she'd never been fed in her entire life.

If he knew how good he looked in his navy suit, he'd never wear flannel again.

"How do I look?" Alex asked him, holding her arms out.

"Like a blueberry."

"Wade!"

"I told you," Alex moaned. "It looks ridiculous."

"It's supposed to look ridiculous. That's part of the experience. Now, let's go so I can get a decent seat."

Alex ducked, careful not to dislodge her square hat, as we climbed into the truck. Wade drove to the high school, a five-minute journey, but by the time we arrived, nearly every parking spot was full. Grumbling, Alex stalked toward the blue-robed teenagers lining up by the fence.

Wade and I proceeded toward the bleachers.

"You're late," Mary said from the middle of the stands. Of course she had the best spot in the house. My heart swelled seeing the entire Londergan family show up to celebrate Alex's day. We—as in Wade, me, and Alex—attended Mary's Thursday-night dinners. That had been one of Mary's conditions when she invested in the blueberry farm.

"Every week—all three of you. That's the deal. No excuses unless you're hospitalized," she'd said. Despite her tone, I'd hugged her, grateful that she'd agreed to be a silent partner and pay the property taxes each year. Wade didn't know it, but Mary had invested in the farm because of him. She wanted to be closer to her youngest son, and caring about the things he found important—like his girlfriend's failing blueberry business—went a long way toward building a bridge between her and Wade. Tough as nails, all Mary Londergan wanted was to see her son each week.

I smiled as we sat and looked out at the white chairs lining the football field from forty-yard line to forty-yard line. A platform had been constructed on the opposite side of the chairs for the teachers and principal to sit on. There was a podium with a microphone for speeches.

Wade adjusted his tie. The open stadium provided no cover from the sun, and beads of sweat appeared in his blond hair. It was odd being at the high school with him, given how we had hardly known each other when we were students here. In my wildest dreams, I hadn't imagined I'd be sitting next to Wade Londergan, my boyfriend, on the bleachers one day.

I smoothed my green dress and straightened my shoulders. I'd promised Alex that I wouldn't cry. An impossible promise that I'd keep for as long as possible.

Wade leaned over to whisper in my ear, "I didn't want to piss off Alex by saying so, but you don't look anything like a blueberry."

"What a compliment." I grabbed his hand, intertwining our fingers.

He looked down and winked.

Ben leaned across Lauren, who was trying to keep Willa from kicking the gentleman in front of her. "We've got the banner and the confetti in the car. Are you guys going straight to the bar after this?"

"Yeah," Wade said as I elbowed him in the stomach. He turned to me. "What?"

I, of course, had offered to throw Alex a party several times, but she'd chosen a trip instead. "I told you she didn't want a party."

"Well, tough," Mary said from behind us. "You graduate, you get a party. Those are the rules. We even threw one for Wade, and Alex did much better than he did."

Wade rolled his eyes but didn't say anything in his defense.

"That's very nice of you," I said, looking at the Londergans, feeling my eyes grow watery. "All of you."

I turned my attention back to Wade. "But remember, we're leaving first thing in the morning for North Carolina. And by first thing, I mean six a.m. sharp."

"Let's not take the scenic route this year."

"You'll go whatever way I tell you to." We didn't have time to continue the spat. At that moment, Wendy Stells walked by wearing a low-cut dress that clung to her curves. I adjusted my bustline, pulling it up to compensate for her exposure. It was hot, but it wasn't *that* hot.

She climbed the steps, stopping in front of us. "Oh, hey, Wade," she remarked, leaning against the railing.

"Wendy," he said politely. I squeezed his hand as hard as I could.

"Remember when you used to be on that field? Throwing the ball?"

"Yup, that was me." He squeezed my hand back as I tried to snatch mine away.

"Actually, I think they turfed it since he graduated," I chimed in.

"Oh. Hey, Felicity," Wendy said, eyes roaming over me, not catching that I was holding Wade's hand. I was just glad that she finally acknowledged me. I thought she didn't know my name at all.

She returned her attention to Wade. "Well, I'll be around. Probably walking down below, if you get bored with the show."

I cleared my throat. The show? "You mean the graduation ceremony?"

"Yeah, whatever." She left and I sensed Wade's smile. It had come as quite a shock to all the women in town that Wade had decided to settle down. Especially when he settled down with me. He'd made the mistake of telling me that he got more female attention when he was unavailable than when he'd been single. I'd let that go without comment as he laughed at the irony.

But today I wasn't worried about Wendy or Vanessa or even Eileen, who made frequent stops at the bar every Saturday and Sunday night during his shifts. No, today was all about Alex. Her accomplishments and her future. I didn't want to miss a single moment.

The students walked onto the field, and the crowd cheered, myself included.

I fished my phone out of my purse. Wade snatched it.

"What the heck?" This was not the time for a game.

"You watch. I'll take the photos."

"I have specific angles that I want."

"I'll take a bunch," he said, holding the phone out of my reach. "I want you to remember it."

"I'll remember it through the photos."

"No," he snapped. "Just watch and think about all the accomplishments or whatever people are supposed to think of at times like this."

"She was a straight-C student who got suspended twice." I wasn't winning any awards for mentorship. Though I was still blaming him for the second suspension. He never should've told her about Mrs. Hanson's poor eyesight; maybe Alex wouldn't have stolen her glasses, then.

"I never said they were *good* accomplishments."

"Keep this up and I'll tell Wendy you're available and on the market."

He smirked but didn't say any more. That satisfied me.

First, the principal spoke, followed by the superintendent, and then the valedictorian. Jeez, it seemed like everybody was giving a speech. Didn't they know it was ninety degrees outside?

Though it was rude, I stood and clapped as Alex walked across the stage and became an official graduate of Elswood High School, the thirty-seventh-best public high school in Ohio. I clapped as loudly as I could from the stands as she shook the principal's hand and moved her tassel from one side to the other. I noted with smug satisfaction that her hat remained firmly attached to her head the entire time.

When it was over, I cried, and Wade laughed, promising to tell Alex that I'd held out until she walked across the stage. I couldn't help it. I was too proud of her not to cry. I cried looking at a sunset, so obviously I'd weep watching my best friend accomplish something significant.

After the ceremony, we filed out of the stadium, promising to meet his family at the bar for the party. I walked toward the parking lot, but Wade grabbed my hand, halting my progress.

"Where are we going?" I knew Alex would be waiting by the truck, counting down the seconds until she could forget this whole high school thing had ever happened. I made a mental note to remind her to thank Mary for the graduation party. She wouldn't be pleased at all by the attention, but like Mary had said: "Tough."

I followed Wade under the bleachers, thankful to be in the shade. Where was he going? Did he drop something down here?

"I should've done this when I was seventeen." Wade looked at the bleachers above us, a smile on his face.

We didn't have time for a detour. "Alex is waiting. Do you want to risk her wrath for making her remain at this high school a second longer than necessary?"

He stopped, glanced upward a second time, then pulled me closer. "I believe I owe you an under-the-bleachers kiss."

I gulped. That was not what I expected. My heart rate increased, the same way it always did when he touched me. I tilted my head to the side as he leaned down and kissed me.

My hands went to his hair as his encircled my waist, drawing me onto my toes. The kiss was better than it would've been when we were teenagers. I was no longer infatuated with the arrogant high school quarterback who had everyone's attention. I was in love with Wade, the man I trusted more than anyone else.

I laughed as my phone rang, and I broke off the kiss. I pulled the cell phone from my purse. My heart lifted at her impeccable timing.

I accepted the call. "I'm on my way, Alex."

ACKNOWLEDGMENTS

To my agent, Laura Bradford, for plucking me from obscurity and believing in my work: Thank you for never giving up on this story.

To Chantelle Aimée Osman, my amazingly talented editor, who turned this writing dream into a reality: Thank you for changing my life forever. I feel so ridiculously lucky to have you and the Lake Union team in my corner. To Carmen Johnson, Michelle Flythe, Dee Hudson, Rachel Norfleet, Sarah Horgan, Jill Kramer, and Emma Reh—thank you for all of your insights and help with shaping this manuscript into its best possible version.

Thank you to my dear friends Olivia and Robin, the first people to read my writing, who provided endless support and encouragement along the way; and thank you to Kristin, Selamawet, Ann, Laura, and Tess for being the very best of friends anyone could hope for.

Thank you to my family—Kelly, Paul, Jacob, Allison, and Annie—for all your love and support.

And finally, to every reader who picked up this book: Thank you. It means the world to me.

ABOUT THE AUTHOR

Grace Demyan was born and raised in rural Ohio and currently resides in Alexandria, Virginia. After graduating from Tufts University and Tulane University Law School, Grace began her career working for the US Department of Defense. When she's not writing or reading, she loves visiting historical landmarks, exploring the great outdoors, and listening to country music. She writes contemporary women's fiction with heart and humor. For more information, visit www.gracedemyan.com.